Dancing With THIEVES

Other Books by Clarissa McNair

Garden of Tigers
A Flash of Diamonds
The Hole in the Edge

Books by Cici McNair

Never Flirt With a Femme Fatale
Detectives Don't Wear Seat Belts

Dancing With THIEVES

CLARISSA McNAIR

FEDORA PRESS
Philadelphia

Reissued by Fedora Press in 2011

ISBN: 978-1-936712-02-1

A note from the publisher: Any typographical errors or any errors in the spacing of the text are due to the imperfect scanning, in 2001, of a manuscript that no longer exists.

Cover Design by Scribe Freelance | www.scribefreelance.com

Visit the author online at: www.mcnairwrites.com

This book is dedicated to Desideria Corsini, a dear friend and gifted painter, who was so kind to me in Porto Ercole.
I also dedicate it to that enchanted fishing village where I wrote this story looking out from my terrace across blue water.

Chapter One

"You are an embarrassment."

The words floated across the white marble coffee table piled with heavy, never-opened art books, their virginal spines intact, past the piano no one in the household could play. It was covered with standing photographs of the family, of smooth lawns in the background, of Long Island Sound sweeping silkily to a distant horizon. Frozen smiles on the tanned, happy faces above pastel clothes. A testament on paper under glass and bound in silver—-to good times. Good times with the Hathaways.

Teddy's face flamed but as she crossed her legs under the Givenchy suit, she thought, Wonder how embarrassed you'd be to know I haven't worn underpants for the entire year and a half I've been your son's wife. She pushed her thick blonde hair back with one hand whose every finger bore a ring. There was the outsized diamond engagement ring Mrs. Hathaway had pronounced vulgar within Teddy's hearing that first lunch on the day of the announcement and there were several cat's eyes topazes from South America and three turquoise rings and the silver bands she'd worn since her first visit to a street fair in Greenwich Village.

"Perhaps 'disappointment' would be also an accurate thing to say so I-"

Teddy forced a laugh and the older woman stopped in mid-sentence, appalled at the breach of good manners. She stood and walked slowly to the windows overlooking Fifth Avenue. A smallish figure with perfectly coiffed blonded hair, pearl button earrings, and a suit from Martha, the shop in Palm Beach. The park was full of snow, it was two hours away from being dirty, and looked clean, though only heaven knows what pollutants came down with it. Yes, but it looked clean all the same. Her mind returned to the girl who had temporarily bewitched her son. Oh, she didn't know for sure what kind of a past she'd had; it was just her irritating way of insinuating she'd done everything. And whatever she hadn't done, Teddy had quipped to one of her husband's partners, "Is on my list."

A disappointment, thought Teddy. Your son has been the disappointment. Stiff and stuffy and tight and worried about the way I make coffee. Worried about what I say to people. Worried about whether my skirt is too short. Why, when I met him they couldn't be short enough. And his tone with me, 'oh, Teddy this and oh, Teddy that' as if I were a hopeless case, a puppy who's missed the newspaper again.

"So I propose that life might be better for all of us—"

"For you? For Jeremy? Surely, Mrs. Hathaway, you are not concerned about how good my life is." Teddy wished she smoked. With great self control she kept her hands folded loosely in her lap of royal blue wool. Relax your shoulders, she told herself.

"No. I do mean for all of us. There's no point in going on with the marriage. People do make mistakes. Jeremy will want children soon and I see no reason for that to involve you."

Children. Jeremy didn't want them, not really. Teddy thought of the half dozen discussions. He always talked as if she were asking to have a too large pet in a city apartment. Something like a pony would come to live with them and "there goes the guest room." Now she felt nothing but anger, for him and for his mother. I would like to spit. Teddy remembered spitting contests at home with the Bradshaw boys. Five feet away. She's in range. I could get her. Don't be a child, she warned herself. Sit up straight and fight. On her terms. War declared on an Oriental rug. Pick your weapon. I'll take the Steuben glass whale. "I am happy that being Mrs. Hathaway has been such a great experience for you. Truly I am." Teddy was standing now. Her mother-in-law faced her in the Delman dark blue shoes at five feet four to Teddy's even six feet. "It hasn't been all that terrific for me so I think—I think you're right." She paused, enjoying the look of surprise that greeted this. "I'll be on my way. Jeremy will be back from Chicago tomorrow. I know that's why you picked today. To spare your son any unpleasantness. How like you." Teddy's face was empty of emotion.

The senior Mrs. Hathaway was suspicious. Surely it was too easy. "I want to clear things up before you go. I want a signed statment— Carson Levitt has drawn it up—saying that-"

"You want…you want…what do you think I want?" Teddy stood at the piano and ran one finger across the keyboard lazily. Adrenalin raced through her like a drug. A rush of energy she tried to still. A higher temperature. Fight or flight.

"I am sure you will not find my check ungenerous. And the paper will simply state that-"

Ping. Ping. Ping. Teddy feigned indifference. Stall. Or start screaming. You can't treat me this way. But on the other hand, I hate Jeremy. I hate the way he makes love to me. Or tries to. I just lie back and think of Alabama. I hate his snooty nose in the air when we go to places I used to go. He's even started to criticize the way the daily folds the towels. And there is something urgent about the way toilet paper HAS to unroll. I hate it all. I hate the way he clears his throat in the morning. I hate being his wife. I hate every cell of every Hathaway.

"Will you please stop that?" cried Mrs. Hathaway.

"Oh? This?" Teddy gave the piano one more 'ping' before looking up innocently. She let her hand fall to her side and stared straight ahead at the Georgia O'Keefe over the mantel. The Hathaways' venture into modern art. The Old Masters circled the globe, shuttled in and out of museums in crates. A secretary came to the apartment five days a week and did nothing but make out itineraries for the canvasses and kept their insurance policies up to date and wrote letters thanking curators for their interest.

Will she take it? wondered Mrs. Hathaway. This restless, annoying scamp. I'm doing my son a favor. If he had more backbone he'd be doing it himself. With anyone else in this day and age it would be unrealistic to think of a woman simply leaving town, rather like the outlaw mounting his horse and cantering away before sundown, but with Teddy...who knew what she would do? Anyone else would get a lawyer but again, Teddy wasn't quite of this day and age. "I want you to accept this check from me. Just to facilitate things. So you won't feel you were deprived of a settlement. Just to get you started again." She tried to put an element of concern in her voice but failed.

Teddy wished she could laugh. "Get me started again? You act as though my life began when your precious son asked me to marry him! May I be the one to tell you it didn't? That I'd been around for twenty years before stepping into this room, before meeting you, before walking down the aisle with your spoiled brat!"

Her mother-in-law gave a sniff of disapproval at this outburst, but resolved to ignore it, to refuse a response. If only this could be over with before half past five when Jer would be home. She wanted to look at her tiny wristwatch but she couldn't see the numerals anymore without making an issue of it and the mantle clock was too far away. Say anything, you little snip! I don't care. Just get it out of your system and go!

"I remember the night before the wedding when you so kindly let me and my aunts stay here—we heard you. We heard you talk about blood and breeding—the way I heard you talk the summer before—plotting to put Jeremy out in a sailboat for the afternoon with that oh-so-cute Junior Leaguer. What was her name? Oh. Yes. Bitsy Kemp. You've been holding your breath all this time waiting for the marriage to be over so that you could pair him up with someone 'more suitable'...yes, that's what you would say."

Teddy's brown eyes were wide and flashed with anger. She was out of control and enjoying it. She felt alive and strong. "And as for talking about me as though I were a mongrel dog...as for your blood..." She realized her thoughts were disjointed and she was almost stuttering. Her eyes shone with tears. "Your blood is blue all right. Surprised it still goes around in your arteries, surprised it isn't frozen." She gulped for air. "Hurray for the Hathaways! I am delighted one of ya'll signed the Declaration of Independence! I just keep wondering..." Her southern accent returned full force. "What anybody's done since then! Jeremy's grandfather had some pizzazz because he made the money but Jeremy's father does nothing but keep it safe on Wall Street and Jeremy just worries all the time about how safe it is and how soon he'll get it." Mrs. Hathaway flinched. "What a life!" shouted Teddy.

"It's not the life for you, my dear." Mrs. Hathaway's lips were a thin line. "I'll make out that check for you." She moved towards the Sheraton desk where she kept the household accounts.

"Forget it! I don't want your money! I won't give you the satisfaction of paying me off! Of sending me packing!"

"I want your signature pledging that you will not use the name Hatha—"

"I wouldn't dream of it!" hissed Teddy. Her hair, platinum blond around her face was like a lion's mane. "I'm Teddy Starbuck from Ace, Alabama, named after my father who had more talent and more guts and more fun in him than all the Hathaways of the last two generations put together! You're not getting rid of me!" Her mother-in-law prayed silently, holding her breath. "I'm getting rid of you!"

Mrs. Hathaway exhaled with relief as Teddy strode from the living room. *Not sure I've seen the last of that tacky girl but at least this is the beginning of a separation. Not sure if desertion still exists in New York State but...oh, Carson can draw up papers and talk to Jeremy over the weekend. I'll have him to Oyster Bay for Saturday lunch.* She walked to the drop front desk and closed it gently. "Quite a performance," she

would say that evening over trout almondine to her husband who had-
n't wanted to be involved.

✳   ✳   ✳   ✳   ✳   ✳   ✳   ✳   ✳   ✳   ✳

"The truth?"

Teddy nodded mournfully. She looked as though tears might slip
down her face right into the vodka. "Come on, Olivier, don't start lyin'
to me now."

He winced behind round tortoise shell glasses, looking like Harold
Lloyd, and nervously plucked at his black bow tie. "Well, you…you blew
it."

Teddy looked down at the two large suitcases. She put one foot on
one, balancing awkwardly on the bar stool with her blue skirt riding
way up above her knees. He went on. "Get a lawyer. It's not too late. A
fight with your mother-in-law, that's all. I'd go back." Olivier began slic-
ing oranges in half behind the bar. Swak. Swak went the knife as it hit
the butcher block. "Go back, talk to Jeremy, get a lawyer, THEN leave."
Swak. Swak. McAllister's was always quiet until about ten. Swak. Swak.

"I can't…she." It was like swallowing an ice cube. That kind of cold
that burns your throat. You know it'll go away, it'll melt and you'll be
fine but that doesn't help the frozen kind of fire at the moment. No one
had ever wounded Teddy with words like that. She feared it was true;
that was why it hurt so much. She could be a mess sometimes.
Sometimes she didn't care and sometimes she did it on purpose. Like
ratting her hair out like a zulu for Jeremy's birthday dinner at the New
York Yacht Club. It had been fun and funny and she'd liked the attention. Jeremy hadn't. Men forgave her. Jeremy didn't anymore. A mother-
in-law like Mrs. Jeremy Taylor Hathaway, Junior, never had. "I hate him,
Olivier. I'd be much happier married to you. I'd be happier married to
the next person who walked in that door…"

It was the owner of McAlllister's who kissed her on both cheeks and said very seriously, "I accept. When's the honeymoon start?"

Olivier was relieved when Teddy laughed. He'd been her confidante since she'd arrived in New York about three months before marrying that pompous jerk. Sometimes Teddy was like a very tall little girl. The tears were bright in her eyes and yet she could forget them with a little stroke of attention.   "How about a long honeymoon and a short marriage?" she quipped. "Actually I'm not big on marriage today. Why don't we just run off somewhere?"

"If I thought you would, we'd be in a taxi for Kennedy," Dirk smiled. Then he saw the bags. "Are you serious?"

Olivier stopped mopping imaginary stains from the oak bar. "She's serious. Tell her to get a lawyer and to—"

Teddy was angry then. "Look, I'm not totally stupid. I know I'm entitled to things from him. What if I just don't want to take them? What if I'm just too tired to fight about it? I mean, after all, I did get a year and a half rent free and all meals were provid—"

Dirk was aghast. "God, you're a dream come true. But Teddy, I like you. Let me see if my pal Blakeley is still-"

"A blind date!" cried Teddy in horror. "My wedding ring is still warm…"

The men laughed. "No. Blakeley is a good lawyer. Honest and tough. He'll take care of you even if you-"

Teddy shook her head. Olivier and Dirk stared at her. It was hard not to. Thick hair, nearly white, the color of children's hair who've played on beaches all summer, sprang from the widow's peak above the nearly square face. Her almond shaped eyes were brown, a warm dark coffee, and hinted of fun, of secrets. Her mouth was wide. Mrs. Hathaway had called it 'rather thick' to her husband after meeting her but Mr. Hathaway had silently decided that it was nothing if not lush, pouting, sensuous. Her nose was straight and fine, inherited from her small-boned delicate mother. After her blondeness, men noticed her legs and said they 'started at her throat' but women noticed a small waist and rather broad shoulders. Her bust was fuller than average and she was used to tying a bandana around it while modelling. Olivier was always surprised when he saw tears, and that had been often since her marriage, for there was some quality in Teddy that bespoke great physical courage—the wild hair of one hundred shades from ash to a Renaissance gold, or the long strides she took in her nearly flat shoes, or the large hands that were almost mannish. Those capable hands she tried to hide. Olivier knew Teddy to be big-hearted, expansive and brave.

It took two hours to convince her, between Olivier tending bar and a long session with Dirk in his little box of an office upstairs, but just after midnight Blakeley arrived and she did talk to him. At two, while waiting for Olivier to tally receipts, her old agent sat down beside her on a bar stool and told her about a modelling job in Rome.

"A one shot deal, Teddy, but you could stay if you wanted and pick up more. Call me if you're interested in that ticket." He drained his scotch as she nursed the eleventh wine spritzer. "First class," John said seductively, winking at her.

Teddy shrugged. She always felt like merchandise around him. She'd told him a thousand times how boring she thought it was. How sick she got of being fooled with. Hair. Makeup. Strapped into things with pins in the side to make them smooth and tight and perfect for the camera when in fact it sometimes felt you had dried twigs in your underclothes. But he'd always gotten her good assignments. Four days in the Virgin Islands after last February's fight with Jeremy. That had been okay. "I'll think about it," she promised.

Olivier walked her to the East End apartment and encouraged her to take everything she owned. She sauntered from room to room and thought, none of this is mine. I came to New York with a red canvas bag from Sears. "Come on," Olivier ordered, motioning her to follow him down the hall into the bedroom. It was as if he lived there, not she.

"I don't care about this stuff," she said as he opened louvred doors and surveyed the racks of dresses. But when he pulled her white mink coat off the padded perfumed hanger she didn't protest. "I'm starting over," she declared standing in the middle of the pale yellow bedroom.

"Fine," he nodded as he zipped yet another garment bag. "Leave this stuff at my apartment until you decide you don't want to be naked while you start over."

"I've done that once. Haven't we all?"

"And tomorrow at nine o'clock, actually today, go to the bank and clean out the bastard's checking account."

Teddy began to laugh. "Olivier! You little sneak! I'm not a thief."

"No one's calling you one," he said as he emptied the top bureau drawer of her jewellery boxes, tossing them one by one, square and rectangular, dark blue leather and maroon and black, into the last open suitcase.

Teddy looked around the room that had cost thousands of dollars to decorate. "Okay, I will go to the bank. And I'll take...half."

Olivier looked up at her and smiled. "Good girl." He was afraid she might cry again. "He didn't deserve you and he wasn't very nice to you either."

Teddy shook her head. Olivier of all people knew that. She realized she was not only leaving Jeremy but this little dressing room of mirrors, the sunken bathtub, the creme-colored raw silk bedspread that took about six months to arrive from who could remember where, and the silver chandelier from France that hung in the hallway with the walk-in closets where she kept all her coats. Beneath her feet was the Aubusson rug that she'd chosen after weeks of boring afternoons with that chattering decorator. For one moment, Teddy felt terribly lost, as though she might be on an unfamiliar street in a strange town without a map, not speaking the language.

"Last chance!" Olivier tried to sound casual, even jaunty. Project, his coach would say. Then he saw her expression. "If you want to stay," his voice was soft. "Then stay. No one ever has to know a thing. Dirk and I…you know how we forget…and…I'll help you unpack."

"No. Seeing Jeremy again won't change my mind. He's not happy either. I wonder if he didn't put his mother up to it." She faced Olivier in the silent room. "Do you think that…" she began.

"Sure. I've missed you since you got married."

Teddy smiled then. "Let's stay up all night the way we used to."

"You're on, kid. I made chili yesterday and the fridge is full of Budweiser."

"You know something, old pal?" Teddy threw her arms around the shorter, slighter figure and the tears fell on the shoulders of his khaki windbreaker. Even in a New York winter, it was his uniform. "My New England blood," he always joked. Seeing her face in the mirror over the bureau Olivier squeezed her hard. Teddy gave a gasp, holding back a sob, and then tried to laugh. "I may live."

*   *   *   *   *   *   *   *   *   *   *

The beige helicopter clattered over the Nevada desert across a pale blue sky. For the hundredth time Chance thought, I'm going nowhere. In a two million dollar machine. Due north, due east for twenty minutes, make sure I'm not followed, then due south until I see the miniature golf course. I should mention that that's the first thing I see and not the landing pad. But Holy Christ! Why fan the flames of paranoia? If I say anything they're liable to make me fly commercial to Seattle and buy a crop-duster or land in Las Vegas and rent a bicycle. Christ. He mopped his narrow face with a white handkerchief and squinted into the glare. The summer suit might as well have been the heaviest wool, made for a winter in Stockholm, for it was soaked with perspiration. Well-cut, expensive, but nonetheless, a damp soggy mess.

Thackery A. Chance was tired. A thin man, who seemed to eat his own weight every day, and then seemed to sweat it away, he was the class sissy grown up; he was the scrawniest kid on the block forty years later. Someone had dubbed the accounting major Take-A-Chance his third year at the University of New Mexico. It was a label for a young man going bald, not interested in women nor men, whose idea of excitement on a Saturday night was a beer and a game of chess. The name pleased him though he was bright enough to note the all too evident sarcasm. But anything was better than being called Thackeray and Albert was worse. Chance was a name for a gambler, a bon vivant; and though the nickname did not change his life he began to drink scotch neat and improved his posture.

The headphones pinched and he adjusted them more comfortably turning to check on Hardware. The Neanderthal Mexican sat beside him, knees spread wide apart, thighs like hams in the worn nearly white jeans. He stared with fascination at what appeared to be a hangnail on his thick as a sausage left index finger. Chance knew that he would be entertained for the entire trip by this.

Forty minutes later Fort Barracuda was below them. It resembled nothing so much as a donkey brown propeller lying in the sand. The golf course extended northward, laid out in the desert like a joke, like an Israeli photograph proclaiming, 'we made the desert bloom.' A satellite dish tilted lazily up at the sky as though sunbathing. If they could paint the grass brown, they would, thought Chance, though they did spend money to keep it soft and green. Maybe soft and brown would be the thing. Extending to the south was what appeared to be a collapsed circus tent painted in a camouflage design. The lumps under it were a pair of vans, a pair of dune buggies and five old Cadillacs. The brothers liked 'the ole fat kind of Caddies' they described as 'real roomy.'

Chance stared down at the sprawling one story ranch house. One wing housed Lesley and Wesley and their bedrooms. Lesley spelled it that way, and not 'Leslie,' to be like his brother. A room, forty feet by sixty, was what they referred to as their home entertainment center. Eleven television screens of varying sizes had been built into the walls;

E-Z Boy loungers in genuine naugahyde sat majestically in the center of the room, little tables beside them to hold the remote control panels and their cans of Dr. Pepper. Pinball machines lined one wall. The brothers kept talking about Chance airlifting in a couple of video games but he hadn't encouraged the project. A second wing extending westward consisted of an enormous white room, its walls almost entirely covered by United States Army maps of the world. They were decorated with pins crowned with miniature colored flags that Wesley and Lesley delighted in removing and resticking. Chance had combed several blocks worth of stationers all over Los Angeles to find just the right pins. "I want the kind a thangs Patton used in that movie," Wesley had insisted. Two more E-Z Boys were in the middle of this room.

The hub of the house was the kitchen, oversized, red linoleum with damp walls and the smell of hamburger gone bad, a place of large metal sinks and steaming cauldrons. Garcia, bow-legged and surly, with a rather oily, precariously balanced pompadour, presided over this territory. He was an astoundingly awful cook and had stayed on after the house had been built, abandoning, with little reluctance, his former trade of plasterer. Now he spent his days making chili that kept the men up at night, belching and wandering the halls cursing him.

The third wing of the ranch was storage for weapons. The room next to the arsenal belonged to Slow, the younger brother of Wesley and Lesley. He had lived with their mother back in their Oklahoma hometown until her death about four years before.

Funny to think, pondered Chance as he prepared to land, that the Barracuda brothers ever had a hometown, or a mother either. He wiped the beads of perspiration from his upper lip and began the descent over the white painted star on the concrete. The brown tarp had been pulled away. Hardware moved beside him, clumsily reaching beneath his seat to gather the red and yellow bags of Fritos. The border of whitewashed tires became clear and then Chance saw the pink metal flamingoes prancing in formation like some mad chorus line out of Alice in

Wonderland. The brothers moved them around constantly in a silly disagreement over whether they should be idealized or, as Wesley thought, appear to be engaged in conversation.

Chance set the copter down gently, turned off the ignition, and pulled the earphones from his head. No sign of life, he thought. The noise had brought no one. Hardware was grunting as he tugged at his seat belt. His brain behind the flat tan face concentrated on nothing but the brute strength involved in freeing himself. Chance would let him go in first. The propellers slowed, were still. Then Take-A-Chance heard it: the familiar strains of Doris Day trilling, 'que sera sera,' and knew that all was normal. The Barracuda brothers were safe for another day. No one else was there; for no one else could have stood their taste in music.

*   *   *   *   *   *   *   *   *   *   *

The church bells began to toll as Teddy pulled her cloak around her and walked quickly through Largo Argentina. Everyone was in a hurry to get home, to get home again, for most had lunched at home at one and returned to their offices and shops at three or half past. At seven o'clock on a February evening Rome was enmeshed in its fourth rush hour of the day. People pushed past Teddy who tried to jam thousands of lire into her pocketbook with several blue plastic bags dangling from her wrists.

"Kiko, Kiko!" squealed Teddy dropping everything onto the sidewalk. The little black chihuahua pranced towards her, between the buckets of violets, daisies, daffodils, and tulips, ready to be petted. The dog led an ideal life—dividing his time between the flower vendor's awning and Paolo's bar. When it rained he went to the bar and very hot summer days were spent reclining on Paolo's ice cream cooler on top of the sports section of Il Messaggero. Teddy loved asking his owner where he was and hearing the answer, "Kiko! Al bar." "You little darling one!" she cooed, oblivious to the young Moroccan who owned the dog and the flower stand. "Per Lei," he smiled as he extended the one white rose.

He shrugged, pleased, hands deep in the pockets of his grey cardigan, when she excitedly thanked him. The dog continued to wag his tail as Teddy retrieved her possessions. "Le piace?" he asked. Teddy nodded and then said helplessly in English. "I adore him." Kiko stood on his hind legs like a tiny circus horse as she called, "Arrivederci!"

The tall blonde made her way through the little piazza and down the narrow cobblestoned street of Benedetto Cairoli. Two Africans, probably in their late teens, greeted her in English as she tried to avoid stepping on their display in front of her doorway. Shining bracelets and earrings, and leather belts and what looked like snakeskin bags were arranged on a yard square piece of red fabric laid directly on the street. Teddy always felt a pang of sympathy for them, huddled in their cheap parkas looking as though they suffered from the chill of the Roman winter more than anyone else. No longer did they plead for her to buy which was a relief, but last week, to her dismay, had given her a pair of copper earrings and refused the few thousand lire she'd urged upon them. She wore them now and they noticed and grinned with very white teeth.

Teddy entered the dimly lit building, thinking that Signora Fabiano, the portiere, must be in if the front door were unlocked. Sure enough, as she stepped into the little cube of an elevator, she could hear the woman shrieking at poor Signor Fabiano in that voice like a parrot. Teddy laughed aloud as she pushed the button for three. She knew she would pass them in Campo dei Fiori the next morning and they would be bickering over how many grams of grapes to buy, but overall, looking quite happy with life and each other. Signor Fabiano had made her understand only the week before that they had just celebrated their forty-fifth wedding anniversary.

Teddy fumbled with the key which looked large enough to be a stage prop and, at last, with arms full, kicked the eight foot tall door open. She hummed to herself as she dumped bags in the kitchen then tore off the black wool cape. The apartment belonged to Heidi, one of the models she'd met her first day in Rome. On her third day, Heidi had told her she was going to Vienna to become an actress and to live with her fidanzato. Literally, this meant he was her fiance, but no one took this expression seriously. "Do you want him?" she had asked again and again at lunch in her German accent, speaking a bit of English and a smattering of Italian.

Teddy was confused, didn't know how to answer. Was this some European custom, to give your lover to a new friend? "You must tell me, Teddy, for I must know. He is very good, really, very pretty, very nice, very big, and with much light and in the centro. He is near the best market…"

Teddy said simply, "I want him."

It was an old building with stone walls and marble floors and green shutters. The apartment itself was white, and high-ceilinged with beams of dark wood. Heidi had hung dozens of old maps, charcoal sketches by an artist friend, and her own watercolors everywhere. The furniture in the living room was arranged around a sofa that could not be seen under its Tunisian rug of bright primary colors in geometric patterns. A pair of large chairs copied by a local carpenter from a photograph of an Egyptian throne sat on either side of the couch. The gilt shone in the half light; the chairs' goat hooves disappeared at the ankle in the white flokati rug. Silhouetted gossamer-clad goddesses etched into each chair-back surveyed the room with dark eyes. These had been abandoned by a former tenant, a Hungarian archaeologist. A rectangular teak table inlaid with ivory had been placed in front of the sofa. On this, Teddy now stood the brass candlesticks in the shape of cobras and the new turquoise candles she'd bought today. "Oh, Lord, pass the incense. This place looks ready for a seance. Maybe I could contact Ramses and ask him what he thinks about Italy's new coalition government or

Hatshepsut could wander in for wine and tell me about divorce in Ancient Egypt...."

Divorce, thought Teddy. Grounds: my mother-in-law. No, not really. She pushed her hair back with the black velvet band. Mrs. Hathaway simply kicked me towards something I wasn't sure how to do. If I ever reminded her of our conversation she would feign amazement and maybe she'd say "Oh, gracious!" No. That's what Aunt Cricket would say. She'd say, "Oh, my dear, really!" and deny "the girl's wild fantasy" about money. Suppose I could have just taken the check and cashed it and seen her the following week for dinner and smiled sweetly. But, frowned Teddy, she knew I wasn't like that. And I'm not.

Jeremy must have read Blakeley's separation agreement and bit his lip the way he does when he's mulling things over. And then he would have said imperiously, "Jones, hold my calls. I'm going out," and Jones, never Miss Jones, would have. Then Jeremy would have stalked to the executive washroom and washed his face and hands if he had been the least bit affected by the letter and then stalked directly to the elevator and down and out through the big granite lobby on Park Avenue and across the street to the Racquet Club for something like a bloody Mary. Not because he really needed one, but so later he could tell Stubbs and maybe Angleton that he 'just had to have a drink.' Teddy scowled. Everything so you could tell somebody later. So you could get credit.

"Boy oh boy!" she shouted. Did we ever get married in a fever! As Aunt Daisy said when I called and told her the wedding was in one week, "Are you trying to get married yesterday?"

Teddy walked decisively towards the blue and white tiled kitchen where she put water on to boil for pasta and began to wash the rughetta for a salad. She grated a third of the fist-sized hunk of Parmesan cheese and it fell in a little pale mountain on the butcher block. It pleased her as did the rich red Chianti in the balloon wine glass.

Maybe, she thought, I'm at the beginning of a happy ending. I feel relieved about Jeremy. No guilt. We were well matched: I was impossible some of the time and he was, too. A lot of the time, actually. Maybe I'm at the start of a happy beginning. Food. Food for thought. After ravioli with butter and garlic and nutmeg and parsley and ground beef and…she sipped the wine. After dinner, I'll know what to do.

$*\quad*\quad*\quad*\quad*\quad*\quad*\quad*\quad*\quad*\quad*$

It stinks. It really has a peculiar smell, thought Chance as he lifted his fork, slowly, suspiciously.

"It's a new recipe," boomed Leslie. "Garcia actually bought hisself a cookbook. Actually Slow sent away for it and Jose drove to Vegas to pick it up at the p.o.and well," he said more quietly, trying to keep the note of optimism in his voice, "it IS a new recipe."

Chance stared intently at the gray matter which clung wetly to the tines of his fork. Wonder if it's something somebody shot. Wonder if it's just plain somebody. Some poor Mexican, some poor wetback, who got too close to the electrified fence and got fried with a big buzz—just one last, big zzzz, for all time.

Wesley had finished and pushed his empty plate away. He leaned back in the wooden chair but his belly stretched forward and still touched the edge of the red and white checked oilcloth. He was engaged in serious tooth-picking with the gold toothpick he'd bought years ago in Tijuana. Or maybe someone had given it to him. Or maybe he'd taken it. He'd had it for years. His face, like Lesley's, was deeply pock-marked from adolescent acne. In Spanish he was referred to as 'cara pina' or pineapple face. The mottled surface was scarred by the long stroke a machete had made. Its inch wide band of shiny pink tissue stretched from the corner of his left eyelid down his cheek to the edge of his jawbone. Like Lesley, he too possessed mud brown eyes that Chance avoided looking into. They didn't shine but instead had irises that were like leather.

Wesley and Lesley, a year apart could have been twins in appearance, in gesture, in their choice of pastel-colored leisure suits and sansabelt slacks. Their voices both rasped hoarsely over the telephone identically; their mouths smiled often, their eyes never.

Chance took a tentative third bite of the mess on the paper plate before him and resisted the urge to grimace in horror. Slow, the third brother, hadn't touched his serving. The midget sat quietly in his blue denim overalls. He was pushed too close to the table like a child in a highchair but had made no objection. His short legs dangled in midair, tiny feet in red and white striped socks, scuffed brown shoes, the high-topped lace-up kind Spanky wore on the Little Rascals.

"I wanna talk to ya, Chance, about what's goin' on in Panama. If there's a political problem with the outfit in Washington and those banks get looked at…" Lesley leaned back and shook his head. "It'll all hit the fan for sure."

Chance spoke evenly. "Don't worry. I've got a good man down there watching things. And he's spreading money where it can do the most good." The drop offs and the pick ups in the telephone booth nearest the National Guard barracks had been going like clockwork and there had been no arrests for two months. No arrests didn't mean our people were getting smarter-it just meant people with badges were getting fat wallets and we all know that money can cause blindness. One of Chance's reasons to exist was to insulate the Barracuda brothers as much as possible from every person possible. He did it well. Chance was their sole link to Los Angeles and the world beyond. "He," Chance began again."He's a little tense about the new police chief in Panama City but so's everybody else so he figures he won't last long."

Lesley then gave an emormous belch, so loud that Chance wasn't sure it had come from a human at all, so deep and rumbling that Chance was reminded of a truck backfiring on a major highway. They all stared. Chance, with his fork in hand, swearing he'd never have dinner here again, Wesley with his dead-eyed look, slack-jawed with surprise, and Slow, blinking. It was Wesley who broke the silence afterwards. He guffawed, "Okay! Thas the best one this year so far but jes you wait!"

Lesley grinned expansively, proudly, exposing square yellow teeth like kernels of corn. He banged his fist on the table and hooted, "yessir-ree bob! I wish I had me a tape recorder!"

* * * * * * * * * * *

Teddy leaned forward reaching for the glass of white wine. The liquid sparkled in the sun giving off little stars of light as she tilted it towards her smiling lips. "Well, I'm glad I stayed. I had a few moments of oh, god, what am I doing here pangs but that seems like ages ago." She put the glass down on the blue linen cloth and looked around at the other tables at the outdoor trattoria. "Now, I wonder why I ever considered leaving."

Diane nodded. "I know exactly the feeling. I've been here for six years. About every four months I am awash with the idea that the world is whirling past me at a great speed—things are happening back in New York or somewhere—-anywhere but here—without me. But I can't leave." She poured herself aqua minerale and sipped. "I guess the scariest part of it all is to think of Rome as a place frozen in time."

Teddy unbuttoned the black and white houndstooth jacket with a great jangling of silver bracelets. Her silver hoop earrings were big enough for curtain rods. "I think it's almost heaven here..." She thought of Massimo kissing her on the bridge the night before or had it been this morning?

Faith laughed. Her name had forced a great cynicism upon her and she often laughed at people she labelled too earnest for their own good. "You DO love it here, don't you?" Her brown curls were shiny, her freckles made her look much younger than her thirty years. Without allowing Teddy to answer, she went on, "Haven't you been attacked by gypsies yet? Haven't you fought with the questura over your papers to stay? Haven't you had the phone company mischarge you thousands of lire because they realize, somehow, in those nasty computers, that you're foreign and you might be calling home?"

"Oh, stop it! You've been having a bad week!" burst in Diane. White paper pale no matter what the season, very thin, soft-spoken Diane was a bright woman who earned a good living as a translator of novels.

"Bad week!"hooted Faith. "More like a bad year! If my darling husbando doesn't get himself transferred to some other embassy I may drink drain opener. Wonder how long it would take an ambulanza to get through the impossible traffic…"

Diane allowed the waiter to place coffee in front of her and then retorted, "You'd better watch out. Brian might get posted to the Philippines or to Warsaw and then you'd look back on these halcyon days…"

Teddy leaned forward and gave Diane the look which meant 'tell me later' and Diane acknowledged it. 'Halcyon.' They were close friends after several afternoons of wine-drinking. It was either lolling on the big paisley cushions on Teddy's living room rug or sitting in Diane's wicker chairs catching the last rays of sun on her balcony.

Their first meeting had been a freak accident; it wouldn't have happened if it had not been an exceptionally warm day in February. Teddy had been given a telephone number for an exercise class and had dialed it in her living room idly staring through her open balcony doors. After haltingly apologizing for the wrong number she had been delighted when an American asked in English what number she wanted. Teddy read from a scrap of paper trying to make herself heard over very loud classical music. "Just a minute," the other woman excused herself. "Let me turn this down." Teddy waited and as she stood there watched some one clad in blue jeans with long dark hair rush into the living room across the street and bend over a table. The music stopped. Laughing, Teddy asked the voice on the line to please look out the window. Diane had, quite perplexed, and then grinned at the tall blonde who waved back at her. They had had wine at Teddy's apartment that evening and talked for hours.

Diane was from Chicago but had lived in New York City, thought that coming from Alabama was very interesting, and was amazed at how much and how little Teddy knew of the world. Teddy thought Diane was brilliant, was convinced she knew everything about Italy and Rome and the Italians. How she wished she could speak the way Diane did. Italian or English. Diane had given her an Italian text and a book by Henry James and she was plodding through both. But if she's so smart about so many things, wondered Teddy, then why does she dress that way all the time? She had a good figure but made no effort to be sexy; she had shining brown hair but it was strictly wash and wear.

"You walk like you're very old and you're only thirty-something," Teddy told her once and Diane had laughed. "Yes, that's probably a fair observation. But next to you, Teddy, anyone is old." The blonde smiled back but wasn't sure exactly what was meant.

Faith was staring down into her coffee. "All jokes aside. I think I'm dying." The two other women were silent. "I mean, it's all very romantic, isn't it, sitting here like this in our light wool jackets when New Yorkers are getting frostbitten, sipping wine under the green leaves, a blue sky, the traffic noises in the distance." At that moment a motorcycle raced by their table. Faith tried to smile. "I really hate my life in Rome and if I can't tell you, Diane, then I shouldn't even bother with Brian…."

Teddy looked to Diane, who'd known Faith for a year, to answer her.

"It's not being able to work, isn't it?"

"A big part, yes."

"There's no equivalent to Madison Avenue here is there?"

Faith fairly snorted with derision. "Hardly."

"Have you talked to Brian?"

"Tried. He doesn't understand. I think he'd love to trade places with me and be able to…to do this…to stay at home all day or meet people for lunch."

Teddy thought, it's not so bad. This. She felt the sun and felt happy that no one would bawl her out for getting tan. No more modelling jobs if I can help it. Three evenings parading up and down the Spanish Steps in glorious clothes with crowds and lights and television cameras and here I am two weeks later.

"You were-you are so good at what you do," Diane was saying. "Brian must know you can't go from a six figure salary at a top ad agency-"

"And a corner office and two secretaries and one personal assistant," put in Faith.

"To being concerned about the cleaning woman-"

"Sicilian and impossible," interjected Faith.

Diane sighed. "I don't know what to tell you. Have you thought about telling Brian you want to commute to Milano where the advertising for this country is?"

"My god," breathed Faith. "What a positively evil and delicious idea!"

Teddy flipped her hair back over one shoulder and stared at her.

"I owe you one," Faith smiled as they divided the check. "Brains, brains, brains. That's all it takes. And plane tickets."

Teddy and Diane walked back to Piazza Benedetto Cairoli through the quiet streets of the lunch hour. All was closed for mezzogiorno from one o'clock to half past three or four or half past four. The grocers didn't open again until five-thirty unless it was Thursday afternoon when they didn't open at all because they did open on Monday mornings when everything else was closed. It was an elaborate system. "Do you think she'll really go to Milano?" asked Teddy.

"No, I don't. I'm sorry I gave her the idea." Diane gazed down at her scuffed penny loafers. "I like her but I don't like the way she'll use the idea to frighten Brian, to get her way about something else."

"How?"

"Oh, a trip home to New York or a long weekend in Paris. She'll throw it at him and he'll think, poor dear, she needs a change and I'd better give it to her. I'd better make her happy and divert her."

"That's awful!" breathed Teddy. She stopped in front of a church and made a face. "That's manipulative and sneaky and so that's what she meant by 'evil and delicious!'"

Diane was trying not to smile. At twenty-two Teddy had a lot to learn. Men were staring at her but she wasn't noticing. Today her hair was a tangled mass of ringlets. Teddy had mentioned reading Italian Vogue with a dictionary and rolling her hair up in socks. She looked golden and healthy and strong.

"I'd never do that kind of thing," growled Teddy as she fell into step with her friend. "Never. Never. I never did in my marriage and I never would in real life either."

Diane laughed. Teddy had never discussed her marriage except to say her husband was a snob and they'd gotten tired of each other. Could anything be as simple as that? One couldn't know with Teddy Starbuck. She'd told Diane that she was her first real woman friend. Perhaps because we're not after the same things. Her reverie was cut short. "I call it terrible, Diane! Could you do something like that? Could you shame-lessly manipulate a man that way?"

Diane's gray eyes looked sad for just an instant before she answered, "I wouldn't know how."

* * * * * * * * * * *

Chapter Two

"It's not as though I haven't thought about it," sighed Teddy, "but what can I do about it?"

"My advice is to do nothing until you're asked…"

"Or until you're on the floor and he is panting in a mixture of French and Italian…"

"Oh, he's not like that!" giggled Teddy. She raised her arms high and twisted her hair into a knot atop her head, then dropped her hands in her lap. She sat cross-legged on the floor of her apartment leaning against velvet pillows. Black leather flats and black lace stockings showed under the hem of the black wool skirt.

Eleanor began to laugh. "Have you seen the latest ads on television? The one where the man with this enormous moustache leers into the camera, I think he's photographed shoulders up wearing no shirt, as if he's just rolled out of bed…"

Diane screamed. "I know that man! I know that man! He looks like the policeman on duty in front of Piazza Venezia from nine to eleven…"

"No, no." Eleanor was adamant. "He looks like every taxi driver you've ever had."

"Had?" laughed Diane.

"Oh, stop it! What are you talking about?" cried an exasperated Teddy.

"Get Massimo to use CONTROL!"

"What is it?"

Diane explained as Eleanor poured more red wine. "This character with the moustache says in this low, sexy, highly meaningful way-'Io faccio l'amore con CONTROL.' and then the camera-"

"I make love with control?" demanded Teddy.

"No, no! Diane, do it right! With CONTROL!"

"And then this box of rubbers appears on the screen…"

Teddy had her hand over her mouth in shock.

Diane felt good after finishing the manuscripts. This was a bit of a celebration after all. She poured herself another glass of wine. "Don't ever do what a friend of mine did. She didn't know Italian very well and was always hanging vowels on the ends of English words and struggling along." She smiled. "Just like you, Teddy. This could have happened to you."

"My Italian is impeccable. Don't be ridiculous."

"Anyway, she was in a grocery store buying some fruit juice and it was just before the one o'clock closing and the place was jammed with housewives. When it was finally her turn to be first at the counter and to ask for her cheese and so forth she held up this can of tomato juice and asked if it had sugar in it and the man said no and then she asked if it had preservativi in it and there was this dead silence in the place. The three men behind the counter got beet red, but being Italian and very polite they shook their heads 'no.' She paid for everything and left the shop to have lunch with me…" Diane started to laugh. "Preservativi means prophylactics!"

Teddy rose to her feet groaning. "On that note, I shall now prepare the sauce for the spaghetti con vongole." She turned in the doorway of the living room. "Eleanor, you're not allergic to clams, are you?"

"I can eat anything, Teddy. And unfortunately, I do!" The auburn-haired woman looked down at her very tight trousers with dismay. "I don't know how you do it, Diane. A week here and I had gained about ten pounds and here I am three years later and I still haven't lost them. I keep my scales by the refrigerator and I weigh myself all the time, but..."

"All the time?"

Eleanor laughed. "You should see me—starving when I get home from Stampa Estera-I mean telexing a story to London about the latest fall of the government makes me die for food—anything makes me die for food—so I charge into my kitchen and weigh myself then I am upset so I begin taking off my jewelry and weighing myself again and then it's off with my sweater and still I'm ten pounds over and pretty soon I'm stark naked..."

"Hey, are you two still talking about sex?" Teddy stood over them holding a dishtowel and a wooden spoon.

They laughed at her. Eleanor began again. "We haven't been much help, have we, Teddy? You asked a serious question about an hour ago..."

"Why don't we move into the kitchen so we can keep talking?" Diane felt protective of Teddy. She was so young in so many ways. Soft. A believer of everything anyone told her. Tender. And yet, a protector. A defender. Why, Teddy had even noticed that the old tom who napped on the hood of the green Fiat by Campo dei Fiori every morning had a new battle scar. "His ear, Diane! If only I could get close enough to put a lit-tle dab of iodine..." Diane had shivered. No telling what diseases you'd come down with if that cat took a swipe at you.

But Teddy didn't consider that. Just that it was a creature smaller than she, most creatures were, come to think of it. But all Teddy saw was something in need of help, specifically her help. Perhaps that came from being so tall, so strong, such a tomboy as Teddy had told her she had been as a child back in Alabama. And there was this affinity for the weaker. She was an earth mother and now, as she poured several ounces of white wine over the clams, she was feeding her friends. But the other side of Teddy could have probably joined Sir Edmund Hilary on his trek and laughed at nosebleeds. Diane felt warm and the wine had relaxed her after the tension of meeting that deadline. Her mind wandered almost dreamily as she leaned on her elbows at the kitchen table. Teddy would have been one of the strong ones, fearless, uncomplaining, able to forge ahead. However, she would have been torn between being the first one to the top or staying behind and encouraging the slowest one.

"Diane!" Teddy was grinning. Blond hair fanned around her face. "Are you with us?" Diane nodded. "Don't you think Massimo is adorable? Don't you?"

"Well, I only saw the top of his head which was nice, but if you say so, I'm sure he is adorable."

Teddy sighed. "You can tell a lot about someone by leaning out the window across the street…"

Eleanor asked how Teddy would describe him. "Besides adorable," she amended quickly.

"This will take a little thought," Teddy said slowly as she ladled spaghetti on the bright yellow plates. The kitchen was warm and smelled of garlic and butter and hot bread. They carried trays of silverware and plates and napkins back and forth to the large round oak table in a corner of the living room.

"Bought this palm tree last week," explained Teddy as they seated themselves. "Don't you feel that we, under this, are on some island somewhere?"

"Absolutely. Nothing less romantic than Zanzibar."

"Come on, Teddy, I want to hear about Massimo. First of all, is he good enough for you?"

"Oh," Teddy looked serious. "Probably too good for me."

The others moaned. "Wrong attitude! Ten points taken away!"

"He's…" sighed Teddy. "Quiet and stable and dependable and so sweet."

"Banker?" quipped Eleanor.

"Why, how did you know?" cried the blonde, her brown eyes wide with surprise.

Eleanor stifled her impulse to laugh when she saw Diane's warning look.

"Wild guess. Go on."

"He's rather exotic. His father is Roman and his mother is Parisian but she's been dead forever, since he was a little boy which I think is so sad." Her voice was wistful. "But he hardly knew her!" she finished brightly. "He has a round face and he wears these little wire-rimmed glasses and has blue eyes from his mother and this jet-black Italian hair. I love the way he smiles. It's a very shy smile. I don't think he's had many lovers which is one reason it might be all right to make love to him but then again maybe he hasn't asked me because I am American and it seems from everything we read that every single person in the United States is either dying in a hospital or walking around waiting for their seven years of incubation to be up..."

The talk buzzed on. It was a warm night for February and the balcony doors were halfway open. Teddy had lit a dozen candles in Heidi's eclectic collection of candlesticks around the big room. Shadows crossed the beamed ceiling high above them. The brass cobras always held a pair of turquoise candles, the glass stars over on the bookcase always held yellow ones; five pale blue candles were in the blue and white candelabra from Tunisia.

Teddy felt at home in the apartment, in Rome. She had told her aunts in Ace only last Sunday that she had found a place that felt better than New York, different from Alabama. A space to be happy in. She didn't feel different here the way she had in New York for she was so different here, first of all being American, second of all being a woman living alone, that any other kind of different, for instance her Alabama accent which came and went, was too minor to consider. Teddy felt sheer delight when she looked around the apartment and held the big key in her hand. The spirit of Heidi was here and she liked Heidi and Diane was across the street and Signor and Signora Fabiano treated her like a daughter, albeit a retarded daughter, so there was no chance of ever feeling lonely.

Loneliness wasn't anything Teddy had experienced in her life, anyway. It wasn't a word she'd ever spoken for she would have said, 'by myself' which connoted pride of accomplishment. Teddy enjoyed being by herself and when someone in New York had talked of being lonely, Teddy had felt sorry for the person who could suffer such a thing, not sorry at all about the situation that induced such an emotion.

This was Teddy's first apartment, at least the first time she'd ever lived alone. Olivier had invited her to live with him and it had been like having a brother and then, of course, the big East End Avenue place with Jeremy. Six rooms with a river view had been nothing to complain about. But this feels like mine. She looked at the faces in the candlelight and thought, so much of the goodness of Rome has to do with Diane. Teddy had never known anyone like her—a woman who lived by using her brain, was entirely self-sufficient and was happy. That friendship was one of the best things about Rome. And maybe the sweetest thing about Rome was Massimo.

Teddy sipped her wine and smiled. It was her little cat smile of pleasure.

*   *   *   *   *   *   *   *   *   *   *

The small figure rocked back and forth sideways on his short legs encased in cowboy boots. The red leather came up over his knees and forced him to walk stiff-legged but the boots did add a good three inches to his height. Slow was also wearing his ubiquitous denim overalls, and a red T shirt which exposed his muscular arms; he had tied a red bandana around his neck. He sang softly as he poured the high fiber cereal into a bowl then strained to reach the handle of the refrigerator. "Milk. Nonfat." He said aloud as though explaining, "We could all live longer. Live to our highest potential if we didn't fill our systems with all the wrong things. With junk. With sugar. With chemicals." Slow sat down in a little blue rocking chair and lifted the first spoonful to his mouth.

The midget's room at Fort Barracuda was all his. No one, not Garcia, not Jose, not Hardware, not his brothers, ever came here. That was the thing he liked about it best. When he'd arrived from Oklahoma at the Las Vegas airport, Jose, who was as beefy as Hardware, had sought him out then packed all his belongings which were considerable into a white van and driven down a highway. Half an hour later he had turned off it and proceeded to the middle of the desert. Slow had worried that he was in the hands of a Mexican madman and had implored him in his self-taught Spanish to let him out, to let him go. But Jose had faced straight ahead, hunched over the wheel as they rocked and bucked over the desert floor.

At last Slow had seen the waiting helicopter, like a mirage, in the distance. Take-A-Chance, in a suit and tie, had introduced himself and he had been pulled inside as Jose transferred the crates and his one suitcase. In minutes they had risen straight up in the sky with Jose a spot below them driving the van back to Las Vegas.

Secrecy hung over Fort Barracuda like a hot unbreathable cloud. Slow had not seen his brothers for years. There had been Christmas postcards with motel swimming pools on them but no return addresses ever. Usually these motel swimming pools were located in Mexico. Acapulco one Christmas, Merida the next. Money arrived for Slow and his mother. Wired. Again usually from Mexico. Ne message. No name. Just thousands. So many thousands of dollars over the years.

Momma hadn't wanted to spend it. She knew her boys. She could never forget how they'd shot up that Texaco halfway to Tulsa, come to her for help, and then when she refused to hide them from the sheriff had waved a gun in her face until she'd given them her cookie jar cash. "Yessirree, Sidney, I know my boys," she often said to Slow. Momma was the only one to use his real name, the name on his birth certificate. As a child, he had been pointed at so often and when people bent down and asked when he was going to grow, his brothers would cackle from their superior heights and chortle, "He will. He's a gonna. He's jes slow." Some folks thought slow meant something different. It hurt his feelings for years and then he stopped thinking about it. They didn't know any better.

Without shoes, the midget was nearly forty inches tall. Slow was too short to pump gas, he couldn't reach the hose. Slow was too little to see over a counter in Sally's Dry Goods or she would have given him a job for she said to everybody all the time "I shore do lak the little feller." So Slow, after high school, the first one in his family to graduate, stayed at home with Momma. They went to the library together every Monday morning at nine and returned six books then checked out three more each which was the most allowed. It was an exciting journey for them both which involved two buses each way.

Once they had made a trip as far away as Oklahoma City just for the adventure of it. Slow would never forget Momma in Sears, trying on all those flowered hats and he'd bought new jeans in the boys' department and five checked shirts of all colors that he still wore. It had been Slow who'd urged Momma to use some of the money for this and he'd been right, she'd said afterwards on the big Greyhound going home. "You was right, Sidney. That money came from somethin' bad, I jes knows that in my bones 'cause I know my boys, but we cain't give it back and so we used it for somethin' good." She rearranged the shopping bags on her lap and pulled out the yards of yellow and white flowered cotton for the new kitchen curtains. Her calloused old age-spotted hand stroked it gently. She looked at her youngest son and he could see her smile in the lights of a passing truck. "Yessirree, Sidney. What a happy, happy day!"

Slow often daydreamed about that day. One of the best days, maybe the best, of his life.

Now he finished the cereal and looked around the room. It was painted an emerald green, "the color of balance, of growth," he had explained his choice aloud. He'd painted it himself not allowing Jose or

Hardware to help. They had been instructed to leave the ladder and the paint and brushes outside in the hall which led past the arsenal to the kitchen. Miraculously they had bought the right color several Nevada towns away involving their usual changing of vans and the helicopter airlift. All the groceries and supplies and mail arrived in this manner. Slow had had a post office box in a little dustspeck a hundred miles from the ranch but it had infuriated Wes and Les and they had shouted at him to mail the key back. Now he had one in Las Vegas which they decided was a big enough city not to incite suspicion. And besides, as Wes said, "Nobody knows we got a dwarf in the family nohow."

"We may not need some of these charts, anymore," he said aloud. Slow rocked in the boots over to the kitchenette and rinsed the spoon and the bowl. Then he pulled a chair over to the wall and stood on it and began to unpin a map of the United States that had all the state capitals circled in red. "I'll leave this one of the stars up because I jes...just like it, but I think the Solar System kin...can come down." He stepped down, moved the chair again and climbed up on the seat and began to remove thumbtacks. "I saw las..last night something in the National Geographic you'd be interested in but I thought it could wait till...until today."

He stepped off the chair and began to fold the paper carefully. Each planet was surrounded by ball point pen markings telling the distance from the sun and from the earth and its diameter, its moons and the presence or absence of oxygen and water. "Yep...I mean yes. There is this tribe in the Amazon that has found an antidote for..." his voice went on. He rocked across the room to a small chair and sat down with the magazine open on his lap and began to read.

"Now listen to this carefully because it's mighty..I mean, very interesting."

The sun shone in the windows through the slatted venetian blinds. Slow spent a few minutes every morning at sunrise tying back the black out cloths he detested and then adjusting the blinds at just the right angle. He took no chances; he wanted no one to see inside his room. Practically square, his favorite color green with a white ceiling. A single bed covered with a Mexican blanket of pink and red and blue and green and black zigzags was in one corner. Slow had a bureau and a shoe rack beside it with four pairs of shoes tilted upwards. All were scuffed and old save the red cowboy boots he now wore because he was too self-conscious to wear them outside. The blue rocking chair was for a child as were the table and the four matching chairs. All the furniture in the room save the metal bedstead bore teethmarks near the floor. There were several bookcases three feet high crammed with volumes—a large dictionary, a complete set of the Encyclopedia Britannica, a thesaurus, several books on gem-collecting and astronomy, history books, and books on health, racehorses, rabbits. National Geographics were arranged by month and year dating all the way back to Slow's fifteenth birthday. Their yellow spines were a bright stripe of color practically the length of the room. Several books on the stock market rested beside a book on the Impressionists. A social history of Plantagenet England stood beside a book on Samurai warriors.

Slow continued to read aloud quietly. "A detailed analysis has turned up 72 different proteins that are fundamental for the healing of wounds in humans and other animals. Some of them actually block bacterial growth. Drug companies have made inquiries about duplicating the secretion but the complexity might preclude synthesizing it." He put the magazine down and continued in a soft conversational voice. "From a fish! Can you imagine? And that isolated tribe discovered it." Slow turned the page as he whispered, "Amazing." It was almost as though he were talking to himself.

∗   ∗   ∗   ∗   ∗   ∗   ∗   ∗   ∗   ∗   ∗

Home is where the phone is. The chocolate brown Mercedes convertible slowed for the light on Rodeo Drive. "What do you mean you can't do it?" Take-A-Chance's voice was hard. "Look, if it's not in L.A. by the sixth, I can't guarantee a thing." He glanced in the rearview mirror before turning. "No.No." His face was a mask behind the Ray-Bans. "No. That's it. No delivery, no money." He listened into the beige phone as he pressed the accelerator down. "Same rules as always, Jack. No exceptions."

Thinking how hot it was, he balanced the phone on his shoulder as he reached down and pushed the air-conditioning control to high. "If it were up to me I'd say what the hell. I know you're good for it. Sure." He glanced at his Rolex and decided the conversation had gone on long enough. "But, Jack, you know it's not up to me." He listened. "Yeah. Okay. The sixth."

Chance hung up and jerked his dark blue silk Sulka tie loose in the stifling heat. It was rare for him to use the car phone. A lousy risk, the Barracudas claimed and he agreed. Cellular phones, too. Out of the question for the business they were in. Can't be too safe. Hardware gave a snore from the backseat, his enormous basketball of a head lolling downward on his wall of a chest. He looked close to drooling on the yellow felt drawstring bag. It was a hundred dollars in quarters all conveniently rolled in red paper cylinders about the size of a package of Life Savers. Hardware could just about handle going into a bank and making the transaction. Christ. Is he my bodyguard or am I his babysitter, wondered Chance as he checked the mirror again. I know he performs two functions even if he is too dumb to know it. Number one: make sure I don't disappear. Secondly, he is my bodyguard. Guards my little body. Chance wished he had time to work out once in awhile. He was undeniably scrawny and no tailor in California for no amount of money could disguise the potbelly on a scrawny forty-one year old male. The python effect.

Chance grimaced. Wes and Les loved those snakes but that old boa constrictor DooDah was the greatest of them all to hear them tell it. He shuddered as he remembered how they'd proudly led him into the snake room for their show. DooDah was 'pretty peppy' Les kept saying. Well, you'd be peppy, too, thought Chance, if you hadn't eaten in five weeks and your next meal was about to be lowered by its tail into your mouth. Chance had gone quite white with disgust. The third rat of the evening was too much for him and he had turned suddenly away claiming he had to call Los Angeles. Trying to sound casual, trying to save face, trying to save his dinner which he lost in the hallway. God. He wiped his face with his handkerchief and drove on.

Hardware snorted. An animal noise. Chance shuddered again. A killing machine. He knew it. He also knew that the killing machine could be turned on him. Quickly, like remembering a mantra or a prayer or not stepping on the crack in a sidewalk, Chance computed how much money he had put away. The money and his possible escape from the Barracudas and Hardware and Jose were all that could calm him these days. He'd told Wes and Les that it couldn't go on forever but they didn't believe him. Chance was a careful man, with an accountant's mentality about some things, particularly about money, and he had planned for the end. He punched in a tape of Carly Simon and thought of the money. The chocolate brown Mercedes convertible purred down the highway towards Los Angeles, his house and still another phone.

* * * * * * * * * * *

"No, I didn't run away from Ace." Teddy reached for more gorgonzola. She and Diane had decided to have a simple lunch in Diane's apartment and the table was spread with bread from the downstairs bakery, prosciutto both crudo and cooked, olives, artichoke hearts. "I love Ace. I am happy when I'm there." She smiled as though about to say something and then stopped.

Diane filled their glasses with white wine. Something new she'd found for a whopping four thousand lire a bottle which came to about three U.S. dollars these days. "What is it? Come on, Teddy! Don't hold out on me."

"Oh, you'd laugh if I told you. I think that growing up in Ace is probably a planet away from Chicago." The expression on her face suggested that wasn't a bad thing.

Diane silently agreed with her. "So tell. What were you like in high school?" Diane had met dozens upon dozens of misfit expatriates in Rome but Teddy Starbuck wasn't one. There were many Americans who came for a year and twenty years later were still complaining about the same things: how provincial Rome was, the rising prices of restaurants, the traffic, the Italian inefficiency, the mezzogiorno. But they didn't leave.

Diane thought many of them were second-rate as writers, as painters, as sculptors and could not have made it back home. What money they had went further in Italy and a garret with a view of church steeples above a piazza had a lot more panache than living in a low rent area of Manhattan or fleeing across the river to New Jersey for more reasonable living space. At least when they bought a cut rate ticket from the VIP Club and arrived in New York or Cincinnati after twenty- seven hours of travelling on Yugoslavian Airways their friends treated them as romantics. For the English of the same mind, it was the same. But they skipped the night in Belgrade and travelled on Ghana Airways, getting on at Fiumicino as the plane refuelled between Accra and Heathrow. Of course, there were the exceptions. Like Gore Vidal.

But Teddy wasn't second best at anything, she really hadn't become anything yet. No college, no ideas of a career. She'd worked in the diner in Ace for a year and 'it was hilarious,' she told Diane. She'd worked in the town's 5 & 10 cent store and 'had a wild time.' Now, at twenty-two, she had only a bad marriage in her past, a bit of a modelling career she hated, and those incredible good looks as a passport to whatever she wanted next.

"Tell me, Teddy. What were you like in high school?" Diane's voice was serious. Teddy was staring out at the sheets of rain, daydreaming. The gutter spouts were splashing bucketfuls of water on the cobbles below.

"Sounds like seven hundred million people have let their bathtubs overflow. I remember at home when it rained like this, my aunts Cricket and Daisy and I would…"

"Are those their real names?"

"My mother was named Beatrice but they called her Birdie because when she talked she always tilted her head to one side like a little bird. So there were these three sisters—Cricket, Daisy, and Birdie." Diane laughed as Teddy continued. "And all of them so tiny! I used to tease them and call them my little chihuahuas and they'd get so crazy and threaten never to speak to me again and in five minutes…" She grinned. "That's prob'ly why I love Kiko so much. He reminds me of my aunts. I swear to God, Diane, I was this giant in the house. Nobody thought I'd ever stop growing and I was worried all the time that I'd go through life with nobody askin' me to dance." Her southern accent returned whenever she talked about Alabama. "That worry started when I was about nine and ended when I was twelve." She sighed. "Three whole years of pre-adolescent panic."

Diane blinked. Pre-adolescent. She'd used the word last week and Teddy had asked about it.

"But anyway, I never knew Birdie which is why I never call her Mother. I just heard talk about her from the time I was about three, I guess."

Something about this rain, thought Diane, must promote the exchange of confidences, and an apartment in Rome at the mezzogiorno when all is still, when the town is dozing. The rain splashed outside the open windows and the white geraniums on the balcony in their terra cotta pots moved their petals like little flags of surrender in the grey light.

"I prob'ly told you, didn't I?" Teddy did not wait for Diane to answer. "She died the same year Daddy did. They say it was a broken heart. That's what her sisters say, anyway." Teddy sipped from the wine and hesitated as though wanting to get it right. "Daddy was..." Her face glowed with happiness. "He was...a hero. Bigger than life. A legend. Everybody loved him, not just my aunts and Birdie."

There was silence except for the gurgling of the overflowing gutter. In between the splash of water in the street below could be heard the shh-hhh noise of the sheets of rain.

Teddy took two bites of bread and prosciutto and then staring into space, chewed and swallowed. "Daddy came into town when he was about twenty. He'd been a goldminer out west, somewhere like Utah or Colorado. Nobody really knows. Anyway, he was so good-looking, so tall, like me, I mean tall like me." Teddy actually blushed with the fear that Diane would think she was vain. She never wanted Diane, of all people, to think that. It was true, of course, which was the best reason of all for keeping it secret. Teddy liked the way she looked. And she liked being able to carry a suitcase nobody else could lift.

"His name was Teddy Starbuck and he had no money at all and he went into one of the joints where men drank. Prohibition hadn't been reprieved then but they had places for drinking and half the population of this little town were bootleggers."

Diane thought, Ace IS a world away. A goldminer! Bootleggers!

"And...almost forgot," Teddy pushed tendrils of golden hair behind her ears. She'd had each ear pierced four times and a pink enamel flower winked in the light beside three tiny gold rings. "The town was called Marker's Junction after this railroad baron from Montgomery that nobody liked. Wardrup L. Marker. He had three illegitimate children. And the town wasn't even quite on the railroad. I mean, really!"

Diane decided it better not to ask any questions. One shouldn't examine legends with a magnifying glass.

"So Daddy got to playin' cards and I guess you could say he was one of the world's best. If you'd learned to play with goldminers, then you really could play." Teddy's face was faintly tan with high color at each cheekbone. She took the time each morning to smudge brown eye shadow beneath each brow bone and the effect was feline. Diane thought she was as beautiful as any angel on any ceiling in any Roman church. "To make a long story short, Daddy won the town in a poker game on the stroke of midnight." She waited for Diane's reaction. "Four aces! He had four aces and the Marker's Junction sign was taken down before dawn."

"Wow!" breathed Diane hoping she sounded suitably impressed. A leap of faith. All these years to be fed this story. I hope she never tells it to anyone who doesn't pretend to believe her. She stared at the glorious catlike creature before her. Tangled blonde hair cascaded below her shoulders, her brown eyes were bright with affection and pride for this man she'd hardly known. Teddy was grinning with sheer delight.

The rain had stopped and sunlight was filling Diane's apartment. "So you see, I never want anyone to ever think I ran away from Ace. Why, I grew up being made to feel I owned the whole town! Sort of a crown princess. Head cheerleader. Homecoming queen. It was my right as Teddy Starbuck, my father's heir." She stopped smiling. "And here's a word I learned last week, Diane. Legacy." Diane nodded. "It was also a legacy to be brave and to be good because that was what the name Teddy Starbuck stood for."

"And do you think you are?" The question slipped out before Diane could stop it. But the moment had taken on such a glow of knighthood, of fable, of fairy tale, it didn't sound inappropriate.

Teddy was serious and then answered. "I know I want to be. From the time I was a little girl I knew about my father. I also knew about my mother and her broken heart." She stopped. "Daisy and Cricket are the mothers for me." She was quiet. "But between the two of them, they

have the common sense of an eleven year old. Of one eleven year old."
Teddy wasn't making a joke.

"What do you mean?"

"I mean, from the time I was about six I had to take care of them.
They get confused, they forget to eat, but that's okay because I love to
cook, they…"

"Are they elderly?"

"No! They're in their forties. Birdie's younger sisters."

"Are they married?" Diane had never heard of any uncles.

"Both widows. Korean War. Awful."

Diane flinched with pity.

Teddy sighed. "I worry about them. I…well, they're probably a little…different. They…for instance, they collect newspapers and once
Chief Abner of the Ace Fire Department came and told them that they
were a fire hazard and I couldn't make them throw them away and it
was only the week after that that Cricket's bedroom floor collapsed."
Teddy suddenly giggled."Her bed came right down on the dining room
table and broke it right in half." She laughed and then resumed the
story."So I went to see Chief Abner and we all made a compromise. That
they could keep newspapers—but only on the ground floor and only
the last seven years."

"How old were you when this happened?"

"I was…let's see, second grade. I was six and a half."

"And you had to go and talk to the Fire Chief all by yourself?"

Teddy shrugged. "I told you, Diane. I was born and given this name
and I have to live up to it." They heard the iron grates of the shop doors
on Benedetto Cairoli and Via dei Guibbonari being unlocked and
thrown open with the great crashing noises that heralded the end of the
mezzogiorno. The sun was bright in the room. Teddy nodded and said
solemnly, "It is my legacy."

∗ ∗ ∗ ∗ ∗ ∗ ∗ ∗ ∗ ∗ ∗

"But Tunisia! Wow! How come Tunisia?! Oh, I wish he'd invite me.

"Well, of course you know the French were there for a long time…" Massimo nodded to the waiter who lifted the empty champagne bottle from the silver ice bucket and rushed away to replace it.

"Oh, of course. I knew. Yes." Teddy swallowed the last of her creme caramel and hurriedly wiped her lips on the pink napkin.

"So Mother always loved the place. My father, he…not so much."

"How exciting, Massimo!" Teddy was starry-eyed but Massimo couldn't see anything but all that golden tan skin. There was so much of it exposed; the dress hardly had a neckline. It was all cleavage. All Teddy. "But do you ever go there? Do you ever go to stay in the house?"

Massimo shrugged. "Tunisia is very dirty, I think. I prefer Paris. I prefer Rome."

"Oh, no!" she cried. "I've seen pictures of the desert and it looked white and clean—"

Massimo laughed. "Oh, Teddy, you are as romantic as any Italian and since I'm merely half I can say that! A trip on the bus is an adventure for you."

She made a face at him but she knew it was one of her cute faces. "Yes, maybe the bus is an adventure for me. You never know who will be standing next to you."

Massimo laughed again. Teddy reached across the table for his hand. It was smooth and soft. Softer than Teddy's for she'd been refinishing a bureau she'd found in a junk shop. Only twenty thousand lire, about fifteen dollars, how could she let it go? Oh, his sweet little eyes, she thought. They look so tired from staring at rows of tiny numbers all day. I wish he would let me kiss his teeny weeny blue eyes.

"So tell me what you did today."

"All my usual things. I went to the Villa Borghese again because Diane has given me a book on Canova and now I know all about Daphne being changed into a laurel tree," she went on. She was excited, animated. "And the statue there of poor Daphne almost made me cry!

Have you seen the way Canova has her fingers turning into leaves as she is reaching out for her lover! It's heartbreaking really…"

Massimo was amused at this American's intensity but didn't allow himself to show it.

"I also bought a probably priceless antique…" she began.

"At Christie's?" Massimo had inherited his mother's snuff box collection and was quite interested in almost anything of the seventeenth century and French.

"No." Teddy shook her head and masses of blond hair moved on her broad bare shoulders. Two tiny straps were all that held the black bodice over her. Remarkable, thought Massimo. "Vie del Pellegrino. You know. It's a little street behind Campo dei Fiori. Behind the French Embassy. Hey, is it true that Cleopatra took baths in those fountains in Piazza Farnese?"

"No, cara. I don't know, but maybe it was Pauline Bonaparte Borghese. She used to have an enormous black slave, or so the story goes, carry her back and forth to the bath."

Teddy looked amazed. Massimo hadn't counted on her grasp of Roman history. "My God. That poor slave. All the way from her palazzo near the Spanish Steps to the French Embassy for a bath?"

Massimo laughed until he had to wipe the tears away with his handkerchief. Teddy didn't laugh. Had she said something foolish? At last, he coughed, took a last sip of wine, and explained, trying not to smile. "Teddy." He had taken his hand away and she sat with hers folded demurely in her lap, wondering if she were in love with Massimo Angelotti after all. "Teddy, the giant tubs weren't always in front of the French Embassy. They were put in Piazza Farnese very recently." Teddy was solemn. "Maybe only one hundred years ago."

Now it was her turn to laugh at him. We are so good together, she thought.

They were the last to leave the restaurant and on the street outside she slipped her arm in his and made sure that he could feel her breast underneath the thin black linen jacket. She knew he did. Why doesn't he stop on the bridge and kiss me, she wondered as they crossed the Tiber in the moonlight. Then it came to her. It was, as the Romans said, SIDA. The AIDS. Hadn't Diane told her only the other night that an article in an Italian magazine said the virus could be transferred by kissing? No! NO! she had protested and Diane had run across the street to get the magazine. Four minutes later, reading aloud in Teddy's living room, she had translated the interview with 'an eminent professore.' Complete with thick Romano accent, Diane had had them howling with laughter. 'Si, si, certo, only by the blood but everyone, everyone has the tiny cuts in the mouth and so you see a kees can be deadly.' Diane and Teddy had decided the newest campaign would not be 'fare l'amore con CONTROL' but something more startling. Giant red lips below a skull and bones on posters all over Rome. The train station, the airport, the fountain of Trevi, absolutely everywhere people might be tempted to kiss.

Teddy looked up at the moon, a silver fingernail in a blue velvet sky, and then down at the river which glistened in the lamplight like satin. She inhaled the faint smell of Massimo's after shave and felt his muscular arm beneath her hand then sighed loudly, feeling cranky. Bernini's marble angels on the bridge bent down as though to bestow silent blessings. No, thought Teddy. Not even an angel can make a mere mortal kiss you on a Roman bridge when we are living in the age of Aids. She frowned, very close to sulking. Massimo is so shy when we are alone, but he did kiss me last week. On another bridge. Maybe the late 80's won't be remembered as a romantic age. Maybe I won't ever be kissed on this bridge. Maybe I'm here in the wrong century.

Massimo turned to her. "Bella. Bellissima. Si?"

Teddy smiled and nodded. He was talking about the view, the night, everything but her. "Si," she answered with a trace of petulance in her voice. They continued walking slowly through the narrow winding streets, past the shop where Teddy's bureau had come from, through the nearly deserted Campo dei Fiori which would be alive with its fruit and vegetable stands, its fishmongers and butchers in a few hours. Teddy looked up and saw Diane's balcony doors open as usual and the yellow glow of her desk light. Working late again, she thought, somehow comforted by her presence in the big sleeping town around her and Massimo.

"Molte grazie per tutto," she whispered, their faces only inches apart.

"No," he shook his head. His glasses shone in the streetlight. "Thank you to you." With that, he gently tapped her nose with his forefinger, as though being affectionate with a little dog. She would later think of the gesture and gnash her teeth in front of the mirror. But now, Teddy only smiled back and then allowed him to open the front door for her. "Ciao," she called to the dark silhouette in the entranceway. "Ciao," he said softly and left Teddy to ascend in the little swaying glass box alone.

*   *   *   *   *   *   *   *   *   *

Twenty minutes later, Teddy lay naked in her big double bed. Like being inside a cake with vanilla icing decorated with Tootsie Rolls, she had decided the first night as she stared up at the dark wooden beams crossing the ceiling. Her bedroom, like the living room, had a sliver of a balcony facing the street and through the open French doors Teddy could see outlines of rooftops and steeples against the pewter-colored sky of early morning. But the view did not interest her.

Why do I want him so much? And why doesn't he want me? I am in love with him. I have this great urge to touch him. To touch his sweet face, his mouth, to outline it with my finger, to stroke that little wave of black hair at each temple. Ohh! She turned over on her stomach. And I want him to come to dinner but I'm not sure he will so I don't want to ask. Is he laughing at me or with me? There are so many things I don't know.

"Not yet," she said aloud. Nothing is too late. And Diane told me I have a good mind, that all I had to do was decide what I wanted to do with it. She leaned up on one elbow, the white sheets falling away from her, making her keenly aware of her bare skin. Diane's light was out. Teddy fell back on the pillows. They were nearly square, the European kind. She pushed her fists under one and tried to relax, then sighed in annoyance; restless, full of thoughts.

I'm going to stay here. Heidi loves Vienna and Olivier sent two suitcases of clothes. Yes. Every shopkeeper seemed to ask why she had come, low long she would stay. She smiled and said, "Forever," the first week and then learned the word, 'sempre.'Yes. I could be happy here for a long long time. But I think I'd better get a job and stop plotting my day around wine with Diane or lunch with Eleanor or a trek to a landmark. Yes, I'll get a job. She frowned in the dark, again twisting over on her back, restlessly. But not as a model. Anything but that.

My Italian will have to be improved but I have that book and Diane can help. She frowned again. The battle with the language began in the morning when she faced the faucets in the bathroom labelled C and F. Nothing comes naturally to me, she had wailed to Eleanor. When Teddy looked, through slitted sleepy eyes, at the C she thought 'aha, cold!' But of course C stood for caldo which meant hot. F was freddo which meant cold. Teddy practiced shivering in front of the bathroom mirror every day for a week saying to her reflection, "oh, it's so brrrr....so very FREDDO." It didn't work. She still reached for the C expecting cold. Now she stomped into the bathroom every morning saying aloud, "It's not what you think it is."

So, I may be the only person in the world who has to learn a language backwards. So what? No one but Diane and Eleanor ever have to know. And I can do it. It may take longer but I can do it. She felt good, making positive decisions in the middle of the night while half of the world was wasting time asleep. And I will get a job. And I won't wait for Jeremy Taylor Hathaway the Third to make my bank account better. I know from Blakeley's letter that the divorce will take a year from when the papers were filed. He said not to expect a fortune as a settlement because the marriage was short-lived. She'd scrawled back on a postcard with the Pantheon on it, "I don't care about the money and make the marriage as short-lived as possible. Hugs from Theodora in Rome."

I'll take care of myself. I always have and I've never needed much money either. She thought of the white mink coat in the wardrobe. It was fun, that's all it was. Fun to have Jeremy give it to me, fun to wear, fun to feel the softness against my cheek. So I have my mink and that's off my list. It wasn't on my list anyway. She held up her left hand in the semi-darkness and ticked off the newest decisions with her fingers. Get a job. Learn Italian. She sighed. Get Massimo to...she squirmed. God. This damn Aids thing. He can't refuse me forever. After all, when I'm really in high gear, I have been called irresistible.

Teddy plotted the next evening. Lots of wine. I'll just keep filling his glass and then I'll make a point of telling him I was totally faithful to Jeremy and that I never fooled around at all before my marriage and why, even back in Ace when everybody, especially the cheerleaders, were doing it at the drive-in, I NEVER did ANYthing. I could even...no, I can't tell him that my nickname was Teddy Won'tFuck. I don't want to shock him. I just want to seduce him. And Diane can help. I'll ask her what she'd do.

Teddy pushed the sheet down to her waist and the night air felt good on her bare breasts "Flaming flamingoes!" she exclaimed. "And what if I can't seduce him? What if he read that stupid interview with that idiotic doctor? What if..." Teddy scowled, feeling that the future was as black as Cricket's cat. "Dammit.." she breathed into the darkness. What if it's true and...what if kisses CAN kill?

* * * * * * * * * * *

Chapter Three

"The inhabitants of the earth spend more money on illegal drugs than they spend on food. More than they spend on housing, clothes, education, medical care, or any other products or service."

Take-A-Chance was reading THE UNDERGROUND EMPIRE under a bright blue umbrella beside his bright turquoise swimming pool. The house behind him was rented and suited his needs perfectly. It was modern, one-story, with two bedrooms, all-white with a mirrored living room wall and a color television. Not only was it furnished, basically in glass and chrome, but it was also well-equipped with sheets and towels, with everything one would resent buying if one entertained the idea of a sudden departure. There was the pool which Chance liked and the afore-mentioned blue umbrella, and a barbecue pit and even tongs to turn a steak. One of its most attractive features was the seven-foot tall cedar fence that enclosed the backyard.

The one-acre plot was located in a residential upper middle class suburb of Los Angeles with nothing much to distinguish it from any other bedroom community. Husbands, clutching briefcases and the keys to their BMWs, kissed their wives goodbye in the kitchens as the TODAY show blared forth over the confusion of getting people out of the house and making a grocery list. Kids rode their bicycles to school down the tree-shaded streets.

Money. Chance closed the book, wiped his forehead with a blue towel and sighed. Not yet noon and baking hot. He'd get in the water soon, just after he went through this last pile of clippings. Money. The

Barracuda Brothers, for all their lack of polish, knew about making money. Most of Chance's work was figuring out where to put it. They were so good at what they did and there was so much of it. He respected them. They disgusted him, repelled him, and frightened him. But they were smart. Maybe that's why they frightened him so much.

Chance kept files on anything concerning drugs which meant his files were enormous, for the subject touched banking, arms, and officials in dozens of governments. The Washington Post article was before him. Chance skimmed and underlined. "In the opinion of many experts, the Medellin cartel, which processes much of the world's cocaine, has become as destabilizing a force as the civil wars in Nicaragua and El Salvador…" He nodded. If Les and Wes don't let me up the ante with Rodriguez they're going to get squeezed out. He made a note on a long yellow legal pad, brushing away the drops of sweat that fell on the page. 'R.- $$-soon.'

Chance wished many times a day that he weren't so involved, that he didn't know so much. Was knowledge really power? He didn't think that anymore. What he knew nagged at him. Worry was always with him, like a blister on his heel that wouldn't go away, that made itself noticeable with every step he took. "Through payoffs and other favors, the drug barons have won the cooperation around the region of key officials in setting up laboratories, using landing strips and ports and laundering billions of dollars in illicit profits." For once, they got it right, thought Chance. Billions. Not millions. Millions per day. Millions per hour in interest in banks. But the rest was so obvious. He smiled. Such a game. And the governments either had their hands out or were wearing blindfolds, like the United States, unwilling to get involved in politics.

Chance put the article on top of the others concerning the Senate hearings and then put the empty bottle on top of that. Chance had developed a taste for good wine and was loathe to throw the bottle away after enjoying it so he used the empty ones as paperweights. This one was a Chateau Lafite Rothschild. A La Tache was holding down the articles on new border patrol tactics from Mexico to California. Hopelessly out of date, of course, he had noted with satisfaction. A Corton Charlemagne bottle held down the latest interview with the U.S. Attorney General and a bottle once holding Le Chambertin was on top of a report in Spanish from a file in the Mexico City police department. It had been poorly photocopied and Chance couldn't read it in the sun.

The thin figure stood and stretched, his blue bathing trunks hanging from his round middle, the baggy shorts making his legs look all the thinner. His feet were long and narrow; his toes gripped red rubber thongs that went slap slap slap against his heels as he proceeded slowly across the lawn. He looked back at the round white table and the forest of wine bottles and laughed aloud. "Surprised I can still walk," he said to nobody and then slap slap slap continued towards the shallow end of the pool.

Hardware's dark square head appeared at the kitchen window briefly and then disappeared. Chance was doing a backstroke that was more noise and splashing than grace and didn't see him. He felt his presence though. It was comparable to having a gorilla live in the spare bedroom. Big. Silent. Watchful. When he'd complained to the Barracudas about the way he dressed and how embarrassing it was to go everywhere with this enormous shadow, Wes had laughed and asked if he'd wanted a butler instead. "He's suppost to be big. Thas the whole point. He's suppost to look mean. You want somebody ta look good beside you then go to Vegas and get yourself one of them gals. You want somebody ta talk to then…" he had snickered, "then use one of them quarters and call me." Chance clung to the side of the pool to catch his breath. Hardware looked out of the bathroom window and Chance waved. The Mexican did not respond.

No, I'm not drowning, said Chance to himself. Christ. He remembered when his life had been different. A small apartment, a small salary with a big firm which prepared income tax returns for normal people who paid normal taxes on normal incomes and worried about the cost of orthodontia for their ten year old. Chance's life had changed in one weekend. Forever. Nothing could bring that life back. Even if he really wanted it back.

Sometimes Chance didn't know. He didn't know even when he gulped Maalox straight out of the bottle for his stomach. He didn't know when he looked down and saw his custom-made Egyptian cotton shirt soaked with perspiration. He didn't even know when he waked at night from dreams of being entangled in the disgusting coils of the long-dead DooDah. There was also the dream of Hardware, who appeared to be nine feet tall, standing over him and holding, of all things, the barbecue tongs.

It had all begun with the weekend trip to Las Vegas. Stan Luffler, an old college buddy who was doing quite well in real estate, had urged him to go. "You're an accountant. You ought to pick up on this. Just see how the place works. Come on, at worst you'll probably make yourself a few hundred bucks and get a tan by the pool. Come on. The flight leaves at five forty-five on Friday."   Stan had surprised him by renting a suite and girls to go with it. There had been too much liquor and music and Chance had left the room to explore the neon-lit palaces of gambling.

The chandeliers glittered above middle-aged men in wild Hawaiian shirts, above white-haired women who wore polyester pantsuits all the shades of Easter eggs. A cross-section of humanity, thought Chance. The enormous rooms smelled of stale cigarette smoke, month-old popcorn. Cathedrals of kitsch. Even the soft carpeting beneath Chance's Hush Puppies felt phony, synthetic, as though plain wool would have had too much character to be in the place.

Chance had lost fifty dollars, his maximum, at the slot machines and then decided to go up and go to bed, hoping there was no one in it. In the elevator he nervously rehearsed what he would say and hoped he wouldn't sound like an uptight wimp, hoped that Stan wouldn't think he was gay. Maybe I could be coming down with flu, he planned as the elevator doors opened on his floor. It was the best hotel in Vegas, Stan had insisted, but the orange wall to wall carpeting made it hard to accept that as truth. Yes, I'll be ill, he concluded as he reached the door of 2714. It was opened for him and he was pulled in.

The crowd was singing 'The Yellow Rose of Texas,' bodies were everywhere, clothed and unclothed though most of the women in Vegas were half naked when fully dressed. As Chance pressed through the noise and smoke, looking for Stan, a woman kissed him full on the lips. When he tried to wipe away the sticky lip gloss, a man laughed in his face and said, "Ya lookin' good! Leave it!" Stan couldn't be found though both bedroom doors were locked from the inside.

Take-A-Chance took the scotch offered to him and sat down heavily on the floor in a corner of the large living room. He wondered why he wasn't back in Los Angeles watching Friday Night at the Movies on television.

The next morning Chance wouldn't remember anything about the money. He would find a crumpled business card in his suit coat pocket and stare at it as the blonde waitress in pink and white gingham exposing her pink and white breasts bent over him and insisted, "Honey, I said one lump or two! Now are you gonna answer me or—-" He nodded and let her stir the coffee for him. Imperial Enterprises. He ran his finger over it from force of habit. Little things made such a difference in presentation, he thought. Printed, not engraved. A bad sign.

That evening he consented to have drinks with whoever Lesley and Wesley Whittle were. Anything was better than another party in their room. At least it'd be empty when he went back to it.

The Whittles were very rich even then. Wesley's machete scar had been a brighter shade of rose which was a bit off-putting but both brothers' acne scars had been helped by a sunburn. Their diamond rings, five between the two of them, twinkled when they made the smallest gesture. They lived here, in the penthouse, which Chance found hard to believe. To live in a hotel was a new idea to him. The view of the city's lights spattered below them was impressive but as Chance lifted his eyes towards the horizon, the total emptiness, the blackness, made him uneasy. Las Vegas seemed like a Christmas ornament dropped in the sand.

Girls were everywhere, they seemed more like pets that one would brush aside firmly but politely without insulting their owners. They reminded Chance of visiting his old aunt when she'd had that poodle that always licked his shoes. You had to bat the dog away without Aunt Alice thinking you weren't crazy about it. Wesley and Leslie offered drinks and sat him and Stan down on sofas that were U-shaped like horseshoes and covered in nylon the color of smoked salmon. A very big chandelier hung over the group; it was modern, of clear plastic as though someone had emptied several ice cube trays in midair and they had stuck together. Chance gulped his scotch as a black girl with a bee-hive hairdo and white lipstick draped herself, smiling like a half naked stewardess, beside him. Stan got the same treatment with a platinum blonde but he immediately clapped a hand on her thigh and looked interested.

The Whittle brothers sat and stared at him. It seems they had all arrived at some sort of conclusion the night before. Chance had obviously agreed to do something for them but he couldn't remember what. The conversation swirled around him until at last he asked. "Why you are gonna make yourself a pile of money, and we are gonna help ya," explained Lesley. Chance squirmed as the girl played with his sideburns. He wore them quite long those days to compensate for what was not on his head. It had seemed so simple, thought Chance now, as he pulled himself out of the pool and walked over to the chaise. A onetime thing. Cash in a suitcase delivered to a hotel room and then off to Switzerland. He liked to feel he'd been roped into it, but he knew better. The money was so much and it was so easy and he must have known that he would want more, that he would do what they asked in order to have more.

They knew it. Stan was in with them and he knew it. So Chance listened and drank his scotch and once in awhile smiled weakly and finally he said okay. They all stood up after the dinner that room service brought and they shook hands and it seemed the meeting was over. Stan went through the door first. Chance turned and looked back at the Whittles. He really had thought he would never see them again.

Chance wondered what his reaction would have been if Stan had told him that he was meeting the Barracuda Brothers instead of Lesley and Wesley Whittle. Of course, he'd never heard of the Barracuda Brothers but wouldn't the name alone have stopped him from getting involved? Within twenty minutes of his return from Geneva he'd heard plenty. The driver who picked him up at the Los Angeles airport had been only too happy to talk. "How're the Barracudas treating ya?" He'd pushed his black chauffeur's cap back on his head and laughed at the accountant's confusion. Take-A-Chance sat awkwardly in the back seat of the silver Lincoln Continental, blue seersucker-covered legs apart, hands palms down on either side of him, fingers fanned on the velvet-soft uphol-stery. He'd blinked behind the wire-rimmed glasses he'd worn before contact lenses and then nervously raked his fingers through his thin-ning yellow hair.

"They call 'em that," the driver delighted in explaining, "because they used to lower people they didn't like into a swimming pool full of bar-racudas." He chuckled. "Story is they'd sit there in lounge chairs and drink margaritas and cheer on the fish. Make bets on-"

Chance stopped listening. He told himself he didn't believe it. At the hotel a half hour later, Stan had paid him in one hundred dollar bills, counting out fifty fresh new crisp ones with Benjamin Franklin's benign countenance gazing up at them. "Oh, that name!" Stan had laughed.

They were on the twentieth floor, the urban sprawl of L. A. halo-ed in smog was below them. Chance paced restlessly back and forth in front of the window. He was uneasy about missing a third day of work, but thought that jet lag had given him a pasty look easily attributable to illness. Stan was mixing himself a drink, bending down over the little frigobar. "They call Wes and Les that because of their car."

"Their car?" Chance hoped they didn't do anything with barracudas in a car.

Stan stood up and turned to him. "You look really pale. Sit down. Lemme get you a scotch." He patted him on the back and noted, not without disgust, that the little blue seersucker suit jacket was damp. Chance sat at the foot of the bed, his narrow shouldered frame slumped like a question mark.

"So, the name." Stan settled himself on the bed, with both pillows behind him; he put his brown shoes unselfconsciously on the pea green bedspread. "When those guys started out, the way I heard it anyway," Stan began. "Well, first they were carrying stuff back and forth between Nuevo Laredo in Mexico to Laredo on the Texas side. Then it was from Tijuana to California…"

"What stuff?"

Stan laughed. It wasn't a mocking laugh. Stan's laugh and his clean-cut good looks had made him one of the most popular boys in Chance's class. "Where've you been?" He grinned and swigged the bourbon. The ice cubes made a clunk noise as he put the glass down on the bedside table. He looked Chance straight in the face and grinned again. "Drugs. Grass."

"What kind of drugs?" Chance was trying hard to be nonchalant. He'd thought of this on the plane. It had to be drug money in the bag he carried.

"Seconal. They got all they wanted from some character who owned a Mexican drugstore. Then there were Black Beauties…"

Chance was reminded of Elizabeth Taylor and that wonderful horse. What a great movie. "Do you know what Black Beauties are?" Stan was asking.

Chance shook his head.

"Amphetamines. They call it speed. It makes you click into overdrive. We used to take'em when we'd pull all nighters, before an exam, at college." Stan could see that Chance never had. "Anyway, they're black capsules and they call them Black Beauties. And, now I'm just guessing, but probably the Barracudas got them for about two cents wholesale and then got a carfull across the border and sold them for, say, fifty cents apiece. You can make pretty good money that way." He reached for the bourbon then remembered the point of all this. "The car they drove was a Plymouth Barracuda. Light blue."

Chance's mind was whirling. The car held no interest for him. "So at that price if they bought a thousand pills and sold each one for a profit of forty eight cents, then they'd make $480 on a thousand..."

"You're right BUT..." he drew out the word and held one finger in the air. "They didn't bother making a trip for only a thousand pills. They'd buy a hundred thousand so..."

"Forty eight thousand dollars?" Chance was amazed."How long did they smuggle the pills, the, uh, drugs?"

"Probably just long enough to get enough money to buy into marijuana. Les and I had dinner alone one night and he can be talkative when his brother's not around. He told me they used to buy it by the ton. The ton!"

"Wow!" Chance had never seen more grass than what half filled a sandwich bag. His roommate had liked it.

"Yeah. Impressive." Stan shook his head. "Sixty thousand dollars a ton. That's wholesale in the old days but think when you get it over into the States and divide it up and throw in a little oregano maybe to...." he grinned conspiratorially, "to just make it a tiny bit more. Then!" He sipped from the tall glass. "Then you are making money."

From marijuana it had been obvious to go to cocaine. With marijuana the problems were transporting it. The Barracudas had been watchlisted at the border and had to resort to hill smuggling which was very tough. Grass was bulky and it smelled in the heat. With cocaine the problem was transporting money south to buy it. Money took up much more space than its equivalent value of the white powder. Stan had talked the morning and the afternoon away in the hotel room on the twentieth floor. Chance had sat like an eager student, all tension and tiredness had evaporated as he heard tales of money. It was quick money, money within reach, and it was so much money, so many zeroes involved that Chance realized he'd had the same rush of excitement when he'd opened a book of pirate stories one Christmas morning as a little boy. The illustrations were on shiny pages and one painting had been of a treasure chest, thrown open, pouring forth gold coins and jewels. The talk with Stan gave him that feeling again. The electricity of possibility made his head swim with delight, made his eyes bright behind his little glasses.

The sun had dried his bathing trunks; Chance lifted his Rolex from the table and was surprised that it was nearly one. There were phone calls to make, to get, and things to decide. The Take-A-Chance of 1988 had three passports, spoke fluent Spanish and looked presentable enough to lunch with a Senator. He hadn't. Not yet. Tomorrow at Fort Barracuda he would recommend that they stop the runs to Switzerland. Amazing to think they'd continued this long. It was not without risk even if the New York contact was eager and liked the money. Ahh! The money, sighed Chance. He closed his eyes and settled himself for another two minutes in the sun.

He remembered that first time in Las Vegas and of his last look back. What should have been his last look anyway. In the doorway of the gar-ishly opulent room, the two brothers standing there, younger and fitter than they were now. Their hair slicked shiny and flat to their heads with Vitalis; their smiles just as greasy.

Chance stood up, gathered his papers, leaving the bottles for the maid to bring in. How well he remembered them! They both wore silk suits, the kind that reflected light, and they both grinned above silk shirts the colors of parakeets, unbuttoned almost to the waist. Gold coins on gold chains were tangled in their mouse-colored chest hair.

* * * * * * * * * * *

Telephones, more specifically Pen Registers and telephone bills, were the reason Chance spent much of his day in the chocolate brown Mercedes convertible. Interested agents could apply a Pen Register to any telephone without a court order because they didn't actually eavesdrop on conversations; it merely determined what local calls were made and received. And so far as long distance calls went, agents could easily subpoena his phone bills for a record of those. Interested agents, Chance consoled himself, for he didn't think there were any at this point. He was very very careful and never used his home phone unless he ordered a pizza or called for a weather report.

No one except the Barracudas called him and that was always Jose from a payphone a hundred miles away from the Fort. The Spanish accent would hiss the same request every time, "Call the Brothers," and then there'd be a dial tone. The Fort phone was illegal, tapped into a line on the highway going towards Vegas. There was no record of it and certainly no phone bills. It was only a phone to receive calls. Calls from Chance. He dialed it only from a pay phone.

An emergency in the South might involve a contact leaving a message with Chance's answering service but no phone numbers were ever left and no names, no real names, ever given. Mexico City was Max, Fort Lauderdale was Fred, and a message to call Peter meant Lopez in Panama City needed to talk before the next check-in call. Not one of the three out in the field were ever allowed to use their own phones to contact Chance's service. They left home or they left the hotel suite, with several pounds of the local coins and, like Chance, sought out a phone booth.

Now, Chance put on the turning blinker and cruised to a stop in front of a dry cleaners ten miles north of Los Angeles. He looked at the empty phone booth, still unmarked by graffiti, and wondered how long it would exist in such a pristine state or even in working order. He also wondered how long he would dare use this number. Seven minutes past three. Hot. Chance wiped his face with his handkerchief and reluctantly opened the car door, got out and then closed the door again on the air conditioned capsule which contained the omnipresent dozing Hardware in the back seat. He walked casually to the sidewalk, read a sign that promised to Martinize his raincoat, and proceeded towards the ringing phone. On the third ring he plucked it from the cradle and listened to the humming over the wire and then the voice asked, "You there? Everything's okay. My grandmother left home. I'm sure you've heard but your grandmother is still the same. My grandmother is not very well actually. Saw my uncle yesterday and he liked the cake."

"Okay. You okay?" Chance asked. Basil Lopez wasn't a bad guy. He'd only met him twice. He drank tequila sunrises and laughed about how much vitamin C he needed. His mother was English, his father Panamanian and he was a big, muscular, blond who somehow managed to carry a U.S. passport and had been a Green Beret. He moved lazily with the slow walk of an athlete. His third wife and two kids someplace in Texas probably didn't see him much.

"Fine. And the weather looks good."

Chance invariably felt like an ass when he talked this way. At some point you have to just take a deep breath, he thought, and use plain English. You have to stop sounding like some Grade B thriller starring Ronald Reagan, and just get it out. "What day?"

"Thursday. Same place."

"Yeah. Make sure he knows it's lunchtime. Only lunchtime." The suitcase of money had to be put in Chance's trunk when the parking attendant took his fifteen minute break.

And next?" For a second, Chance didn't understand and then read from the slip of yellow paper. "Same area code. 534-9989. In three days, right?"

"Right." Lopez hung up.

Take-A-Chance replaced the receiver and then looked at his watch. Four thousand dollars for a watch. He still loved looking at it and being reminded of how he'd paid cash. Of how casual he'd been in front of the salesman who'd asked if he should wrap it. Chance smiled, thinking of the most flamboyant gesture he'd ever made in his life. He'd actually said he'd wear it and dropped his old watch, a high school graduation present from the aunt with the poodle he'd never liked, right into the wastebasket behind the counter. The timepiece that cost minutes of his time, that would have cost months of his accountant's salary, now told him that it was three twelve. He stepped outside the booth and looked at the highway, watched the shiny cars whizz past and then waited for the phone to ring a minute later. It didn't. He gave it another eight minutes then walked back to the Mercedes. Must be okay, he told himself.

Chance started the car and pulled away from the curb. Pen Registers, he thought. What a damnable way to get caught at something. But, he concluded, if anyone knew who I talked to, who talks to me, they'd know my life. They could follow the phone wire from here to everywhere: to Bogota, to Carlos in Mexico City, to Lopez in Panama City, to Jason in Fort Lauderdale.

Chance thought of himself as one link of a chain. He and the Barracuda Brothers were at the top. And one link down was Lopez but Lopez didn't know Carlos or Jason so Chance's seniority was clear to him. Jason and Carlos were ignorant of each other and of Lopez. None of the three had any idea that Chance, or they themselves for that matter, worked for the Barracuda brothers.

That was the way it should be. Each link connected to a smaller one and each person only dealt with his immediate inferior or superior. There was no skipping up the chain unless your superior got out which didn't happen often unless it was related to ill-health or disappearance. Stan had disappeared and then been found, in very ill-health, actually quite dead in his car which had plunged over a bridge somewhere outside San Diego. The coroner had ruled accidental drowning and the idea was that he had fallen asleep at the wheel.

Chance sighed and pushed in a cassette of Linda Ronstadt. He'd felt cold and sick with fear and lain awake for nights on end after the body had been discovered. But that had been almost fifteen years ago and now Chance only thought of Stan as the high-living University of New Mexico pal who'd taken him to Vegas for the weekend. Who had, very casually, made Take-A-Chance a part of something that both fascinated and terrified him.

Farthest removed from Fort Barracuda in the Nevada desert was the peasant farmer in Peru or Bolivia or lately Brazil, Venezuela or Ecuador, the Indian who only knew that growing coca would provide him with many times his usual annual income. His standard of living was raised, his children had shoes. He often chewed the leaves himself and forgot that he was tired, forgot that he was hungry.

After the coca leaf is picked, it must be treated by a chemist who literally cooks it to cocaine base and then to crystals. Sometimes the base or paste is sold and made into crystals hundreds or thousands of miles away; at any stage of the transition it is precious. A laboratory with beakers, flasks, potassium carbonate, kerosene, drying ovens, takes up little space whether it's in a jungle or a city. Colombia used to be known more for being a processor than a grower of the crop.

When the cocaine has become pure cocaine or snow, it must then be taken to market. The most primitive way is by a carrier called a mule who transports it into the United States. By the mid-1970's, crates from Colombia were routinely searched so the mule who 'wore' it was invaluable. Since nearly every traveler from the country was suspect, mules often used hand-held false-bottomed suitcases; they put it in their clothes; and the women even carried it en el conejo which is what customs officials call 'vaginal caches.' Mules masquerading as nuns and priests had the powder sewn into their flowing black robes. One man imported tropical birds; most of them arrived dead and had, in fact, begun the journey that way. Stuffed with cocaine. Another imported tropical fish. Again, dead on departure, dead on arrival.

The most dangerous method of transport by a mule is to carry it in his stomach. The uvas or grapes are capsules wrapped in part of a surgical glove. X-rays can spot it at customs and of course, this results in immediate arrest, but it is a far worse fate to have a capsule caught in the intestine. The carrier waits for it to dissolve and for the imminent horror known as White Death. A torrent of pure cocaine into the system results in a heartbeat like a jackhammer, a raging temperature, bleeding, convulsions, and paralysis of the respiratory system.

There are mules who elude customs inspectors and arrest who get as high on the thrill of it as they could on the drug itself. Some carriers have made countless successful trips over borders with either imprisonment or thousands of dollars awaiting them on the other side of the frontier.

Before the mule sells to a dealer it is very likely he (or she, for the best mules are said to be women) will add something to it to increase the weight. The wholesaler will later do the same. Nanitol, a baby sugar, was one ingredient used. The test for purity is simple. Cocaine melts at a far higher temperature than what most wholesalers use to cut it with. Coke liquifies at 150 degrees Fahrenheit while the cut will blacken and smoke long before that-at between 75 and 100 degrees. Wesley and Lesley learned early on how to test for quality by rubbing the cocaine on the web of skin between the thumb and the index finger. The purest coke melts immediately and is absorbed by the skin.

The cocaine will be cut again and re-sold in smaller and smaller portions, less and less pure, until at last it reaches the user. He may sniff it in a line through a tightly rolled hundred dollar bill or from a gold coke spoon. He may inhale it quickly in a back alley from the back of his hand. He may be on the spike which means he injects it intravenously. He might be snowballing which combines coke with morphine or heroin or he might be free-basing which involves heating the cocaine and inhaling the vapors.

From the small bushes some Indians call 'little birds' the trip is a long one. Every person who touches the coke is taking a risk and becoming richer or poorer or going to prison.

The Barracudas have their own plantations growing 'little birds.' They pay off local guerrilla groups to protect their harvest on its way to their own laboratories to be processed. The Barracudas don't use mules to move their coke; they have their own fleets of planes and ships which arrive at secret airstrips and at hidden docks. They have pilots and sailors who work for them. Cocaine is moved by the ton, not by the kilo.

For Take-A-Chance, who refused to even try the powder, the beginning of the pipeline is millions of light years away. And the end of the pipeline, too. Chance liked to imagine cocaine as a party drug, something glamourous people shared after dinner in Beverly Hills. To offer guests a few lines of the powder on a coffee table spoke of success. Cocaine gave the user the illusion of power. Who didn't want to be stronger, smarter, sexier? And if coke made you feel those things, in a great rush, you were bound to like it. Coke also made you want to feel that way again and again. Addiction and crime were problems Chance read about. They comprised articles he stacked neatly under his empty wine bottles. Take-A-Chance didn't deal in dope; he managed money. He told himself he was the financial advisor for an empire. Sometimes he told himself it was a vast agricultural empire.

It was six in the evening of the same day as Chance and Hardware stood outside Fort Barracuda on the flagstone path. The pink metal flamingoes did the can-can behind them. Garcia opened the door after the doorbell had played a chorus of Jingle Bells, after Chance had thought again how hot it was.

Lesley was in an expansive mood, swigging Dr. Pepper out of a can, his enormous belly completely obscuring the buckle and the front half of his leather belt. The back seemed to be beaded in a multi-colored Thunderbird design. He wore light pink trousers which were one half of a favorite leisure suit, a white T-shirt and white loafers that needed to have the sand brushed out of their seams. They were penny loafers but each sported a bullet instead. Black socks showed between shoe and the high water trouser cuff. "Chance, come on out to the home entertainment center. Wes has got a rerun of the las' Oklahoma Oilers game and after that...."

After that, Chance and the Barracuda brothers had gone into the map room to talk about Panama. Chance picked the metal card table chair, as he always did, and turned it towards the maps and away from what Wes called his living cemetery. "Don' they look jes about to start breathin'agin!' He would gloat. And Chance thought, yes, they do, and that's what makes it so utterly disgusting. The Barracudas had found a taxidermist in Utah they thought was a genius. He didn't stuff animals, he freeze-dried them, "Lak the coffee beans!" the brothers had chortled when they'd explained it.

First, they'd shipped him Radar, the Rhodesian ridgeback who'd gotten run over by Lesley in a dune buggy race. Radar was such a success, complete with shining red gums exposed in a snarl for all eternity, that DooDah who'd choked to death on a rat had been next. Now DooDah coiled behind Chance's chair, black and brown scales shining in the light, beady eyes staring at nothing, well-fed forever. There were the rabbits, but obviously not any they'd machine gunned, and there were several prairie dogs so well done that you hardly noticed the bullethole in their skulls. Chance couldn't decide which was worse: to face the dead animals or to feel they were about to resume life behind him as the tiny hairs on his neck stood on end.

The Barracudas mounted their enormous E-Z Boy lounge chairs and leaned back with a great deal of sighing, both from them and from the chairs. The air conditioner whirred at top capacity pouring frigid air into the room. It may have been the only place south of Canada that Chance didn't think was too warm. He tried to concentrate on what Lesley was saying. "What does Lopez say?" he finished.

"About five hours ago when we talked, everything was fine. He said Noriega was where we want him and that the President..".

"Shit," barked Wesley. "Delvalle is nowhere. And we don' want him nowhere."

Lesley turned to his brother who now stood beside a thirty-five square foot map of Central America, holding a flaggged pin in his hand. "Thas what Chance is saying. He is nowhere, no power, nobody, nomore."

"No shit," concluded Wesley. He pushed a pin topped by a purple flag in the spot marked Panama City.

"In a nutshell," sighed Chance. "Noriega is using the U.S. opposition to him to make him more popular. Now that the Justice Department says it won't drop the drug charges, it won't make a deal and let him go into exile-"

"What crap!" exploded Wesley. "I bet thas exactly whut happens-"

"Look, all we care about is that Noriega stays or that whoever takes his place is of the same mind," put in Chance.

"Chance is right. Has Lopez been givin' money to the right people?"

"He thinks so. The new president is as weak as Delvalle and with Noriega controlling the army-"

Their meetings were always full of interruptions, but somehow the three of them managed to exchange information and to make decisions.

"I think Chance might oughtta git some more money down there. It cain't hurt right now. If Lopez is sure he's payin the right people."

"Okay." Chance thought a hundred thousand would do it. Day after tomorrow he'd tell Lopez to tell Jack to keep it aside. That's when you realized you had to trust someone—when there was no way to check. Jack could take out a hundred thousand dollars and run away with it, but no, it wasn't enough when so many times that went through his hands every week. Or Jack could put aside one hundred grand and simply forget to leave it in General Guzman's office. Those things happened. He risked having the whole caper collapse on him though. More than likely, Jack would only put fifty grand in the briefcase and leave it in the office. That made more sense. And he'd think, no reason to throw money away when you don't have to. When it feels so good sticking to your fingers.

Wesley put another plug of Bull of the Woods in his mouth. "What are we gonna do about that guy in Miami?"

"Who? Martin?" Chance asked.

Lesley leaned back in the E-Z Boy and stared down at his white loafers. "Martin won't talk. He won't talk. The DEA guys, the FBI, Dade County, everybody can work him over for forty nine years and Jason swears he won't talk."

Chance was often surprised at the Barracudas' reading of human nature. They'd never met Martin, why, neither had he, and they'd never met Jason but they remembered conversations he'd related to them months ago. He spoke. "Jason is thinking of getting Miguel out. Just paying him off. Calling it quits."

"Still the Quaaludes, huh?" Les shook his head. He and his brother had burned themselves out on tequila years ago. Neither one had ever gotten turned on by drugs. Now they stuck to rootbeer and Sprite and Dr. Pepper mostly. In cans so cold it hurt to hold them for long.

"'Fraid so. He can't shake it. And he's basing the coke…he won't last long."

Wesley threw up one hand. "Jason has good sense. He kin run things but tell him you highly recommend that Miguel go. If Miguel were in the hands of the Feds we'd all be…." he giggled. "Well, I'd ruther be freeze-dried than…"

The meeting was disrupted until the Barracuda boys could control themselves. Chance smiled weakly.

"Carlos says the price is going down. There's so much coming in all the time.."

"Then why the hell's he keep on payin' thousands to that Cuban, that Luis…?"

"Luis refuses to lower the price. Says he's not just charging for a simple delivery, he's charging for security measures."

"Lak whut?" demanded the brothers in a chorus of indignation.

"Luis lives in a compound almost to hear Carlos tell it. All the houses on his street, both sides, are owned by family members. So Luis says he is paying for lookouts and security guards and armed escorts…"

"Armed? Are they armed?" guffawed Wesley. "We're not dealin' in lingerie, for christ's sake! 'Course they're armed!"

"Well, the bottom line is…" Chance liked the phrase. It gave him the illusion, short-lived though it was, that he was actually controlling the conversation. "The bottom line is that Carlos says Juan is threatening to dump Luis and his pilots if Luis doesn't lower his price. Luis says he can't change the price. It's his family that determines the price and…"

"Hell!" snorted Lesley just before using the brass spittoon on the floor perilously close to DooDah. "Why don' he go back to Jaime then. At least-"

"Uh, Jaime's dead." How soon they forget, thought Chance. They had told Carlos to 'have him fixed up' and somebody had.

"Oh, okay. Yeah, I remember now." Les nodded.

The Barracudas were all business. Like bankers foreclosing on a mortgage, sometimes it was necessary to have somebody 'fixed up.' And like bankers, they didn't get a kick out of it, but they didn't run around bawling either. It was straight business. Chance tried to close the discussion. "I'll tell Carlos to ask around. Quietly. I'm sure there's somebody down there who fits the bill. It's just tough on him starting all over again…with the new drops, a whole new set of characters." Chance wanted the brothers to say, oh, stick with Luis. It's just a few thou different and we're making money faster than we know what to do with it anyway. But they didn't. Chance had known they wouldn't.

"Tell Carlos to git somebody else double quick!" commanded Lesley making a fist and banging the arm of his lounge chair.

"Yeah," echoed Wesley. "We're gittin ripped off!"

"Okay. No other problems that I can see." Chance looked down at his crossed legs and unconsciously stroked the little stirrup on his Gucci. "It occurred to me today that you may want to stop the Switzerland runs and leave the accounts as they are or simply transfer it all down to the Caribbean…" He used the plural. Accounts.

Sentimental about DooDah and Swiss bank accounts, both brothers rose inches out of their E-Z Boys. Wesley's was dark red and Lesley's was dark blue. The chairs snapped to the down position in unison. "Chance! Whut are you sayin', boy?"

"We need those Swiss accounts! I mean where would anybody be without a good solid Swiss account? Think of the Shah, think of Marcos, think of Bebe Doc, think of anybody who counts…"

Chance put up both hands."Okay. I'II leave them alone." He stood up. "Anything else?"

"Thet covers the whole blinkin' ball game," nodded Wes. The plug of tobacco made his plump face ever rounder.

Les stood and stretched. "You're invited for supper you know. We decided ta eat late jes because of this late meetin'…" "Oh, thanks, but I can't. I have…" Chance was a lousy liar. "I have a lot of paperwork to catch up on."

Wesley was behind him now. He gave him a big slap on the back. "Okay, boy. You're doin a real good job. I keep meanin' to tell you."

Chance was caught unawares. Praise was not something he expected from the Barracuda brothers. He felt himself near blushing and prayed he would not. "Gee, thanks."

They walked him down the red linoleum hall, both stocky bodies swaying sideways and almost bumping the opposite wall. Chance smelled Garcia's newest poison and then heard Lawrence Welk's peppy rendition of "When My Baby walks Down the Street," and told himself not to run for the helicopter. Hardware was already standing beside it, a linebacker next to a dragon fly in the spring darkness. As Chance waved good bye, his briefcase in one hand, the Barracuda Brothers had already forgotten him. He could still hear their voices, arguing about the positioning of the flamingoes as he turned the ignition key and the rotors began to turn.

*　*　*　*　*　*　*　*　*　*　*

Chapter Four

Teddy hurried down the street in a cloud of Jeremy's aftershave. But it wasn't really. She had worn Lord's long before she'd met him and he'd liked it. But after they'd married, he'd objected and given her perfumes, real perfumes he'd called them, with names she couldn't pronounce and then, of all things, taken to wearing her Lord's himself! Thoroughly unsentimental, she'd bought a new bottle in Rome and an hour ago had literally poured it between her breasts and on the inside of each bare arm. Hell for leather, she thought to herself. The cobblestones beneath her gold ballet slippers almost hurt. New meaning, she sighed. Strangers turned their heads to both inhale and gawk at six feet of long-limbed glory. She wore a black and white striped linen jacket and under it a black cotton dress, nearly backless. Cascades of blonde hair fell to her shoulders and were decorated with several black velvet bows tied here and there in a half-hearted and wholly unsuccessful effort to create order. She'd given up wearing rings on each finger but a cluster of pearls was at each ear. "Tayd—ee! Ciao, Tayd—dee!" She grinned and waved at the Africans who sipped coffee in the doorway of Paolo's bar. Paolo waved from his perch on a stool behind the cash register. "Ciao!"

Teddy Starbuck was oblivious to the stir she caused as she concentrated only on running towards the right bus which would soon arrive at the center island of Largo Argentina. The great orange elephants wheezed past every ten seconds during rush hour, stopping only long enough to allow the seven o'clock crowds to funnel themselves forward to the door and up the three steps to the steambath interior.

Glad I'm tall, she thought, clutching a metal bar high above the dark heads of the Romans. The bus lurched, squealed to a halt, threw its passengers backwards then forwards en masse several times, more people squeezed aboard, people cried out, 'scendo! Per favore!' and still others tried to move aside to allow them to exit. The Italians seemed ever-polite, ever-good tempered. Teddy was always amazed when she stepped on someone's foot and apologized only to be greeted with a musical, "Prego!" as if it had been quite a nice experience and would you mind crushing my instep one more time?

Twenty minutes later Teddy was standing before the liveried young man at the portals of the palazzo. He asked her name and then squinted at his list in the fading light. "Si, si! Buona sera, signorina!" He directed her through the lobby which dwarfed them both, and up the wide stone stairs to the secondo piano. An evening of jazz, Eleanor had said. Please come, Diane won't and I would love to have at least one other American in the room with me. Eleanor, for all her aggressiveness in tracking down a story, or wangling an interview from a reluctant subject, was sometimes shy in social situations. And with Enrico out of town covering the music festival at San Remo, she was sorely tempted to barricade herself in their flat at via del Plebiscito watching Dallas and Dynasty. Don't knock it, she defended her taste, until you've laughed yourself silly over the way J.R. says, 'Ciao, Sue Ellen,' or until you've seen Joan Collins have a temper tantrum in machine-gun fire Italian.

A second liveried servant opened the tall front door and Teddy crossed a reception area and entered a crowded room. Many of the men were greying at the temples, and most of the women looked as though they'd been married to those same men for a long time. "No mistresses here," whispered Eleanor in her ear. Teddy turned with a grin of recognition. She'd never seen Eleanor so dressed up. The beige linen suit with gold buttons across the double breasted jacket was a far cry from her daily uniform of trousers and T-shirts.

"What are you talking about?" Teddy laughed. "But before you tell me-it's been hell to find this place—is my hair all sticky outy?"

"Your hair is ALWAYS sticking out! That's one of the reasons everybody is staring at you."

"Oh, God, don't say that!" Teddy was pleased though and wanted to say, 'oh, really. Tell me who.' "Okay, what's the story on mistresses? I've never met one. Why, I've never been in the same room with one!" Teddy was nearly gasping with excitement.

"You're too much. You may not be in the same room with one tonight but this is a rare occasion. Seems the men have decided this is a wife only party." Eleanor was pensive. "Don't know if they use the phone or it's some en masse instinct the way those birds suddenly decide it's time to cross the ocean..."

Teddy looked around her with great curiosity. She'd been to her share of parties in Rome-all because of Diane who hated them. Diane was a loner whom Teddy had seen actually flinch when invited to dinner. Then recovering, she'd speak into the receiver,"May I bring a friend? An American. Oh, she's such fun..." she'd say several times. Teddy had been delighted and then on the appointed evening had rung Diane's doorbell only to have her lean out the window and swear she had stomach cramps or a migraine. Teddy, dressed in her perpetual black or white—black wool cape of winter or white silk shawl of spring knotted on one shoulder—would stand with arms akimbo and shout curses and threats up at her friend.

"Blast you, anyway, Diane! Darn it! You know I don't know these people and I can't walk in like some gatecrasher and sit down and eat their food when I wasn't REALLY invited and you really were! Now put on that red sweater and your good black trousers and get down here! Now!" she would shout. "Or do I have to come up and dress you myself!" Diane would tell her to go on ahead and promise to come if she felt better by nine o'clock. Teddy would call her a liar and then Diane would notice, usually during a lull of Teddy's yelling, that she was not the only person leaning out a window. Teddy would then call again. "I can't simply walk in and plant myself in a strange living room and..." But the truth was, Teddy could and Teddy did. Diane thought her trickery was well-founded. Teddy needed to meet people and people loved meeting Teddy and she, Diane, would get invitations forever, she moaned, and not have any desire to accept them.

But this party was different. It wasn't a room full of expatriates with a few token Italians gathered for red wine and spaghetti and it wasn't the journalists of all nationalities she'd met with Eleanor at Stampa Estera. 'The salon of the palazzo was thronged with elegant middle-aged Romans whose old names were prefixed with 'Conte' or 'Principe' or 'Barone.' There was the sense of raffinatezza, of refinement; the guests were relaxed with one another and at home in the massive marble and tapestried palazzo.

The ceiling thirty feet above them was frescoed with plump angels, chubby cherubs, and cumulus clouds big enough to qualify as fog banks. A large refectory table was set with bottles of Scotch which was a favorite, and various wines and champagnes had been opened; rows of shining glasses stood in lines upon silver trays. A buffet was spread in the dining room and people milled about the table, talking and balancing plates and wine goblets beneath a chandelier of one thousand twinkling prisms. Eleanor handed Teddy white wine and then a tall man stepped between them.

"Oh, you speak English!" she sighed with relief.

"My Italian is indescribable and I thought you didn't look a bit local-"

"I'm insulted. I think I'm moving on," she pouted. He was fortyish and not a tad attractive, she decided. But at least he speaks English and I don't have to make an idiot of myself getting all my verb tenses wrong so I'd better thank my lucky stars and stick with him.

"Insulted? Why?" He was better when he smiled. A large hook nose loomed above thin lips. Heavy, even bushy black brows sprouted over small eyes and then decided they would be one long horizontal brow instead. He had oily skin that was shiny in the light.

"Well, I'd rather look like a typical Roman in this room than like a typical American." Teddy had been trying not to stare but she could easily see that the men were beautifully tailored right down to their glove leather shoes and the women had a sheen of confidence, of elegance, that only comes after thirty, if it appears at all. They wore silk suits and good jewelry and held themselves very straight at their husbands' elbows as they chatted and smiled and bobbed their well-coiffed heads.

"Typical, you're not." He sipped mineral water and shook his head. "And typical, they're not."

Teddy didn't answer that. "You are American, aren't you?"

He nodded. "Half. My grandparents were born in Calabria, you know the heel of the boot, and went to the States, Ellis Island, the whole bag, when my mother was a baby."

Teddy thought, he talks without punctuation and there is no accent at all. He talks like a disc jockey.

He'd barely paused for breath. "And where are you from, my little southern belle?"

"I thought I'd lost it," she smiled faintly. "Alabama."

He was warming up to her, quickly. "And the stars fell on Alabama. Well, hot damn!" he put on a southern accent. "Imagine meeting a bona fide Alabama belle-"

"He's tacky," she hissed to Eleanor minutes later in the dark blue bathroom. Eleanor seemed to be ignoring her opinion and commanded her to touch the wall. "It's velvet," Teddy agreed and then went on. "But I want to meet Italians. I don't want to stand there with some character from the United States!"

"You won't be for much longer. The concert starts in about fifteen minutes. Giovanna told me everything's ready. It's just getting people away from the buffet and sitting them down...."

Teddy was reapplying coral lipstick and then patting gold sparkles above her cheekbones. Suzanne, the model from Paris she'd worked with once in Martinique had taught her. It was especially effective with a tan.

Eleanor was distractedly brushing her rust-colored hair. She looked at Teddy's little nothing dress and realized she looked better than any-one at the party. It was as if she'd sauntered in after a day in the sun. Hers was an effortless, natural kind of beauty that couldn't be copied. You just had to be Teddy Starbuck to look like that.

"But really, Eleanor. He's kind of a creep. Couldn't you come over and say that I simply had to meet your very best friend who's here from Afghanistan for only ten minutes?"

"Oh, Teddy! Stop complaining! I'm limping along with a man old enough to be my grandfather but at least he's telling me the truth, well, maybe not, about Prime Minister Goria...and you know what else?"

"No, what?" Teddy was adamant about ditching the American, with or without Eleanor's help. She put the silver-backed hairbrush back on the marble dressing table.

"The creep you're talking to...he looks so much like this movie tycoon. Can't think of his name. I've seen his picture. He owns the stu-dios outside town. A big takeover by a California group...." Eleanor dabbed perfume from a tiny bottle at each wrist. "He does look like him."

Teddy fumbled in the bag she'd made by knotting the orange silk scarf she'd bought from the Africans last Thursday. When she found what she wanted, Eleanor shrieked.

"What is the matter?"

"I simply don't believe you, Teddy! That bottle! So that's why you smell exactly like someone I used to be in love with in New York!"

Teddy methodically dabbed the after shave at her temples and then across her collar bones. "Don't get any ideas, okay?" She lowered her voice to a growl. "I'm straight."

Giggling, Eleanor grasped the ornate silver doorknob and opened the door. Arm in arm, they strode down the marble hallway towards the lilting Italian voices, towards the laughter, towards the movie mogul lookalike, towards the truth about Goria.

*   *   *   *   *   *   *   *   *   *   *

"You've given up the modelling? For good?" he was asking. His eyes were admiring, in a sleazy way, thought Teddy who was pressed beside him on the dark green brocade sofa. The cushions were filled with down and she hated being this close. He'd managed to squeeze himself between her and Eleanor the minute they'd found a place to sit. Eleanor had winked at her and given her a 'now, be nice,' look which elicited one of Teddy's darkest scowls. Teddy shrugged her bare shoulders and Eleanor thought the man looked as though he might lick one. Nobody ever acts like that around me, she thought. Actually Enrico does and he is quite enough. She felt lucky to have him when she saw how solitary Diane's life was. And now, when she saw what Teddy was putting up with. All because Massimo had been unable to come.

Creep was the right word.

"I think if I keep on modelling it's just more of the same," Teddy was saying. "I know basically how and I don't want to be the best in the world and so the next assignment is just that—an assignment. I'd like to do something else."

The buzzing conversation stopped then. Sixty or seventy guests had arranged themselves on the sofas and various chairs in the salon. A dozen people stood in the doorway of the dining room and opposite them were another dozen clustered in the entrance to the hall. Giovanna was before them, exceptionally pretty with dark hair brushed back from her face. She wore a yellow shantung suit and a necklace of twisted pearls around her neck. "Buona sera," she began and then introduced three black American women, all dressed in black, all of whom bowed self-consciously when their names were mentioned. The applause was enthusiastic as they tuned their instruments and by the time they had actually begun to play and to sing, the crowd was theirs.

Teddy was transported to another time, another place. She was back in Alabama, at home with Cricket and Daisy, and Billie Holiday was crooning on the record player, singing of lost love and of being mistreated by men. The black women themselves affected Teddy. They were American, Southern and so far away from what they sang about. Teddy was beginning to recognize the Ethiopians she saw on the street. Poor things running away from famine, from war. And having to run to a city of white faces to begin again. Teddy was lost in a dream as the music floated through the rooms of the sixteenth century palazzo.

A man stared at her from the dining room doorway. He noted the parted lips, the shining dark eyes with gathering tears of emotion, and the profusion of blond hair. She looks, he thought, like the wild younger sister of Botticelli's Venus. She could stand up and step from the waves and away from the sea shell and no one would think she was impersonating anyone. He was jarred from his thoughts when Flavia put her hand on his arm and squeezed. He looked down at her but did not smile. He didn't smile often these days. Flavia stepped inches closer and made sure he could see down the neck of her green silk dress. If he'd look, he could see, she thought. Pero, non interessa a lui. No. He is not interested. She sighed and wondered why the Romans were so mad for jazz.

As the clapping, interspersed with shouts of 'Brava!' and 'Bravissima!' swept over them, the man tried to speak to Teddy. "Have you ever done public relations?" he asked. "I said have you ever done public——"

Teddy shook her head and continued to applaud. "Would you like to?" he insisted.

She looked blank and then saw Eleanor lean forward. Her lips moved and the man turned towards her and away from Teddy.

"Brava!" "Brava!" The Romans were on their feet now and the women musicians were basking in the appreciation. The trio held hands and like prizefighters lifted their arms over their heads and shook them in triumph. There was an encore and then another and another and at last the crowd, chattering, animated, was on its way towards the front door where Giovanna and her husband Giuseppe kissed everyone on each cheek and thanked them for coming. The American, still beside her, smiled and presented Teddy with his card. She took it without looking as he bent to kiss her hand.

Over his bowed head, behind him, she saw a man with white hair and very pale blue eyes. His face was tan, handsome, fine-featured and devoid of expression; he looked straight at her, staring without embarrassment or apology. The directness of Teddy's gaze matched his. Neither looked away and it was only the intrusion of the American as he stood that cut the tension between them.

"Goodbye," smiled Teddy, thinking how wonderful it was that he hadn't asked for her telephone number. Safe. Home free.

He smiled slowly, the nose like a jib above the narrow lips. "Until Wednesday."

"Come on, Teddy!" It was Eleanor digging her fingers into her bare arm. "If we're going to meet Enrico and Massimo we have to hurry."

"What? Oh, sure. Yes. Of course. Massimo." She turned towards Eleanor and they took small steps forward in the throng of milling people. "What are you talking about?" Teddy hissed when they were a few feet away. "And what is this Wednesday business?"

Eleanor gave her a look that plainly said, shut up if you know what's good for you and Teddy amused herself by admiring the jewel box of a ceiling as they edged towards the door. Incredible. Now Eleanor has two jobs. And I don't even have one. It's a shame I was stuck with that man all evening and there were so many divinely attractive older types. The room was exploding with them. Wonder who the man with white hair is. His face is so young. She turned around and saw him again and then looked forward immediately. "Eleanor," she whispered. "Don't look now, but wait a minute and then tell me if you know the white-haired man with the blue tie and the blue and white striped shirt. He's next to creep of all creeps."

Humming under her breath, Eleanor looked back and then turned to Teddy. "Oh, boy. That's Vittorio della Venturini. Don't bother getting excited."

"I'm not excited," Teddy said a bit huffily. "But," she couldn't resist. "Why shouldn't I bother?" Oh, God. He's gay. He's in the last stages of AIDS. He's got two weeks to live—

"Because he doesn't." Teddy waited for her to explain. "He doesn't get excited. He doesn't bother. Women fall all over him. Tonight he's with a countess from Florence and he might as well be alone. Don't think he's gay. He's just—I don't know. Passive?"

Teddy was thanking Giovanna for including her and then Giuseppe was saying in very flowery Italian that she must come again for she was from the South, wasn't she? Evidently these evenings of jazz were held about once every two months.

Once down the stairs and out into the street, Eleanor turned to Teddy and said, "Congratulations!"

"For what? My great Italian? I was pretty good, wasn't I?"

"No!" laughed her friend. "Your new job."

"My what?" Teddy stopped dead in the middle of the sidewalk, arms akimbo, orange bag hanging from one wrist.

"You, my dear Teddy, have a job. And it's perfect because you won't need working papers or residency or-"

"What were you and that troll discussing when I couldn't hear?" she demanded. "And what's this about Wednesday?"

Eleanor smiled and took her arm. "Come on. Diane's still up, I'm sure of it. She'll give us vino and I'll tell both of you at once."

Half an hour later, in Diane's living room, Teddy leaned back in the wicker chair and sighed. She'd had so much to drink, she was nearly past caring about jobs or promises of any sort. Wednesday seemed as urgent as the next century.

"You with us, Theodora?" Diane had brushed her long hair back into a rubber band. Her face was pale and quite pretty in the dimly lit room. She and Eleanor smiled at each other. Teddy was their little sister, the naive new kid in town and she, with her Alabama background, was slightly unreal.

"Present, marinated, but with you," Teddy then splashed wine all over the front of her dress. She was unconcerned. "Oh, well. It's due for the garbage anyway."

"You're throwing your dress away?" Eleanor stammered. "Because white wine comes out."

"Hey, I bought it six weeks ago at Campo dei Fiori. It's really long past its prime." Teddy brushed the drops away and sat up straighter.

They were aghast. "You bought that dress at the market?"

"Yep." Teddy couldn't understand what was so extraordinary about that revelation. There was a place for sweaters and socks and underwear and shoes behind the flower stall. It was strictly open air, clothes lines strung under the canvas lean-to's.

Eleanor who'd seen her at the party with a slice of Roman aristocracy, with many Qf Rome's richest and most chic, simply had to know. "How much was it?"

"Six thousand lira, I think. Maybe five."

Diane shook her head and sat down across from her. "You paid four or five dollars for that dress?"

"Not bad, is it?" Teddy asked seriously. She looked down at the black cotton. It was simple. Empire waist. The back was the best part. Teddy thought everyone bought clothes the way she did. At least once in awhile. Couldn't understand designer clothes. Oh, there was the white mink. Fun. Just fun.

Eleanor sighed. A five dollar dress to that party! She would have been terrified to wear a five dollar dress TO the market to buy lemons let alone—

"Come on, Eleanor, I'm not going to be sober forever..." It was Teddy's sleepy voice. "Did you tell that sleaze I would work for him?" Teddy glowered.

"Just last week you said you wanted a job. Now, you have one. Be happy." Eleanor turned to Diane. "I kept thinking this character was a dead-ringer for Ernie Melville. I know you know this man! The character who bought the old studios about thirty miles outside Rome. He's California. Los Angeles. Remember about six years ago when there was the big scandal and Lorenzo Mancini got caught for income tax invasion and skipped town? Actually, he skipped the country. Until last year the studios were sitting out there in a field and then poof! Enter Melville and his crew. A marriage made in...well, not in heaven. But let's call it an affair between the Californians and the Italians. And they're making movies like sausages."

Diane was nodding. "I do remember this story."

"Well, what's this about Wednesday?" Teddy's voice was tense.

"You are having dinner with Ernie Melville who will be your new boss. But not really..." She held up one hand as if to stifle Teddy's moans of protest. "He won't be your boss because he doesn't spend much time in Rome. You will work here and you will hardly ever see him. And don't worry. You have Massimo, remember?"

Massimo. Teddy looked down. Massimo had lied about not being able to come tonight. She knew he had. And he hadn't kissed her, not even good night, the last three evenings they'd spent together.

"All I told him was what he could see for himself. That you are a natural for public relations." And that you never bothered with college since your modelling career began with a bang in New York right after high school. "A natural," she repeated.

"I am?" Teddy asked suspiciously. "I met someone who did that once in New York and there were publicity people always hanging around the fashion shows-"

Diane was glad. This would be so good for Teddy. A salary. A position to challenge her. She'd be learning something. "You're on the right track, Teddy. You do know about publicity and public relations. More than you think you know."

Teddy was pensive. Wednesday. She was hoping Ernie wouldn't try anything, wouldn't expect anything. They toasted her. Then they toasted Hollywood. Then they poured more wine and most of Teddy's went down the front of her dress. She smiled slowly. "Yes, I can do it. Thank you, Eleanor,"she said formally. Her southern accent had returned. She grinned crookedly and raised her glass. "Here's to true friends." She swallowed and then held the nearly empty glass aloft once more, tipping it perilously towards her lap. Diane and Eleanor gasped in unison but Teddy didn't appear to notice. "And here's to public relations," she collapsed with giggles, sinking even lower into the chair. They stared at her. "Well," she laughed, "it sounds like sex in the street!"

*   *   *   *   *   *   *   *   *   *   *

"My Italian's not terrific yet but-"

Ernie Melville shook his head. "Doesn't matter. You're a winner."

Teddy smiled and touched the damask napkin in her lap. No matter what happens now I can at least have a fit for about thirty years about getting picked up in the white Mercedes. Diane had almost fallen out her window and she'd been dying to give her a little wave the way the Queen does and then slowly oh, how blissfully slowly they had hummed down the narrow street! And the Africans and Paolo and Sharif, the Moroccan flower vendor and probably even

Kiko had all been open-mouthed. Too bad the Fabianos had missed it. But Signora Pace had been outside her profumeria so they'd hear about it. The whole neighborhood would know before breakfast time.

"Do you like the wine?" he was asking. "I have a vineyard in the Napa Valley. It's only a hobby of course but -"

"Where are you from?"Teddy insisted.

"I'm really bicoastal now. I wouldn't know what to-"

"But you must have grown up somewhere, been born somewhere..."

He twirled his wine glass as if studying it for sediments. "Why don't I say that I live-"

Teddy stared at him. Maybe she shouldn't've asked. Maybe he'd been born in a women's prison and had worn striped diapers till his mother was paroled. Maybe he....

Ernie Melville realized she was waiting for an answer, wouldn't let up. He sighed. "Hackensack, New Jersey."

"Hmmm," she answered.

"I think..."he said to the waiter. "We'll start with pasta primavera for me and-" he nodded to Teddy.

"Spaghetti con vongole." She had to remember not to save the shells. They were so pretty and she planned to drill holes in them and make jewelry. Diane had been horrified and had told her never to do it in front of anyone except her or Eleanor again. Teddy had promised. She thought, oh, what a waste, though. To throw them away and I bet this restaurant has great shells.

"Tell me what growing up in Alabama was like."

Teddy laughed, completely forgetting that this man was offering her a job. "Am I grown up? Are you?"

He stared at her. "I...I don't know."

"Why do you say you don't know?"

"Because....because I still worry about stepping on the cracks in the sidewalk." He felt ridiculous. Why had he answered her?

Teddy nodded "Oh, God. So do I. Break your mother's back." She pushed the mother of pearl comb deeper into the waves of golden hair and sighed. "And sometimes I feel so awfully old."

"Why? You?"

"Oh, I miss things. Things have changed. And I think when you look back on the good ole days then you're old."

The pasta came and they ignored it. "But what do you miss?" Ernie insisted.

"I miss making wishes on Coke bottles. Did you ever do that? You have to drink the Coke first and then at the end you look at the bottom to see where it was made and if you're not there and it's foreign—" She could see he didn't understand. He was older. "Well, let's say I'm in Ace and the bottle says Montgomery. That's foreign." Her dark eyes were shining. "So you get to make a wish and you're lucky for a long time afterwards." She lowered her eyes. "And now. No more glass bottles. You can't wish on a can for pete's sake. No more wishes."

"You can still wish on stars."

"I know. I do."

They began to eat. Ernie Melville watched her. She ate carefully, as though she were admiring the shells. She plainly adored food and looked as if she burned it off by running around. High energy level. He really should talk to her about the job. For a split second all kinds of lascivious thoughts paraded before him.

"You'll be the liason between Rome and Los Angeles. That means that the L.A. office will get your reports on everything that goes on here regarding the making of a film. It'll be your job to be on the set, to interview the actors, the director, the producer, everybody, and to write about it."

Oh, God. Nobody said I'd have to write anything. Teddy tried to look calm. Tried to look as if she'd had lots of jobs like this one. Her silver ballet slipper fell to the floor and she resisted the impulse to slide down in her chair and find it. Her bare foot with lavender toenails was arched and searching blindly under the table.

"These reports will be then given in the form of press kits to journalists in the U.S. You'll write a synopsis of the film and that will go out to the reviewers. For magazines, for newspaper critics and so forth."

And so forth. Teddy felt little and young as she listened. This is a real job, went through her mind. This is real and he expects me to do all this and in return he will pay me. This is not standing around in clothes and being quiet and looking stuck up. Teddy squared her shoulders and took a deep breath which nearly took Ernie's breath away. Diane had told her to go ahead and wear the low-cut black dress and she had. "Yes," she said definitively. "Yes." Remember Aunt Cricket. Whatever's going on, whatever anyone asks you to do—you stop and ask yourself one question. And that isn't, can I do it? The one question is: what's the worst thing that can possibly happen if I fail? And when you decide what that is, you just put your head down and go towards it.

Teddy appeared to be absorbing every word that Ernie Melville uttered. He felt important and very pleased with her respect. A free spirit, he thought, but bright. The pasta was stone cold and the wine was undrunk and still he elaborated on what would be expected of her. Teddy did not flinch in the face of it. She told herself that at the worst, she would be fired. That wasn't so bad. So she would try. No, she would do it. Because my name is Teddy Starbuck, she nearly whispered aloud.

Ernie Melville had finished. She was going to be great for the job. She seemed to thoroughly understand the ramifications of publicity and the importance of keeping L.A. on top of things. He smiled with those thin lips. "Teddy," he said solemnly. "You're a winner."

*   *   *   *   *   *   *   *   *   *   *

"It's a circle, Diane, and I can't seem to break it, change it, get out of it." Eleanor leaned back on Teddy's couch with an expression of despair.

Teddy reached for another strawberry from the blue bowl on the table and bit into it. Diane leaned forward from an Egyptian chair and crossed her blue-jeaned legs. The brown sandals are the kind those nuns wear, thought Teddy. She'd seen loads of nuns on the bus lately. She'd even seen one wearing topsiders under her black robes. A Yuppy nun. Diane spoke. "Have you told Enrico that you think it's all in his mind? That he is changing things by imagining them?"

"Of course I have!" Eleanor's exasperation was evident. "This jealousy of his is like a poison. He adores me, he is wonderful to me, he thinks I am divinely attractive. All splendid so far, right? And then we get to the snags. Enrico's mind seems to work on the level of- If I think she is so attractive, then so does every man in Rome. Then we have the next truth and that is- women like Eleanor or maybe all women need sex and if I'm out of town and not able to please her then any of the other several million men in Rome will."

"And of course, even though you say you love him, the flesh is weak and you have succumbed...." Diane finished for her.

"So then with the accusations, come the arguments, the denials from me, and the declarations of undying love...."

Teddy was shaking her head. She put her hands over her ears. "What is it?" demanded Eleanor.

"I can't stand it. I can't stand how complicated it is. It makes me crazy."

The older women laughed as she stood up and headed for the kitchen. "What you need is colzetti alla polceverasca," she said as she left the room. Eleanor looked at Diane. She was mystified.

Diane smiled. "Teddy says she doesn't speak Italian but she does speak Italian cuisine. Amazing girl."

"Anyway," sighed Eleanor. "I simply can't make love anymore. Can't bear the thought and that's the last of the circle." She pinched the stem of the wine glass so hard her finger tips went white.

"After the fighting?"

Eleanor nodded. "You know the scream and let it all out Italian mentality and then the passionate make up routine—" Her eyes filled with tears. "I guess I'm just too Ohio to handle it."

"You're straight and honest and Italian men can't always handle that. That's all."

"Maybe." Eleanor reached behind her and fumbled for a kleenex in her beige leather bag. "I think he wants me in hysterics then he wants me to fall into bed and prove to him how much I love him and that's another thing…." She looked at Diane and said, "I feel like Teddy. Like covering my ears and saying I can't. It's too complicated."

Diane smiled. Their funny Teddy. Massimo problems were never discussed these days but he did still call her for she would give news of his latest trip to Paris or to Milan. Evidently he was interested but didn't ask her out. It was so strange, for Teddy was obviously pining for him. Men stopped her on the street to flirt, to ask her for a coffee and she was not the least bit interested. Thank God, thought Diane, because if she were she'd go. It wasn't a sense of decorum that kept her from accepting those invitations-it was Massimo. She did go out with groups once in awhile. They met at Othello's or some pizza place in Trastevere and drank lots of wine and beer until early morning and then walked home in pairs. But Teddy wasn't interested in anyone her own age. Why should she be fascinated by a hippie from Vienna who sits on the Spanish Steps all day or someone who hadn't experienced half of what she had in New York? No, Teddy is perfect for an older man, say, mid-thirties. She would adore him and he would, rightly or wrongly, polish her a bit but be self-assured enough to find her eccentricities endearing.

"The second phase of this," Eleanor was saying, "is worse than the first. He-" she took a sip of wine. "He came back from San Remo. He came back and instead of quizzing me about what I'd done, who I'd seen and telling me he'd called Stampa Estera and they hadn't been able to find me and that I hadn't answered the phone at eleven o'clock on such and such a night…now it's something new." She sighed. "He told me that the new stringer for the Daily Mail is very attractive and has made it clear that she would like to sleep with him."

"Oh, God," Diane turned down her mouth in disgust.

"Yes. Exactly my sentiments." Eleanor ran her fingers through her copper colored hair. "And that means I am to look at him and think, oh, what an attractive man I have! Aren't I lucky that other women want him and shouldn't I jump on his bones and show him how much I love him and how lucky he is to have me!"

Diane nodded. "Well, I couldn't. I know it's expected by certain Italian males but maybe I'm just too Ohio, too."

Eleanor managed to smile. She thought of Diane as one of the most sophisticated women she'd ever known. She read books, mostly novels, in four languages, she thought about things, she absorbed ideas on a different scale from Eleanor's quick gleaning of day to day politics. Her perception was keen about matters of the heart, though it was strange, thought Eleanor, that she had never heard her speak of being in love. There had been no marriage for Diane and as far as she had confided, no love affairs, no passions.

Teddy had padded barefoot into the room and was setting the table behind them. Wonder if she thinks we're like her two helpless aunts, thought Eleanor. Diane had told her about Teddy's father, her mother, and of Daisy and Cricket. And then there's Teddy who storms through it all with guts and instinct spurning the intellectual arguments. Fearless and strong. Does she simply not know enough to be frightened of anything? Has she ever been hurt?

"I wonder if Enrico-" Diane was speaking slowly, carefully. "I wonder if it's possible that he's been unfaithful to you?"

Eleanor was perplexed. "I don't know what you're-"

"I'm playing with this and maybe it doesn't mean a thing. Psychologically. Let's pretend we were writing a novel. When a character suddenly changes a behavior pattern there is a reason and the reason has to be presented to the reader or you lose the thread of that character. The plot sinks. Now Enrico wasn't like this a year ago, was he? What has changed? What has happened?"

"He's been promoted. He's gotten a raise. And he's gotten….. a very good barber." Suddenly Eleanor thought of the new clothes he'd bought around January. That was out of character.

"So he's gotten generally more attractive and more sure of himself through professional recognition. And good ole RAI, the state-owned television has had a great deal to do with it."

"You think Enrico has had an affair," began Eleanor.

"I don't know. I have no way of knowing," Diane sipped the last of the wine in her glass. "What if he had and he felt so guilty about it that he almost wanted you to confess to the same thing?"

"You're nuts." Teddy's voice was quiet. She stood over them with the steaming bowl of pasta and butter and marjoram and then placed it on the dining room table.

Eleanor was not answering, deep in thought, as they seated themselves. Violets were in a small round glass vase in the center. Teddy lit two lavender candles in the little glass star holders. "So that we could really erase the slate and begin again? So that he could free himself from this? So that he could confess and be absolved?" Eleanor was finding it difficult, though not impossible to consider. It was a highly imaginative scenario.

Diane sat down. "Maybe Teddy's right and I'm simply nuts. But I think there are lots of corners to this. Enrico is complicated."

Eleanor smiled. "You're right about that, anyway."

They poured wine and then Teddy passed the bread, the cheese, the sliced roast beef she'd cooked earlier in the day. The watercress salad in the blue ceramic bowl was worthy of a photograph: each avocado section was aligned exactly with three bright pink shrimp. Whole walnuts had been sprinkled on top.

"Okay, Theodora," said Diane. "What do you want from us?"

"Why, whatever do you mean?" Teddy grinned.

"I mean that this is a feast. Diane and I are known to eat tuna out of the can standing over the kitchen sink. So we will do it. We surrender. What is it you demand of us?"

Teddy didn't miss a beat. "Tell me everything you know about the movie business and teach me how to do an interview, help me write the first one up, and let me borrow those three books on film-making, the ones in English, I saw on the bookshelf near your bedroom door."

＊　＊　＊　＊　＊　＊　＊　＊　＊　＊　＊

It was two Roman subways—-one to the train station and the second to almost the end of the line—-to EUR. The suburb of the Italian capital had been originally planned for Mussolini's 1940 exhibition which never took place but now it was a zone of modern office blocks and apartment buildings designed in the worst possible Fascist style. Teddy sprinted up the steps to street level, to the now familiar bar with its telephone.

"Si, si. Anna? Buon giorno. Sono Teddy Starbuck. Si. Sono arrivata. Grazie." She hung up and looked at her father's watch tied with a red plaid ribbon around her wrist. The original leather strap had disintegrated during a mud fight with the Rainey boys just before her eleventh birthday. She'd found it flung safely on the bank of the creek and run all the way home with the big cheap Timex cupped in her hands like a wounded bird. Since then Teddy had amassed a collection of straps and ribbons, though the scarred brown leather curves reclined in a jewelry box like priceless artifacts.

It usually took fifteen minutes for a studio car, anything from a little red Fiat to a black Mercedes, to arrive and honk twice for her. Mario, one of three drivers, looked a pimply fifteen. He entertained ideas of the Grand Prix and pronounced seatbelts 'per le donne' or 'for women.' As the radio blared the latest Italian hit single, the car sped over the highway with a terrified Teddy envisioning her own funeral. They whipped past green fields complete with grazing sheep and soon they were turning off the highway towards a low, very large, grey, concrete building which reminded Teddy of nothing so much as what a high school should look like. A guard in a guardbox nodded them through and pressed a button to raise the candycane striped barrier. Teddy always thanked Mario with gritted teeth and clutching notebooks to her chest, fairly ran towards the building, up the stairs, and down the hall to Salvatore's office. "Ciao, Teddy! Caffe? Luisa just brought this up from the bar. Sit. Per favore, stia comoda! Make yourself comfortable!" He always welcomed her to his office as though it were his home. The walls were papered with black and white glossies, and shooting schedules thumbtacked at all angles; the desk was piled with cameras, lenses, orange boxes of film, notes, and usually a ringing phone. "Ciao! Come stai? Si. Si. Si," he'd sigh and then roll his eyes at Teddy and breathe "Certo," into the receiver before hanging up.

'Sair-tainly. Sair-tainly," he translated with a grin.

"So, how is everything?" Teddy smiled back. "Everyone wants it yesterday, right?"

Salvatore's ringlet-covered head bobbed up and down as he laughed. He was a small man from the south of Italy, with all the good qualities they were said to possess. He was open, friendly, generous, and appreciated a good joke, a long coffee with friends, a four hour lunch. This week he had been told to show Teddy Starbuck the studio, answer all her questions, and decide if they could work together. He handed her the cappuccino and leaned back in his swivel chair.

She sipped, trying not to let her notebook slide off her lap and onto the floor. "Did you get the still shots of the Devil last night after I left?"

"Si," he nodded. "Just before the nose melted and fell off on the victim."

Teddy burst out laughing. "Oh, ugh! As if all the blood and goo weren't enough! It FELL on him?"

Salvatore nodded. "They're making a new one this morning. And they want all my stills to duplicate it exactly so that...." He waved his hand. "You know the story."

Continuity. Teddy was catching on. Each person involved in making a film or publicizing it was one piece of the puzzle. She had been told on Monday what each did and only yesterday, on Thursday, did she begin to realize how they worked together. Salvatore was to provide Teddy with stills to send to Los Angeles to go in the press kits, but he also could pinch hit in an emergency on the lot. The nose emergency, for instance. The continuity shots taken just before each scene hadn't been detailed enough to show the exact location of the black warts so Salvatore had been called in to blow up his stills. "The Polaroids aren't good enough?"

Teddy's question was rhetorical. She'd learned that often the Polaroids weren't good enough, but the continuity woman was having an affair with the assistant director so they stumbled along hoping, as Salvatore put it, "that she's better between the sheets than behind a camera."

Teddy went off by herself after coffee so that Salvatore could answer the perpetually ringing phone and try to get to his darkroom. She left the building that housed the offices and strode, in her gold flats and black miniskirt, across the grass towards the sound stages. They sat like enormous barns with open doors exposing the urgent activity inside. There were carpenters bent over sawhorses, there were electricians on ladders shouting down to assistants, there were men in three-wheeled trucks careening around corners honking their horns. And above all the din of incidental noise there was the perpetual wail of a buzzsaw punctuated by hammering. Several of the men nodded and smiled at her. They'd all been introduced the day before. "Ciao," she called back.

"Ti piace?" asked Lorenzo as he pointed to the small house they had nearly finished. It stood with only three walls, open like a doll's house, but furnished, wallpapered, complete with living room, dining room, bedrooms, bathroom and kitchen.

"I do like it. I can't believe you're not going to cook lunch there."

The set designer smiled. "I can't believe we'll finish it before the shooting starts after lunch." He shouted an order Teddy didn't understand to two men laboring under the weight of a piano and then turned back to her. "Ci vediamo," he patted her arm and walked quickly away.

Teddy stepped over the lumber, the toolbox, and behind the wooden crates and out into the sunlight. She knew she should begin the interviews next week. Nothing to it, Eleanor had said. I'll rehearse you, Diane had promised. Teddy nodded at one of the actors who passed her and waved. They were all American, about her age and had been rescued from the stopgap careers of parking cars and waiting tables. Thank God my interviews will be in English. It won't be hard. I'll just ask what I want to know, she said to herself.

Teddy opened the door of the next building. This was what she liked-the idea that she was now part of all this-that she had free rein to open doors, look at everything, ask questions. The interior was black but in a few seconds Teddy could see that canvas had been draped over the doorway. Cables like snakes were beneath her feet but there was a path to stumble along on tiptoe; it reminded her of entering the house of horrors at the Alabama State Fair. She heard shouts of 'silenzio!' then the curse of someone and a crash. Then another voice called a bit angrily, "Silenzio!" and then "Azione!"

Teddy froze. She heard the voices of the actors speaking their lines in English for a moment and then,"Cut!" She walked towards the light as the great relaxing sigh of many in unison signalled the end of the shooting. Voices rose and fell, a director in a canvas chair sat with a script in his lap and a clipboard. He was American but directed in an interesting mixture of Italian and English and everyone moved when he spoke even if they didn't understand his command the first time. Teddy walked away from the cameras through thirty or forty people who fanned out from the set. Blue jeans, bright jerseys or T shirts, desert boots or running shoes, were what everyone of either sex wore.

Teddy, in her miniskirt and black and white striped blouse, was openly ogled, but then the company publicist was usually more dressed up. The last publicist had swept in and out of the drafty studios wearing diamond clip earrings and a full length mink. "Gone Hollywood," remarked an actress and the quick retort was "No. FROM Hollywood." She hadn't liked Rome and often complained about this and that little quirk of living there. "It doesn't agree with me," she often said of the city, as though it were a bad clam she'd eaten. With her departure, the position of publicist had been open for exactly five weeks.

Teddy leaned on a sawhorse well away from the set which depicted a clearing in a pine forest. Real trees had been planted here and there among the masterpieces created by Lorenzo's art department. Teddy opened her notebook and looked for her notes on this particular movie. It was titled, "The Devil In You" and starred two never-befores directly from Marina del Rey, California. Salvatore had told her of the has-beens and the never-befores, all willing to work for pennies.

Yes, Monday I'll start my interviews. I'll get the list of hotel phone numbers from Anna and call everyone over the weekend and set up times. Teddy smiled to herself as she pencilled in notes. And there's the director, the producer, the special effects team to talk to—when they finish that nose, of course. I can do this, she decided as she crossed her ankles. It'll be like homework back in high school.

Chi e questa ragazza?" a grip asked an electrician.

"Teddy Starbuck," was the response. "Americana." "Every day she comes here. You mean you haven't noticed?"

There was laughter as the electrician climbed a ladder to adjust a spotlight. "He is legally blind. That's why he lost his car last week." More laughter.

The grip, a Roman of twenty-five, paid no attention to them. He was mesmerized at the sight of Teddy, hair almost white under the bright lights, like a cloak falling over her shoulders. Her legs in red tights were long, slender, perfect. Blissfully unaware of the attention, Teddy kicked off one ballet slipper and arched her foot. She continued to write.

"Lunedi, she arrive with black dress, long, down here," explained a carpenter. "Martedi, a short dress, white. Wow!" He shook his head, grinning at the memory. "Mercoledi, a very little black dress with white buttons down the side."

The grip took up the description. "And yesterday, also, something black with…" he sighed. "With so much leg showing."   "So that's the new publicist," put in the electrician.

"Sposata? Divorzata?"

The electrician was pleased to know more than the others. "Not married now. I asked Salvatore and he said she didn't mention a divorce but she was married."

The grip tried to turn away from the sight of Teddy, head down, intent on her ideas for interview questions. At last, he looked at the others. "Well, if she was married and she's not now and she didn't say separata and she's not divorziata then all that black only means one thing…."

The carpenter stopped hammering just as shouts for 'silenzio' began again. The electrician quietly folded his stepladder. "It means she's a widow."

The three of them stared at the legs and the blonde hair and the long lean figure. "Una vedova?" repeated the carpenter. Teddy Starbuck didn't look like any widow they'd ever seen before.

There was another urgent demand of "silenzio!" just as the grip whispered, "Well, maybe she fucked him to death."

*   *   *   *   *   *   *   *   *   *   *

Chapter Five

Slow had finished his lunch of sardines, sliced onions and steamed beets, a recipe for long life, and had washed and dried the dishes. Now he sat in the blue rocking chair teetering back and forth in silence, reading HOT HOUSE PEOPLE by Jane Walmsley and Jonathan Margolis. It was the only book he didn't read aloud and he hoped it wouldn't hurt Edith's feelings. She was eating popcorn, her favorite snack, under his bed. Crunch, crunch, crunch. Slow looked up for a second. Nothing he said improved her manners, but manners weren't important in the grand scheme of things.

Slow read quickly, skimming the pages he had read so many times before. "Debate continues over what age should the stimulation and education of the human being begin. Some organizations, particularly in the United States, are convinced that hot housing should begin in earliest infancy, even before birth." The dwarf nodded. "Some common sense educators decry hot housing as creating geniuses who have been denied carefree childhoods, geniuses who never develop social skills necessary for happiness." Slow turned several pages. "It has now become widely accepted that a deadline in a child's development is reached by his third birthday. At that age he has acquired some seventy-five percent of his adult language ability."

Very loud crunching came from under the bed. "Any discussion of the value of hot housing seems to throw up three questions. (1) If you intervene and accelerate children already identified as gifted, do you make them into geniuses? Is that how nations should develop their own

Einsteins? (2)If you try it on 'average' children, can you make them superior? (3) Perhaps most important of all-if you systematically hot house disadvantaged children, can you repair early social damage-or better still, prevent it?"

Slow flipped towards the last chapter and found his place. The words were underlined in red ball point pen; "If children are expected to become more intelligent, an important piece of research published in 1968 showed that their teachers will then perceive and treat them as such, aiding this kind of growth." So much of this is the degree of involvement of the parent, the midget said to himself. He closed the book and said, "Edith? Edith? Are you coming out soon?"

The crunching stopped and the Mexican blanket hanging nearly to the floor moved slightly. "Edith?" Slow's voice was low, soft, gentle. "Whenever you're ready. There is something I'd like to read to you. And then I thought maybe we'd play chess. I kinda think it's a good day for a game of chess, don't you think?"

The blanket moved again and out popped the white face, the eyes as black as JuJubes, the long black and white ears tilted back. The twenty-five pound spotted rabbit pom-pom-pom approached Slow. Her passage across the red linoleum floor was nearly silent, as though a powder puff was not quite hitting earth after each spring of the strong back legs. Effortlessly, with natural grace, innate ability, Edith the Educated Rabbit leapt into Slow's lap nearly knocking him and the rocking chair over backwards.

The midget embraced her, putting his face in her sweet-smelling fur. She pressed her body against him and vibrated with happiness. It was Edith's answer to purring. Slow waited until she was comfortable and then reached down beside the chair where several books were stacked. Awkwardly, he managed to pick up the N volume of the Encyclopedia Britannica. "Let's see," he said. "I put the marker yesterday right on...yes, here we are." Edith looked up at him, her face only five inches from Slow's, as he arranged the big book with difficulty at the fork of his tiny crossed legs.

"Yes," he said smiling down at her. "Yes, I know you're ready. Okay." He found his place and began to read. "Nijara. In Jaina religious belief of India, the destruction of karman (merit and demerit). For the soul to achieve….."

Edith's ears were straight up, her black as licorice eyes shining. The two of them tilted back and forth, back and forth in the blue rocking chair as Slow continued to read.

*   *   *   *   *   *   *   *   *   *   *

The silver Lamborghini sped under the archway and with a growling of gravel under its silver spoked wheels spun to a stop in the usual parking place. Prince Vittorio della Santini Venturini jerked the key from the ignition and then leaned back in the black leather bucket seat and closed his eyes. He was very tired. After a few minutes he stared straight ahead at the bougainvillea already in bloom, branches so heavy with fuschia flowers they bent towards the ground under their weight. He seemed to be summoning energy to leave the car and approach the palazzo.

At last he opened the door and pulled his suit jacket from the hook in the back seat and walked towards the colonnade. Taking the white marble steps two at a time his tall figure reached the front door and hesitated. Cesare loved to open the door with great ceremony but he never heard the bell anymore. Vittorio used his key and soon stood in the magnificent entranceway of the Venturini family quarters. Vaulted ceilings were above him; gilt eighteenth century chairs, commodes, and tables furnished the large salon before him. The large Oriental rugs covered only small sections of the black and white marble floor. Paintings in heavy gold frames fought for wall space. Paintings, he thought. All we've got. And too many of those. We must put some of this up in

Umbria. That poor castle's nearly empty. If only Mama weren't so attached to every single....

"Vittorio! Ciao, bello!" came the voice of his father. Dressed as always in one of his many three-piece dark suits as though he had just returned from a morning at the Caccia which was his favorite club, he limped forward. The elderly man leaned heavily on an ebony cane whose ivory handle was shaped like a turtle. All four legs and tail and head spiralled out in six directions.

"Ciao, Papa." The son and father kissed each other warmly. Both men had the same pale blue eyes, the same olive complexion and fine head of snow white hair, which had gone white in their late twenties. "How is Mama?"

"Boh!" the elder prince shrugged. "The same. Go in and see her. She is with the movie magazines all day. Won't talk to me. Something about Princess Stephanie has upset her. See what you can do."

Vittorio smiled and putting his coat over the back of one of the Baroque chairs in the reception hall, strode quickly down the corridor towards his mother's apartment. The marble under his handmade shoes resounded behind him and then died away as his father watched him proudly, thinking what a strong, good looking son he had.

Vittorio prepared to knock but the door was opened for him by Cesare who shouted in surprise. The major domo had been with the family since Vittorio's birth and his father before him, too. "You scoundrel!" he cried. "You like to sneak up and down the halls like a cat! You all do it!"

Vittorio tried to calm him but his every word was met with a loud "Prego? Prego?" as Cesare cupped one hand to his ear. Vittorio clapped him on the back and smilingly, pushed past him in the doorway. Cesare, in the livery of the Venturini family which was dark blue with silver buttons, shuffled down the hall muttering to himself.

"Vittorio! Precious one!" came the voice from the lavender brocade chaise. The Principessa lay supine upon it with pink chiffon falling to the floor; pink satin mules peeked from beneath the hem of the evening dress. Her white hair was pulled back from her face and into a knot atop her head. Two pink feathers adorned the chignon and bobbed when she spoke. "I have been thinking just this moment that it's time for the candles. In the spring you know it's getting darker later so that I have…"

Vittorio bent to kiss her on the forehead, hardly listening. Then he backed away and struck matches to the candles in the gold sconces on the wall above her and at last to the ormulu candelabra on the table. When the two dozen candles were lit he turned back to her. The sun was setting outside, dipping below the corner of the roof across the courtyard, but the light now was the light he usually saw his mother in. Very grey, fading, the silhouette of her regally reclining at dusk, after a day of being waited on, catered to, by old Cesare, by his adoring father. Her face, though wrinkled and pale, had a sweetness to it so that Vittorio could understand his father's devotion.

"Mama, come va?" he asked as he pushed magazines off the little boudoir chair next to her. He sat down and took her hand. Rings on every finger and every one with its history. The diamond from Napoleon given to his sister Pauline and left in her will to her best friend, Vittorio's great grandmother. The emerald from Napoleon himself to Vittorio's great grandmother. Vittorio sighed.

"Darling!" she crooned stroking his face. Abruptly her voice dropped in anger. "Have you seen that?" She pointed at one of the gossip magazines on the rug.

He shook his head and reached for it. Italy must churn out these rags by the thousands every week and Mama reads them all.

"There!" She sat forward. "Princess Stephanie is set on destroying that family! She's about to marry a rapist in California. It says so! Right there!" She was adamant about it as Vittorio tried to suppress a grin.

"Mama-"

"I believe it!" she said decisively. "Poor Prince Rainier. I've been keeping up with Stephanie's escapades ever since her mother died and

Vittorio, that's another thing. I read yesterday—did I tell you-I read in
Gente that the Mafia killed Grace…"

"Mama-"

"Mio Dio! What would your father do if you decided to marry a
rapist in Cali-"

"Mama-"

Vittorio saw Cesare enter the sitting room with a glass of Campari
and, with great relief, he took the glass. A slight breeze caused the gauzy
undercurtains to blow and the candles waved back and forth casting
eery shadows on the frescoes above them. A crack of thunder outside
announced the advent of another spring storm. In seconds, as Cesare
struggled to latch the outside shutters, Vittorio's father limped into the
room. Then it was Angela, Cesare's granddaughter and only living rela-
tive, who was preceded by her qreat stomach under the white frilly
apron.

Everyone in the household was frightened of storms save Vittorio
and they clustered around him for luck when it thundered. He took his
mother's hand as his father pulled a chair towards the tableau. The candles flickered but did not go out. His mother complained about nature
being such a bore but clung to the hands of her two principes as though
she were in the worst throes of labor. When that thought crossed
Vittorio's mind he turned to look at Angela who stood beside the fireplace murmuring over her rosary. Early summer by the looks of it.
Vittorio sighed then looked down at the hands locked together resting
on the pink chiffon. His father's cuff was frayed with wear and his suit
was nearly as shiny with age as Cesare's livery. He glanced at his mother
who attempted a brave smile and then closed her eyes in terror when a
great crack of thunder followed lightning that illuminated the room.
She was dressed in the height of fashion. La Bella Figura. Yes, the height
of fashion. If it were 1968.

Angela gave a little cry as the rain began to pelt the windowpanes with great force. Yes, thought Vittorio with a sigh of exhaustion. Early summer or late June. Another mouth to feed.

✳ ✳ ✳ ✳ ✳ ✳ ✳ ✳ ✳ ✳ ✳

"My Lord, look at this storm," sighed Teddy. She stood, in blue jeans and black T shirt, staring across the rain-swept street at her own apartment.

"Hey! Come back here if you want help!" Diane cried.

Eleanor punched the tape recorder rewind button and they listened to Teddy's voice asking an ex-waiter how he felt about the Academy Awards. "Now, can you take criticism, dear girl?"

"Sure I can. Blow me away," Teddy grinned as she plopped cross-legged in between the two others.

"I think you're getting out of bounds with that question. You see, this, what's his name? Ricky. He's about as near an Academy Award as I am and that doesn't have any bearing on his part as a groundhog who eats an entire kindergarten..."

Teddy was nodding. "Okay. Agreed. But what about his feelings about being an actor?"

"That part's good. Leave it," put in Diane.

"I think you should keep in mind that this is to be read by someone like me," said Eleanor. "Someone who doesn't have too much time and wants straight clear writing. The old who, what, where, why. Think of the way you read a newspaper."

"Oh, but can't I be creative with this stuff?" Teddy was excited by her interviews. She liked standing on the set all morning, waiting for someone to be finished with their lines so that she could spring upon them with her brand new little tape recorder.

"Well, think Hemingway," said Diane.

"Hemingway," repeated Teddy. "You mean Margaux and Mariel's grandfather?"

Eleanor and Diane were silent. They didn't dare look at each other. High school in Alabama. Okay. Not Teddy's fault.

"I've never read him," Teddy continued. "But I've read all of Faulkner. Suppose I don't want to write like Faulkner." She laughed at the looks on their faces. "You know! The eight page sentences!"

Diane took a gulp of white wine. Full of surprises. "So you studied Faulkner at school?"

"Oh, no, at home. Cricket loves him. Daisy is more...more Steinbeck. We read them aloud to each other at night after dinner." Teddy snorted. "My aunts are a tad out of touch. There was the idea of keeping me out of school and having them teach me at home. That would have been terrible. I would have had no friends probably. And they know all these writers and nothing, I mean not a thing, about math or science. I would have been this lopsided person."

Eleanor laughed. "Lopsided?" Teddy's accent was strong, her expressions were different whenever she mentally returned to Alabama.

"Well, not well-rounded."

Diane smiled. "What else do your aunts read?"

"Dickens. Fitzgerald. O'Hara. John Updike. You should hear Daisy reading a sex scene. Oh, Cricket and I just about die!" She grinned. "But...well, the only newspaper they read is..." She stopped and they waited. "Never mind."

"Tell us," insisted Diane. "Come on, we're impressed beyond words at this point."

"This will DEpress you," said Teddy licking her pencil point. There was silence in the room. The sheets of rain hissed outside the window and the gutter gurgled loudly. A crack of thunder made them all jump. "Okay. The only other thing they read is the...National Enquirer."

"You're kidding!" burst out Eleanor. "That trashy paper where Siamese triplets are born to a ten year old girl in Peru and grow up to be brain surgeons and operate on themselves and get married to identical triplets and have..."

"Yep." Teddy put her head down and began crossing out all the questions and answers about the Oscars. She cared what Diane and Eleanor thought of her.

"I think it's great. A very eccentric lively imagination is at work here," said Diane decisively. She stared levelly at Eleanor over Teddy's bowed blonde head.

Teddy looked up and grinned. "You mean I shouldn't try to talk them out of the five year subscription?"

"Certainly not!" said Eleanor. "It sounds like your aunts have a lot of fun."

"They do," nodded Teddy. "And actually..." she began shyly. "They got me an international subscription and so if you ever want to borrow any of mine...I've got every issue starting with the woman who was raped by the extra terrestrial in that trailer camp outside Alberquerque...."

* * * * * * * * * * *

The next night they met for dinner at Teddy's apartment and between bites of ravioli and fried shrimp they talked about her new job. "Two hundred and fifty acres! I can't get over how big the place is! And they're doing twenty movies this year! It's big, big big!" exclaimed Teddy.

"So they import Americans and pay them peanuts and the Italians make lots because..." Eleanor was trying to figure   something out. "Didn't you say you got paid last week?"

Teddy nodded proudly. "Yep. I thought it would be a disaster not having work papers but no one cared. I tried to explain-"

"Did they give you a check?" Eleanor asked. Diane tore the head off a shrimp then shelled it.

"No, I just lined up with everybody else out in the hall and one by one we were allowed into a room with a cashier and a poodle." "What does the poodle do?" Diane asked.

Teddy grinned. "Guard dog for all that cash, I guess."

"So they gave you lire?"

"Of course they gave me lire! Eleanor, you sound suspicious! Lots and lots of lire. About seven hundred dollars worth which is the most money I've ever made in a week, except for modelling, of course." She stabbed the last bit of ravioli on her plate and popped it into her mouth. "I must say it's all pretty casual, leaving out the poodle, even. It's just this man named Piero with a big moustache sitting at a card table with a metal box in front of him. He had me sign something saying I'd gotten ny money but he didn't give me a receipt. He tucked the paper away in a bureau drawer and said, "Ciao."

"Another black and thriving concern," murmured Eleanor. "What's that mean?" Teddy demanded.

"No records and no taxes."

"Non fa niente!" laughed Teddy. "It makes nothing! It doesn't matter!"

"Nothing better for you to learn than that phrase," agreed Diane.

Eleanor looked at her watch. "Have to go. Enrico's due home in half an hour from that reception he's covering. Trying to get a word with Goria. Hope he did." She thrust her arms into the dark blue cardigan around her shoulders and stood. "Teddy, thank you for the feast! Diane and I would starve to death without you."

As she reached for dishes, Teddy waved her away. "Don't! It's easy! Go!" Teddy beat her to the front door and held it open. Eleanor raced through it and down the stairs calling, "Ciao, ragazze!"

Teddy sighed heavily and sat down again. "I've done the first six chapters of the Italian grammar you lent me. If I think very hard before I go to sleep at night then I think maybe it will be absorbed by my tiny…." her voice faded.

"What is it, Teddy? You're not entirely here."

"Oh, I guess irregular verbs aren't what I think about in bed."

"Massimo?"

"Si." Teddy reached for the bread and then took a slice of the gorgonzola she loved so much. "Don't know why I-"

"You miss him, don't you?"

Teddy nodded. A black velvet band held the torrents of wild hair away from her face. Her dark eyes looked sad. "I wish I understood myself better. I mean, look at you and Eleanor. Eleanor has someone and he gives her problems but she handles them or him. And you-" Diane waited with interest to hear the younger woman's opinion of her. "You live so well by yourself. I admire it but it amazes me. Don't you ever go to parties?"

Diane shook her head. "Rarely. If someone I've known forever arrives from the States-"

"But what about men?"

"I am not looking."

"But—but do you want to get found?" insisted Teddy.

Diane smiled. "I don't think so." She sipped the Frascati.

Teddy spread the lumps of marbled cheese on the bread and then lifted it to her mouth. Church bells began to ring out in the piazza. "Well, I know," she said after she'd swallowed. "I want someone. I think he is Massimo. I want someone older, who knows lots of things I don't know. I want someone who thinks I'm fun instead of laughing at me and thinking I'm funny."

Diane felt a sudden pang of sympathy for this sometimes gawky, but always beautiful creature who had somehow arrived in Italy, an ocean away from Alabama, a world away from familiarity. Not even New York was as far from Ace as Rome. "I want someone..." she stopped. "Sometimes I think I want someone to take care of."

Teddy looked up, wide-eyed, awaiting Diane's reaction. Diane often said she wished she could teach her plants to water themselves, that she was so tired of all that dependency.

"You miss your aunts, I know."

"I do. But it's not that. Definitely not." Teddy was adamant. She wasn't saying it well and she wanted it to be so clear. "I think it's the idea of belonging with someone wonderful and having him think I'm wonderful, too."

Diane smiled. Such a simple statement. A plea for something old fashioned and sweet in an era of women's liberation, male confusion and AIDS. "Sounds like heaven to me. Ever thought of going back to Ace and marrying the boy next door?"

"No. I didn't run away from anything in Ace and it's not that I think I'm too good for anything there but I left because I had the idea there was a lot more." She stopped. "And there is. I like the way the men look in New York. And in Rome. And I like pretty apartments and I like food like this instead of sweet potatoes and collard greens." Amazing. Diane had never imagined that Teddy might have come from a poor family, but the possibility appeared and she was filled with awe yet again. "And I like wine instead of beer. Would you like a little more?" Teddy asked as she tilted the bottle towards Diane's glass.

"And Massimo?" asked Diane as she nodded for more wine.

"I think he is the best I've found in Rome," Teddy said quite seriously.

"You sound so—so calculating."

Teddy nodded. "I told you. I do want someone. I'm ready. Jeremy was a wrong turn. That's all. I learned a few things from him. From his family." She remembered Mrs. Hathaway's cold voice describing her as 'an embarrassment' as she sat on the couch in that big living room high over Fifth Avenue. Never again will I marry anyone who would think that. Never again will I allow anyone to get away with thinking that. "Massimo is the right age and I am very attracted to him, though he-" Diane waited. "He resists me. Or else he is not attracted to me physically. I don't know." She swallowed wine. "I do know he is good for me and I'll play it out with him. As far as I can."

"You sound as if your mind is made up."

Teddy nodded. "It is. Massimo is what I want. I only wish I could make him want me."

"You're not as fey and romantic as I thought you were."

Teddy bolted from the table and stood at the bookshelf until she found it. Webster's. "F-A-Y?" she called.

"With an 'e,'" answered Diane, folding her blue and white checked napkin. Dear Teddy. Someone to take care of. And Massimo isn't sure he wants that. She looked at the remains of the meal, at the blue candles burning low. Somewhere in Rome there is a man who would adore Teddy's brand of attention. Actually there were probably millions. But would they be the—

"Diane! Would you come to dinner if I invited Massimo? Would you help me? If I get up the nerve to ask him will you come?" Teddy looked up from the dictionary.

"Teddy, I don't know how I can help-"

"Yes. It's perfect. I'll wait til next week and then I'll call him and he'll come and even if- well, you can give me your honest, no nonsense opinion of him. And with you here...he'll like you. He's half French, remember? And you can speak it to each other and I'll listen. It'll be great." Diane nodded, unsure of the idea. Teddy replaced the dictionary and turned back to her. "Fantastic," she nodded. "I knew you'd help me."

*   *   *   *   *   *   *   *   *   *   *

Take-A-Chance mopped the beads of perspiration from his suntanned head and with dismay felt how few silky threads still adorned it. He grimaced into the receiver and let the phone continue to ring. Christ. Ninety nine percent of the population has an answering machine, thought Chance. Why doesn't Roger use his? There are probably people in California with answering machines instead of washing machines, instead of hair dryers, he grimaced again, thinking he'd go to some shop in Beverly Hills and buy a really good looking hat.

"Roger! You're home-"

"I was in the shower. What's up?"

"Sorry, but this is important. Can you get—no, can you call me?"

"Sure. Give me a number."

"Same area code. Say, two hours. 567-3321."

Roger's big hairy body was wrapped in a yellow and white striped beach towel. The paper was spattered with drops from his just shampooed hair as he clutched a ball point pen and scrawled. "Got it. Talk to you later."

Chance hung up and looked down at his tablet. Five phone numbers and five check marks beside them. Not much time. The Panamanian national airlines had cancelled all flights to Miami. Les thought this was so the U.S. couldn't seize their jets as assets. A cash crisis in Panama. Seven million a month would stop as payment for the canal. A pittance, really, but things were grinding to a halt.

Chance walked towards the Mercedes and got in. Noriega is staying and the U.S. is trying to strangle him economically and there are no dollars in the country except drug dollars, coca dollars. Chance sighed as he slammed the door. And so much of it belongs to the Barracudas. He pulled his seatbelt across his soaked with perspiration suit as Hardware waked with a grunt. Take-A-Chance slipped the chocolate brown Mercedes in gear and pulled out onto the highway. So much money. Too much money. And I've got to get it out of there and sprinkle it somewhere else as soon as I can. He looked down at his four thousand dollar watch and said, "Too much money and too little time."

* * * * * * * * * * *

The tall man in the tan wool suit stared into the wardrobe mirror as he jerked the dark green silk tie into place. Hermes. Vittorio slitted his eyes and turned sideways examining his face critically, first the right profile then the left. The side part was a straight, clean, definite line across his scalp; he'd shaved very very close with a new blade and his eyes were clear, his very white even teeth just brushed. He turned the corners of his mouth down and walked across his bedroom. La bella figura. The country runs on it. Good impressions. Good intentions. Vittorio laid his silk handkerchief out on the big canopied bed and then plucked it from the linen sheets and with one little flick of the wrist pushed it, just so, into the suit jacket pocket. He stared at the unmade bed and then looked at his watch. Seven o'clock and he'd been up since four. Looking out the window and listening to his heart pound.

He strode over to the seventeenth century bureau and scraped the loose lire coins off the lavender marble top. The fifty and hundred thousand lire bills fanned out like a paper flower in his gold money clip. Questa and questo and questa. This, this and this, he said to himself as he filled his pockets. He walked to the ormolu table supported by carved dolphins beside the bed and picked up the prescription. A dozen white pills rattled in the plastic bottle. His Gucci briefcase of black calf lay on the sleigh bed's blue brocade cover; the shutters and the window above it were open to the courtyard. The Roman traffic could not be heard over the twittering sparrows who nested in the ivy. Cesare had to cut it back periodically for the delicate young tendrils crept right into Vittorio's bedroom and on several occasions in the spring he had discovered his desk decorated with dark green leaves twined around his great grandfather's silver and onyx penholder.

Principe Vittorio della Santini Venturini stood at the window for a moment, briefcase in hand, listening to the birds. He shrugged his broad shoulders in the suit jacket as though adjusting armor and then frowned again. The bank, he thought. Eight thirty. The bank opens. He looked at his watch which was flat and gold and simple and from Bulgari on the via Condotti. Always the bank. Always the money.

✳ ✳ ✳ ✳ ✳ ✳ ✳ ✳ ✳ ✳ ✳

"No, no, I love Italy. My roots, ya know," Ernie put down the unlit, never to be lit, Cuban cigar and fumbled for a breath mint. The speaker phone on his polished granite desk barked back. "How did it go the last time?"

Ernie tilted back in his black leather Eames chair and then swung his feet up onto the stool. "Great. The whole team's churning 'em out. Maybe get twenty films in the can this year. 'Course that August holiday stops everything. The whole country goes to the beach, ya know."

"Moneywise, how do we stand?"

"Nothin' to worry about there. "High School Vampire" and "Chainsaw Sisters" aren't goin' to win any awards but-"

"That's not what I asked." The voice was strained, attempting to leash impatience. He didn't have much time to decide. Then there was the flight before dinner so the briefing could be in person.

"Don't worry. We're losin' money hand over fist and I've got every confidence we'll keep on losin' money."

"Could you make use of more money?"

Ernie Melville put his feet on the floor and sat up straight. The skyline of Los Angeles was like a painting, still and big, outside his window of the city's tallest skyscraper. "More money?" he repeated. Zephyr Studios was almost a hobby for him but more money—

"More money for more horror films, Ernie. You understand, don't you?" How he hated talking to anyone on their home or office phones and to have to spell things out with Melville wasn't putting him in a better temper.

"Sure. Sure I do." Ernie's little eyes under the long black caterpillar of a brow lit up. More money, more money. MORE?

"Okay, that's it." He prepared to hang up, praying that Ernie Melville who was a whiz kid film producer turned mid-life crisis independent backer, wouldn't call him by his name. Not on this line anyway. "I'm arranging everything. Just wait. Things will be in gear by the end of the week."

Ernie couldn't stop grinning. He leaned over and reached for the soggy-ended Montecristo number five where it lay like an old dog turd in the pink marble ashtray. More money. "Okay. Don' worry 'bout a thing. All under control. Everybody laid back," he drawled into the phone.

The caller was all set to replace the receiver when he heard it. "Bye, Chance." Take-A-Chance banged the phone down and yanked open the glass doors in a rage.

Ernie felt so good he thought he might light the cigar. He hadn't had a smoke in seven months and eleven days. He tasted the bitter tobacco leaves on his tongue and wondered if he still had a match in a desk drawer. Then he wondered, spinning around to look out the window, if anyone out there might make a citizen's arrest and get him right in his own office. California, he shook his head. Then he picked up the phone to call his newest wife. Sharon had said to call him whenever he felt like smoking because, "if you start it again, we might as well be lepers, Ernie! You know that no one will have us in their home! And," she had added solemnly, "where would our marriage be without parties?" She had a point.

The phone rang in the petal pink bedroom and in the petal pink living room and in the sauna and in the work out room and in Ernie's study and in all ten bathrooms and in the kitchen and in the eleven guest rooms and in the wine cellar and in the poolhouse and in the equipment room by the tennis courts. No answer. Ernie was disappointed. Out shopping, of course. And the maid's afternoon off. Maybe he'd buy Sharon something pretty on the way home. Something to wear. Something like a diamond necklace. Ernie's face was split by a big grin under the aquiline nose as he thought of it again. More money!

✳ ✳ ✳ ✳ ✳ ✳ ✳ ✳ ✳ ✳ ✳

Vittorio had seen the sheet of lined paper lying on the sidewalk beside the front door and, with a reflex wholly unnatural to most Italians, had picked it up intending to throw it away. Instead he'd been stopped in the hall by Anna who wanted him to see a telex from L.A. and then there'd been one of the directors who invited him to dinner that evening. Vittorio had put his arm around the American and winked slyly, "Non posso. I can't."

"Oh, you're busy!" grinned Sam delightedly. "I've heard about you, Vittorio! Oh, the things I've heard!"

Vittorio called, "Ciao," and walked rapidly down the hall to whatever seclusion his office would provide.

He looped his tan jacket over the chair and rolled up his shirt sleeves. Then he sat down behind his desk and put the telexes in order, marking each one that required an answer with a thick red pen. Then he printed responses for Anna to send. His work day was over. One hour maximum at the banks in the morning depending upon the centro traffic and the long drive out here and now he could turn around and go home. Don't think about it, he told himself.

He reached for the notebook page with the serrated edge and started to toss it in the wastebasket. What was this? he thought as he read the half English, half Italian scrawl. A list of things to do.

cut hair- first sharpen scissors in Campo dei Fiori
wax legs-ask D for painless person
more candles-blue, white, orange, green

decide agnello al forno but where do I buy rosemary?
or arista di loin of pork but where do I get rosemary?

Vittorio continued to read. Someone was pazza for rosemary.

decide betw. mussel soup or fettucine al doppio burro
strawberries in cream or zabaione or choc. mousse
ask wine man what goes with pork or lamb—
study irregular verbs on page 79
type the last part of synopsis in S's office
find black nightgown just in case

Vittorio shook his head. Black nightgown! Just in case of what!? After she's plied him with rosemary and zabaione! My God-the lucky man. Lucky if he can get away from the table the way this woman intends to feed him! Lucky if he can stand up afterwards. And then in the candle-light to have her come after him with her new haircut and her smooth legs in the black nightgown. Vittorio was still smiling as he put on his jacket and thought about leaving for the day. He stuffed the paper into his suit pocket and grabbed his car keys from beside the telexes. He closed his office door and thought, someone should find this man and warn him.

* * * * * * * * * * *

"Well, shit, Juan!" shouted Lopez into the phone. "The flight's in two hours!"

"I'll be on it! I've got the money and I'll be there!"

Juan was as skinny as a thirteen year old; a little Clark Gable mous-tache sat on his narrow upper lip as though it had been pasted there for Halloween. He hung up with a bang and began to run around the hotel room, looking under the unmade bed with its tangle of sweat-soaked sheets, then under the orange molded plastic chair and at last standing in the doorway of the bathroom and helplessly raking his hands through his shiny black mop of hair. All he wore was a small pair of white cotton briefs with the words 'Olympic 1988' printed all over them.

The phone rang as he stood there, a brown statue caught in a state of indecision. Juan cursed then sprang halfway across the bed and on his knees picked up the receiver and listened.

"I know you," 'said Lopez, "so I'm sending Pedro over. Fifteen minutes." Juan hung up without speaking. Muy bien.

Pedro arrived in ten. "Look. I think it's better for you to wear it." He looked at the narrow body then at the suitcase packed tightly with hundred dollar bills and shook his head. "Let's see your clothes."

Juan opened the unpainted plywood closet door and displayed a cotton shirt printed with red, blue and green parrots and a pair of not very clean blue jeans. Dozens of empty black wire hangers jangled on either side of his wardrobe. Pedro looked down at his khaki trousers and then began to take them off. They got caught on his heavy soled lace-up work boots and he cursed.

"Okay. You're gonna wear some and you're gonna check some. First, give me those jeans. And the shirt. And anything in the bathroom." Juan began throwing things on the bed. Pedro took money out of the suitcase and began to wrap the packets in the jeans.

"Hey! I gotta wear those! You can't pack'em!"

"Don't worry." Pedro was busy building a mound of dollars and clothes and towels in the little suitcase. "Now, you got another pair of shoes?" Juan shook his head. Pedro threw in his. "This may not be necessary. You want to check this or not? You know it's your skin if Air Panama fucks up."

"I carry it."

"Okay. What I'm doing is putting in a few things the security guard will recognize when this sits under the x-ray. They see shoes and they think 'aha,shoes!' and don't bother about the mess of things in the middle. Juan handed him a snaggletoothed black comb then snatched it back to use.

The suitcase would barely close. Pedro looked depressed as he stared at all the thick packets of green bills on the bed, on the floor. He looked at Juan again. Maybe he'll spend some of the two thousand on food. Poor little guy. Pedro knew what the money mules went through. You sweated off ten pounds at each airport, leaving and arriving.

Juan tossed the comb in with the big work shoes. "Right. Now come over here and let me tape you up." Juan held the adhesive and the scissors as Pedro hurriedly wrapped packets of bills in the torn plastic dry cleaning bag he'd brought. "Otherwise, you get to L.A. and you wring the money out. As it is you just drip all the way."

Juan looked dubious but lifted scrawny arms as the tape went round him. A layer of thousands of dollars was soon a carapace over his torso. Then Pedro began with the legs; the inside of the calves first and then a few bundles on the outside of his thighs. "You're wearing my old khakis so don't worry about anything showing. They're baggy 'cause you've lost weight. Right?" Juan smiled. "AII these spectacular Panamanian restaurants." Pedro was Colombian and didn't think much of Panama. He'd been close to Lopez for the last two years, going everywhere he went. He snipped another yard long strip of tape and wound it round one skinny leg one more time.

"Try walking. Just to the door and back. Relax." Juan had all the insouciance of the Tin Man in the Wizard of Oz. "You're terrific. Muy bien."

Pedro looked at his watch and swore. "Here. Put this on." He pulled his sports shirt over his head without unbuttoning it and Juan tried to do the same and it got stuck. Swearing in Spanish the two of them managed to get it on him without any of the money becoming dislodged. "Now, these." Pedro stepped out of his trousers. "Careful. Let me help. Sit. Don't move. I'II just pull them up on you."

In another minute the suitcase was zipped. Juan had been pronounced perfect. He said breathlessly in the doorway as he wiped his brow, "I sweat a lot. Now. Even now."

"Don't worry, baby. Everybody sweats a lot." Pedro patted him on the shoulder gingerly, wished him luck in Spanish and handed him the suitcase. "Oh, si, fifty bucks for taxis. You know where to go in L.A.?" Juan nodded. He still looked like a little kid. Fatter but still very young. His face and the way he held the suitcase were like a boy spending the night away from home for the first time. "Okay. Now go! You'll make the flight if the traffic's right. If you miss it, sit in the airport and get the next one."

Juan was already hobbling down the hallway. It smelled like urine and cornmeal. Jesus. The poor of Latin America, thought Pedro. Gotta get out of this place. He looked down, abruptly went back inside the cheap hotel room and found the phone. "Hey, Lopez, it's me. Yeah. He's gone." He listened then said, "Don't hang up. Send somebody over here. I'm in the Hotel Buenas Dias with no fucking clothes!"

* * * * * * * * * * *

Seven black and brown patterned yards of DooDah, thick as a man's thigh, coiled behind Chance's chair. The coral snake, the diamondback rattler, the black mamba and the green mamba, "all his little friends," as Wes put it, spiralled around him in homage to the biggest of them all.

"Look. The banks are closed. That's a fact. We cannot touch anything stashed in Panama. All we can do is not put any more in." Chance was trying to be precise. "And hope that the banks open up and we can get the stuff out."

"Delvalle is finished. Poor bastard. Nothin' to do but shower and shave and make home videos of hisself-" Wes sipped from the Sprite can and then put it down on the little table beside the E-Z Boy lounger.

"Noriega's about to go. The minute he cain't pay the army-" Les chimed in, crossing his white-loafered feet. The bullet was shiny in each shoe and his socks were pale pink. "The army of that country has changed leaders five times in the las' ten years." Lesley was absolutely horizontal in the chair gazing up at the ceiling. His belly mountained up hugely; the effect was of a pregnant woman in a psychiatrist's office.

"He opened the banks today to pay the army and the police but you're right. All fifteen thousand'll turn against him in a minute if they're hungry." Chance listened to the hum of the air conditioner. He considered some of this his fault. Oh, not the trouble in Panama but the trouble with the banks. He should have gotten that money to the Bahamas. Anywhere. He should have realized what was brewing. Damn. Chance had discovered that Merrill Lynch had closed their Panama City office and moved the whole show to the Cayman Islands. A month ago! Shit! A whole goddammed month ago! "Here's the way I see it," he began forcefully." The money is going through Panama with or without the banks, through Miami, through Mexico City. It's okay. We leave the pipeline as is. Lopez is a good guy. Moving the money is harder than moving the drugs. It's just so damn bulky." Chance sighed. The proceeds of a cocaine sale can weigh five times as much as the drug itself."The only thing we change is where we put it. So instead of using Panama- we just need to use another Caribbean bank-say, Belize. That's the up and coming country for this, the way I see it. Or we can put more in the Bahamas. Any one of a dozen places will do Just fine." But Panama had been more than fine. The country had more banks per square mile than any country in the world.

Chance knew the Barracudas well enough to know they wouldn't panic but he was surprised when Wes slammed down his chair into the 'sit' position and crowed with delight. "Hey, Les! Time to hit Vegas again! Whaddya say?"

Oh, no, sighed Chance.

"I'm a rarin' to go!" bellowed Lesley. "Whoooooeeeeee! Git out the purtiest gals in town! The Barracudas are on the way!"

"Hey, but look-" Chance began.

"You comin' wid us?" Wesley had a lascivious grin on his pock-marked face though his eyes were the same dead unshiny brown. "Let's take the big red Caddie! Jes fill it up with dollars and root beer and broads! Whoooeeeee!"

This happened about once a year. A trip to Las Vegas meant forty-eight hours of playing games—-at the tables with chips and in a suite upstairs with whores. Under the guise of business they went, but Chance likened the binge to a dieter who suddenly eats an entire chocolate cake and then looks up with icing on his face and says, "Give me another one and then I'II go back to the celery."

"This is the ticket. We'll change all the money you kin git us-"

Chance shook his head. "Go to Las Vegas and have a good time but don't think about handing over more than, say, twenty thousand each a day. Then get the cashier's check." He'd spoiled their fun, the room was silent. "Or just get the chips and don't use them."

These trips worried Chance. The brothers attracted so much attention. For three hundred and sixty three days of the year they were paranoid and for the other two they were high rollers in their brightest leisure suits barrelling around Vegas in a cherry red Cadillac convertible, vintage 1955, with Hardware at the wheel and half a dozen hookers squealing and giggling in the backseat. Christ. Every spring.

"Most casinos in Vegas can have the money credited to another casino out of the country. Why don't you credit some to one in Monte Carlo and then I'II get somebody to pick up a cashier's check over there and walk it across the street to a bank. How's that?"

"Chance, you know the casinos don't have that silly 10,000 dollars requirement lak the banks. They don't have to tell nobody how much or who. Why-" Les leaned up on his elbows and said seriously,"thas the whole point of me and Wes goin to Vegas." Silence in the room. Wes looked solemn as though he were offended that their advisor would imagine that the trip were for fun. For girls. For adventure.

"I know. I know. I worry that you two…well, you stand out." Chance hoped he'd phrased it all right. "Don't forget that's why you live here. Why you stopped those runs to Mexico all those years ago. Too many people know your faces. Too many people-"

"He's right as rain," Lesley said to his brother.

"Yep. Too many people'd like to…" Wes turned and looked at the writhing shapes on the floor. "lak to freeze dry us…" He snorted in unison with Les. "Or worse."

It had been a long day and Chance was tired. He stood up and put his hands in his pockets trying not to notice the snakes behind him. He gazed at the map in front of him instead. The little purple flagged pin was still stuck on Panama City. "Go to Las Vegas and have a good time but don't change too much money. Lopez has got a few mules comin' up with cash tomorrow and all next week. Somebody arrived this afternoon. I can have it put all over California in packets of nine thousand nine hundred and ninety nine but-"

"Cripes! Thas the ole way! That'll tek you forever to git to all those banks," put in Wesley.

"I can have it wired over that ten grand mark-"

"No. I don't lak pieces of paper floatin' round with figures and bank account numbers on 'em." Wes was dogmatic.

Chance thought, if these characters could put it under their beds in shoe boxes, the way they used to, they'd be happy.

"Jes cash. Jes the real thing. Let's be ole fashioned and get it moved."

"You don't want to wire it?" Chance said with the lilt of hope in his voice. It was the Bank Secrecy Act of 1970 that he found himself constantly tiptoeing around. It required the specific reporting by banks and financial institutions of cash movements over $10,000. The casinos were exempt from this as were wire transfers so it was far from an impossible little wrinkle in the game. The Barracudas hated records of anything though so a wire was anathema to them unless they planned to use it as proof of something later on for one of their legitimate business transactions. As for depositing cash directly into the banks, it was necessary to go below the ten thousand limit again and again and again and using all the damned aliases was a pain.

"Christ no!" Wesley shouted. "Whaddaya think I jes said about them little bitty pieces of paper! A wire is a steak for one of them Fed guard dogs to come sniffin' at one of these days." He shook his head. "No wires."

"Right." Chance nodded. He hadn't even discussed Zephyr Studios with them, but it was such a small project when you considered their vast real estate holdings including a race track, seven hotels, the apartment complexes in Fort Lauderdale, Denver, Chicago, Minneapolis and Boston, not to mention the coca plantation of 360,000 acres in Bolivia. It was damn near half the size of Rhode Island. How many millions would the production plants in the jungle fetch if they were to go up for sale? And the fleet of planes that moved the snow? And the ships? Zephyr was small potatoes. A tax write off. Zephyr was going to make more films. High School Vampires Parts II, III, and IV if need be.

Chance slipped on his suit jacket as the Barracuda brothers decided whether Jose or Hardware should drive the Caddy to Las Vegas, where the chopper should drop them and if Garcia could be trusted to get a four-wheel drive to a pre-arranged spot in the desert. Chance sighed. Sometimes the logistics of everyday living threatened to overwhelm him. Ernie Melville. A sleaze. Roger. A doper who liked fifteen year old boys. Hardware. Jose. The Barracudas themselves. He jumped when Wesley clapped him on the back.

"Hey, Take-A-Chance, don' you worry bout nuthin! Switzerland, here we come! We gonna git that money outta Panama quicker than butter melts in a skillet! Yessirree bob! Git those boys off their asses, buy some suitcases, and fill em with cocabucks! Whoooooeeee! Git'em first class on Swissair!"

*　*　*　*　*　*　*　*　*　*　*

Chapter Six

Olivier grinned as he plucked it from his mailbox in the lobby then took the unread postcard out the front door and down the steps. He sat on the bottom one at 307 East 92nd Street and stared at the Colosseum's crumbling majesty below a too blue to be true Roman sky. Then he polished his tortoise shell rimmed glasses and turned it over and read: 'Dearest 0! This place is getting better every minute and I thought it was bella bella bella the second I arrived. Have job with film company-can you believe it? Still waiting for next installment of divorce saga. If you see Blakely or Dirk tell them I'm not getting married but want to know what's happening. I miss you molto. Wish you had a magic carpet. Read for any good parts lately? Any commercials? Write me. Tons of love, Theodora.'

"Oh, Teddy," he said softly as he stood up and stared out at the Second Avenue traffic. "You goofy girl." He started to walk downtown towards McAllister's. His black trousers, white shirt and black tie under the khaki windbreaker announced his status as staff, probably waiter, maybe bartender. Olivier was one of an army of would-be actors, at four thirty in the afternoon, who was making his way across New York City to perform for rent money, for money to live. Performing for love, on a stage, in front of a camera, would come later. Olivier was sure of it.

He tucked the postcard in his back pocket, careful not to bend it. But how wild, he thought. Teddy may be closer to stardom than I am. He stopped at the curb and watched the Don't Walk sign blink and then stay red. Spring in New York. Another one. Two auditions on Friday morning. Maybe....he fell into step with the crowd as it surged forward across Eighty-sixth street. Maybe.

* * * * * * * * * * *

Teddy sprawled on the white fur rug, leaning on her elbows, tablet in front of her. With her yellow pencil she checked off all the articles needed for the Los Angeles office. "A press kit contains," she said aloud. "A list of the credits, a synopsis of the script, then the interviews." She sat up and cross-legged began to sort through pages and pages of transcripts she'd scrawled in her own brand of shorthand from the tape recordings. There was the lead, Brian Kennedy. She pushed pages into a pile and paper clipped them together. Then Gail Grosvenor. Teddy put a candlestick on top of her pages because she needed a lead sentence. Then there were interviews with three supporting actors, at one page each. Eleanor had written one as an example and, of course, it was best of all. The guide for all the others.

Teddy had talked to the director and to the producer at three pages each so that left only the special effects team. Diane had told her she learned very quickly and really, it wasn't that hard to do, if you thought of every single interview as English homework. She twisted her hair up a la Gibson girl and secured it with the black combs. "Flaming flamingoes!" she yelped. The synopsis. Teddy stood up and ran in her silver ballet slippers to the dining room table. There it was. A nice fat script called "Creatures from the Crypt." Teddy winced but grabbed it and flounced down on the sofa, kicking off her shoes and putting her feet up. She read two pages and groaned. Never mind. Maybe the next script, the next movie would be better. She put the bound text aside then got off the couch and began to crawl on hands and knees across the flokati rug littered with papers. All were on the same yellow stationery with the bold letterhead 'ZEPHYR STUDIOS' emblazoned across the top. Teddy found the spring shooting schedule and hurriedly skimmed the typed page. There it was. The next film. "Revenge of the Baby Vampires."

*   *   *   *   *   *   *   *   *   *   *

Take-A-Chance leaned back on the sea green bedspread and pulled the two pillows up behind him. A first class hotel. A phoney name on the register. A room with a view of Los Angeles outside the length of glass above Hardware's bullet head. The massive Mexican sat staring into space in his best clothes- a pale blue leisure suit straining at the seams with trouser pockets lined with grime from his not often washed hands being thrust into them. The jacket hid his holster and the what-ever number gun it was.

Chance hated thinking about guns and refused to know about them. Part of my life, he thought. Suppose I will always, though an accountant basically, struggle to remain a romantic. He knew that the Barracuda brothers maintained a veritable armory- from handguns of the Saturday night special variety to Uzi machine guns. They had the U.S. Army-issued M-16s, several AK47s and the Colt 9MM machine gun that was now being issued to the Feds. Lesley had raved about it a few weeks ago. "Light, easy to handle, and it knocks off 52 rounds in a few seconds!" The room nearest the kitchen was stacked with dynamite, nitroglycerine and timers. Christ. The place would go up like the fourth of July if Garcia spilled any of his chili on the floor.

Chance looked at his watch. Maybe the flight was late. This was the seventh day in a row he'd checked into this hotel and waited for the flight from Panama. Suitcases of money. He wondered why the sweaty, nervous little Panamanians Lopez was recruiting as carriers didn't disappear with their loot into a barrio of Los Angeles. All of it, thought Chance. Not just two thousand upon arrival. But, it must be the promise of more. The idea of another run. He pulled the pillows up a little higher. Like me. I won't cut bait until the end.

This was where it had all started. In a hotel room with a green bed-spread with Stan. Chance realized he had become the heir apparent to the Barracuda boys. A crown prince to two kings of coke. Through default, really. The others, like Stan, had simply dropped away. Take-A-Chance had steadily ascended; he had stood the test of time and all the other tests, too. Fort Barracuda had been his idea, the combination car/helicopter security measures, his brainstorm. He'd gone along with what the Barracudas had wanted almost always. He HAD talked them out of killing all the workers on the house. They'd compromised with blindfolds and several different flight plans, a few threats, and then at last dropping them off in a Land Rover with phony Arkansas plates in downtown Las Vegas. God! Chance had thought. It's like the ancient Egyptians getting buried with all their servants. Wes and Les had said 'They're only wetbacks. Nobody'll miss em.' The most awful part of it was-it was probably true. Anyway, Chance could always think that he'd talked two people out of murder and saved seventeen lives. But, deep down inside, Chance knew he hadn't stood up for a belief, he simply realized he would have had to sever himself from people who would do such a thing and the truth was—he didn't want to abandon the possi-bility of all the money to come. He didn't want to have to make that decision. That break would have been harder for him than his logical stand over why it was unnecessary to kill all those Mexicans.

Worries niggled away at Chance's peace of mind. Somehow Les and Wes had the idea that there were scores of couriers going to Zurich and Geneva each week. Christ, thought Chance as he reached for the glass of Heineken on the bedside table. There's only that one courier Roger has a link-up with. Nobody else. Glad I didn't shut down the Swiss run entirely last September. Came close. Still have the account in Geneva and, he grimaced with distaste, Ernie Melville still has access to it. Two years ago some of the Zephyr money had gone through it but now it was just another of about a hundred and fifty Barracuda accounts in banks in eleven countries. Chance sipped and swallowed. He liked keeping that money in the Caribbean. No reason for the Barracudas to know there's only one Swiss account. Maybe it was their original. The one he'd been a courier for. Chance smiled wryly and put the glass down.

Chance looked at the sea green phone on the pressed wood table. A little plastic open box held two inches of loose white pages proclaiming themselves to be 'for your convenience with compliments from the management.' And then, in case your IQ was too low to catch on, they were labelled 'Messages.' Chance sipped the beer and stared out at the greyness of the sky on the other side of the glass. Hardware was staring out, too.

"Hardware!" The enormous head turned on the broad shoulders. He appeared neckless, like a gigantic shy turtle. "Do you play chess?"

* * * * * * * * * * *

"Hey, Ollie, would you do me a favor?"

"Sure. What is it?" Olivier stood in his white apron, wiping his hands. McAllister's was packed. And everyone was thirsty. The noise was a part of the air, like heat, and was only punctuated by someone's bark of a laugh or the sound of ice crashing into a glass. Wall to wall Yuppies except after the October crash you weren't supposed to call them that. Okay, thought Olivier, wall to wall post-Yuppies.

"Two gin and tonics, three white wines, a spritzer, and a scotch on the rocks, no water."

"Five glasses of house red, one martini."

The waiters stood by the cash register and gave their orders, trays in hand.

"I'm going to be sick on Thursday night. Can you come in for me?"

"One Campari and soda and a Perrier."

"Sure. Happy to do it." Olivier was very happy to do it. That was one of the best nights of the week for tips. He splashed Perrier into a goblet and quickly hung a lemon section on the rim.

Olivier was so busy it was almost half an hour later that he took the few seconds to turn and look at Red and to replay the words. 'I'm going to be sick,' he thought staring at the red haired, freckled bartender. What did he do on Wednesday nights? Pakistani restaurants? A long weekend didn't make sense because he never missed a Saturday. Olivier nodded at Dickie who recited,"J and B, no ice, two white wines, and one kir." Olivier worked quickly. As he allowed a few drops of cassis to color the wine, he thought, and the beat goes on.

$$* \quad * \quad * \quad * \quad * \quad * \quad * \quad * \quad * \quad * \quad *$$

"Come on," she insisted. "Something racy. I've heard all about the mechanical stuff. And yesterday I sat behind Alex for four hours at the drawing board. I know about fiberglass and molds and oil-based clay. Help me spice this up." Teddy in a black T shirt dress, long legs ending in gold ballet slippers, clutched her notebook to her chest. Her tape recorder sat on a workbench among rolls of electrical tape, a pair of pliers and clumps of what looked like black human hair.

"Teddy, I don't think you should write this but I'll tell you a secret." Charlie from St. Louis was one of the four special effects crew. They designed and built the many monsters used for Zephyr Studios and then hung around the set all day long making sure they moved properly, growled on cue, savaged the right actor, and bled the right shade of red.

Teddy plopped down on a foam rubber mattress in the workroom. "What a teaser! I'm supposed to be Brenda Starr, Barbara Walters and Dan Rather all in one—you can't get away with that!" She tenderly stroked the nose of a ferocious looking ape's head that hung above her. "You can't hold anything back once I turn on my tape recorder."

"Okay," he lowered his voice,"but don't quote me."

Teddy pushed the 'record' button. "An anonymous source says…" Grinning, she held the recorder towards him. Charlie, twenty-five but looking nineteen, cleared his throat nervously and began. "AII I want to say is that the drool we use is K-Y jelly and the glistening stuff we coat the wounds with to make them shine in the most disgusting manner possible has a chemical name about fifteen letters long but is really the stuff they use as thickener in milkshakes at McDonald's."

Teddy fell backwards laughing. "I used to live on them!"

Charlie tried to look serious. He was holding a paint brush and dabbing at the black wrinkled body of what would become a baby vampire. "That's the stuff of scandal, Teddy. Remember the power of the press…"

Dale Alby, the head of the special effects department, stood in the doorway. "My God, she's here! She's there! She's everywhere! It's SuperTeddy, star reporter!"

"I'm supposed to give ya'll maximum coverage and I am!" She struggled to her feet. "This goes right to Los Angeles and will probably make you famous. Professionally you're about to take off." Teddy paused with a sense of the dramatic. "With my help of course." She picked up the tape recorder and then turned to Dale who was smiling at her. "Do you have any last words?"

"Yes."

Teddy pushed the 'record' button and held the little machine towards him. He looked serious and said in a low voice. "Get paid before lunch if you haven't been." She looked surprised. "They're running out of money."

"Happens all the time," put in Charlie not looking up from the black winged puppet he was coating with shellac.

"I'm on my way. Thanks." She turned before leaving them and said, "Guess there are worse things happening in the world than baby vampires."

* * * * * * * * * * *

Vittorio sat in his silver Lamborghini and tried to read Il Messaggero. He was parked directly in front of the bank, the bank he visited every Monday. The morning traffic in the piazza buzzed around him—motorcycles, taxis, belching, groaning buses, three wheeled miniature delivery trucks, and automobiles ranging from sturdy Mercedes to Fiats to the little cinquecentos that had once sold for the bargain price of five hundred thousand lira. It was a bright spring day with cool grey shadows resting in the lee of the fountains nearby but Vittorio didn't notice. He looked at his watch again and then crumpled the paper and tossed it on the front seat.

"Caro! Vittorio!" The pretty face was thrust into his window and the red lips were upon his. She sighed, exuding the strong scent of Opium.

"Daniela!" he greeted her "Come va?" He took one of her hands in his as they rested on the window frame.

Her full lips turned down in a pout. "Missing you, darling." Daniella took a deep breath of exasperation in the red sweater which emphasized her full breasts; she shook her head at him as though scolding a schoolboy. "You never call. You never take me to parties. You never took me to Porto Ercole even once last summer…"

"I am very busy these days. Always working," he lied easily. "You see, even now, I am waiting to meet with the capo of the bank. Always working." Vittorio tried to smile, to be cajoling, but his heart wasn't in it. Daniela was silly. To go to bed with her once had been enough.

She leaned forward and kissed him on the mouth and then breathed in his face, "I miss you. Caro, please call me."

Vittorio nodded. "Si. But I am always working. Ciao, bella."

She was already a few yards away, turning to wink at him, a voluptuous five foot two teetering on spike heels.

Vittorio picked up the second paper, La Repubblica, ignored the headlines and anxiously looked at his watch again. Eight seventeen. The pounding in his chest began and he gripped the steering wheel, willing it to stop. Oh, heart, don't do this to me. You are me, a part of me. Don't be so disloyal. He stared at his watch for the doctor had told him to focus on something else, on anything, when it started. The tiny gold hand moved three dots. Three minutes had elapsed. The beating was loud in his ears now. Vittorio was surprised that pedestrians on the sidewalk did not hear it and come over to him. With cold fingers he fumbled for the prescription and then put the white pill between dry lips. He looked at his watch again. Eight twenty two. Eight more minutes before the guard would unlock the glass door and it would slide open and he would walk through. Eight more minutes until he smiled as confidently as he could and said, "Buon giorno," to Alessandro Pertini. And ten minutes from now he would have signed the receipt yet again. If the money had arrived. Vittorio swallowed hard once more, forcing the pill down. His heart hammered on, in his head, in the veins at each wrist, and beneath the fine grey flannel of the two million lire suit. Vittorio stared straight ahead at the fountains, at the pink geraniums peeking through the iron railing of a balcony across the square and thought that every time he did it it was more difficult. His heart continued to pound. Vittorio dabbed with his white handkerchief at the faint perspiration that was cold on his temples. His hands were like ice. "Si," he said aloud. It only gets worse.

* * * * * * * * * * *

Chance stood beside the Mercedes for a moment and then slammed the door and walked slowly to the sidewalk and then into the drugstore. He walked up and down the long aisles enjoying the air conditioning as he looked for his old standby in life, Maalox. He picked up the largest size and then turned back and took two more. He stood on one foot and then the other, waiting to pay, behind a man buying band aids and a girl clutching nail polish remover. He wondered if he should twist open a bottle now and pour some of the soothing liquid down his throat right in front of the cashier. Like some junkie, he thought, trembling with anticipation at the sight of his next fix.

Chance's stomach was not in good shape. He returned to the car and swigged the medicine in greedy gulps, wincing horribly between swallows as Hardware watched. He wiped his mouth and then his tongue on tissues he kept in the glove department and then when little shreds of kleenex stuck to him he had to rise up in the driver's seat and open his mouth in the rear view mirror and pick them off in disgust.

He looked at his watch and got out of the car again. The phone booth was three yards away when the ringing started. Jason. On the nose. He held it to his ear and heard "We got trouble." Jason's voice was low, and every word was precise, every syllable drawn out. "Big trouble."

"Shoot."

"A DC 6. Gone."

Chance moistened his lips. "What do you mean? Crashed?"

"Worse than that. Julio may have been fucking up the drops. Anyway, seems that it was on the airstrip at Rosario all ready to go. All packed." Jason sighed in Miami.

Chance groaned audibly into the receiver. A DC 6 could carry twelve tons of cocaine. That was about a billion dollars worth of snow. Wholesale. "I'm listening," Chance managed.

"Due to take off at midnight and at eleven it wasn't there."

"Holy Jesus!" shouted Chance, unable to control himself.

"Julio says he talked to all ten guards and it was strictly a case of see no evil, hear no evil. All dumb. No news from a one of them."

"You believe him?"

"Julio?" Jason hesitated. "I don't know. There are a couple of possibilities. One is that he hasn't been making the drops and one of the National Guard got brave and had it flown away. Sort of nationalized it, if you like." Chance waited. "The other idea is that Julio paid the guards a lot to keep quiet and had it flown away himself. Another possibility is that some hot shot from another group down there decided he needed a DC 6 and just took it."

"How much would you have to pay a guard to keep quiet?"

Jason thought a minute. "For a caper like this. I mean, this is big, isn't it? I think…." he raised his blond eyebrows and looked out at Biscayne Bay. "I think, gee, I dunno, maybe forty -fifty grand each."

"Could Julio raise that by himself?"

"Might be able to. Or he could borrow it and then….when the plane is somewhere else…." Jason stopped. "Ordinarily that kind of money would be nothing for Julio but lately…well, he's blowing his profits straight up the old snoz."

Chance swallowed the bile in his throat. And the Barracudas were off to Vegas tomorrow. He'd let it wait. He'd say it happened tomorrow when he told them. "Okay. Keep on it. Anything else?"

Jason managed a humorless laugh. "Not in comparison to this."

"Okay. Tomorrow. You still have the number we used ten days ago?"

"Yep. Same time?"

"Fine with me. Adios, amigo." Chance hung up and started back to the Mercedes. The pain in his gut was like fire. The Barracudas would have a fit. And they would send him down there to find out what had happened. Chance was soaked with sweat. He reached the car and tried to open the door. His fingers were unable to grip the metal. Chance thought, oh, shit. A whole mother-fucking DC 6 and then he doubled over in the parking lot and lost his lunch and then his breakfast.

* * * * * * * * * * *

The two of them were in Wes's bedroom, side by side on the king size bed, pillows propped against the orange naugahyde- covered head-board, bedside lamps aglow. Like a compatible, long married couple they sat in silence, reading comic books. Dozens were piled between them, an assortment of Superman, Batman, Spiderman, and Mandrake the Magician. Several cellophane wrapped cupcakes lay in the valley between their two bodies. A Twinkie, golden yellow, had been torn in half beside Wes's left hand and Lesley picked at something that looked like a tennis ball covered in pink shag. The gold crest-shaped label nearby called it a strawberry coconut pompom.

At the opposite end of the large bedroom stood a large glass cube, about five feet square. It was supported three feet off the red linoleum floor by four iron legs on wheels so that it could be pushed from one brother's bedroom to the other's. They took turns. The glass cube and its contents were so important to them that they had specified that the bedroom doorways be wide enough and tall enough to accommodate it. Inside it lay a foot of sand, some leaves, and many branches and even two full-sized tree stumps. Rocks were in one corner, several grey ones piled in a mound and two long nearly flat ones. The brothers usually had to stare for a moment until they saw anything more than the vegetation. It was like leaving the light and walking into a dark room. It took a moment for shapes to form, for the eyes to adjust.

Then the silent, steady writhing came into full focus. The glass cube was full of adders, vipers, mambas, rattlesnakes, cobras, and several asps. A coral snake, twin to the one in the map room, slipped gracefully along a branch. A diamondback rattler lay in a torpor on one of the rocks as though soaking in the heat luxuriantly. The brothers had always been fond of snakes but their mother had refused to allow them in the house. Maybe this was a way to get back at her, to say we're grown up and we can do anything we want and we want to sleep with our snakes in our rooms.

Other than the bed, the snakes, and a bureau, the bedroom was nearly empty. Not one picture adorned the walls, only a comb sat on the chest of drawers. Lesley's room was identical.

Les looked up as he turned the page. No way Mandrake was gonna get out of this one. He put the comic down when he saw his brother staring into space wearing a rather goofy grin. "Whattsa matter with you?" he demanded.

"Aw, I'm thinkin 'bout Vegas, thas all," he pinched off another clump of the pink sponge cake and licked it off his fingers with loud smacking noises.

"Oh, boy, we gonna have us a party!" agreed Les.

"I like wimmen, you know that?"

"Sure, I know that. You know I do, too! Only them damned fairies who don't!"

There was silence. They both stared as the black mamba, skinny and graceful, navigated the chasm between one branch and another. "Hey, Wes, you ain't gittin like you git every spring, are you?"

Wesley shrugged. "I jes think it would be...."

"Come on! I lak em as much as any man but that don't mean we need to keep one in the house!"

"Okay." Wes looked down at his comic again, trying to find his place. "I guess you're right."

"Of course, I'm right about it! Jesus H. Christ! Not in the house!"

The Barracuda brothers went back to their literature, the snakes continued to sleep or slither in the glass cube and a few hundred yards away in his own wing of the house, Slow continued to read. He rocked back and forth in the miniature blue rocking chair, his feet leaving the ground in the red cowboy boots with every backward tilt. Edith rocked with him, her body adapting to the motion like a passenger on the heaving deck of an ocean liner.

Suddenly Slow stopped the chair and put the astronomy text on the floor. "I think if we turn out the lights we can move the black-out cloths and look at the stars firsthand, Edith." She jumped off his lap as he stood. "I mean it's silly to jes...I mean JUST read about them when they're right there." It took a few minutes for Slow to decide what would be a good platform but at last he dragged the table across the room to the window he judged to face north. He took the Mexican blanket off his bed and folded it carefully so they would be comfortable and then he turned off the ceiling light and the lamp on the bookcase. In the darkened room he made his way to the window and pushed aside the curtains and raised the blinds all the way up. The cool night air hit him in the face like rain.

Edith, with a little pomp noise, landed on the table beside him. They settled themselves in front of the dark window frame, Edith sitting up nearly as tall as Slow who dangled his legs down over the table edge, with knees touching the window sill.

The stars glittered cold as chips of ice over the black desert that stretched away from the dwarf's window. He saw them as hanging by invisible threads like diamonds in a dark closet. He saw them as bits of mica resting on the bottom of a clear deep sea. Edith pressed herself against him and he put one short arm over her rabbit shoulder. Slow decided not to spoil the moment with talk of constellations and planets. That was too orderly for the glorious disorder of the sight before them. The midget and the rabbit sat for a long time, framed by the square window, gazing at the clean pure sweep of sky that stretched endlessly away from Fort Barracuda. The starlight shone down bright upon them.

*   *   *   *   *   *   *   *   *   *   *

Vittorio kept to himself at Zephyr. He usually parked his car and walked quickly to his office where he spoke only to Anna in the adjoining room and then closed his door, read the newly arrived telexes and wrote answers to them. So it was not surprising that he had not yet seen Teddy. She, however, was all over the lots, and into everything. Teddy was taking notes in the canteen, interviewing an actor with his mouth full of spaghetti at the cafeteria, and following the prop men around asking them for anecdotes. In one morning she'd cover all the sets, plop herself down with Charlie in the special effects department for a half hour, have coffee with a director, and go through the latest black and white stills for California with Salvatore.

Vittorio was standing with his back to the window his hands in his pockets when he heard her. It was a light feminine laugh like a child's, he thought, and wondered if it were some daughter of an actor. He was especially sensitive to the idea of a laugh today for he'd met one of the American directors in the hall and the man had had the nerve to make a joke about his never smiling! Not true, Vittorio said to himself. Not true. Then he had set his face in a glower and frowned all the way back to his office. Now there was all this laughing. Coming from next door. Then Anna's laughter and Salvatore's. Vittorio strode over to the door and swung it open. This tall person, towering over everyone else, was wearing an enormous gorilla head. White blonde hair showed behind the hideous mask; the body below it was very female in a black and white short wool dress and gold ballet slippers.

Muffled and giggling came the voice, "So you tell whoever runs this place that if there are no bananas in the commissary by tomorrow's banana break—then I'm off this picture!" She banged one fist on Anna's desk as they all shouted with laughter.

"Where's my lawyer! Get me an avocado pronto!" They turned and saw him then and the laughter began to die. Vittorio Venturini never laughed. Teddy couldn't see out of the mask and continued, "I demand a banana clause in my contract-"

There was silence as Vittorio leaned against the doorframe. Teddy thought, what has happened? She reached up to lift off the papier mache head as Charlie stepped forward to help. Salvatore looked at Vittorio who was smiling.

"The new gorilla, Queen Kong," he laughed as Teddy shook her head free and then looked directly into the face of the white haired man from the jazz party. Teddy gave him her broadest smile.

He stood apart from the others. Management, went through her mind when she saw his suit beside Salvatore's rumpled corduroys and

Billy's blue jeans. "Io sono Teddy Starbuck," she extended her hand. He took it, halfway smiling back at her.

"Vittorio Venturini. I'm in a position to do something about the banana situation so you won't have to quit the picture."

Salvatore could hardly believe his ears. Vittorio never joked. He was a familiar figure striding through the building with the corners of his mouth turned down. The temperament! Salvatore had often suspected he wasn't really Roman. Teddy laughed. It was a young girl's laugh having fun after school. She turned to Charlie. "See, Charlie, I told you if you get tough you get your way!"

* * * * * * * * * * *

Diane poured the red wine, handed Eleanor a glass and then Teddy. "You'll NEVER guess who I saw today!" Teddy leaned back in the wicker chair, coming perilously close to tipping it over entirely.

"Goria," said Eleanor quickly.

"Oh, no, better than Goria!" Teddy winced.

"Craxi?"

"Oh, for pete's sake! Guess somebody good...somebody sexy...somebody tall...and he's a prince, too! Salvatore told me so."

"We give up, but Teddy there are a million princes in this city . I mean if you want to have a party you can just telephone Dial-A-Prince and they'll send one over, clean and...."

"Well, I don't care if you're excited or not! I met Vittorio Venturini. PRINCIPE Vittorio Venturini."

"Watch out," said Diane immediately.

"Where?" asked Eleanor.

"At the studio. He works there. Has the office next door to Anna and I spend half my life running in and out of there. I don't know why I had to meet him today. I was being a nut and suddenly there he was..."

"Being a nut? You? You're never being a nut. Teddy, tell us." Eleanor was teasing.

"I was wearing a gorilla head and demanding bana-"

"You weren't. Tell us you weren't."

Teddy nodded. "I got it off and there he was. He is terribly, outrageously sullen, isn't he?"

Diane was firm. "He's slept with every woman in Rome. Once. Just once. Stay away from him."

Teddy grinned. "Oh, that lousy in bed, is he?"

Eleanor and Diane exchanged glances. Teddy had never shown a prickle of fear or caution concerning anything. Principe Vittorio Venturini had been called forbidding, but obviously Teddy didn't agree. She was delighted to have met a prince and was merely curious. A hero from a hundred fairy tales had materialized and worked for Zephyr. Diane sighed as she picked up her wine glass. She remembered her first prince. It's heady stuff for an American.

Eleanor spoke. "Prince or not I think he's strange. I don't think he washes his face and shaves in the morning."

"What do you mean?" demanded Teddy. Of course he did! He looked so absolutely well-groomed, so nearly perfect, so just out of the shower. And it had been in the afternoon, too.

Eleanor finished. "I think he goes somewhere and gets airbrushed."

Teddy made a face at her. "I'm not attracted to him but no one could say he isn't stunning to look at."

"Theodora, might I remind you that you are planning a major seduction dinner for Massimo?" It was Eleanor. Diane had hoped the idea would be forgotten.

"I am! But how can I seduce him with hundreds of miles between us? Nobody's arms are that long...."

"Florence?"

"No. Paris."

"Speaking of absent friends, Diane, I think you're right about Enrico. "I've been dropping hints. It adds up. He's had someone else for awhile."

"I'm sorry," was the quick response. "Are you going to make it up with him? Does he even know you know?"

Eleanor shook her head. "I think it'll die a natural death when I go to London. There's an international conference for correspondents for ten days and I might stay on for awhile afterwards. I have a flat in South Kensington and....I'll see how I feel about coming back to him."

Italian men, American women, considered Diane. She put all her female friends in her address book under their first names. It saved all the scratch outs when they left their husbands. There was silence. Both Teddy and Diane felt sorry for Eleanor, but she obviously wasn't in the mood to talk about it. "Speaking of other absent friends I think we should call Faith and have her over for Saturday lunch or something. I haven't seen her since that rather depressing lunch with you, Teddy."

Eleanor spoke. "I called her only three days ago to invite her to a film festival. It was four in the afternoon and so I thought she'd be free."

"How was she? Did she go with you?" Diane's voice was concerned.

"She told me everything was just fine in her life. And when I asked her what had happened she said she was having 'extensive dental work done.' I thought I'd heard wrong, but no! She has a Canadian dentist she really likes and his hygienist is from North Carolina and she said she went every day."

"That desperate?" shrieked Teddy.

"Rome does awful things to some expatriates, Teddy." Diane turned to Eleanor. "But, is that all she said?"

"She said...." Eleanor took a sip of wine . "She said she was quite happy because the appointments gave her day some structure."

No one spoke for a moment. Diane refilled their glasses and they each took a swallow. It was Teddy, overcome with sympathy in the face of such obvious depression who finally erupted. She put down her glass and breathed, "My God. She decided to go to the dentist instead of Milan."

*   *   *   *   *   *   *   *   *   *   *

Teddy didn't see Vittorio Venturini again that week or the next one, but he saw her. He would be drawn to his second story window and then would hear her laugh, or would see her crossing the grass with a cameraman or Salvatore. She would be taking those long strides of hers, always in the flat gold or silver shoes, as if she were being easy on the smaller Italians around her. Her hair fascinated Vittorio and he watched it fan out in the wind, then whip across her face, then would see her twist it up quickly and pin it back. It occurred to him that she looked like she'd just gotten out of bed.

She seemed to be always talking in broken Italian to everyone as though she were at a great big party. A grip would explain why he was building a miniature track for the camera, the costumista would be interrogated as she bent over her sewing with a mouth full of pins. She badgered a neurotic producer from Beverly Hills mercilessly until he spent a solid hour with her and her tape recorder. "You want this picture to really go, don't you?" she had demanded as she ruffled through pages of notes, looking for the beginning questions. "Well, this is my job. This is promotion!"

Leonard Saperstein had smiled, nervously. Could anyone be that excited over the success of "The Return of Frankenstein's Mother in Law?"

Teddy Starbuck was so ingenuous that several in the California contingent once spent an entire lunch in the big shot dining room arguing over whether it was faked or not. They decided it wasn't.

The pale green days of spring were passing. Teddy had dinner with several sets of arriving and departing actors who came and went in the span of three weeks which was the time it took to get a film in the can.

Teddy met them when they were jetlagged and confused by the pandemonium that was Zephyr, saw them every day as they perspired under
heavy make-up and monster heads, and then went to their farewell din-
ners where they gave sentimental toasts about leaving Rome.

Teddy thrived on the chaos. The shouts in Italian, half understood,
amused her. The make-up artist who spoke in a fierce Romano accent
regaled every actor who sat in the chair with the most lurid accounts of
her bad marriage. And every actor, nodded in agreement or said yes,
yes, while the mascara went on, as if matrimonial conflicts were univer-
sally comprehended. The American directors yelled, "Azione!" and
"Taglia!" while the Italians, ever sensitive to their foreign colleagues,
shouted "Action" and "Cut!"

Teddy's interviews were recorded, transcribed, typed in Salvatore's
office and sent to Los Angeles. They were all right and getting better. It
was as if she were seeking a voice and after a few weeks she was finding
it. She followed her instinct to find out what she wanted to know. How
did you decide to become an actor? Did you go to school for this?
Where? Is this your first movie? Other experience? Your favorite actor?
Why? What do you think of horror movies as a genre? Do you like
Rome? Is it different warking here in Italy? Better? What are your future
plans?

Her approach to the older 'character' actors was different. She let
them reminisce about the good old days and their successes which
might have been one Broadway show in 1949 and then she asked them
what had surprised them most in their careers. Teddy hated to call them
'has beens' but perhaps that's what they were. One of the actors, in his
early seventies, wrinkled and grizzled and slow moving, was playing a
corpse for almost two thirds of the shooting. He said the biggest surprise of his career was how restful being dead was.

Teddy was happy with her work, had made a place for herself at the
studio, had friends she could meet for dinner any night of the week, but
missed Massimo. She had gone to his building and been told by his

portiere that he had come down with pneumonia in Paris and had gone into the hospital there. The plump Roman in the flowered shawl and big sturdy black leather shoes pointed to his full mail box. It was stuffed with letters behind the glass door.

Teddy suffered. She wasn't worried about him so much as worried that he wasn't worried about her. "Doesn't he even miss me?" she shouted at Diane. "Not a word. Not a letter. Not a phone call."

"He's sick, Teddy. All that takes strength. And anyway, your phone is broken," consoled Diane and then decided to change tacks. "Look, tell me why you are so enamored of this man. I want to hear it."

Teddy frowned and didn't answer.

"Listen to me! You are this amazingly attractive female. Men gawk at you on the street, the actors are always asking you out, you go to parties every single Saturday night and you are always busy for Sunday lunch." She waited. "Why are you so fixated on this Massimo? Isn't there anyone within reach, who probably adores you the way you deserve to be adored, who attracts you? Can't you give another man a chance to…to come after you…to…" Diane was at a loss for words which was uncharacteristic. "To woo you, to court you?"

Teddy burst out laughing. "Woo me?" she grinned.

"Come on, Teddy! You're being evasive. Please."

Teddy's brushed the back of her hand across her face. Her eyes, golden brown in the late afternoon light, sparkled with tears. "I told you why I wanted Massimo."

"Do you think he needs taking care of?"

Teddy nodded decisively.

"But does he want to be taken care of? Have you thought of that?"

Teddy breathed out in a big sigh of resignation. "I have thought a lot about Massimo…and there are a couple of things that bother me."

Thank God he isn't perfect, thought Diane. "What are they?"

"Well, I know that I love his little glasses. And I loved Jeremy's glasses, too. Before we got married I used to lie on top of him and pretend I was Marilyn Monroe in "Some Like It Hot" with Tony Curtis....."

"You've lost me," Diane said hesitantly.

"Well," sighed Teddy walking to the window. The black cotton dress barely reached her knees. It was chic and in style but Teddy's waist was so small and her legs so long that it did look a bit as if a child had begun to grow out of it. "Well, I think that Tony Curtis and Jeremy and Massimo have a lot in common."

Yes, thought Diane. You and/or Marilyn Monroe. She listened carefully. Teddy's attempts at logic were imaginative.

"All three of them are rather bookish, intellectual types which turns me on like fire." Teddy smiled. "And they are shy and unsure of women which is where I step in imagining that I'm this mad sex goddess who can have my way with them. But..." she held up one finger. "First, I have to take off their glasses."

Diane was staring up at Teddy who was pacing around the room like a six foot tall cat. She leaned back on the red couch and concentrated as hard as she could on the monologue. "You like to be in control, is that it?"

Teddy grinned and her black and white star earrings caught the light. "I don't like to, particularly. I just always am. It's a fact." She hesitated then used one of Diane's expressions. "A fait accompli."

"Okay, let's come back to that. Tell me what you mean about taking off the glasses."

"In "Some Like It Hot" Tony Curtis plays a man who can't do anything with women. He's shy and inexperienced until Marilyn comes along and literally fogs up his glasses and then gently takes them off. Then of course he is free to have fun, to be sexual-"

Diane had seen one Marilyn Monroe movie in her life and obviously the deep significance of the plot had eluded her.

"And in a way, I did the same thing to Jeremy."

"Go on."

"Well, when I met him at a party he was the only man who didn't climb all over me, the only man who didn't approach me and ask about this sort of strapless, frontless, backless dress I was wearing. And I was curious." Teddy's almond shaped eyes narrowed to slits. "Who is that? I asked someone. Not very interesting, I was told. So I was very curious and when I met him and he moved away from me instead of towards me, I…." Teddy stopped. "I didn't think I had so much to say."

"Go on. You're making sense. Sometimes it helps to say things out loud."

"Well, when he finally made love to me it was…" Teddy stood over by the bookcase and stroked the spines of several paperbacks with one manicured fingernail. "It was Christmas and Hiroshima and Bastille Day all at once."

Diane winced at the description. Pure Teddy.

"So it was a big adventure. I stopped wearing underpants because we went wild in taxis, I…." she stopped. "I guess that gives you an idea." Diane laughed lightly and nodded. "And when I met him he was so serious and so solid and so responsible and I loved taking him over and making him misbehave and love sex. I loved taking off his glasses when the kissing got serious."

"And Massimo?"

Teddy made two fists and shook them. "I can't get that close to him. His kisses, ha! the ones I vaguely remember, are…what was that word you…oh, yes, chaste. They are chaste."

"But you realize, don't you, all the similarities between Massimo and the way you just described Jeremy?" Diane hadn't known anything about Jeremy's personality except he was 'boring,' until today.

"Both responsible, bankers, logical, clear thinking, and I…I have this great desire to take over them and take care of them." Teddy sighed. "I can't figure any more out." She sank heavily into the wicker chair across from her friend and stared up at the coffered ceiling.

Diane looked at her. "You think you know what you want but I don't think it's another Jeremy in Massimo's beautiful Italian suits."

"You don't?" There was great surprise in Teddy's voice.

"Because…after you've quote 'taken off the glasses' and won them over they aren't exciting enough for you…not Jeremy, probably not Massimo and Tony Curtis is too old for you by now."

"Oh, Diane! Some shrink you'd make!" Teddy threw a bright yellow pillow at her.

Diane caught it by the corner and dropped it on the sofa beside her. "I'm serious. You take unfair advantage of these men who have never met anyone like you. You storm into their lives like some bigger than life fantasy and they can't help themselves. You need someone to storm into your life."

Teddy ignored the last sentence. "You say they can't help them-selves?" She smiled. "You mean you think I can still have Massimo fall in love with me?"

"Teddy!" shouted Diane standing up. "You are impossible! Haven't you absorbed a word of all this?"

Teddy pushed the black and white striped plastic bracelet almost up to her elbow and then gave one of her little cat smiles. "I told you, Diane," she said patiently. "I'm going to play it out with Massimo as far as he'll let me go." She looked pleased with her decisiveness. "So I'm still plotting that dinner and I'll let you know the minute he says 'yes.'"

Diane stared at her. Teddy then spoke. "I know what you're thinking and if Aunt Daisy were here, she'd say it for you."

"What? What am I thinking?"

Teddy laughed. "Stubborn as a mule."

*   *   *   *   *   *   *   *   *   *   *

Chapter Seven

Chance pulled on his blue bathing trunks and tied the little drawstring around his paunch. Then he pushed his feet into the red rubber thongs and flop-flop-flopped out of his white bedroom and through the white living room. He caught sight of himself in the wall of mirrors and briefly considered the merits of sit ups. Briefly. This noise, he thought, is making me crazy. Hardware sat like a mountain in one of the white modern armchairs. His t- shirt and khaki trousers were clean which pleased Take-A-Chance, but that didn't mean he could forgive him everything. The giant stared at the big color television, totally expressionless, as though the program were being broadcast in Finnish. This damned noise, thought Chance, as he gathered up his papers and his sunglasses.

"Beep beep!" shouted the Roadrunner cartoon. There was the sound of skidding tires and the screech of brakes as Chance closed the sliding glass doors behind him. He flop-flopped through the grass to his table with the umbrella beside the shimmering blue water of the swimming pool.

There were six wine bottles with the labels which gave him so much pleasure. But there was no time today for his articles and his filing. Chance had far too much to decide; there was so much to be done. He thought of that miniature purple flag over Panama City as he laid out the records. The Barracudas were convinced, at least he had insinuated, that there were no records. They actually labored under the impression that he had it all in his head. Christ! smiled Chance. I'm smart, but I don't have a photographic memory.

The list of bank accounts in the United States was put under the Chateau Latour. There were three hundred and forty two held in nearly as many names in fifteen different cities. They weren't that important actually. They had been opened in the beginning when he'd been feeling his way; now they were a pain in the ass.

Next, Chance, placed the five pages of information regarding Panamanian banks under the white Burgundy bottle that once held Corton Charlemagne. These, he would come back to.

Most of the Barracudas' shell companies were in the Bahamas though several were also in Panama. There were forty-one of them all told. The great advantage of a shell company is that it's capitalized by bearer stock with no owner of record. So these companies had two stockholders, just Wes and Les. The shell company could deposit money in a bank—of course, a bank protected by secrecy laws was the best choice—for its offshore clients. Banks in Panama protected the depositor by, like Lichtenstein and Switzerland, strict laws including big fines and jail sentences for any bank employee violating secrecy laws. In Panama, a depositor does not have to give a name or an address. Chance remembered once, in the Bahamas, sending a courier into a bank with a green plastic garbage bag of bills. No one batted an eye but they did charge a one percent counting fee.

Chance stared at the list of companies and smiled. He'd named them after creatures of the deep so he'd recognize them easily among the Barracudas' more legitimate enterprises. There was Anemone Associates, Goldfish Global, Limpet Enterprises, Carp Incorporated, Salmon and Son, and Amalgamated Minnow. The list had grown and grown until finally Take-A-Chance felt a bit of an ichthyologist as he skimmed his paperback called All About Fish, usually a half hour before landing in the islands. The shell companies were put under an empty bottle labelled La Tache.

The sun was hot on his shoulders and back. Chance pushed his sunglasses up higher on his nose and continued to open and close manila folders. One held his Gucci notebook chronicling that hopeless saga of seven years ago. Take-A-Chance had flown to Port-au-Prince to talk to Bebe Doc Duvalier which was easier to do than he'd imagined it to be. He'd had an afternoon appointment in the big white palace that looks uncannily like the White House and had waited in line with another dozen nervous, foreigners, just in from the airport with a quick stop at one of maybe five good hotels for a shower and a fresh shirt.

They all had a lot in common. They all wanted something from the President for Life and they were all fidgety, tense, bored and perspiring. From arms dealers to soft drink company representatives, they stood on one foot then the other, awaiting their names to be called in a French accent by a khaki-uniformed Haitian, holstered and unsmiling.

Duvalier, massive, very black and quite dignified, had said 'non'. 'No' to his request that he cede the island of Gonave as a center for global banking. Chance had been on the next flight to San Juan where he had changed planes and flown to Costa Rica. In return for pumping a percentage, two percent, of his clients' banked money into Costa Rica, Chance wanted an autonomous piece of the country. This area would become a center for gambling and banking. World class, not just Caribbean in category. It would be modelled as a headquarters for offshore finance. The President of Costa Rica had been all for it, but, the plan had hit a snag with the parliament when they proved reluctant to hand over sovereignty of even a little piece of their country.

Chance failed in his mission, but followed the progress and the subsequent failure of other similar schemes in the Caribbean. Plans for a free banking zone using Dominica, Anguilla, and Montserrat also met with defeat. About ten years before Chance's try at Haiti and Costa Rica, there had been an attempt to effect the secession of a tiny island from the Tonga group in the South Pacific. It was to be free of all taxation and annoying banking regulations but unfortunately the entire island disappeared under several feet of water with every high tide.

Chance skimmed page after page of phone numbers and notes taken at meetings, in hotel dining rooms, at private clubs. This man and that man, all smiling, all friendly, all eager to help. All with their hands out. Take-A-Chance had decided, on that specific trip, his first foray into international affairs, that greed had no nationality and was edgeless, infinite. Nothing was enough and the promise of more, the excitement of additional treasure put the same gleam in the eye of the richest or the about to be richer. How much was enough? Chance had asked himself as he relaxed by a swimming pool at a cabinet minister's villa outside San Jose. He sipped Dom Perignon as the buffet of lobster and smoked salmon flown in from Scotland was served on silver trays in the shade of a gazebo large enough to qualify as a house. Servants in white linen jackets criss-crossed the green lawns carrying drinks for the guests who lazed in the sun, talking almost soporifically of parties in Madrid, of friends in New York, of shopping in Paris.

Chance sighed then dropped the notebook in a manila envelope labelled 'island shopping' and walked barefooted back to the house for a beer. Hardware had not moved a muscle and seemed mesmerized by the squeals of the crowd as the Wheel of Fortune was spun. Vacuous White was beaming. No, nothing was ever enough, he decided as he snapped open the Heineken in his large kitchen. He returned to the pool and opened the folder labelled with the initial 'D.' Diamonds. Dutch Guilders. Money was taken in a suitcase from Los Angeles to New York's 47th Street, just west of Fifth Avenue where diamonds were bought. Small, easily transportable, that very day they were on a KLM flight to Amsterdam. Eight or ten hours later, Frans had sold them for about ninety-nine percent of the price he'd paid and the money, in guilders, had been deposited in a bank in the Dutch capital.

Chance sorted the real estate transactions by city. There was Chicago, Las Vegas, Boston, Minneapolis, Fort Lauderdale, Houston and now

Oahu since he'd bought three houses there last week. Hawaii was full of Japanese investment and he'd turn them over soon. The yen was so strong against the dollar that Tokyo businessmen were buying several houses at a time. Chance put the copies of the leases in other folders labelled hotels, apartment complexes, undeveloped property, shopping malls and miscellaneous. The race track was miscellaneous. Tax deductable mortgages churned on and on. But cash could buy things more cheaply.

It's all a game, thought Chance. What Gorbachev said, who happened to be President, what was happening in Nicaragua, riots in the Left Bank, the war between Iran and Iraq. All of it affected Wall Street, interest rates, the price of oil, the price of gold, the currency markets, and the Barracudas' chips. Their fortunes rose and fell like a boat on an ocean, but the boat was so big and so heavy and so solid that the waves were only noticed by Chance. The waves were the tiniest ripples lapping at a fortune. Losing ten million was a ripple for there was so much more, so much sucking in interest in banks in so many different countries every minute of the day and night. And deep in the jungles of Bolivia the coca leaves got sun and rain and kept growing and were picked and were prepared and the value multiplied as the snow moved north. There was no end to the river of dollars rushing towards Take-A-Chance.

He wiped the perspiration from his face with the edge of the light blue towel and took a last swig of the Heineken. Six wine bottles stood like soldiers before him guarding the secrets of the Barracuda boys. Wes and Les might not initiate a real estate transaction or decide a new company was needed but their acumen in reading human nature was formidable. Their instincts were sound about the probable behavior of men they'd never met, men they only heard of secondhand, through Chance's descriptions, through Chance's reported conversations. They could predict when a contact on the spike was no longer reliable; they could suss out a coward or a turncoat long before Chance. That had to be a reason why two brothers with a seventh grade education from a town in Oklahoma, a place that had no oil, a place Chance imagined was like the old black and white photographs of the DustBowl, had generated an income that rivalled a Fortune 500 corporation.

Chance estimated the Barracudas were producing, preparing and shipping and selling a million pounds of cocaine a year. Not all of it destined for the United States. That was worth over four hundred million dollars.

Chance stared at the clear turquoise water shining in the sun before him. If, in the beginning, in the good ole days as they called them, the days of holding up gas stations with sawed off shotguns, they'd had more balls than brains, that had changed. Then there'd come the wild days of Mexico and smuggling Black Beauties and grass into California in the pale blue Barracuda, and when the borders were tough, the hill smuggling. Through some instinct, they had surrounded themselves with men who could deliver, men who didn't fail them. And the men who defected weren't around long enough to brag about it. The Barracudas weren't susceptible to guilt so far as he could see. Or fear. The decision to do or not to do wasn't complicated by morality.

Chance took off his sunglasses and rubbed his tired eyes. Yes, they were shrewd. And yes, they frightened him. Chance looked down at his thin, veined hands. Could they sense, could they smell, that he was plotting defection? Did they know? And did they know that he thought of it as escape?

*   *   *   *   *   *   *   *   *   *   *

Diane walked to her balcony, looked down at the crowds and the traffic below, and shrugged. Too noisy. She unknotted the blue and white print scarf from around her neck and began to wave it back and forth wildly.

"What on earth are you doing?" called Faith from behind her in the living room.

"Teddy's phone has been on the fritz forever," sighed Diane as she continued to flail. "This is how we communicate."

"I don't know whether to laugh or cry. I thought you were surrendering."

"No. I'll never surrender. This town is completamente pazza, too crazy to be real, but one has to keep fighting."

Teddy stepped out onto her little bedroom balcony wearing only a red bath towel and lifted her hand with two fingers. Then she nodded and went back inside.

Diane flipped the scarf into a triangle and tied it again as she returned to the living room. "She'll be over in two minutes. How do you feel about wine?"

Faith said cynically. "Will it help?"

Diane shook her head. "Faith, where's your spirit? Your optimism...your...your faith!"

There was a pounding on the door before she could answer. Teddy came prancing in, grinning, her white miniskirt well above her knees, her silver ballet shoes making scuff noises on the stone floor. "Now we celebrate!" she laughed.

Diane was glad to see her. Alone with Faith was tough these days; Teddy was a godsend.

"Faith! How are you?" Teddy bent down and kissed her on both cheeks quickly. "Been so long-"

Faith smiled. She hadn't realized Teddy was so tall. And thin. She was like a colt. All legs and hair. "What are we celebrating?"

"Il mio telefono! Funziona! Funziona perfettamente!"

"I'll drink to that!" sang Diane as she handed Teddy a glass. Faith took hers from the coffee table and stared. She didn't think it was funny, anymore, the way this country ran or didn't run. It just wasn't fun. It was a waste of time, a headache, an exercise in frustration. How could

Italy have overtaken the United Kingdom last year with the standard of living index? Not possible. The Italians probably cheated.

"How did it happen?" demanded Diane.

Teddy sat down on the red sofa. "You know I've been calling that repair number at SIP every single morning for all these weeks, every single Monday, Tuesday, Wednesday, Thursday, and Friday."

Faith was simply staring at her.

"And you know how someone always takes my number and says 'domani, domani,' and nothing happens." Teddy sipped the wine. "This morning at the studio I suddenly thought, it was something Salvatore said, that I was approaching this from an American vantage point. What was needed was an Italian approach. So this time when I had the man on the phone I told him my phone was blank blank blank and my address was la de da and he had a nice voice so I-" Teddy's face broke into a very self-satisfied smile of triumph.

"I told una piccola bugia," she said. "Just a little lie."

"How little?" insisted Diane.

"Well, I told him that I was very upset about the phone because I was living alone and he sounded sympathetic and I couldn't stop myself." She spread her hands. "All true so far."

"You're not having dinner with him?" screamed Faith in horror.

Teddy shook her head. "I couldn't possibly. Not in my condition."

"Teddy...." Diane said with a 'what have you done now' tone of voice.

"I merely told him I was seven months pregnant with my first child and I was very nervous because my husband was in New York at the moment and you know how Italians are about mothers and babies..."

Faith wasn't amused and simply shook her head. Diane was laughing. "So your phone was fixed the day you decided to be seven months' pregnant?"

Teddy nodded and took another sip of wine. "Within the hour!" She held up one finger. "I dialed my number and it rang normally. I think this morning illustrates the true meaning of when in Rome do as the...oh, you know," she waved her arm and only one wide silver bracelet gleamed. Teddy was toning down the jewelry.

Faith spoke. "I'm losing my sense of humor and you two haven't and I wonder if it's because of our personalities. It doesn't bother you, Teddy, to play helpless and female whereas I'd rather dig ditches and you, Diane-"

Diane was irritated. Faith was walking clouds of gloom. Maybe she should get on a plane and go home. How did Brian stand her? "Oh, for crissake, Faith! Loosen up! Lighten up! It's a fucking broken phone! Yes, it's an inconvenience. Yes, it's annoying. But Teddy hasn't slashed her wrists over it!"

Faith's face had gone very white. She stood up and slammed the glass down on the marble-topped coffee table. "How dare you talk to me like that!"

"Like what?" Diane said carefully. "Nothing is good here for you. Nothing is pretty, nothing pleases you. You have become hyper-critical and just generally hard to be around. This is Rome. This is not New York. And it doesn't work like New York. The toilet paper is different in the public bathrooms, the phones don't work, the plumbers come and sing opera and ask for corks to plug a leak but, my god! The sun is shining and the bakeries are turning out fresh bread in every neighborhood and the clothes are the most elegant anywhere and every balcony has its little garden of flowers and the wine costs two dollars a bottle." Diane could hardly breathe after her impassioned monologue.

Faith was at the door. "I hate this country, and I hate the phone company and I hate all the plumbers."

"Oh, come on, Faith! Come back and sit down and let's talk! I didn't mean to explode at you." Diane was standing now.

"No. I hate Italy and I hate Rome." Tears were streaming down her cheeks. She clutched her dark blue leather pocketbook under one elbow. "And I won't be torn to pieces by you or anyone-"

In seconds, she had opened the door, gone through it and slammed it so hard that Diane's favorite icon hanging on the wall nearby crashed to the floor. Teddy walked over and picked it up carefully. "Not broken," she announced as she gently laid it on the coffee table.

Diane filled their glasses and they sat together in silence and drank what remained in the bottle. Then Diane dialed Faith's number and when she answered began to speak. "Look, let's forget this. Let's meet for...."

Faith didn't allow her to finish. "No! You're right! Nothing pleases me here! So I'm leaving and you and Teddy and the people who put up with this Italian mentality can stay and rot for all I care!" And with that the phone was banged down.

Teddy couldn't help but hear it all and without a word went into Diane's kitchen and began to saute garlic cloves in olive oil. When the spaghetti was al dente she returned to the living room with napkins and bowls and forks and the big wooden pepper grinder. Another bottle of white wine was opened and splashed into their glasses. It was dusk and the light changed from a rich gold color to a pale pinky grey.

Church bells began to ring as Teddy spoke. "If it helps, I agree with you." She pushed back her hair and leaned forward on the couch. "Campo dei Fiori with its tomatoes, its artichokes, its watermelon, is like the Garden of Eden. The wine is cheap and the bread is fresh and every piazza has its fountain and its flowers." Diane smiled at her over a forkful of steaming spaghetti. "No matter how many churches there are in New York I never heard the bells sound like this."

They listened to them peal a few last times and then there was the return of the traffic noises outside the open balcony doors. Teddy went on. "I want to stay here forever. I want to marry and have my children here." Diane was silent. "Because," finished Teddy staring at the lovely yellow color of the wine. "Everything you said is true. It's only a fucking phone."

* * * * * * * * * * *

"Massimo?" Teddy could hardly inhale she was so excited. She held the receiver with both hands and listened. "It's Teddy! How are you? How do you feel? Are you well? Is everything all right?"

"Bene! Sto bene e tu?"

"Oh, I'm terrific," she breathed. He was back! Massimo was back in Rome and had finally answered his telephone!

"Il tuo lavoro? Va bene?"

"Yes, yes. The studio is fine. A little bit pazzo," she said. "Everyone is having affairs, love affairs, you know. Except me. Of course I'm not! But these California men are so gay and how can they…."

Massimo was laughing. "You are still having your adventures!"

"Massimo, I was thinking….I am a good cook, you know…well, you don't know! And I wonder if you would come to…to dinner…at..at my apartment. You've never seen where I live." She told herself to stop there. To not jabber on. To not rephrase it twelve times. Just do it the way I rehearsed it and then keep quiet. Don't plead with him and don't beg and when he says 'no' be very casual and cool and say, "oh, another time perhaps."

Teddy spoke. "Oh, well, another time perhaps." Massimo was laughing again. "Teddy! I said 'when!'"

"Oh! Oh! You can come?" Teddy was fairly jumping up and down. "We can…what about tomorrow night?"

"Si. Va bene."

"Okay. Va bene. Yes, si. Okay." Teddy's heart was thudding and her mouth was dry.

"A che ora?" he was asking.

"Eight o'clock!"

"Ci vediamo!"

"Si! Okay! Yes!" Teddy suddenly realized she was listening to the dial tone for Massimo had hung up.

* * * * * * * * * * *

"Edith!" Slow had his short, thick arms akimbo and his hands on his hips. "Edith! How could you?"

The big black and white spotted rabbit stopped tearing at the pages of the 'G' volume of the Encyclopedia Britannica and looked up at him. She didn't stop chewing though. Her entire face moved back and forth, her black eyes unblinking.

The midget walked to the open book and stared at the page half torn from it. "Gorilla," he read. "Well, we passed that a long time ago." He smoothed what remained of the page flat and closed the big volume. "Edith!" The rabbit the size of a cocker spaniel stared at him. "I'm not angry at you, don't worry," he said softly reaching down. She hopped pom pom pom over to him and pressed her ears back flat so that he would stroke the top of her head.

Slow smiled. His mother had bought Edith for him when she was a tiny little thing you could hold in your hand. It had been the Saturday before Easter. The owner of the pet shop had sworn she would never get any bigger. "That's a Dutch rabbit," he had said. "Can tell by the black spots. Nossir! Won't ever grow!" Then he'd looked at Slow and gotten embarrassed. Slow had taken her home on the bus with his mother. They'd both anxiously leaned over every few minutes asking if she were all right, if she were afraid of the noise, if she were liable to jump away. But no. Edith had pressed herself to him that first afternoon and forever after. And she had grown. The next time, a month later, Slow had gone to Paysonville taking Edith with him in a basket. The man at the pet shop had been amazed at her size. "She's Polish! I never woulda guessed it!"

So the Polish Edith had continued to gain weight and grow. And Slow continued to read to her, to talk to her, to educate her. Edith the Educated Rabbit was a giant among rodents.

Slow now went to the refrigerator and unwrapped a plastic bag where he kept what was best for Edith's teeth. They had to be constantly used or they would grow too long. No wonder poor Edith gnawed on the legs of the rocking chair. "Come on, Edith. I know you like this." Slow put the month old tortilla down on the floor. It was the size and the consistency of a frisbee. Garcia couldn't figure out what Slow wanted with them. "And yes, I know it's the middle of the afternoon and a good time for this." Slow poured one glass of lemonade for himself and a teacup for Edith. She pom pom pommed eagerly over to where he placed it beside the bread.

After a few sips her narrow face with the eyes placed peripherally puckered so much she had to stop and lift her head. She liked it as sour as Slow could make it. He drank his as he stood over her, smiling down at her excitement. "Yes, Edith. It's all right. Don't worry about the Encyclopedia. I think you have a great hunger for knowledge. Don't worry."

Edith stopped drinking at the sound of his voice. She looked up at him, ears back, onyx eyes shining. Another kick of tartness hit her and she sucked in her cheeks. Her eyes slitted but did not close and did not leave his face.

*   *   *   *   *   *   *   *   *   *   *

Teddy sat on the front steps of Zephyr Studios and stared at her watch saying, "Mio dio, mio dio, mio dio and oh my God, oh my God." Her blonde hair was in curly profusion over the shoulders of the black sleeveless dress. Her tan arms were crossed in front of her. Head down, she continued the chant of "mio dio, mio dio."

"Anything I can do?" Vittorio bent over her. His shoes were dark brown and shiny and looked new. They were the first things Teddy saw. She looked up. "No, I'm in trouble, that's all. I'm desperate and I'm late and my life is ruined." She sighed. "But there's nothing you can do about it."

"Are you waiting for a driver to take you to the station?"
She nodded.

"Andiamo. Come on. Let's go." He watched her stand up, clutching notebooks and scripts across her breasts. "I'll take you. Don't know if it's faster for you to take the subway or to let me drive you but I'm going to the centro."

"You are?" Teddy was recovering. All was not lost. "Wow!"

Vittorio smiled. She was like a kid. An American teenager he'd seen in movies. She was a 1980's Yvette Mimieux. Yes, he remembered her in the movie "The Light in the Piazza." "This way. My car is nearby."

She ran to keep up with him and noted with surprise that he was the first man she'd been beside in Italy who wasn't shorter than she or, like Massimo, exactly her height. Massimo! In less than four hours he'll be in my apartment and I'm not ready and I've lost my recipes, she suffered. They were in this notebook. I know they were here. Long before Massimo succumbed to pneumonia in Paris.

Vittorio unlocked her door of the silver car first and helped her in and then went around to the driver's side. It was a small sports car, that's all Teddy could tell. When he started the engine, he looked at her and said, "Yes?" and she said immediately, "I was thinking that this car smells good. It smells like a new doll at Christmas."

The Principe put the car in gear and reversed expertly. She's right, he thought. I never would have said a new doll but certainly a new toy.

"Traffic's not bad yet." He glanced at his flat gold watch and then at Teddy. "It's only four-thirty, shall I drive you in?"

"That would be fantastic," she smiled and stretched her bare legs before her as she rearranged various papers, a notebook and an Italian dictionary in her lap. Teddy wanted to ask him what it was like to be a prince and was his mother a queen and was his father a king and did he live in a palace with plenty of gold and did he have lots of servants in fancy uniforms and had anyone ever bowed to him and how did he sign his checks?

Vittorio suddenly asked, "Why do you only wear black and white or one or the other?" His accent was more English than American and he spoke very well, very clearly.

"I'm in mourning," said Teddy and when he didn't respond she continued. "For my dead marriage."

"Ah," the tone was cynical. "Broken promises."

"Shattered dreams," her tone matched his.

"You're recovering very nicely, I think."

"Think so?" Teddy bit her lip.

"I see you." He put on the blinker and the car smoothly changed lanes. "Sometimes."

Silence in the little car as it sped down the smooth grey highway. Looks like chewing gum, thought Teddy. One miles and miles long piece of Juicy Fruit. "What do you do for Zephyr?" she asked.

"I'm in charge of money."

"Ha! So you're the one!" she hooted, turning to face him.

"What do you mean?" His tone was noncommittal.

"I haven't been paid for two weeks!"

"Money is coming," he said calmly. "Don't worry."

Teddy scowled.

"Well, are you about to be thrown out into the street, are you starving?" he persisted.

"No," she admitted. "But money is nice to have."

He nodded and knew that she was staring at his profile. She was like a big cat, the way she moved, the big steps, the free movements. He could feel her brown eyes examining him from his ears right down to his foot on the gas pedal. A child. Too young to be embarrassed or…to have manners.

He had to ask. "Are you going to tell me why you're in such a hurry to get back to Rome? Why your life is ruined? Why you were murmuring 'mio dio' on the steps?"

"Oh," Teddy groaned. "I invited someone to dinner, actually him and my friend and then I called him back and told him to bring a friend and they're all coming at eight and I've lost my ideas for what to cook and I had it planned so carefully and it was going to be special and now it'll be only normal and not wonderful the way I wanted it to be." She sighed and rested her elbows on her knees and her face in her hands.

Then he realized. Teddy must be the author of that delightful list of things to do. The black nightgown just in case list. He resisted the urge to ask if she'd ever been able to find rosemary. "Sounds like quite a dinner party," he said lightly.

Teddy turned to look at him. "Are you making fun of me?" she asked.

"No," he said seriously. "I imagine you are a very capable cook. You look as though you have a healthy appetite for many things…" He hadn't meant to say that. If she'd caught it, she didn't respond. Vittorio had an idea that Teddy could eat an ox and would enjoy tearing it apart with her bare hands. The feline face wasn't all that conveyed that idea, there was something that seemed almost feral. Teddy Starbuck probably appeared delicate in repose, but not many people had seen her in that state. The moment her dark eyes turned their attention to something, the instant she moved, the great energy in her became apparent. Vittorio had the impression she wore shoes because her parents had told her she had to. He decided she probably had atrocious table manners.

"How old are you?" she asked.

Vittorio was surprised. "Thirty five," he answered. Silence. "Anything else you'd like to know?" He meant it as a joke, but Teddy said "oh, about a million things. When did your hair go white?"

"I was in my twenties."

"Was it fright?"

"No!" he laughed suddenly. "It's hereditary. My father has the same hair."

"Well, I only asked because there's somebody at home whose hair turned white when his dead wife came to visit him and his new wife on the wedding night." Teddy's voice was matter of fact. "Are you married?"

He shook his head and passed a red Fiat. God. How American she is.

"Not ever?"

"Once I was. We fought for eleven days and had it annulled."

"Ha! Really!" exploded Teddy.

A child, thought Vittorio. A prattling child.

"So you live with your parents now?" Teddy had become accustomed to this with the nonmarried adult Romans.

"Yes. My mother and my father."

"I miss my aunts, Daisy and Cricket, back in Alabama. I miss them a lot," said Teddy softly almost to herself. "They're crazy and silly and it'll be good for them to become more self sufficient while I'm away but I still miss them." She sighed. "Do you get along with your parents?" she insisted.

How very American she is. "I do. We love each other very much." Vittorio hesitated. "My mother isn't very well but she is always reading, always talking, always having a little party around her in her bedroom. And my father-" Vittorio wondered why he was elaborating. "And my father adores her, loves being nearby even if she is impossible late in the afternoon."

Teddy was smiling. She was imagining a king and a queen both with crowns, both with books, books bound in leather with gold tooling, and both monarchs would be reading. Perhaps they would read in Latin. And they would read important things, like documents of state, or per-haps poetry.

Vittorio glanced at Teddy who gazed straight ahead. This half hour had been the only segment of time since last night's call that she hadn't thought of Massimo, but now her mind went back to him. What shall we eat. What shall I wear. Will I have time to buy flowers. Of course he'll stay for brandy and we'll sit up all night kissing and maybe...oh, I would love to make love, thought Teddy. Vittorio looked at her profile, at the softness of her expression and imagined her running down a sloping green lawn welcoming her distinguished genteel aunts home from Atlanta. Vittorio had seen "Gone with the Wind" and knew all about Tara and Miss Scarlett.

The Lamborghini coursed over the highway at 90 kilometers an hour, towards Rome, towards the Venturini Palazzo and, towards Massimo.

* * * * * * * * * * *

At five minutes of seven Teddy was in the bathtub, at one minute after she was wrapped in a pink towel, applying mascara and grey eyeshadow and at four minutes after she was perfumed and pulling a silver lame minidress over her head.

Diane, across the street, was reading a novel by Moravia for the second time, wondering why on earth she'd said yes to dinner. The pounding at her door made her jump. "Vengo subito!" she called.

"Look at you! Look at you!" Teddy stormed in carrying a small overnight bag. Diane looked down at her blue jeans, her brown sandals. This was her normal outfit. Teddy disappeared into the bathroom, turned on the bath water and came back. "Now speed it up!" she commanded. "I'm waiting for you!" She put what looked like a dark green tackle box on the coffee table and began to rummage through the little compartments for pencils and brushes.

"What are you doing? I didn't know this was black-tie and if you make me up, it'll be Halloween."

"Take a bath, Diane, and then we'll talk while I'm doing your face." Teddy's voice was stern.

Ten minutes later Diane was in a white bathrobe on the couch, head tilted upward as Teddy stood over her. "Open. Look to the left. Okay. The right. No, try not to blink. Okay." Teddy sighed and placed a palette of eye shadows on the table.

"Teddy, I have to feel like myself! I don't want to look like anybody else. I just—"

"Genius at work," breathed Teddy as she expertly smoothed ivory cover-up under Diane's hazel eyes. "No talking til I'm finished. Then you can wash your face if you want—I'll even supply the cleanser—but let me have fifteen minutes of your life first." She rooted around in the box until she found a large sable brush with a bright red wooden handle. "Now for the cheekbones." She softly applied the dark blusher and then the lighter on top. "Diane, you are a beautiful, beautiful, outstandingly-boned person!" Teddy smiled radiantly, then gave her one last dusting of the matte powder. "Flaming flamingoes!" she cursed. "You just reminded me, I have to run home and baste the lamb!"

Teddy was torn, afraid to let the lamb dry out and afraid to leave Diane at this point either. It was crucial that she be given positive feedback. So it was Diane or dinner. What was it—a sacrificial lamb? she worried. "Now, you are not wearing jeans. I assume you do not have two wooden legs so I brought-"

"I haven't worn a dress in years!" moaned Diane putting one hand up to her face.

"Don't touch!"commanded Teddy. "Look, I have something black that'll be knockout on you and if your legs are hairy wear these." She pulled black lace pantyhose from the blue canvas bag. "Come on, Diane," she insisted.

"Do I have a choice?" Diane began to pull on the stockings. When the silk dress was in place Teddy zipped it. "You're as thin as I am. I knew this would fit." Teddy stood before her looking very satisfied with her handiwork.

"May I look now?" Diane asked for the fourth time. Teddy nodded and followed her towards the full length mirror in the hall beside the bathroom door.

"You look fantastic," said Teddy softly. "Absolutely dazzling."

Diane was silent. Yes, I do have cheekbones. Yes, I do have a flat stomach and nice legs. She didn't speak.

Teddy was throwing equipment into the green metal box when Diane returned to the living room. "Boy! I interviewed three werewolves from

Chicago today, then I did you, now I take care of the lamb and later I take care of Massimo!" she panted. "A woman's work is never done!"

* * * * * * * * * * *

It wasn't going as Teddy planned. Oh, the lamb had thrived on inattention and had obediently absorbed the flavor of the garlic slivers, the rosemary sprigs and the bacon. And Massimo had had three helpings of the pasta with creme. Three bottles of wine later, the four of them leaned back companionably in their chairs in the candlelight and talked. But it wasn't going as Teddy planned. Federico is nice, she thought, but Massimo is divine. I do not want to tell Federico my life story. I want to have Massimo tell me anything. Anything! Like what he had for breakfast.

Federico was asking what Alabama was like and Teddy was smiling her head off. She could hear Massimo asking Diane what she thought of de Chirico. "I hope he isn't your favorite and I hope you don't kill me, but I think he's overrated," she was saying. "If you put him alongside the others of that same generation in France or in the U.S. who..." Massimo was attentive to the point of being hypnotized.

"Well, it's hot," Teddy was saying. "And there aren't any big cities. Montgomery is the capital." Teddy thought I'm boring myself. I sound like a social studies film for third graders. She went on, hating herself, hating Diane for looking so beautiful, hating Diane for being so bright, for knowing about things that Massimo knew about, hating her own dinner party. "It was one of the states before the Civil War where cotton was king." She stood up. "Excuse me, but would anyone like chocolate mousse?"

Delighted moans met her question. "Oh, you're a witch, Teddy," smiled Massimo. "I had no idea you were such a cook."

Teddy looked adoringly at him. She loved his haircut, she loved the blue and white striped shirt and the dark blue tie.

Diane spoke. "You have no idea what it's like to have her as a neigh-bor. I've never been so well taken care of in my life." Teddy felt a twinge. Not only was Diane taking over Massimo but she knew all Teddy's secrets. Diane continued. "She's incredible. I might have five things in my refrigerator, all going bad, and Teddy will march in and whip together something so creative…"

Massimo laughed. "Your refrigerator sounds like mine."

Teddy turned and walked into the kitchen. Federico followed her and asked if he could help. She tried to be gracious and pointed to coffee cups on the top shelf. As she arranged fresh strawberries in a circle on the surface of the mousse she heard French coming from the next room. One big fat tear fell into the chocolate.

Two hours later, very long ones, they all stood in the doorway kissing good bye. Massimo's face was pinkish from all the wine and his blue eyes were bright behind his little wire-rimmed glasses. Federico held Teddy's hand an instant longer than was necessary which, in Italy, often meant more than the little brushes of kisses on either cheek. Diane was thanking her profusely as Massimo bent forward and kissed her lightly on the cheek.

"I'll talk to you tomorrow," Diane was saying. Massimo winked, "Ci vediamo," and she knew he didn't mean it. He always said that and never called. Federico hung back as the three of them started down the stairs and Teddy thought, no, not you, you idiot! Massimo is supposed to ask for the brandy. But he didn't and she smiled bravely until her guests had disappeared on the first landing. She heard their footfalls on the stone steps and their laughter. Massimo laughing was the last thing she heard as she closed the door.

* * * * * * * * * * *

Teddy tore off her silver dress and cleared the dining room table stark naked by candlelight. The cool spring air felt good on her bare skin and besides how easy it was to wipe her wet face on her bare arm instead of getting her dress spotted. Then she moved the Tunisian candelabra into the kitchen and washed the dishes. She blew her nose on a paper towel thinking Scott towels and Coca Cola...the Americans are taking over the world. Damn it! she stomped her bare foot on the blue tiled floor. Just when I learn Italian they had to speak French! Teddy bit her lip and gave an enormous sniff as she stared at the four wine glasses, clean, shining, lined on the drainboard. Diane had looked radiant. Teddy had never seen her at a party, never seen her even talk to a man except the news dealer or the butcher.

The platter the lamb had been on sank in the suds and she began to slide the cloth back and forth in the warm water getting rid of the grease. Had she tried to attract him? wondered Teddy. She held the blue plate under the running water and doubted it. It was so natural for her to talk like that. That's the way she talks with Eleanor. That's what she reads all the time. Teddy sighed. I wish Eleanor weren't in London. I wish....oh, how she wished Massimo had stayed and let the others go. The tears began with a stinging in her nose. But he hadn't wanted to stay.

Teddy dried her hands and blew out the candles. It may not be the end, she said to herself. He might call me. She walked through the dark living room. It smelled of paraffin and daffodils. He might call and say he was dying to speak French and to please forgive him if he had been rude. She went into her bedroom. He might call tomorrow. Now that he's back in Rome, cured of pneumonia, and my phone works since I'm pregnant. Teddy still had not turned on a light. She stood at the foot of her double bed and felt very lonely. Diane was still up. It was past midnight and the traffic noises were far away on the other side of Largo Argentina and sounded curiously like the ocean. Teddy's eyes widened as she stared across the narrow street.

Diane was standing with her back to the fireplace still wearing Teddy's dress. She was holding a brandy snifter and talking. Massimo walked in front of the window towards her. He had taken his suit jacket off. He put his glass on the mantlepiece and reached out and touched her hair gently. Teddy had both hands over her mouth. Diane was shaking her head and staring into his face. She turned to the side as he reached for her and the brandy seemed to spill. As Teddy watched, Massimo folded Diane in his arms. She pushed him away and held her head back at first and then she seemed to change her mind. Naked and shivering, with tears rolling down her cheeks, Teddy imagined she heard the crash of the brandy snifter as it fell on the marble floor.

* * * * * * * * * *

Chapter Eight

"I don't give one itty bitty flyin' fuck what Noriega's doin'!" Wes was shouting at Chance as he paced in front of the map of Central America. The purple flag continued to wave valiantly over the Panamanian capital.

"I'm just saying that-"

"Chance! Have you lost your marbles? Those spics are riotin' in the streets, the banks are closed, nobody has any dollar bills, the troops are firin' tear gas into hospitals! And you think things are gettin' better?" The word 'better' was bellowed deep from Wes's big belly in two distinct syllables.

Chance didn't answer. God. We're all so tense. Let him exercise for awhile and then he'll call Garcia for a nice cold root beer and tilt back in his chair and this'll blow over.

"That bastard's organizin' a meetin' with other countries down there. They're thinkin' bout printin' their own money! You know what that means?"

Chance let him go on. He stared at the deep red angry face. When either of the brothers lost their temper their old acne pockmarks seemed more deeply pitted, as if the skin around them actually swelled with the heat of wrath. The machete scar became particularly ugly. Chance wondered how a woman could go to bed with one of the Barracudas. He wondered how the trip to Vegas had gone. He wondered if they'd taken his advice and cooled it on the money. Wes was shouting, "Garcia! Get your cockroach ass in here with a root beer! Pronto!"

Les lay on his E-Z Boy in the horizontal position looking like a beached whale awaiting a conservation group. He turned his head slowly and gazed at Chance as if signalling it was time to speak.

"I'm not happy with the mess in Panama either. But all I propose is the obvious: that nothing else go in there. We don't disagree. Not at all. But neither do we have a multitude of choices. Not a multitude." He liked the word. Chance continued. "What's in the banks down there has to stay. No way to get it out today but it isn't lost. They have to open the banks sometime and the minute they do I'll just wire it to a couple of the shell companies in the Bahamas. From there some can go to Belize, Costa Rica, Lichtenstein, some to Switzerland."

"Dammit!" Wes grabbed the bright red can out of Garcia's hand. The little Mexican in jeans exited quickly. His legs were so bowed that from the waist down he looked like a blue denim horseshoe. "Goddammit! I don't want no more wires! I don't care if you have to ride on airplanes yourself! No more of them wires!"

Chance sighed. "Right. Suitcases. That's what you want. Suitcases."

Les snapped his E-Z Boy in the upright position. "Chance, there ain't nothin' complicated 'bout this. Buy your boys some Samsonites and get movin.'"

Chance nodded. He stood up and turned to lift his jacket off the back of the metal chair. He faced DooDah and felt his stomach lurch with revulsion. The mouth was wide open and the black forked tongue danced obscenely towards him. "Right. If you need me I'll be back in Los Angeles in a few hours." Chance walked quickly from the room and down the hall as Lawrence Welk led his Champagne Music Makers in "Polka Dot Polka." He left the house and hurried past the flamingoes towards the chopper. He knew he would dream of DooDah all night long.

* * * * * * * * * * *

The phone was ringing in the kitchen. Oliver turned over clutching his pillow with both hands and tried not to hear it. The glowing pale green numbers of his alarm clock said three eleven. The phone continued to ring. It was shrill, insistent in the silence of the dark apartment and suddenly Oliver thought it might be Teddy and ran barefooted, his baggy blue pajamas flapping round his legs like sails, down the hall. "Hullo," he panted. He rubbed his head as though it hurt as he listened and then he said, "Christ, Kelly! Why'd you call me now?"

"Look, I'm in the hospital. Roosevelt. Yeah. I'm not having you on." He was talking very softly and Oliver was straining to hear. "I knew you'd work til at least two and I couldn't call you at McAllister's."

"Are you okay?"

Kelly began to sweat again when he remembered the pain. "I thought I was going to die. Kidney stones. Two of them. I just walked around my apartment doubled over, crying, until I called an ambulance."

"Kidney stones! How did you get a kidney stone?"

"The doctor told me it was too much acidity. You know how I take a hundred and thirty five vitamins a day? That did it. Vitamin C. A killer."

"My God," breathed Oliver. "You sure you're allright?"

Kelly was nodding weakly. The room was dark but he could see the nurses' station light reflected on the polished linoleum outside his partially open door. "Ollie, can you do me a favor? Don't say yes unless you really can or I'll be in big trouble."

"Well, give me a hint." Oliver's feet were cold on the kitchen floor.

"You know how I sometimes don't show at the bar? Well, that's because I do errands for some guy. I take trips for him and make deliveries. It's real simple. Nothing to it and they pay my ticket. First class. And they give me..." Kelly hesitated. He needed Ollie to do it but he didn't want to give him all the money. "They give me five hundred bucks, too." Oliver was listening. "Are you with me so far?" Oliver didn't answer but Kelly went on anyway. "I can't make it. They're letting me out of here tomorrow, that's today, at nine o'clock, but I'm just too weak. I'll be home and if you want to do this, you come by and get the suitcase and I'll give you the ticket."

"Five hundred bucks? Is it drugs fer Chrissake?"

"No! It isn't! I promise it isn't drugs."

"Where do I have to go?"

"Switzerland. Geneva. First class ticket. First class hotel paid for two nights. All meals. Only thing that comes out of the five hundred is taxis." Kelly stifled a yawn. "A cinch."

"Okay. Where do you live?" "Eight one five Park. Corner of Seventieth Street."

Oliver inhaled. "Be there at nine-thirty." He hung up the phone. Park Avenue! Red Kelly lives on Park Avenue and he tends bar three nights a week and wants to be an actor! Olivier stumbled into the bathroom shuffling like an old man. "Park Avenue!" he marvelled aloud as he switched on the light. "This, I gotta see."

* * * * * * * * * * *

Oliver leaned back in the green upholstered seat and smiled. He'd never felt so free in his life. Not since graduation day at the University of Vermont as he'd stood in the sun wearing his mortarboard harboring the delusion that the world was his tomato, or his oyster. His whatever. The champagne tickled his throat. Tasted better high in the sky than it did sipped between customers on the wrong side of the bar. Oliver pushed his seat back a little further and smiled more broadly.

"Are you comfortable, sir?" asked the blonde flight attendant in a sweet voice. Oliver nodded. He couldn't smile directly back at her; he was already generally smiling his entire width.

Oliver James Richardson, known as Olivier to one Teddy Starbuck, drank champagne, ate filet mignon, and smiled all the way across the Atlantic. He was still smiling when the captain came on the intercom and announced, "Please fasten your seat belts, we are beginning our descent towards Rome's Fiumicino Airport and will be landing in approximately twenty-five minutes."

＊　＊　＊　＊　＊　＊　＊　＊　＊　＊　＊

He called all day and there was no answer. He didn't have her work number so he took a taxi to the Colosseum and gawked at it and then he took another taxi to St. Peter's and gawked at that and at five-thirty this little southern accent said 'Pronto," into the telephone.

Teddy started to cry when she saw him. "Oh, I've missed you so much!" she kept saying. "How did you get here?"

"Alitalia. You know those planes that go from Kennedy to the Eternal Citta every single day…."

"Stop it! Oh, Olivier! Please stay with me forever! There's a great couch, yes, that one and see my very own little balcony, two of them, and you're going to love Rome!"

Teddy started to calm down as she sauteed the garlic. Cooking calmed her. He could tell something was wrong. Yes, of course, she'd missed him but not to the point of tears.

They talked all night. His auditions. His preliminaries better known as cattle calls. She was divorced. Blakely had sent her a form to sign for Jeremy's 48 hour quickie in the Dominican Republic. He'd advised her to hold out for more than $50,000, but Teddy had signed and celebrated. "He could've had my signature for much cheaper. For one nickel," she now grinned. How was McAllister's. How was Dirk. Had he seen Jeremy. No.

"How are your aunts getting along without you?" Olivier tried to keep up with the news from Ace. He wanted to go there someday with Teddy as a tour guide.

"Olivier! You know how I thought my going to New York would make them more independent?" He nodded. "And how I thought

· 172 ·

coming to Rome would be fine?" He nodded. "Well, I got a letter from Cricket who is…well, the poor woman is out of her mind with worry…" Olivier interrupted. "What's happened?" Teddy took a sip of wine. "Daisy wants to join the Peace Corps!"

Olivier burst into laughter then Teddy did, too. "There's no age limit she says and the thing is they might even accept her! Cricket wrote, 'she'll end up digging wells in the Sudan when she could stay home and dig wells right here in Alabama.'"

Teddy leapt up and returned with another bottle of wine. It was nearly four o'clock in the morning. "Teddy," he said. "You can't fool me. What's happened?"

She threaded her fingers through the tangled thick blonde hair and sighed. Then she bit her lip as if she were holding her breath. "I guess I made a mistake, Olivier. And I made a fool of myself."

"Making a fool of yourself never bothered the Teddy I used to know."

She made a fist as if to hit him. They were sitting on the floor leaning on pillows against the couch. The wine bottle was beside one leg of an Egyptian throne chair. "I thought I was in love with someone, an Italian, and….I guess I wanted to be in love with him. And I chased him and thought I had a pretty good chance of…"

"Pretty good chance!" exclaimed Olivier. "What was wrong with him?"

"Not him, Olivier. Me." She took a swallow of the wine. It tasted very red at this hour. "What was wrong with me."

"Maybe he was legally blind. Maybe he couldn't see what you look like, what you are. You, Teddy, are like the sun! You are like the rain in a desert! Like the…"

"Olivier," she said seriously. "He didn't want me but he did want my best friend. I had them to dinner and poof! They got on like ham and eggs, Sears and Roebuck, Jekyll and Hyde."

Olivier couldn't help smiling. "Is she still your friend?"

"I don't know." Teddy looked very sad. "I can't seem to talk to her. I keep hanging up the phone. She keeps calling. We used to see each other every day but…" She pointed out the window. "She lives right there. We met looking out the window. She never used to pull her shades." She hesitated. "So I know he's there."

"Oh, shit." Olivier frowned. That was pretty rough. Poor Teddy.

They killed the Chianti and the last wedge of cheese and thought about going to bed. Olivier helped Teddy make up the sofa in the living room and they both remembered all the times the situation had been reversed. Olivier's West Side apartment had once been her haven. She had lived there, stocked the refrigerator, done the laundry, and watered the plants. Olivier looked around the immaculate living room, thought of the delicious dinner, and thought, God, what a jerk is Massimo. Teddy put a clean towel in the bathroom for him, "It's blue for you, and white for me," and then kissed him on the forehead. "So happy," she smiled and then padded down the hall to her bedroom.

Olivier was still half awake at dawn when the church bells began to ring. He still hadn't told her everything. He hadn't told her he'd quit McAllister's and he hadn't asked her to get him a job at Zephyr Studios. Darling Teddy, he thought. If I'd had a sister instead of a brother, I would have wanted her to be you. The rush hour traffic was beginning to buzz and growl in the street below when Olivier finally fell asleep.

✳   ✳   ✳   ✳   ✳   ✳   ✳   ✳   ✳   ✳

Chance stood under the shower letting the hot water pelt his face and then stream down his body. He reached up and adjusted the fancy shower head turning the spray to sharp needles. It felt good on his shoulders. Take-A-Chance tried to decide what was bothering him, causing his muscles to tighten like twisted ropes, causing his stomach to flip frighteningly every few moments. He wondered if he should carry a little white disposable bag in his briefcase. Maybe he could steal one off a plane. Or get one of the couriers from Panama City to bring him a few. One for the road. He tried to smile as he soaped his feet, separating each toe carefully. If I were female I'd think it was morning sickness, but I'm not and besides it's every hour of the day. He adjusted the nozzle again and stood with eyes closed beneath it, face tilted upward. Take-A-Chance resembled a sad religious figure, a lost supplicant blindly gazing at a heavenly sunburst.

＊　＊　＊　＊　＊　＊　＊　＊　＊　＊　＊

"Look, I won't talk to you on your office phone," Chance's voice had a sharp edge to it. He was not in an amiable frame of mind. "That's final. Now get your ass out of that building and call me from a pay-phone…"

"Hey, Baby!" Ernie was standing up now, hands out, shoulders raised in the grey sharkskin suit. "Whattsa matter with you?" He was talking to the speaker phone on his big desk. "Just tell me what's happening. That's all. Just…."

"Take this number. Same area code. 472-3244. Got it?" Without waiting for a response, Chance barked, "One hour," and hung up.

＊　＊　＊　＊　＊　＊　＊　＊　＊　＊　＊

"That's good. Yes. That's good. And go look at Piazza Venezia and at the balcony where old Mussolini used to make speeches." Teddy laughed. "No. I repeat do not go to Piazza Navona without me." She smiled into the telephone as Anna looked up from her typewriter. "No! I'm taking you there tonight. Tre Scalini is the place for tartufo." Teddy laughed again. "Oh, you're pathetic. I'm going to have to lead you around like a pet monkey." She listened, winding the cord around one finger. "No later than six. Maximum. And look, tomorrow why don't you plan to come out here with me? Sure. Okay, ciao." Teddy hung up and sang, "Grazie, Anna," and then ran from the room.

Vittorio saw her racing down the stairs, hair flying, and thought, she's like a kid. Could she be twenty? he wondered. He heard her pleading for Salvatore to come with her to take pictures of the Martians on Stage Five and shook his head. She dared call him 'Sally darling' and he liked it! Vittorio closed the door of his office and called to Anna that he was leaving. As he left the building he saw her crossing the lawn towards the sets. Salvatore's short legs were hard put to keep up with her though she was nearly walking backwards and waving her hands trying to convince him of something. Her hair was nearly white in the late afternoon sun, her knees were exposed in the short black dress and she was smiling. Vittorio turned towards the parking lot wondering how the dinner of the week before had turned out. The new publicist. A rambunctious, funny child.

*　*　*　*　*　*　*　*　*　*　*

Two days later Vittorio heard her voice as he was about to open the door to Anna's office. She was speaking her fast strange Italian that was comprehensible once you understood her system. First of all, everyone was formal, even dogs and children. Saves time, she told Salvatore, and everyone thinks I have elegant manners. And any irregular verbs remained in the infinitive. Until I have time to get them right, she insisted. Sometimes people stared at her, fascinated, and couldn't answer, but most of the time the Romans were imaginative enough to grasp the content.

Vittorio stepped away from the door and returned to his desk. He waited fifteen minutes and then checking his watch once more decided that he had to interrupt. He knocked and then opened the door. Teddy looked stricken, ill; there was no color in her face at all. "Scusate, pero…" he began. "Anna, this telex should go off to Los Angeles before five so that it will be on his desk when he arrives at nine."

Teddy stood slowly and said, "Anna, grazie," and then left the office quickly.

"Is she allright?" he asked the secretary when the door had closed.

Anna shook her head. "She's a little upset but I told her to wait until tomorrow to do anything." She read the telex and then flipped through the book for the telex codes. "I don't think it's serious."

        *   *   *   *   *   *   *   *   *   *   *

It was an unusually warm April evening and the trees were green and full along the via Veneto. Roses, daffodils, violets, and zinnias at the stall on the corner of via Ludovisi seemed to scent the air both up and down the hill. The outside cafes were crowded with laughing men and flirtacious women in bright dresses; many of them were sun-tanned after Easter weekend in Porto Ercole or on the Costa Smeralda. Vittorio slowed the Lamborghini in the bumper to bumper traffic as he crawled past the Hotel Excelsior and wondered if he dared double park while he ran to the newsstand. Sometimes Piero saw him and sent his little son out to him, but tonight there were so many people, couples strolling on the sidewalks, crossing the street, window shopping, that Vittorio doubted he would be seen.

"Merde!" he swore as the Fiat in front of him swung into the parking place he'd been counting on. He continued up the hill then turned and went down again. Twenty minutes later he had parked in the Borghese parking lot and was walking back to buy his magazines. He passed under the archway which had once been part of the city's walls and was making his way between the sidewalk tables of Harry's Bar when he saw her. Teddy? He stepped into the dark interior and there she was—atop a bar stool, bare legs ending in gold ballet slippers. One had fallen to the floor leaving her left foot decorated only with scarlet toenails. The most recently arrived producer from Beverly Hills was talking to her as he patted her knee. She didn't appear to be paying the least bit of attention to him but instead was folding and refolding the little square cocktail napkin as though intent on teaching herself origami.

Myron Firestone, pink and balding, was perspiring with excitement. As Vittorio approached them he heard him say, "Sweetheart, have you ever had acting lessons? You have IT. I know my starlets and sweetheart, you are a natural." Teddy took another gulp of what could have been water and didn't answer. A natural. A winner. People are always saying that. She leaned precariously backwards instead and Vittorio decided it probably wasn't Perrier after all. The third time Myron called her "sweetheart" Vittorio stepped forward.

"Myron," he extended his hand. "I found you." Teddy didn't speak, she had both elbows on the bar as if she intended to support her head on her hands but had made a mistake with depth perception. Vittorio turned while still talking to Myron and clasped her shoulder firmly to prevent her from falling to the floor.

"Victorio!" beamed Myron. "Join us for a drink. I just bumped into our beautiful publicist and we've been talking about painting the town red! Come on! What'll it be?" We waved at the barman in the white linen jacket.

"I have to steal our publicist away," Vittorio said firmly. He pulled Teddy from the stool and supported her between him and the bar. Her knees kept bending and Vittorio was sorely tempted to throw her over his shoulder like a sack of meal. The Roman continued smoothly. "A problem with some telexes. Teddy is the only one who knows how to straighten this out and since," he looked at his watch quickly, "it's still Friday before lunch out there I think it's not too late." Myron looked helpless. "But she said she…"

"Oh, I'll get her back to you as soon as I can. But," he shrugged apologetically and used an American phrase. "Business comes first." Vittorio put his arm around Teddy's waist and firmly propelled her out of the bar and into the afternoon sunshine.

* * * * * * * * * * *

Teddy kept hearing someone calling her. Was it Aunt Cricket? "I'm coming," she moaned. "I'm...." Then someone began to shake her. "Leave me alone. I won't be late for school. Just five more min-"

When she opened her eyes she saw him staring down at her. His blue eyes, crystal clear, were examining her as though she were a new species. His white hair and olive skin make them seem even paler than they were and the difference between the blue iris and the dark pupil was astonishing to Teddy at such close range. Wavering between conscious and unconscious, she thought, he looks exactly like a Husky dog. "How did you get here?" she demanded, struggling to sit up. She realized she was in a car, she remembered the smell of leather and then sank back with her hand over her eyes. How did I get here?

"Tell me where you live," Vittorio was saying. He'd dropped her at the market before. "I'll take you home."

"Piazza Benedetto Cairoli, number....oh, god, I don't know where I live," she moaned. "It's green. The door is green." She whimpered. "And tall." She halfway sat up and tried to pull her short skirt over her knees and then she pushed the hair out of her face and wondered if she'd just been sick or was just about to be.

"Don't worry. We'll find it."

Teddy rested her chin on the open window frame as the silver Lamborghini cruised slowly over the narrow cobblestoned street. "That one." Vittorio patted her on the back. "Brava," he said and she moaned again.

He parked easily and went around to help her out. Luckily, her shoulder strap bag had been looped around her neck-protection against the purse snatching motorscooter thieves. In Harry's Bar? thought Vittorio as he unzipped it and began to look for the keys. A silver compact, two lipsticks. a bottle of purple nail polish. Ugh, he thought. A kleenex, some old bus tickets, an address book and a Swiss army knife. No keys. "Teddy," he said firmly. "Where are your keys?" Her eyes were closed but she was sitting up which was progress. She heard him and pulled up her skirt. Two keys were safety- pinned to a black lace petticoat. She'd lost one set already and decided she probably wouldn't lose her petticoat. Vittorio fumbled with the pin trying not to touch the lean suntanned thigh.

The minute he unlocked the door of her apartment Teddy ran to the bathroom and was very sick. She was too weak to flush the toilet, too weak to brush her teeth and passed out on the bathroom rug in a foetal position. "Oh, no," she whined when he picked her up and held her over the sink like a rag doll. Vittorio had taken off his jacket and tie and rolled up the sleeves of his pale blue shirt. He wet the washcloth and washed her face as if she were a child as she begged him to go away. "Oh, please. I can't have anyone see me like-"

"No. I'm not going away until you're sober enough to listen to me."

Teddy focused on his face. She was now sitting up on the couch bare- footed. "I have to brush my teeth," she said and walked slowly towards the bathroom. Teddy felt herself sobering quickly. What have I done? she wondered. Vittorio in my apartment. I threw up. Not on him, at least. I was at Harry's Bar. She ran hot water and washed her face and hands. She brushed her teeth twice and then her tangled hair. Teddy looked down at the black dress and saw no spots and besides what would I put on anyway? went through her mind. Her creme silk bathrobe hung over the back of the door on a padded silk hanger, but it weighed about as much as a spiderweb. No. The dress, she decided, stays.

"Feeling better?" Vittorio was sitting on one of the Egyptian throne chairs, looking totally at home. But he always does, doesn't he,thought Teddy. Mr. Cool. And he had to watch me get sick.

She nodded. "Thank you. I can manage now. Thanks." She wondered why he didn't stand up and go home. Remembering her manners she waved at the liquor bottles on the hammered brass tray. "Feel free to make yourself a drink. Wine is in the fridge." She felt weak. "I think I'II have a glass of water."

He poured the aqua minerale into a wine glass and handed it to her and she nodded, "Grazie." He sat down again and leaned forward. His voice was stern. "Do you know who you were with at Harry's Bar?"

Teddy shrugged. She didn't like the way he was talking to her. "Sure, I do. Myron what's his name."

"Do you use coke, Teddy?"

"No! Of course not!" she erupted. "But what if I did? What are you being like this for?"

"Because you were with one of the biggest—" Vittorio was angry. "Myron Firestone can't make a phone call or sign a memo or pick out his tie in the morning without snorting coke. What do you think that means for you ? When you're too drunk to know where you are? When you're too drunk to notice his hands all over you? When you're too drunk to—"

"Stop it!" she shouted at him. "Get out of here! Just go away!" At that moment her eyes lit on the green and white plane ticket on the table behind his head. Teddy remembered why she'd been drinking. Her hands clutched the stem of the wine goblet as she thought of the last three days. She hardly heard the crack of breaking glass, she hardly felt the pain.

"I think this is the last. Hold still." Vittorio's white hair shone in the lamplight. Teddy's open palm was on his lap which had been spread with a dark blue towel. He put the tweezers down and held her by the wrist. "Now, let me look one last time." He turned her hand back and forth under the light. "Do you feel that it's all out?"

Teddy nodded. She didn't trust herself to speak. He looked at her face. "Did I hurt you that much?" Her brown eyes were filled with tears. She shook her head again and her blond hair moved on her shoulders. "Iodine. In the bathroom?" He stood up and left the room. Laying the towel on the coffee table he took her hand again. "This'll burn, but I'll be fast. Just don't move. I'll blow on it." Teddy obediently put her hand palm up on the table and allowed him to put the stinging rust-colored antiseptic on all the little cuts. Then Principe Vittorio della Santini Venturini leaned forward and blew. "Okay now?" She nodded. Teddy suddenly looked very small to him. "When did you last have food?" It was the kind of question Teddy asked. "I don't know. Probably today."

"If I make spaghetti will you eat it?" Teddy nodded and he stood up and hesitated. "I know this must be a line in an old American film, but I'll say it anyway. Would you point the way to the kitchen?" Teddy did and then she leaned back on the Tunisian blanket and tried not to think.

"I'd like a glass of wine, too," she said and when he hesitated she said, "I don't have meals without wine anymore. This is Rome, you know."

They sat at the dining room table which Teddy had set with the blue plates and yellow napkins. He poured white wine for her and then spoke. "Were you going to throw that glass at me?"

She shook her head. I can't go into it again. Telling Anna was enough. "Thought I'd scare you." She took a bite. "Good spaghetti."

Vittorio was staring at her. Tears were rolling down her cheeks and she appeared not to notice. "Teddy Starbuck." When she looked up at him, he asked, "What is it?" She didn't answer, but took her napkin and wiped her face and continued to eat. "It must be hard to taste the delicate flavor of my old family recipe when you're crying." Teddy kept chewing and then gulped the wine. Vittorio put down his fork and waited. "Who lives here with you?"   Teddy looked surprised and said, "Nobody."

"That's funny. There's shaving cream in the bathroom and those look like men's shoes under the chair."

Teddy took a big gulp of oxygen and decided to stop crying and tell him.

Fifteen minutes later he had the bones of the story. "And he went out sight-seeing and he hasn't come back?"

Teddy nodded. "I saw him on Tuesday morning asleep and left the note and my second set of keys and I talked to him from the studio that afternoon. He wasn't here when I came home. Wednesday I stayed home, thinking he'd call, but he didn't and Thursday I talked to Anna who told me to calm down and today I went to the American Embassy but there was a big line at the consulate and no one could see me. I walked out and Myron what's his name was lurking in front of the Cafe Paris and he said you look like you need a drink." Teddy paused. "You know the rest."

Vittorio picked up the plane ticket. "But I don't understand. This is a one way ticket to Rome. What is this about Switzerland?"

"He said someone in New York, Red is his name, asked him to deliver something to Geneva. When Olivier found out it didn't have to be there before Friday he decided to come here first,"

"So this Red person must have given him a ticket to Geneva and—"

"It had to be that way. Olivier couldn't've paid for it."

"So he cashed it in and bought a one way to Rome and then thought he'd go by train." Vittorio was walking in front of the window. "Teddy, is there any chance he left for Geneva suddenly and couldn't tell you? That he had to leave that minute?"

"He'd call me," she said in a whisper.

"What was he taking to Geneva? Could he have taken it and planned to come back here afterwards?" Vittorio was hoping that was the case.

Teddy shook her head. "As far as I can see, he left this apartment to go sightseeing. You saw his razor and his toothbrush in the bathroom," her voice broke. "And his luggage is in the big hall closet."

"Shall I call the hospitals?" Vittorio's voice was calm.

Teddy took another bite of the now cold spaghetti. "If you think that...." She couldn't finish.

"Do you think he had his passport with him?"

"Yes. Because when he was asleep, his plane ticket and his wallet and the passport were all together on the coffee table. I put the note beside them."

"Monday morning at nine o'clock you call the American Embassy and tell them you want to know if Olivier has been reported to have had an accident. They will tell you." Teddy was thinking, not of Olivier for one moment, but a part of her brain was impressed by how well Vittorio had phrased that. Better than lots of Americans. He sounded English sometimes. Then the panicked, terrible ache began again after the seconds' respite and she swallowed and nodded.

Vittorio was putting on his suit jacket. "Go to bed, Teddy." He left her standing in the middle of the living room, barefooted with tousled hair. She was pale and silent as he closed the door behind him.

*   *   *   *   *   *   *   *   *   *   *

Saturday morning the phone rang when Teddy was in the shower. She didn't realize what the ringing was at first and then raced, dripping and slipping, down the hall to the living room. Holding it in one soapy hand she cried, "Pronto? Pronto?" and heard only a dial tone. She stood, cold and wet, over it for what seemed like ages, waiting for whoever it was to try again. Whoever it was, didn't.

At noon Teddy went to the market and bought armfuls of flowers and bags full of peaches. Then she tried on shoes and bought black patent sandals with one inch heels, bare slingbacks. Sexy, she decided as she inspected herself from the back in the shop mirror. Wonder how I lost a shoe yesterday.

Then she went home and noticed that Diane's shades were up but the windows were closed. She had gone away. Teddy was glad. One thing I don't have to think about is the two of them behind the shades together. She put on her red bikini and settled herself in her bedroom on a towel. With the balcony doors open she had several hours of bright sunlight. She drank Nastro Azzurro beer which she proudly knew translated as Blue Ribbon and ate prosciutto and cheese with her fingers. I am trying to be happy, she thought. Her hand hurt when she held the cold glass and she was reminded of Vittorio and the tweezers. He wasn't as aloof as she'd thought.

The phone rang again at three and she arrived on the third ring. No one hangs up on the third ring, she thought, but they did. Slowly, she put the receiver down wondering if Olivier were trying to signal her, were in trouble. She walked to the hall closet and opened the door. There were the two suitcases. One was the dark blue canvas duffel bag she'd seen him carry a hundred times to the gym and the other was a large Gucci suitcase. Can't imagine Olivier buying that, she thought. It's not like him. The red and green stripes were pristine. It looked brand new.

Teddy closed the door with a terrible pain in her throat. She realized she had never been so frightened before. No one she loved had ever been in danger. Her parents had died before she'd ever known them so it was secondhand sadness that amounted to melancholy on her birthday, at Christmastime, but not grief, and it was too late for fear.

She went to the kitchen and opened another Nastro Azzurro. It foamed all gold and cold and lovely in the tall glass. Then she turned on the television and watched Rita Hayworth in "Gilda." My Italian is not too bad, she thought as the credits rolled. Then what seemed to be an advertisment flashed on the screen. The camera panned in on a woman's hand as an orchestra played, then a man's hand closed over the woman's. She was shown lying on a pillow smiling, in ecstasy actually, her head moving back and forth. It was obvious that someone was making love to her. Then the camera showed the hands again. Holding onto each other. The music played on. Teddy couldn't imagine what she was watching. Then there were both faces on the pillow-a man's and a woman's in delight, in orgasm. Suddenly they became skeletons. Teddy gasped, horrified. "L'amore e ancora una cosa meravigliosa?" "Love is still a marvelous thing?" flashed on the screen. "It depends on you." Another AIDS ad. Public service. Thank you, thought Teddy and punched the television into blackness.

The weekend took a long time to end. It was on Sunday afternoon that she went to the closet for a second time and stared at the suitcases. Maybe one of them held a clue as to where Olivier was. She sat, in her green bikini this time, on the floor in the hall and unzipped the blue canvas bag. Shirts, Olivier's khaki windbreaker. She touched it almost tenderly, thinking he wouldn't leave this behind. How many times had she spattered tears on the shoulder of it way back in New York and thought gee, I'm glad it's waterproof? Teddy put everything back and zipped the bag. Then she stood and pulled the big Gucci suitcase from the closet. It was heavy. She lay it on its side on the floor and examined the little padlock.

Heidi had a bottom drawer in the kitchen jammed with screwdrivers and a hammer and nails and wirecutters and string; the lock surrendered in two minutes. "Excuse me, Olivier," sighed Teddy as she opened the suitcase. She stared in amazement, closed it carefully and then put it back in the closet and slammed the door. Then she paced around her apartment from room to room as if checking to confirm she were in fact alone. When the phone rang that evening she gasped, "Oh, it's you. Can you come? Can you? Please?"

Vittorio was there within fifteen minutes. He was wearing khaki trousers and brown slip-on shoes without socks and a green polo shirt. She'd never seen him without a suit. He'd never seen her in a bikini. They stared at each other and then she said, "I want to show you something," and he followed her into the hallway and watched her open the suitcase.

"Mio dio," he said three times. They looked at each other and then without speaking, began to count it. The entire suitcase was filled with packets of hundred dollar bills. The sheer grey greenness of it was a shock but then it was necessary to absorb the idea that beneath each bill was another and another and another making the stacks six inches deep across several square feet of suitcase.

"Would you like a glass of wine?" asked Teddy. The suitcase had been put back in the closet. Vittorio turned to look at her in the doorway. She was as unselfconscious of her body as an athlete after an Olympic tournament and stood before him in a few narrow strips of green cotton. "Si, per favore."

She returned wearing a man's blue shirt which came to mid-thigh as if she could read his mind. "Okay. Two million one hundred thousand dollars. What do we do?" She handed him the white wine and sat down across from him.

"You haven't heard from Olivier?" He hated to ask the next question. "How well do you know Olivier?"

"Extremely well," she said with determination, ready to fend off any accusation, any slur.

"He's gotten himself involved with something very big. Either he knows about the money or he doesn't. Maybe he didn't intend to make the delivery to Geneva. Maybe he did." Vittorio stopped. "But he has your apartment key. And the money is here. Someone is waiting for it. Was waiting for it the day before yesterday."

Teddy was staring at the green and white plane ticket which still lay on the coffee table. "What are you saying? That someone will come here for the suitcase?"

He nodded. "May I use your telefono?" He dialed from memory and then asked for someone named Rolando. Teddy understood only something about a door, a key, a lock, tonight. Vittorio hung up. "The lock will be changed in half an hour."

"But what about Olivier? What if he tries to come back and his key doesn't work?"

"Then he will ring the bell or he will wait for you at the bar in the piazza." Vittorio was calm. "I will wait for whoever Rolando sends. If you'd like me to. Do you think I might have another glass of wine?"

*　*　*　*　*　*　*　*　*　*　*

Teddy wasn't sure about the locksmith. A small swarthy man arrived wearing a white apron with a Rorschach of tomato sauce across the front, greeted Vittorio effusively and then put a brown burlap bag of bread down on the floor. Teddy, now in white levis and a black T shirt, watched him turn the bag upside down. "Excuse the crumbs," he smiled at her, and dumped out his instruments which clanked on the stone floor.

She gave Vittorio a look but he merely nodded at her ever so slightly which was the Roman way of saying, "Calma" without speaking a word. After a few minutes, Teddy moved into the living room and he followed her and they both sat down in Egyptian chairs. "I forgot to tell you that someone has called and..." Vittorio's face was grim. "Once may have been a legitimate hangup but the second time I'm sure they heard me say 'pronto.'"

He leaned forward. His forearms were muscular, and they looked tan. Probably looked like that all the time, thought Teddy. It was that olive skin. "Have you ever been to Switzerland?"

"No. But Vittorio, we don't know where in Ge-"

"You aren't going to make the delivery. You are going to..."

"Ho finito," sang the locksmith. He extended his hand with two new keys in it. "Vuole provarla?" he asked Teddy and she took one and inserted it in the lock. It turned easily.

"Molte grazie," she nodded. "Cuanto costa?"

He grinned, his face went pink, and he adjusted the burlap bag more comfortably in his arms. The bread went 'clank.' "Niente! Niente!" He shook hands with Vittorio as Teddy protested that she wanted to give him something. "Niente!" he smiled and closed the door. The new lock made a respectable 'click' noise behind him. "He's a friend, Teddy. Don't worry about the money."

"Well, for once it's not as if I can't afford to pay him." She glanced at the closed hall closet. "Speaking of money, what were you saying about Switzerland?"

"I think you should call the Studio and be sick as soon as possible. Then you should get on a plane or a train— Geneva's closer than Zurich though it doesn't matter which city- and open a bank account. Put the money in and wait."

"Wait? Wait for what?"

"I don't know. For someone to claim it. Which might never happen. Wait for Olivier to come back." Which might never happen, either, is what he kept to himself.

"Do you think he will?" Her voice was soft, wistful.

"I don't know." Vittorio walked to the door. The two bright brass keys lay on the hall table beside a silver candlestick with a yellow candle in it. "Here's my phone number at home. I'm very nearby, three piazzas away. Call me if anything happens. My parents never sleep so don't worry about waking anyone—"

Teddy took the engraved calling card. "What do they do all night if they don't sleep?"

Vittorio shrugged. "They play cards."

This news delighted Teddy. She hadn't laughed for days. Just like Daisy and Cricket with their gin marathons that went on for thousands of points from Thanksgiving to Christmas while they made fruit cakes to give away as presents. Everything happened on the kitchen table. The cards were marked with flour and once the scorekeeper pencil had been lost and old Mr. Crabtree almost broke a tooth on it.

Vittorio left her laughing in the doorway. The hall light behind her amazing hair made it look like a halo designed by Picasso. It was not the time to remind her to call the Embassy first thing the next morning. She was barefooted and tonight her toenails were orange and matched her lipstick. Teddy stood on one foot like a stork in the white jeans and laughed joyfully as he went down the stairs.

* * * * * * * * * * *

Chance sighed and tilted the air conditioning vent so that the cold air hit him full in the face. Then he looked at his watch and got out of the car. Third call this week from Ernie Melville. As if Panama's going down the drain wasn't enough. A fat woman in red stretch short shorts and pink foam curlers was behind him and gaining fast on the payphone. Chance stepped inside quickly and picked up the receiver pressing the button down. He chatted with no one for forty five seconds as the woman tapped her foot impatiently on the hot sidewalk outside. All her cellulite jiggled as she moved. When the phone rang Chance almost threw up. He managed to say "Okay," forcefully as he swallowed.

"Hey, baby, it's me, Ernie," came the voice Chance had grown to loathe.

"I know," Chance said with resignation. Christ, who else would it be at three oh five at this phone number on Sunday afternoon. "I've been making calls since we talked on Thursday and some things are not clear to me."

"Anything you wanna know, just zing it by me." Ernie sounded his usual, laid back self. He also sounded as though he were rolling a Tootsie Roll around in his mouth. He was. Sharon had convinced him that gnawing on those cigars, lit or unlit, was "debilitating" their social life. So now, for Sharon, Ernie was ruining his teeth. "Who is picking up the money in Rome for Zephyr Studios?"

"Ha! Great question, Chance! I'm glad you asked me that!" Chance winced. "Okay. Before you answer me, tell me this: why does the money appear to be coming out of Geneva instead of New York?"

Ernie was perspiring. The green silk shirt was damp under the arms. "Because it is coming out of Geneva."

"Okay. Why?" Chance was holding his temper. He told himself it was all his fault. He shouldn't trust anybody to do things. They fucked up.

"Because no one will ever know how much mo-"

"Wrong. You're a little confused, Ernie. I'm not going to waste your time with a lot of details but the whole point of Zephyr Studios is to make films that lose money."

Chance felt a churning sensation in his stomach. He could see several pounds of cellulite out of the corner of his right eye. It was vile, it made him think of butter, or churned creme. The pink rollered head turned when she saw him looking at her and her flesh began to quaver again as she tapped her Adidas-clad foot. He opened the glass door and said, "Lady, this is important, it's from Hong Kong and he called me and we're going to talk for six hours. Now will you please push off?" Chance realized he was beginning to sound like the Barracudas. All four of her chins shook in indignation. At that point, Hardware got out of the brown Mercedes and the woman glanced from Chance to the surly Mexican and then ran to her Pinto, her behind wiggling horribly in the red shorts.

"You still there?" Ernie was asking.

"Yeah. The money is supposed to come out of New York so there's a record of how much money Zephyr is losing."

"Oh." Ernie was not sure he understood or maybe Chance didn't understand. That was probably it. "For taxes, right?"

"So I found out on Friday that Zephyr money is still in Citibank and has been for five months. How do you explain that?"

"Well, I thought, gee, Chance, I thought that the best thing would be to have..." He spit the Tootsie Roll on the floor of the phone booth. It was distracting him. "And Switzerland was closer."

Chance couldn't figure out if Ernie were devious or simply dumb. What would he gain by the transaction, hummed through his head. Do I toss him out now or do I wait and watch him? If he's skimming more than I think he is and he stays, he'll panic that the party's over and try one last big grab. Or he'll cool it and plot the last big grab for later. If he's dumb this may scare him into thinking a little bit. Into being more careful. The wires were a record of how much had been sent. For once the wires were a good thing. Even Ernie must know this was on the record. "So if money is going from Geneva to Zephyr, who picks up the wires in Rome?"

"That's the beauty of this whole deal!" Ernie was delighted to be able to tell what he'd done. "I've got an Italian picking up the money at the bank every week!"

Chance was confused. "But it's not legal for an Italian to have any currency but lira and you can't wire lira from Switzerland because no lira is supposed to ever leave Italy."

"I know. I know. But I found a bank that hates the paperwork. The bank manager is a little sly one. And anyway, the money is in DOL-LARS."

"But what's the Italian involved for? Why doesn't one of the Americans, any lost soul with a U.S. passport, pick up the money?"

"Because," said Ernie. "The money doesn't get sent to Zephyr."

Take-A-Chance pulled his handkerchief from his trouser pocket and wiped his bald head very thoroughly. The sun was making the glass box hotter and hotter. Greenhouse effect, decided Chance. "Ernie, tell it to me slowly." Christ. What had this idiot done? The story was getting worse.

"I found a guy in Rome, impeccable credentials, elegant to fall down for, what a guy! And he has no job, see? Because he's loaded to the gills with dough. I mean his family is rich rich rich. So I meet him and I like him and he likes me." Ernie talked as if he and Chance were sipping whisky at the Beverly Hills Polo Lounge. Chance was considering taking off his shirt and wringing it out. "So we talk a little and we drink a little and I make nice with him and everybody in the place knows who he is. Everybody! I ask him if he wants to be in the movie business and I tell him that if he'll write the checks, we'll reimburse him every week."

Chance was pop-eyed with horror. He feared he knew what was coming next. "So this man pays the bills for Zephyr, is that it?" Chance's mouth tasted like lead.

"You got it, baby!" Ernie was ecstatic at his brilliant maneuverings. "So he goes around in his car and picks up the money IN HIS NAME every week. Meanwhile he's written checks amounting to thousands of dollars all over Rome. You know how much it costs to rent a camera? Oh, Baby, wow! And every film, low budget or low as in the cellar low costs a minimum of $800,000. But see everybody knows him and trusts him to make good." He paused. "And in Italy, your check bounces in the morning and the polizia ring your bell in the afternoon."

"What does he get out of it?" Chance couldn't believe his ears. He wished he were talking to a wrong number.

"I give him a few thousand a week. Jesus, not that he needs it! But think what I've set up. It's genius!"

Chance spoke slowly. "You're telling me, Ernie, that the tax write-off I set up two years ago —-" Chance took a deep breath and continued. "You're telling me that Zephyr Studios has ceased to exist?"

"Exactly!" exclaimed Ernie. He was ebullient." It doesn't pay taxes in Italy OR in the U.S.! The IRS-nobody-will ever find it!" He was feeling much better than he had ten minutes ago.

Chance hung up the phone and walked slowly back to the chocolate brown Mercedes. Ernie Melville. He opened the door and got in. Wheeler dealer. IQ of an onion ring. Laundering money that was clean. From the wrong bank. The wrong country. Dynamiting a legitimate tax loss.

Chance was swigging Maalox straight out of the bottle when he heard the phone ring. It woke up Hardware who snorted like a hibernating animal from the backseat. Chance stared at the ringing phone halfway expecting it to shake angrily the way they did in Hardware's cartoons. Then he screwed the top on the stomach medicine, belched, and started the car. With my luck, those garbage movies will start making money. He grimaced as he tasted Maalox in the back of his throat and turned the Mercedes onto the highway falling in with the Sunday afternoon traffic. Chance thought, just one more thing to keep from the Barracudas.

* * * * * * * * * * *

Teddy's voice was thin and childlike. "I can't come in today. Tell Anna." She took a deep breath. "I couldn't seem to call her before this."

"What did the Embassy say?" asked Vittorio. It was strange to speak to her on his office phone.

"They said—they said they'd let me talk to a consular officer and he told me that…they had his passport." Vittorio pressed the receiver to his ear. He was leaning forward in his chair holding the phone in one hand and with the other he gripped the edge of his desk: "They said he was run over and he's…" her voice faltered and then she said it quickly. "Dead."

"Teddy, are you alone?"

"Mmmmm," she nodded as tears gathered in her throat again. Other tears were literally splashing on her hands and bare arms. Like rain. Wasn't that a song, she thought absurdly.

"I'm driving back to town. I'll be there as soon as I can. Forty minutes." If I drive like Monza."Va bene?" Vittorio was standing. He held his jacket by one index finger and was about to swing it over his shoulders.

"No. Don't come. I'm all right." She was trying to be reasonable. The Teddy who cried over a bird with a broken wing. Oh, when anything at all happened to a man who wore glasses Teddy's heart splintered to pieces in her chest. And this was her adored, her darling Olivier. "It's…" she began and Vittorio waited. "It's too late. There's nothing we can do. Can you hear me?"

"Si. Si, I can hear you."

Then she asked the question Vittorio didn't want to hear. "Do you think it's because of the suitcase?"

* * * * * * * * * * *

Chapter Nine

Red Kelly was standing in the middle of his gargantuan living room talking on the phone in his gym clothes. The early morning sun was streaming in the windows which looked out over Park Avenue. The fourteenth was a good floor-good view, bright light, traffic noise reduced to a gentle hum, and not impossible to climb the stairs if there was another blackout. Red was standing on one foot and then the other. His bare legs above the thick white socks were pink and the hair on his shins glinted like copper. Shit. Shit. Shit. He fucked me up. That goddamned Ollie. Fucked me up. "Yeah. Look, I don't know what to say. I trusted him. I'll find him. I'll get the money back." Red realized he was pleading.

Roger's threatening voice changed. What was this game, wondered Red. Good cop, bad cop? Red looked at his watch. Only four a.m. in California. Yeah. Roger hadn't wanted to miss me. The faraway voice sounded reasonable, "Take my advice. Forget it. Forget your pal, forget that suitcase." Red held the phone away from his ear and stared at the smooth white plastic. "I just want you to concentrate on the future." Red looked at the Andy Warhol silkscreen of Marilyn Monroe over the fireplace. He looked at the modern sculpted steel and black leather furniture.

"I want you to be on call for deliveries every Friday from now on."
"Starting when?"
"Starting now. Today is Monday. Can you leave on Thursday night?"
"Sure. Sure I can. Roger-"

"Don't thank me yet. You're gonna be hustling your buns. You're gonna think jet lag can be fatal by the time I'm through with you."

Red Kelly was smiling. "Roger, I want you to know I really appreciate-"

"Can it," growled the voice from the West Coast. "Just don't fuck up again." The line went dead.

Red Kelly did a handspring on the emerald green wall to wall carpeting and then stood up and whooped. One phone call. I must have lost four pounds. Then he said aloud, "Down the tubes, forgiven, then in the money all over again." He grinned at his reflection in the five foot tall stainless steel sculpture that resembled a sailboat or maybe just a sail. Then his mind went back to Oliver. He could hardly believe it. It was not in character. Or was it? Did anybody know anybody? Red shook his head in amazement at the balls it must have taken to pull it off. Jesus Fucking Christ! Where did that son of a bitch go with all that money?

* * * * * * * * * * *

"Yes, yes," Teddy was nodding. "I understand. Please come in."

The American Embassy's vice consul was perhaps in his early thirties, round, balding, with a look of confused interest, as though he had a cigarette in his mouth and were patting his pockets in a futile search for matches. He had been in Rome for twelve days and had been a vice consul for the last eight. His eyes darted around the apartment with curiosity.

"Would you like a cup of coffee?" asked Teddy as they sat down in the living room.

"No, thank you, Miss Starbuck. I think the sooner we get this over with…"

She nodded. "I have to know everything you know. Please. I…" Her eyes were filled with tears. "Have you told his parents? They're in Vermont…"

"I observed the protocol of the Embassy and when the police gave us his passport I telephoned his family and then followed it with a telegram." Graham Snodgress seemed to be seeking approval. "You see, under Italian law they must, as next of kin, tell us if they want the body shipped or interred here."

Teddy's face was as white as paper.

"There has been an autopsy and an inquiry and the body was shipped..." he flipped the pages of a brand new red notebook. "Yesterday. Yes, it went off yesterday. Alitalia." He skimmed his tiny blue ball point pen notes. "Steel-lined casket." He looked up.

Teddy wanted him to go away. She wished Vittorio would come, wished the phone would ring, thought of yelling 'fire' to get him out of her living room. "Now, Miss Starbuck, as vice consul I become the provisional conservator of Oliver Richardson's estate..." She didn't know what he was talking about at first. "That means that I must take all his belongings with me and when his parents, since he was not married, can send an affidavit showing they are legally entitled..."

Teddy was hardly listening and then she heard herself saying, "Yes, that's what he arrived with. I've put his toothbrush..." She couldn't finish the sentence. How she wished she'd taken his windbreaker to keep. If only I had known.

Vice Consul Snodgress shook her hand in the doorway and managed to get into the elevator and wave good bye. If he'd had a hat he would have tipped it. Then he was gone.

* * * * * * * * * * *

"You just missed him," said Teddy as she opened the door.

Vittorio was staring into her face. She looked drained, empty, older than her years. He thought she'd been crying and had reached a plateau of sorts. Her eyes were dry.

"Who?"

"The American Embassy sent their Vice Consul to see me."

"What did he say?" Vittorio was holding a bottle of white wine in one hand and a nosegay of violets in the other.

"Not much. Oliver's on his way to Vermont." Her mouth trembled and she bit her lip. "He said he was the...let me get this right...." She smiled when she noticed the violets. "Thank you. Oh, thank you." She was near tears then. "You'd better open the wine. I think I need a glass of something."

It took a moment for her to get goblets and the cork crumbled so that held them up but at last, Vittorio asked again.

"As vice-consul he is provisional conservator of Oliver Richardson's estate and so he....he took Olivier's things."

Vittorio didn't say a word for a very long moment. Teddy sat in an Egyptian chair and thought how good the wine was. "You gave him Olivier's things." Vittorio made it a statement.

She looked over at him. He stood in front of the window in a tan suit holding his wine glass. The sunlight was behind him. Teddy's voice was soft. "I don't know what came over me. I...I took him to the closet and said 'this is what he arrived with' and opened the door. We stood there and he took the blue bag and I made a deal with myself. Do you ever do that when you're waiting for the light to change?" She went on as Vittorio stared at her. "I told myself that if he asked he could have it, and if he didn't...."

Vittorio put down his wine glass and ran to the hallway. When she heard him laughing, she started to laugh, too, and then she started to cry again.

*   *   *   *   *   *   *   *   *   *   *

Necessary. Vittorio said it was necessary. He didn't take her hand or her elbow but was simply beside her as she walked down Piazza Benedetto Cairoli and then past via Guibbonari and then another three minutes towards Campo dei Fiori. She felt cold and had pulled a black sweater over her black cotton dress. More than cold, her bones ached as if she had suddenly succumbed to flu or Aunt Daisy's rheumatism. Ailments. I'm ailing, thought Teddy.

Campo dei Fiori at dusk was so changed from the piazza at dawn that one could swear they were not the same place. At dawn it was alive with the vendors setting up their stalls to sell fish, flowers, vegetables, fruit, and even pots and pans and socks and underwear at the far end near via del Pellegrino. By mezzogiorno all the stalls have been cleared away and after mezzogiorno noisy little boys in knee pants slam a soccer ball over the cobblestones and shout at people to watch out. Dogs race around with tails in their air like pennants and cats catch the last rays of sun on the hoods of parked cars.

After the shops have closed at seven, and the crowds have thinned, the dark statue of Giordano Bruno presides over the Field of Flowers. Burnt for heresy in 1600, he stands with his cape outspread looking sadly towards what is now a very good bakery. After eight the restaurants open and their twinkling lights and the gold glow of their warm rooms make Bruno appear less alone. Their tables spill out onto the piazza and laughter and voices loud with wine and good humor take the place of the morning's fish mongers. Campo dei Fiori spans all its seasons in a day.

Vittorio was embraced by the padrone of the small restaurant in the near corner and he laughed and joked for a few moments before they were seated outside at a table with a red tablecloth. A tall carafe of wine was brought immediately and poured with much smiling then plates of warm pastries filled with meat and shrimp and cheese appeared. Teddy ordered penne alla vodka with the pasta shaped like quills and Vittorio chose spaghetti with mushrooms. "Mangia," insisted Vittorio. Several times during dinner, the owner, small with a handlebar moustache waved at Vittorio and cheerfully called, "Subito!" but he was plainly very busy with customers.

At last as Teddy stared down at the nocciola ice cream Vittorio had ordered for her, he appeared at their table. Vittorio introduced her, "Tay 0 dora Star book," and he bent to kiss her hand and said,"It is a pleasure. I am Rolando."

Vittorio began to speak to him in a very low voice. Teddy heard the word 'money' and 'valigia' which meant suitcase and then she heard her own address and 'terzo piano' which meant third floor. She was furious. What was he doing? When he had pretended to be so worried about the money? Then, as Teddy watched, he took a key from his pocket, it looked very much like one of her new keys, and dropped it onto the plate with the remains of the spaghetti. It disappeared in the creme sauce like a rock in a lake.

Rolando smiled and waved at a waiter to come and clear the table. The plates were taken away as Teddy watched in anguish. "Vittorio!" she began and he gave her one of his 'calma' looks and continued to talk to Rolando who was beginning to resemble in the half light a very eager, quite happy weasel. Suddenly Rolando looked up and excused himself. Teddy leaned forward, but Vittorio shushed her. "Guarda!" She turned to look and there were two policeman towering over Rolando who was built like a fireplug. They were nodding and smiling and he was asking about their health and they were asking about business and then he was signing a paper that one held for him.

Vittorio explained. "Rolando is Il Re delli Ladri di Roma. King of the Thieves of Rome. He is out of prison now but every night that the restaurant is open, every night but Sunday the carabinieri come and make him sign a paper to prove that he is here, that he is living an honest life."

"King of the Thieves! Great! You gave him the key to my apartment and you told him about the suitcase!" Teddy's face was flushed in the light of the candle that wavered under the hurricane lantern.

"It is the safest thing." Vittorio was definite. "In Rome, when something is stolen you come to Rolando and he will get it back for you. A fur coat, anything. Sometimes you must buy it back, but at least you can decide if the price is fair instead of losing it forever." He shrugged. Teddy thought, you maniac. You…you Roman! "Rolando is a much higher class Porta Portese. Do you know this market?" Teddy shook her head. She wanted to scream. These people are foreign. And crazy. "Porta Portese is open on Sunday morning for antiques, for bicycles, for clothes, everything you can think of. If your house is robbed on Saturday night you must go to Porta Portese on Sunday morning." He took a sip of his wine. "There you will find it."

"You're out of your mind," Teddy said slowly and distinctly. "Competely pazzo. Crazy. Understand?"

Vittorio stared at her and then shook his head. "No. I am Roman and this is Rome."

Teddy stood up to leave. "So what if I go home and the suitcase is gone? I call the police and tell them I want to report a theft but my Roman friend gave my apartment key to the King of the Thieves in a plate of spaghetti!"

"Sit down. I want you to say 'good bye' and 'thank you' nicely."

Rolando bent to tickle her hand with his moustache once again and wouldn't allow Vittorio to pay for their dinner. As they stood to leave, a short man in an apron very stained with tomato sauce nodded at her from the doorway. The locksmith. Teddy felt sick. She and Vittorio walked back to her apartment in silence. He took the elevator up with her and unlocked the door. "You've never been so safe in your life," he said. Teddy didn't answer. "Now go to sleep. Try to sleep."

His voice sounded far away. Too much had happened. He'd been with her all afternoon. She hadn't poured out all she'd been thinking but on the contrary had retreated into silence. "I feel fragile suddenly," she had said at one point. Vittorio had read the newspaper in the living room when she took a bath, when she tried to read, when she worked on an interview. Then he had insisted on this dinner. Teddy was getting used to him. He didn't seem as old as thirty five. She'd never known anyone that old, at least no one that old had ever taken her to dinner before. Dinner. Rolando. "Grazie, I think."

He almost smiled. "Don't think too much. Dorme. Sogni d'oro." The tall figure turned and went down the stairs. He never used the elevator. Teddy closed the door and stared at the shiny new lock and then thought of the suitcase in the hall closet. Sogni d'oro. Dreams of gold.

* * * * * * * * * *

They both hated to check the suitcase. Both watched the Alitalia man at the counter casually loop the little elastic around the handle; the cardboard said GVA. Then a foot pedal activated something beneath it and there was a bump noise as it bucked onto the black rubber conveyor belt, fell over on its side as though wounded, and disappeared behind a seductive little curtain of black rubber streamers. Gone.

In two hours they were standing together watching another conveyor belt go round and round. "So this is Switzerland," said Teddy. She sniffed the air. "Smells the same." Vittorio looked at her. "What are you, a dog?" he asked.

"Yes. Part dog." She said it so definitely he decided not to pursue the matter. "Beagle blood."

They stared, with the other one hundred and four passengers who had been transferred from an airport in Italy to an airport in Switzerland, as unfamiliar suitcases went round and round. Teddy glanced away, feeling almost hypnotized. She was determined to be casual. "There!" she pointed and Vittorio prepared to grab the large Gucci suitcase, but a hand from his left took it instead. "Scusi," murmured Vittorio. "Gee whiz, what's to prevent anyone from making a 'mistake,'" said Teddy.

A mistake, thought Vittorio, in the taxi after they'd dropped the money at the bank called Colbert et Cie. Teddy had insisted they each know the account number. She had insisted it wasn't her money. He had said to her in front of the bank officer, "Do you realize this is like a grandissimo checking account and I could come here and take it all if I wanted to? If you give me the account number then...."

She had gazed back at him, sitting up very straight in the leather chair with the brass nail heads around the armrests. "But you won't do that. I know you won't."

"Miss Starbuck, the Principe is making a valid point and I think you would be wise to consider..."

Then she had said it again. "He won't. I know he won't because I know him."

Vittorio ordered lunch for both of them. Teddy was wearing a black and white linen dress with a jacket over it. For once, thought Vittorio, she looks older than fifteen. Perfect Swiss bank attire. The wine came and she sipped. "I feel good, Vittorio."

"I'm glad." He allowed the waiter to pour his wine.

"I think I want whoever owns that money to come to my apartment so I can tell them what I think of them. And then when I've said it all maybe I will kill them." Teddy looked serious. "We've been over this. Remember the two options?"

She nodded "Go to the police and tell them everything and give them the money or forget we have the money but put it in a safe place and wait to see if anyone comes after it. Rolando's territory." She carefully lifted the backbone from the fish onto the little plate at her elbow. Jeremy taught me this, she thought. Vittorio was admiring her finesse in dealing with the sole. Many Americans were boorish, indelicate to say the least, and even used a handkerchief at the table. Well-bred Italians left a train compartment to blow their nose in the corridor. But Teddy Starbuck had lovely table manners. "But Vittorio, you're forgetting one thing."

He looked at her over his tilted wine glass. It sparkled in the sun and reflected the bright blue of the lake beyond the window. "Si. Cosa?"

Teddy smiled one of her brightest, most determined smiles. The expression on her face was defiant and slightly wicked. She looked like a great big tawny, brown-eyed lioness as she whispered one word. "Revenge."

* * * * * * * * * * *

"Right. Right. Sure thing. In two hours at…." Roger quickly scribbled the number on the white lid of the pizza box. He circled the '2' beside a large grease spot. "Catch you later." He hung up the phone and cursed. The hotel room was a shambles; he'd left the DO NOT DISTURB sign on the door for three days. Roger kicked a damp towel across the room towards the bathroom doorway and then sat on the foot of the bed, head in hands. He wore only yellow jockey shorts and a gold ID bracelet engraved, "Roger." Inside on the curve of metal that touched his skin was the inscription, "to darling R with love always, your Eric." Roger toyed with the links as he stared into space and then read the words. Your Eric. My Eric? He could hardly remember an Eric. He did remember Stu. Stu had left fifteen minutes ago. Roger smiled as he stared down at the bracelet. Always. As for always, always wasn't very long, was it? Roger stood up and thought, time to go home.

In two hours Roger had showered and shaved and put on slacks fresh from the plastic dry cleaners bag. His yellow polo shirt outlined his large torso like a second skin. He wore topsiders without socks and felt good. Pretty good, that is. He'd been so tense he'd had a little go with the nose candy and felt fine, ready for anything. But Christ! he worried. Could he know so soon? Should I risk telling him or should I risk not telling him? I can't win unless he'll never find out. Roger looked at his watch and then jingled the quarters in his pocket. He was standing in front of a package store twelve feet from one of his favorite phones. So I tell him and he cuts me out. I tell him and he thinks I'm an idiot. I tell him and he forgives me but watches me like a hawk for the next eleven years. I tell him and…..oh, shit. Roger bit his lip. I'm not going to tell him. But then, if he finds out, he thinks I stole it myself. Then I pay it back or he sends some Colombians to my house some night and they cut me into hors d'oevres with a chainsaw. Oh, shit, Roger whispered. Those boys from Colombia love chainsaws.

Roger picked up the phone and put the quarter in and dialed. Take-A-Chance answered on the first ring. "How are you?"

"Fine, great. Good weather huh?" Roger swallowed and hoped it didn't make a noise on the line.

"I want to know if you can double the deliveries?"

"What do you mean exactly?" Roger's voice was even. Coke was great for the nerves. Snow was a great stress reducer.

"Make twice as many. Get more couriers. Going over more often." Chance sighed. "More suitcases on Fridays." He put in. "And more of a cut for you. Sure. That's obvious."

A trap? Roger didn't think so. Chance sounded a little strung out. "Yeah. I can handle it. I might want more boys in New York but I can get them." And if one of them is a friend of a friend but we're in a bind and he loses a suitcase in the near future it won't come down so hard. Because I was doing double the usual. Roger felt better. "So two deliveries every Friday?"

"No. About five."

"Jesus! That many?"

Chance nodded. He nodded on the phone alot. He talked more on the phone than he did face to face. "Panama is a powder keg and we're trying to sidestep it altogether for awhile. So five per Friday for at least a month."

"Mmmm." Chance usually didn't tell Roger a thing. This was interesting. "Okay. Suitcases come to me the same way?"

"No reason why not. Just make sure your guys are at Kennedy for the Thursday night flight. I want to know when I wake up in Los Angeles on Friday morning that it's all in the bank."

"Right. And the same hotel in Geneva and the same frog?"

"Yep. He's been good so far. No sense in dropping him. Just make sure he knows how many couriers to expect."

That hotel room's gonna be like Grand Central Station, thought Roger. "Okay. When do we start?"

"Now. You'll have a delivery this afternoon." Chance started to hang up and then thought of something else. "Oh, and Roger, how much are you paying for the NY to Geneva trip?"

"A first class ticket, two nights at the hotel and a thousand bucks." Roger first felt a little offended that Chance would ask, would check up on him. Then he thought it was a good thing. The more involved Chance was the less he could be blamed IF anybody ever disappeared with a suitcase.

"Maybe you oughtta Jack up the perks a bit. Keep them honest. Make it two thousand and they'll want to do it again."

Roger wrinkled his forehead. Was this a hint that he knew? "Right. I will. Two thou it is."

"You need anything, just leave a message on my service." The line went dead.

Roger, known as Mr. Roper to Chance's service, hung up and wiped his forehead. He felt like driving home and taking another shower. Did he know? Could he know from the frog somehow? Roger didn't think so. He didn't think there was any link between Pierre in Geneva and Chance in L.A. except him and he sure as hell wasn't waving phone numbers around. Roger unlocked the front door of his navy BMW and slid into the driver's seat. Oh, shit. Oh, shit. I didn't tell him. Maybe the whole sweet conversation was a joke. Roger was frightened. Those boys from Colombia just loved chainsaws.

*   *   *   *   *   *   *   *   *   *   *

Vittorio sat in the silver Lamborghini reading Corriere della Sera. Eight fifteen and he was ready. This time he'd take it first. He put down the paper and with cold fingers untwisted the cap and shook out a white pill. Then he fairly threw it down his throat and told himself to take deep breaths.

Amazing that Teddy Starbuck would give him that account number. No, would insist he have it. He shook his head. Poor Olivier. His body was being sent to his parents in some little town in Vermont. He'd talked to an Embassy official and insinuated that he was Oliver's boss at Zephyr. Well, Olivier was an actor and Zephyr does make movies, if that's what you want to call them. It all fit.

The pounding began. Vittorio thought, can almost set my watch to it. In seven minutes I face that little weasel and sign the paper. I break the law once a week with someone who offends me as a witness. But I am safe for he breaks the law when he hands me the pen. Vittorio's fingers held onto the steering wheel. The heartbeat seemed triple what it should be. Any minute, any minute now, he consoled himself, the pill will take effect. He thought again of Rolando and was sure he had done the right thing to give him the key. He had links all over town. Everyone checked into that trattoria at Campo dei Fiori every night, not just the carabinieri. Si, decided Vittorio, I would trust Rolando with my life. He sighed, thinking of Olivier and of the suitcase full of hundred dollar bills. Si, with my life. But Vittorio hoped it wouldn't come down to that.

* * * * * * * * * * *

Teddy was in Salvatore's office with a chair pulled up to the side of his desk. Her head was down as she flipped through one contact sheet after another inspecting photos not much bigger than postage stamps with an oversized magnifying glass. Salvatore sipped cappuccino and talked on the phone. "Si, si. Certo. D'accordo. Subito. Ci vediamo." He hung up and Teddy smiled.

"All your phone calls sound just the same, Sally. You should just make a recording." She held the magnifying glass up as if it were a big transparent lollypop and then tilted it towards her ear. "Yes. Yes. Yes. Okay. Sure. Right away. See you." She mimicked his accent and then pretended to bang a telephone down. He made a face at her and unsuccessfuly feigned annoyance.

"When you've finished with those, there are more." He waved his hand at the large brown envelopes stacked on the table behind him. Teddy sighed. "They're all good. Really. It's hard to pick. If I wanted to send L.A. just one of the swamp creature do you think it should be this head shot or this full length where the slime shows?" She pushed the sheet towards him and pointed.

"Go for the slime every time," came the voice in the doorway. It was Charlie. "Speaking of slime, is anybody ready for lunch? The canteen's concocted another unmentionable...."

It was one o'clock. They all walked across the grass together to the other building that housed the costume department, make-up, the snack bar, more offices, and the canteen. Vittorio happened to be looking out his window.

＊　＊　＊　＊　＊　＊　＊　＊　＊　＊　＊

That evening Teddy watched the news as she did sit-ups in front of Brown Wasp. Well, his real name was Bruno Vespa, but she preferred Brown Wasp. He was a good newscaster, too. She took a long hot bath and slipped into her 'spider web' and then poured herself a glass of red wine. She couldn't decide between an old John Wayne film, "Butterfield Eight" or "Picnic." Dallas was on! Teddy leapt up from the couch and dialed Eleanor, but only her answering machine responded saying she was in London for business and would return her calls 'as soon as possible.' Teddy barked, "This is Theodora. And soon as possible means now! I want to talk. It's eight thirty in April." She hung up and looked out at

Diane's closed windows. This was the dangerous time for Teddy. It took so long to get dark and the seamless moments between Teddy's workday at Zephyr and the time she went to bed were the times she thought of Olivier. "I can't believe you don't exist anymore," she said to no one. "I can't believe I have seen you for the last time." She sat on the couch and put her hand on the wool Tunisian blanket. Right here. I saw you here. Would it have been easier to have gotten a letter from New York telling me you had died there? No. I had one last great bull session with you. She tried to smile but when her cheeks moved the tears rolled down them very quickly. And we talked about Massimo. How my life has changed! Diane and Eleanor warned me of this. It's just the way Rome is, they told her. You meet someone and you become friends. It's called Instant Intimacy in capitals, Eleanor had laughed. Then they go away and you meet somebody else. So you have a string of close friends in the span of a year, like a little girl in third grade with one best friend at a time.

Teddy sipped the wine and stared at the Egyptian goddess on the back of the chair. "I'm glad you got to come to Rome," she said aloud. "To sit there and drink a lot of wine."

The phone began to ring. Teddy put down the goblet and hurried to the table. "Pronto! Pronto!" She realized she hadn't given up hope. "Pronto!" she cried for the third time. The voice said, "Teddy, Teddy—" and then hung up. Teddy was shouting. "Don't hang up! Please!" long after the disconnection. A minute later she put the phone down and walked to the window. She felt too warm, almost feverish. Who was that? It sounded vaguely familiar. Teddy leaned on the window sill looking down at the darkening street. The street lights had not been turned on yet but the shops were shuttered, closed for the night. The Africans were folding up the scarlet cloth. One saw her and waved and she waved back. Someone knows where I live and knows my name and is checking to see if I'm home? No, they wouldn't have to speak to know that.

Church bells began to ring in the piazza. She looked over at the doorway of the bar and saw the locksmith or baker, whatever he was, staring up at her. He was wearing a blue nylon shirt and blue jeans today. He nodded at her ever so slightly and she made a small movement with her hand. Rolando. Vittorio. The suitcase is in Geneva. The voice. Could it have been the person or the people who kiled Olivier? She turned back to her living room and began to turn on lamps. I want them to call again, she thought. I want them to dare to come here. Teddy felt her face flame with anger. How could anyone hurt Olivier? I need music, she thought, as she put a cassette of Gershwin's "American in Paris" in the tape deck. The notes filled the apartment as Teddy poured herself another glass of wine. She blew her nose once more and stood up and marched into the kitchen decisively.

"Oh, Olivier," she said aloud." I wish you were here and I bet you do, too, because I'm going to make zabayon and eat it all myself." Teddy tore off a paper towel and took a vicious swipe at her tears, then opened the refrigerator and began to count the eggs.

* * * * * * * * * * *

Take-A-Chance was sitting up in bed with papers and folders piled around him on the white sailcloth bedspread. A chrome tensor lamp cast a bright light on the pages of figures in his lap. The lamp was on the chrome bedside table between a box of white kleenex and the omnipresent bottle of Maalox. Chance said aloud, "I don't feel well," and immediately felt a wave of sadness that no one could hear him. Nobody cared that he threw up twice a day. Take-A-Chance suddenly missed his mother. He blinked and put down the gold Cross pen. My mother left my father and my father left me with my aunt and then I left her. And then she died.

Chance frowned with a face that no one could remember which might have been an advantage in the life he led. He could have sprung full-grown out of the sandy Nevada earth like a cactus for all anyone knew. His personal history was so slim; for the last fifteen years it had become a past punctuated by expiring passports. But before that in school, in college, he'd simply put in the right number of days and been given his diplomas. He'd been pleasant. He went along with the group, making no waves, taking no stands, smiling enough, irritating no one. The most interesting thing about him was his name. Chance thought, I'm under stress. Stress is mental or physical reaction to an event, according to an article he'd just read. He wondered if he could swallow a bit more Maalox or if he might overdose on the stuff. White pages instead of flowers would be strewn around his body; pages listing the Barracudas' secret accounts.

Chance was listening to hear if Hardware still had the television on. A re-run of the Munsters. Canned laughter was coming from the living room. He pulled a file from under the sheet and opened it carefully. The letters on the front were in pencil: "TAC." I'm well fixed. Anytime, he thought. I can bail out anytime. It's enough. I've reached the point where I think it's enough. He used a bank in Zurich for some of it. There were the Channel Islands for the rest. Chance liked the idea of their being so close to London. London was cool, grey, mist-filled with all that fog and rain and he didn't hear of people sweating in London. He quickly skimmed the numbers, small and clear, in his own hand-writing. It was safe in dollars, safe in banks in places without dictators, without palm trees. He closed the file and put it under another stack of them near his left foot. Yes, a hotel like the Dorchester until the dollar rises a little against the pound and then cash for a place in Mayfair. Maybe Knightsbridge. Take-A-Chance wiped the thin film of perspiration from his upper lip. The air conditioning hummed from across the room as though reminding him of its efforts. He leaned back on the pillow and wished he had someone to play chess with.

* * * * * * * * * *

"Aw, Wesley! Stop! At least slow down! I cain't see nothin' the way you're goin'!"

The Barracudas reclined at forty five degree angles, in the red chair, in the blue chair. All the giant screens were lit around them. CBS news blared on the left, NBC in the center, ABC to the right and CNN to the right of that.

Wesley extended his arm and click click clicked his little remote control channel changer. The screens flashed off and on, Dan Rather drowned out Peter Jennings, and all the while his brother shouted, "I hope you sprain your thumb!"

At last, he found what he was looking for. A map of Panama, without a purple banner, flashed on the NBC screen. "There! There, you dumb bastard! Stop!" They listened in breathless silence. Wesley with arm still outstretched, Lesley with frosted can of root beer halfway to his lips. It was as though they were paralyzed with the impact of the newscast.

Then it was over and they began to scream and shout. This was normal. Noriega's pilot had just defected to the U.S. bearing tales of weapons from Cuba. "Them Commie pricks are fillin' Panama up with weapons! Jesus H. Christ!" yelled Lesley. "Planeloads of guns goin' right in under the Americans' noses! That Noriega's got some nerve when WE still own that mother fuckin' canal!"

"You're damn straight! It's ours! I'm glad Rockin' Ronnie got the sense to send in those troops!" Wesley swigged root beer and belched. "Yeah, 'cept I bet it was Nancy's idea!" "Wahoo! Couldn'ta been, Lesley! Ronnie would ask her and she'd say 'no.' She's the 'jes say no!' gal!"

They both hooted with laughter at this. Then it was Peter Jennings' turn to solemnly intone the latest from Panama. Silence in the room as they absorbed the impact. "Goddamit," said Lesley quietly when ABC had moved on to Israel. "Goddamit. The banks have been closed for over three weeks now."

"I know. And the National Guard's just an eyelash away from a coo."
"How's Chance doin'?"

"Okay, I guess. He's comin' out tomorrow to fill us in."

The national newscasts were over. The local news began. Both brothers stared at the screens around them, eyes flickering from one enormous wall panel to the next, afraid of missing something important. Then a map of the southwestern United States was blipped directly before them. They stared reverently at the man in the dark blue blazer who swirled a pointer at this 'high pressure system' and that 'low pressure system.' Then the camera panned in on Nevada. Lesley sat up, springing his E Z Boy into the upright position. "Clear skies and warm ranging from fifty six degrees Fahrenheit, that's thirteen degrees Celsius to eighty Fahrenheit which is twenty-six degrees Celsius." Lesley seemed excited by the forecast though it had been the same for roughly the past twenty days. "Wow! Hey, Wesley! You hear that?"

Wesley took a swig from his can and grunted.

Lesley was pretty keyed up. "Let's play miniature golf all day long tomorrow!"

"We cain't. Chance is comin'."

"Well, till he comes." Lesley loved miniature golf."You think he's been actin' strange?"

"Yeah, but it's jes nerves. Noriega's gettin to me, too. He's got a bad stomach. I can see that on his face."

"I don' think he takes to DooDah in a real big way either."

"Well, shit, I don' care one fuck about his stomach or whether he likes snakes or not. I jes want him to bail us out of this Panamanian pandemonium." Wesley liked the sound of that.

"You don' care 'bout ole Chance? He's been around a long time." Lesley was sincere in his question.

Just as sincere as Wesley in his answer. "He's a hired employee to work for us. We are chairmen of the board and Chance is our financial officer. He works for us. Nothin' more. No better'n Garcia or Hardware or Jose."

Lesley considered this for a moment and then said. "Yeah, I see what you mean. Only thing different-"

"Is what?" Wesley thought he'd made his point. He didn't appreciate being contradicted. Perhaps that was why he bore the machete scar.

Lesley grinned, holding the red root beer can near his lips, and said, "Chance ain't no spic."

The brothers laughed companionably and Wesley flicked the screens into blackness. From the wall speakers placed in the corners of the room came a perky rendition of "Rudolph the Red Nosed Reindeer" sung by the Lennon Sisters.

* * * * * * * * * * *

More money for more films. Those words kept coming back to Ernie Melville. Great! He looked at his watch and added nine hours then punched out the number of Zephyr Studios. "Hey, babe!" Anna always jumped when she heard the rough voice. "Is the Prince around? Yeah, it's Calfornia callin'. Tell him it's Ernie on the line."

Anna didn't speak very much English but she knew he wanted Vittorio. "Si, Signor Melville. Subito."

Vittorio picked up when the buzzer sounded. "Si. Grazie, Anna." He punched the lit button and spoke. "Buona sera." Ernie Melville was so obsequiously informal that Vittorio distanced himself without realizing it. He imagined Ernie smiling and talking as he breathed directly into his face. Another of the plastics from Beverly Hills. Ernie thought Vittorio was a snob, but what the hell—he's a prince, right? They approached each other like two dogs, sniffing for anything unusual, anything that might cause them to revise their opinions. And so far, they'd never had to change their minds.

"How's it goin'? Takin' care of the Eternal Citta for me?"

Vittorio tried to be friendly, hating himself. Hating his alliance with this man. "Everything is molto bene. Tutto bene. Fine." He paused. "And you? Los Angeles?" Ernie never called. He telexed. Vittorio was alert.

"Couldn't be better, pal. Listen! I just got the word- more money for more films! Great, huh? What I want to do is-"

Vittorio's heart begin to pound. He licked his lips and swallowed. No. It's tension, it's not really my heart. I won't die. I'll get over this. He listened to Ernie's gravelly voice and thought he sounds like that American with the big nose. What was his name? Si! Jimmy Durante. He thought of Ernie's big nose. Like a jib. An eagle nose. He thought of the eagle on the dollar bills.

"So the idea is that money comes on Fridays and I can have the wires off on Mondays. Immediate pick-up. Same deal. When the bank opens on Monday morning. Now what I want is four more films before the August holiday and that means more cameras, more crew flying in from the States and...well," Ernie was talking very quickly plainly very excited. "All that means for you is you have to write a few more checks but 'course you're covered 'cause there's more money on the way." Ernie paused and changed the white phone from one ear to the other. He didn't use his speaker phone for Italy. Usually too much static on the line. He began to unwrap a Tootsie Roll from the dozens piled in the heavy pink marble ashtray. "You with me? You get my drift?"

"Si." Vittorio could feel the vibration of his voice like a deaf person putting his finger on a tuning fork. He could only hear his heartbeat. "Certo." He swallowed. "How much more money in checks are we speaking of?"

"Ah! Four more films at a million each. That's a million bucks not lira!" He laughed and got the candy lodged perpendicularly in his mouth and panicked. It was like a stick between an alligator's jaws. Vittorio's heart was making so much noise he didn't hear Ernie's gasp of relief as he managed to extract the sticky brown log. It was plopped, streaming with drool, in the ashtray. Looks almost like a cigar, thought Ernie as he fumbled for his handkerchief.

Vittorio was trying to think. More risk. Even more risk. "I assume," he spoke carefully, "that this means…"

"Sure it does! Don' even haffta ask!" Ernie was the soul of benevolence. He was leaning back in his Eames chair and he sounded like a man leaning back in an expensive chair. "I'll see that there's more for you. Don' worry about that!"

Vittorio nodded. He could feel the pill lodged in his throat. Damn. Damn. He wanted to gasp as though waves were washing over his head. He imagined someone drawing a velvet rope around his neck. He thought of himself falling down a satinlined mineshaft. More money.

"So go to the bank on Monday mornings as usual but the wires'll be for more. A lot more. I'll telex the info about the new films tomorrow and the expense sheets will be on the way soon as I can make'em up. Okey dokey?" he boomed into the phone.

"Va bene," Vittorio managed. His wrists hurt at the pulse, his temples hurt, he felt as if the veins lay on the outside of his skin like lengths of spaghetti. "Si," he sighed. "Va bene."

*   *   *   *   *   *   *   *   *   *   *

Red Kelly was carefully patting on the white cream as he stared into the make-up mirror. Okay. Avoiding the eye area. Rest quietly for twenty-five minutes. It was already beginning to harden as he flipped off the square constellation of 300 watt bulbs and left the large black-tiled bathroom.

The phone rang as he touched his white nose to his now white knee in the forty-seventh sit up. Red, looking like an Irish geisha, stood up and answered it on the second ring.

"Oh! Oh, I'm great! Sure, I'm ready. Fuck! Three?" He scratched his head. "The same day? Friday delivery?" Red recovered quickly. He didn't like showing what he was thinking to old Roger. He'd never met Roger; Roger was just a voice but Roger had power over him. Over his money. Over whether he could live on Park Avenue or not. Roger had been bequeathed to him by Tim, a McAllister's bartender who'd moved to Toronto. What a fool was Tim, Red often thought. You could have stayed and moved to Park Avenue if you hadn't been so nervous. "Right. I'll arrange for the doorman to know. Yeah, he's good. No problem." Red hesitated. "Look, don't pick another one like the other one. I'm letting that go by because it's your first fuck up but it better be your last. Get some guys you trust. Careful guys who need the money and by the way, it's two thousand a trip now. You shouldn't have any trouble getting some out of work actors to jump at that. Just make sure they want it every Friday." Roger paused. "Not just a one shot deal. No repeat of last time." His voice was grim and meant to be.

"No problem," repeated Red. His face was beginning to feel like it had been dipped in plaster of Paris. He'd left it on too long. What if he couldn't get it off? Tomorrow morning there was the orange juice commercial audition that his agent had promised would 'open doors.' "Right. Three suitcases. Same hotel on Friday. And the envelope with the tickets and expenses will be in a brown envelope just like always. Okay." Red tenuously patted his cheek. It was hard as a rock. "Don't worry. No problem," he repeated.

"Remember," said the voice from California. "I'm giving you another chance. Be careful who you pick." Pause. "No more fuck ups." The line went dead. Red slammed down the phone and went squealing into the bathroom to wash his face.

*   *   *   *   *   *   *   *   *   *   *

Teddy could not sleep. And when she did, she dreamt of Olivier. They were the catnap dreams. She would look at the big red alarm clock on the bureau and see that it said twelve-forty. Then she was with Olivier walking up Third Avenue and they were holding hands and laughing. Teddy would open her eyes and turn over, the sheet tangled like a shroud around her, and see that it was twelve fifty-five.

How could anyone have so much money? And how could they put it in a suitcase like that and ask a total stranger to do an errand? Blackmail money? Drug money? Bank robbery money? Teddy didn't think so much of the amount that she and Vittorio had counted on the hall floor that Sunday night as much as she thought of what it looked like. All that pale green and grey. Such an expanse. Then her hands became knotted into fists and she thought, but who could kill Olivier for a suitcase full of money? Did they think he'd double-crossed them because he didn't go to Switzerland right away? Did they think he never intended to deliver it and caught up with him? Maybe they were watching him all the time? Maybe it was a test?

Teddy asked herself the same questions over and over again and nothing changed. Nothing except she was tired. And the only thing that surfaced in her mind with every dawn's early light was: those bastards! How could anyone kill Olivier? And why do they have to get away with it? Teddy turned on her side and punched the big square pillow. No. Things shouldn't go on as if nothing has happened. They should pay for what they did. Olivier can't come back. Her eyes were wet. But they should be punished. Whoever they are.

Teddy stared at the ceiling as light filled the room. Yes. I meant what I said to Vittorio in Geneva. There's only one thing he didn't take care of. She stared out the window at the pink light on the terra cotdta rooftops across the street. Revenge.

∗　∗　∗　∗　∗　∗　∗　∗　∗　∗　∗

"Tutto bene?" It was Vittorio.

"Certo. Tutto bene. You haven't been up to Swtizerland to clean out the account yet, have you?"

"No. Probably tomorrow. Will you have me sent to Regina Cieli?" Leave it the Romans to call their big prison, 'The Queen of the Skies.'

"Yes!" she said definitely. "But I might feel sorry for you after ten or eleven years and send Rolando over with keys in a plate of lasagna."

"Are you all right? Davvero? Really all right?"

"Mmmm. I lie awake at night but I'm fine. I never see you at the studio. You haven't been fired, have you?"

"No. I'm in town a lot these days. I—"

"Vittorio?"

"Si?"

"You are the only person who knows everything. Would you…could you…I wish…"

"It's almost eight o'clock. May I come for a glass of wine?"

Teddy wiped a tear away quickly. "Please. Ci vediamo."

$$* \quad * \quad * \quad * \quad * \quad * \quad * \quad * \quad * \quad * \quad *$$

The cool green smell of spring was in the apartment. Teddy had found a cache of vases, as assorted as the candlesticks, in a top cupboard over the refrigerator and had spent twenty thousand lire at the Moroccan's flower stall. Daffodils, coral roses, carnations the color of orange sherbet and white iris were in a pair of copper pots, a silver bowl and a white china urn. Teddy looked around the apartment critically. Everything in place. She wondered if she had time for a bath. Three piazzas away. She ran for the card he'd given her. Had he meant it literally or was it an expression like 'a stone's throw?' The card was on the bookshelf where she'd dropped it that night. Teddy touched the little engraved crown over his name and smiled. She didn't recognize the address. Piazza del Drago. Square of the Dragon.

Teddy decided to risk it and was neck deep in hot water when the bell rang. Accidenti, she cursed. She didn't know what it meant yet but Salvatore said it every minute. Mio dio! realized Teddy. He's gotten up the stairs! She called "Vengo subito!" from the middle of the living room and then ran into her room and pulled a white dress over her head. It was halter-topped with a short skirt and she impulsively wrapped a wide brown cowboy belt around it and sprinted to the door in her bare feet.

"Ciao!" he stepped in the hall and looked at her.

"I know I'm a mess," said Teddy. "I know it." She backed into the living room and then disappeared into her bedroom looking for a hairbrush. Why do you always look so perfect?" she called to him.

Vittorio stood at the window, not hearing her, and looked down at Nino in the doorway of the bar. The men nodded.

"Wine? Vino bianco o rosso?" she asked from the kitchen as she reached for glasses. Teddy hurried into the room on a cloud of shaving lotion. Her blond hair billowed in wide waves of gold on her bare broad shoulders. Her strong wide face was flushed.

"Sometimes you look like Natassja Kinski," he said. "White, please."

Teddy handed him the bottle and the corkscrew then began to pace the room. Don't cry, she told herself. Not again today. "What's Nino waiting for?"

He filled the glasses halfway and sat on the couch. "The last time I was here we were counting money," he said. Teddy stared at him, willing him to answer her question.

"I don't know but I think you shouldn't be alone. If Diane were here I'd say move across the street with her. I've even considered having you come home with me." Teddy raised her eyebrows. "It's only been two weeks since…" he sighed. "I've called the Embassy three different times for information but they seem reluctant to give it out. The case is closed. I've been Olivier's boss, his friend from New York and even pretended to have seen the accident."

"You don't think it was, do you?" Teddy walked to the coffee table and picked up her glass. Then she sat in an Egyptian chair and waited.

Vittorio stared at her. Her eyes were daring him to answer her. "No." He sipped the wine. "A motorcycle in front of San Silvestro. And no one got the license number and he sped away. Two men were hit and one is in a hospital in Rome but the Embassy doesn't know his name." He stared at the seascape water color on the opposite wall. "So no chance to question whoever he is." Teddy waited. "I have called the polizia and they have no name for the second person, because he had no identification. Isn't that odd? I think only if you are committing a crime would you leave your carta d'identita at home. Every Italian carries it. But not this man and now he is in a hospital and because he has no name we cannot find him. The boy on the motorino was frightened they said and ran away. An unfortunate accident."

"Was it?" asked Teddy again.

They sat in silence. Flowers and Teddy scented the big high ceilinged room. Dusk was making soft grey shadows across the ceiling, but they were paler and paler as the light faded. "You know how I felt about Olivier. I told you, maybe I never told you after all," she said softly. "He was my brother I used to tell him, except better, since we never fought and he never had to know me when I was truly awful." She smiled. "I was awful for about five years but I'm getting better."

"How were you awful? Dimmi tutto." Tell me everything.

"I just thought I was the greatest thing since miniature marshmellows and wondered when I was going to be crowned queen of the universe." Vittorio was staring at her. "Small towns can do that to you."

She grinned and looked down at the wine. "I went to New York on a dare and got a few surprises and Olivier was always right there telling me to stand up straight and not let anybody push me around just because I talked funny." Vittorio resisted the urge to tease her. She did not speak like any American he had ever known. "And I modelled and made lots of money and we used to stay up all night and watch old Bogart films and drink beer." Teddy told her eyes not to fill up with tears but they didn't pay any attention to her.

"And we jogged in Central Park and we did goofy things on Halloween. You don't have that here, do you?" Vittorio shook his head. "And we rented bicycles and raced each other all the way to Wall Street, the bottom of Manhattan," she explained, "on a Sunday afternoon." She smiled bravely, determined to make him understand. "Anyway, we were great pals. Sometimes you meet someone and you think you've known them all your life. It's that simple." Teddy spread her hands. "And whether you order pizza and sit around listening to Gershwin or it's your birthday and you get dressed to kill and go and drink champagne at Tavern on the Green...." she smiled again. "The feeling inside you is just the same."

Vittorio didn't speak. Teddy poured herself another very full glass of wine. Then she said, "I can't help it, Vittorio." He looked at her sharply. She breathed it in little more than a whisper. "I think about it all the time." She had to tell him, there was no one else to tell. "Revenge."

He reached for the bottle and grasped it by the neck. The fading light caught one shining coat of arms cufflink as he splashed wine in his glass nearly up to the top. Teddy waited for him to say something. Anything. That she was a fool. That it wasn't too late to tell the police everything. That she was to forget it. Vittorio looked at her and repeated, "Revenge." He nearly smiled but it was nearer an expression of irony. He lifted his wine glass and said, "Shall we pursue it together?"

*   *   *   *   *   *   *   *   *   *   *

Chapter Ten

Vittorio didn't know how much to tell her so he began at the end and tiptoed gingerly around the edges of all he knew. "I have an idea about the money. I may be wrong but we won't lose anything but time and airfare to Geneva to find out." Teddy nodded. "I know that money for Zephyr is wired on Monday from Geneva, from Credit Suisse. You and I know that Olivier was to make the delivery on a Friday. We don't know where he was to leave the money or even if it was to go to a bank but I know that Zephyr money used to come from New York." He stopped. "It may be a coincidence, nothing else."

"Tell me anyway."

"I know that Zephyr would wire the money the minute it was available and if it arrived from somewhere on a Monday they'd have to wait until Tuesday to wire it. So, unless they're letting it sit, and I don't think so because the interest is nothing, the money is arriving on Fridays." His blue eyes were shining. It was possible that the Gucci suitcase was full of Zephyr money. Perhaps not probable but possible.

Teddy breathed the words in a whisper. "You mean revenge would be to get their precious money away from them?"

"It would bother them." Vittorio felt a sense of lightness, of excitement. He thought of Ernie Melville, of Pertini the bank manager, of all the checks he'd written and signed with cold hands.

"But that's stealing!"

"I don't think it's their money, Teddy, or it wouldn't be going to Switzerland. It's illegal for an American to have a Swiss bank account.

It's illegal to take more than $10,000 out of the United States without declaring it. Dollars are wired to Zephyr every single week and it's illegal for an Italian to pick them up at the bank." He decided not to pursue that. Not now. "It's all so that Zephyr pays no taxes. A fraud. To steal from Italy. And money from Switzerland means Zephyr pays no U.S. taxes either." He paused. "What I don't understand is why those movies are allowed to lose so much money. That part doesn't make sense."

"But whose money WAS it?"

"My guess is drug money."

Teddy was shocked for a split second and then nodded. "I should have guessed that myself." She filled both their glasses once more. The bottle was empty. "So we'd be stealing money that doesn't exist?" He nodded as she continued. "Remember what I said in the Geneva airport?"

Vittorio frowned. "About being part beagle?"

"No!" she protested. "I said...." She hesitated dramatically. Her eyes were full of mischief. "I said it would be so easy to take the wrong suitcase."

* * * * * * * * * * *

"I insist and I am your papa!" The elderly man rapped his cane on the marble floor making a loud noise.

"Papa! Si, I know you mean well but I...."

"Alberto is arriving in twenty minutes. You must. We decided two years ago. It is necessary."

Vittorio sighed. This caused him an almost physical pain. Yes, we did agree but I can't do it anymore.

His father limped towards him and put his arm on his shoulder. "Si. La bella figura. You know what that is all about and you have since you were a very little ragazzo. And more important than ever with the

California people. They think because you are a prince you are rich. They must continue to think that."

Vittorio looked very tired. He surrendered. "Hai ragione." You are right. After all, if Ernie Melville didn't think he could handle all the expenses of the film company then he wouldn't have the job with Zephyr or the money that went with that. Which was all he had. A job of signing papers on Mondays after writing potentially bad checks all over Rome the week before. Paper tricks. Shadow boxing. An expression in English came into his mind. Oh, yes, check-kiting. "Pero, Papa, don't you think we could make do with the suits from last summer and —"

Principe Arturo shook his head and looked as if he might rap impatiently on the floor again. He was such a gentle man that the cane seemed to have been recently handed to him from offstage, a prop to lend vigor to his fatherly commands. "Vittorio," he spoke to his son almost tenderly. "We talked for so many hours before you told the man from Los Angeles you would go to the bank the first time." Vittorio hated talking about it, hated thinking about it. He couldn't decide if it were better or worse that his father knew. He was sorry he had to know and yet his knowledge was approval of a sort. "They are using you. And you are using them. But if you walk a fine line between what they think and what is real, you must continue to wear the most elegant shoes." His son managed to smile. "Was that original, Papa?"

Principe Arturo smiled and nodded. "Now the suit fitting is this morning and tomorrow morning the new shirts." The tailor and the shirt maker and the shoemaker always came to the palazzo. They had for years, for Arturo and for his father and now, for his son. And they, at least, understood. All about la bella figura, all about being a prince, and all about credit.

Cesare was shouting from the reception room. Alberto must have arrived. The two princes, white-haired and handsome, put their arms around each other and walked slowly in to greet him. Vittorio sighed. La bella figura. Wasn't it the only way?

* * * * * * * * * * *

Lou Ann had waited a week to call him, a week to calm down, a week to think. God, an accident, but the least he could do was not act as if it were solely her fault. Why had she ever slept with him once, let alone every weekend for a month? Why? Because she liked him at first. At first. She held a kleenex in one fist and then held her breath so that he would not know she was crying. Her face was dark pink and her blond hair was damp with perspiration. She wore blue jeans and a white sweatshirt and sat cross-legged on the floor in the very center of her space in Manhattan. This was a twenty-four by sixteen foot studio apartment on the corner of First Avenue and 90th Street.

Lou Ann took a deep breath and spoke slowly. "But you're the only person. How can you think…" She was panicked. It was like being on a ferris wheel when it first starts to move and your gondola tips and you realize you're airborne and it's too late to say, 'No, I don't want to do this.'

She listened, disbelieving and then when she knew she was in this all alone, she burst out, "You bastard! You horrible selfish pig!"

Red Kelly almost smiled. "Come on, Lou Ann. This is 1988. I'm actually relieved. I thought you were going to tell me you had AIDS."

Crying, she hung up the phone. She would not have his baby.

* * * * * * * * * * *

Slow closed the "N" volume of the Encyclopedia Britannica with a joyful sense of accomplishment. "Well, what do you think, Edith? From NAACP all the way to nymphomania." The rabbit surveyed him with her black as ink eyes and said nothing. She lay on his bed in the center of all those colorful Mexican stripes like a giant fur muff.

There was a knocking at the door which surprised Slow. He stood up and called, "Coming," immediately alert for a problem, for the news of some unusual occurrence. No one ever knocked at his door unless Take-A-Chance were staying for dinner. Then Slow didn't mind being included. He didn't mind sitting at the table with the skinny lawyer. But it was still mid-morning and Chance never came until afternoon. "Edith! Get under the bed! Go on, now! That's right!"

The midget walked stiff-legged in the tall red boots across the room and opened the door. It was Jose who had just returned from Las Vegas with his mail. The trip required a van and two cars when Chance wasn't around to fly them part of the way.

"Thanks." he nodded and happily accepted the latest National Geographic, eleven Wall Street Journals and the half a dozen envelopes. The man before him was so big in the khaki trousers and blue work shirt that he blotted out the light from the hallway. Jose grunted and turned to go. He, like Hardware, was not a talker. But he turned back to Slow as the door was closing and pushed it open.

The dwarf asked, "What are you doing?' but with horror he knew. Edith pressed herself against his left cowboy boot as Jose looked down in amazement.

Slow closed the door in the Mexican's astonished face. Now he suffered, too upset to read his mail. Would Jose tell his brothers? He wasn't even positive that Jose and Hardware could talk, let alone would talk.

The little man sat in his blue rocking chair with Edith in his lap and began to cry. He knew what his brothers had done to his cat all those years ago. His first pet. He remembered what they'd done to the neighbor's dog, Rusty. The police had come about that and there had been threats of reform school but they'd only been eleven and twelve and so they'd been forgiven. In a way. The neighbors sold their house and left town.

Edith pressed herself against the body which now shook with sobbing. She looked up at the contorted face as the tears fell in her black and white fur.

*   *   *   *   *   *   *   *   *   *   *

Take-A-Chance closed the file labelled 'Panama' and grimaced. Fifth day of a general strike, Noriega holding on, the nation in turmoil. He'd talked to Basil Lopez yesterday afternoon who advised him to stop everything for the time being. Stop the coke, stop the money. Sidestep the capital entirely until things were settled one way or another. Chance was taking his advice for the situation had to be critical for him to halt all the action for it meant no commission, no income. Obviously things were a lot worse than even the Barracudas thought.

He heard Hardware in the kitchen and hoped he'd go outside with his peanut butter and banana sandwiches. A minute later, like an answered prayer, he heard the screen door slam and saw the hulking figure walk slowly to the lawn furniture in the shade. Hardware was balancing a Dr.Pepper on top of a six inch mound of sandwiches on white bread.

Chance shook his head. There was no reason for him not to carry the can in one hand, the sandwiches in the other. No reason not to use a plate. Hopeless. And Jose was just as dumb, just as big. Jose had lived with Chance all winter. One oar in the water. The elevator doesn't go to the top floor. Cerebellum in neutral. Warning: chili can kill brain cells.

The bodyguard wore his light blue leisure suit which was grimy at the seams. Perhaps he should encourage him to go back to the blue jeans for they didn't show the dirt so much. Chance wondered if what Stan had told him was true. He'd heard that Hardware and Jose had been paroled after years in San Quentin. No one knew why Jose had been in but Hardware had been an enforcer for loan sharks in Chicago. His favorite for people who defaulted on their loans? Dragging them behind cars.

Chance winced and wished he could stop thinking, could turn off his brain. He envisioned a button labelled 'Stop.'

He looked out the window again to confirm that Hardware was, in fact, outside and then opened the next file on his lap. The other six lay on the white sofa and in front of him on the glass and chrome table. 'TAC.' Okay. Jersey, Guernsey, and the Isle of Man. Leave it there. All safe. The last time he'd been in New York they'd sent someone to pick up a briefcase for him. A small charge but a nice touch. $200,000 in twenty dollar bills in each briefcase. There had been three and they'd fit neatly into the suitcase and then been taken to Kennedy and then to Heathrow and then had arrived on the little flower-covered island of Guernsey before bank closing time the day after Chance had shaken hands with the courier. Chance much preferred that kind of service. Professional all the way. So far, Roger had been all right but Chance hated the haphazardness of it. But, he remembered, it isn't my money, it's the Barracudas'. I handle mine differently.

Chance closed the file. All cash. Safe places. He felt almost feverish with the heat and wondered if he should try to eat something. He would be flying out to Fort Barracuda tomorrow for another briefing on Panama. The Barracudas had taken the loss of the DC 6 astoundingly well but since then everything was tighter and getting tighter all the time.

The plane had been taken by a rival gang and not recovered but thank god, it wasn't some defector I hired or who was hired by Jason. Then I would have been blamed, as it was I was merely yelled at. They're watching me. Chance could feel it. Maybe I should stay for dinner and try to talk about other things, try to be more social. Nothing worse can happen to my stomach. And since the demise of DooDah, Garcia has stopped rat farming with a vengeance. Chance shuddered. It was disgusting to think of the cook raising rats in his spare time.

He put the folder under the others and thought, I can see it happening. The money is safe and I'm ready. At last I am mentally ready to get out of this. To start over. He heard Hardware open the screen door. I just can't visualize the last scene. I don't know how I will physically get away. Chance had the other passport, the fourth one, the one the Barracudas didn't know about, in the safety deposit box, and there was more than enough money for the ticket to be bought at the L.A. airport. He would carry no luggage, nothing from this life. What am I waiting for? he asked himself as Hardware snuffled into the room still chewing. Chance put down the 24 karat Cross pen. A sign. Something will trigger this and I'll make the escape. Maybe the long-awaited coup d'etat in Panama, he thought. Maybe something else.

* * * * * * * * * * *

"Domani. Domani e venerdi." Tomorrow is Friday. It was Vittorio's voice on the phone.

"I know it is. And I'm ready. Should we buy our tickets at Fiumicino?"

"No. I have them now." Vittorio hesitated. "Teddy, we don't want to look conspicuous so perhaps you-"

She understood immediately. "Wasn't I fine the last time we dashed into Geneva? Wasn't I absolutely great?"

Vittorio thought, a kid. She sounded as if she were asking to be complimented on how well she'd behaved at the movies. A Walt Disney film, certo. Of course. "Si. Va bene. Domani. I'll pick you up at seven."

"Seven? My God, Vittorio. I don't stay up all night playing cards!"

"We have to arrive about the same time as the New York flights, otherwise there's no point in this...." He couldn't think of the word.

"Stakeout," she chirped. "Hai ragione." You're right. "I'll be ready." Teasingly, just before he hung up, she said, "Are you nervous about this? If you are, don't be, Vittorio."

"I am not the least bit nervous," he protested with dignity but then decided her taunting voice was irresistible. "But tell me why you say I shouldn't be."

Teddy was fairly gloating. "Because you may be a Roman and know all about the King of the Thieves, but I'm American and the Americans invented the stakeout." She laughed merrily. "So stick with me, kid, and you'll be all right." Teddy put down the phone still laughing.

*   *   *   *   *   *   *   *   *   *   *

Teddy felt better this week than last. She felt she was doing something, other than grieving, other than trying to forget. Little jagged pieces came back to her at the strangest times. How disappointed he'd been about losing the part in the Francis Ford Coppola movie. It should have been his. Everyone said so. The time he'd cut his finger with the paring knife when they'd been making paella. Even the good things made her ache inside. Olivier was just beginning. His life span was seventy something as an American male and he didn't even make it one third of the way there. The subway on the way to EUR was the worst place for this sadness. The roar, the anonymity of the metal car, surrounded by strangers, was conducive to a summoning of all kinds of memories. It was as if she carried a bottle instead of her shoulder strap pocketbook and a wicked genie was freed when the train began to move.

Now she walked to her closet and surveyed the dresses and skirts critically. Vittorio was right. Yes. And he always looked so elegante beyond words. Teddy pulled a black and white striped dress off the hanger and frowned. Do I look like a six foot tall zebra? she asked herself. Yes. With several false starts she decided upon the black and white houndstooth dress with a wide belt of black patent and the new black patent sandals. She looked in the hall mirror. Vittorio never saw me in my ring phase. That is probably a good thing. She decided on

· 231 ·

black and gold cluster earrings and a black enamel bracelet with gold lion heads. She'd twist her hair up and wear make up since she was pale as a ghost in the morning.

At seven she was downstairs in front of the bar when the silver Lamborghini materialized. "Mio dio," he said when she got into the car.

"What's wrong?" she asked.

"Buon profumo. E meraviglioso." The perfume is marvelous.

Teddy smiled. Nothing like a decent after-shave to pep up one's day. "Tickets? Passport? Everything?"

"Tutto bene," he said as they purred along the Lungotevere, the road along the river. The Tiber was a silver-green streak that shone in the early morning sun. The green leaves of the plane trees were dappled in the bright light as the Lamborghini raced through the nearly empty city. And Rome, as it had for hundreds of thousands of mornings, wakened and yawned.

Two hours later beside him on the plane, she glanced down at the tan linen suit sleeve on the armrest and wanted to touch it. We have never touched each other, she realized. Except for that evening when I was drunk and he dug broken glass out of my hand. How strange for an Italian to not touch another person.

"Sì?"

"Oh, I was wondering what we'll do when we get there. What happens after we look for Red? What if he's there?"

"I look on this as a..." He nearly smiled. "A stakeout. All we will do is look for Gucci suitcases and a red haired American."

"But we don't approach him?"

Vittorio shook his head. His hair was so very white, his skin so dark, his eyes so pale. "This is only to see if what I suspect is true." When he saw Teddy's disappointment, he added, "But we'll be back." He hesitated. "You'll come back with me, won't you?"

She nodded as she fingered the gold lion heads. "I know when I see him .." she licked her lips and sadness crossed her face. "I'll want to grab him and say 'why did you do this to Olivier? Why did you send him on such a dangerous errand? What are you doing with such dangerous people? Why?'"

"It's called money, I think." Vittorio looked out the window at the Italian Alps. They must be past Milano by now. The peaks appeared to be covered with powdered sugar. The biggest pastries imaginable.

"Money? Yes, we use it instead of clamshells or pebbles but when you have what you need to live, when you have enough…." her voice lapsed into silence.

"What is enough?" he asked and she didn't answer. "What about extenuating circumstances?" His voice was pleading.

She shook her head, "I don't know. A person can only wear so many clothes, so much jewelry, and only eat so much food." She was wondering what he meant. "I can't think of anything else."

"Then what about money for fun?"

Her face came alight. "Fun? Oh, yes! That's my white mink! Yes, I understand money for fun! That's going to the movies money and money for chocolate and money for taxis when you only have to walk five blocks and money for…."

Vittorio looked at her. Sometimes the thought crossed his mind that maybe, just maybe, Teddy Starbuck wasn't entirely hopeless, after all.

* * * * * * * * * *

Red Kelly hadn't slept all night. And he'd told himself he wouldn't drink but he had had two of the small bottles of red wine and then two brandies after dinner and all that'd been after the pre-dinner champagne. I should be blizted or at least groggy, he marvelled. I'm really wired. Wired to the point of screaming. It was the coke before the movie and then the coke when the screen went blank due to 'technical difficulties.' He lifted the shade an inch and the bright light was like a needle in his eyes.

"Shit," he said aloud. The man on the aisle had his head thrown back and his mouth wide open. Red envied him. He spun the hand of his watch six hours forward and leaned back in the seat resolving to close his eyes and relax.

In a few hours it would be over. Simple operation. He'd paid the overweight at Kennedy and checked the bags. Now all he had to do was pick them up as they came around, put them on the luggage cart and wheel them through customs. Anybody stops me, I smile and say, I'm here for a long skiing holiday and my wife is coming later. I laugh and say, you know women. So many outfits per day. It adds up. And the man smiles and nods and I'm home free. A taxi to the Hotel Richemond. Hi, Pierre. My couriers and I consolidated. This is it. The whole load. Six thousand for yours truly. I then check into the hotel, into a double room, cancel the others, and later tell Roger that Dick is such a great pal we shared and that Harry——no, not Harry, nobody trusts anybody named Harry. Not even the little one in England. Robert. Good solid name. Robert stayed with his stewardess friend.

Nothing to it. Six grand, tax free. Plus those cashed in Swissair tickets. Red's eyes kept snapping open against his will. Come on, he murmured looking out the window at the snow covered Alps. The peaks looked sharp, dangerous, but then Red wasn't a skier. He didn't like the way they looked. Come on, he thought, urging the Swissair jet to go faster, let's get this show on the road.

* * * * * * * * * * *

"There he is. Don't look now, but there he is." Teddy leaned towards Vittorio and tried to keep her voice low.

"You're right. Stands out like a neon sign."

Teddy wanted to say and you, with that absolutely white hair, don't stand out? I'm the only one around here who is not being pointed at! But she didn't. She was practicing being subdued this week. Or maybe just today. She turned her head a few inches to the right once more and gave Red another look. He was tense all right. He didn't look like anyone she remembered meeting with Olivier. Good.

Vittorio stiffened at her side and she followed his eyes to the luggage carousel. A large Gucci suitcase was in sight, and then a second one. She watched Red who visibly brightened at the sight of them. He struggled with the first and then the second. God, they are heavy, aren't they? All that money. If it were in hundreds it would be two million one hundred thousand all over again. Times two. He pulled them on the luggage cart and then resumed his watch. Five minutes went by. Teddy and Vittorio pretended to be looking for their bags. "Oh, you'd think the airlines could be more efficient," Teddy said in a bored voice. Five minutes passed and then there it was. A third Gucci. Matching money, thought Teddy. Wildly chic. Vittorio felt a rush of triumph when the red-haired man reached for it and with difficulty hoisted it on top of the others which lay on their sides. They let two other people get between them and Red for the parade past Customs then watched him push the cart through. Teddy smiled at the young Swiss officer in the dark blue uniform. "Nothing to declare," she said breezily. "We came for lunch." He spoke enough English to laugh.

Red was in front of the terminal helping a taxi driver put his luggage into the trunk when they walked out into the sunlight. "Why don't we hit him over the head and hijack his cab?" asked Teddy.

"I have a better idea." He opened the door of the next taxi in line and practically propelled her into the back seat. Vittorio spoke French to the driver as he slammed the door. "What did you tell him? What did you say?" demanded Teddy.

Vittorio looked sheepish. "Follow that cab."

They did and it led them to the Hotel Richemond, perhaps the most elegant in Geneva. They watched Red get out and motion a porter to take the bags. Vittorio paid their driver and then he and Teddy walked into the lobby and sat down on a velvet loveseat. "What next?" she whispered as they saw Red and his trio of Guccis disappear behind closing elevator doors.

"I wonder if whoever he's delivering it to will come down with the luggage or will make one hundred trips with briefcases or will sit on it all weekend. What's your guess?"

"Gucci all the way," said Teddy definitely.

Thirteen minutes later, Red walked past them, looking satisfied. Six minutes after that a short man with black hair and a dark blue pin-striped suit got out of the elevator and walked to the long dark mahogany reception desk. Then he stood in front of the cashier as they prepared his bill. Three large Gucci suitcases came out of the elevator on a trolley a moment later. The young bellhop stood a discreet four yards behind him, awaiting the merest nod of a command. "Get ready," hissed Vittorio. When the man had paid and waved that he wanted a taxi, they were right behind him. All the way to Credit Suisse. Vittorio leaned back in the taxi and sighed with satisfaction.

"Dimmi tutto," demanded Teddy. Tell me everything.

"Zephyr's bank. Olivier's suitcase. All those matching Guccis. It has to be Zephyr's money. Being laundered. Right in front of your big brown eyes."

Teddy blinked. "Wow."

"Flown in from the States, stashed in Switzerland tax free, no questions asked and then wired to Zephyr to make films so bad......." Vittorio frowned. One thing he still couldn't figure out. If they weren't paying U.S. taxes and they weren't paying Italian taxes what was the point of losing all that money on movies like "Bloodsuckers from Outer Space?"

Vittorio spoke to the driver again in French. Teddy asked, "Who are we following this time?"

"No one. I told him we want the very best restaurant in town." He leaned back and the cab began to move in the Geneva traffic. "With a view of the lake," he added as Teddy opened her mouth.

"But Vittorio, we haven't really done anything yet. Don't you think it's too early to celebrate?"

He shook his head. "I'm amazed at how much we have done. You're coming to Geneva next Friday with me, aren't you? That'll be the payoff."

Teddy smiled. Her hair caught the sunlight and shone a rich shade of gold. "Wouldn't miss it for the world or even for three vampire interviews." She was silent for a moment, lost in thought, then she asked seriously, "Vittorio, do you think thieves are born or made?"

"Made. By circumstances." Maybe I will tell her at lunch. He looked at her open trusting face and wondered why she had such faith in him. Unmerited. Maybe I won't tell her at lunch.

"You trust Rolando and his…his retinue." A Diane word. "And you know they steal. Why don't you worry that they will steal from you? Or from me? They could have taken the suitcase."

"Don't you know about honour among thieves?"

Teddy shook her head. "I guess not. Until all this with Olivier I have never even known a thief."

*   *   *   *   *   *   *   *   *   *   *

Chance spotted the miniature golf course and saw that the little windmill had been rebuilt for the fifth time. Les liked to shoot curious jackrabbits with automatic weapons and an Uzi played havoc with that windmill. Chance began the descent over the white star on the black concrete. He loved the idea of being able to pilot a plane and a chopper. It was romantic, it was dashing. If I were a woman, he considered, maybe it would even turn me on. He set the machine down very gently, as always, and turned off the motor. The rotors still spun but were slowing down as Hardware grunted over the complexities of his seat belt. Chance always let him go in first. He remembered photographs taken at the scene of the Sharon Tate murder and swallowed hard. These came back to him, the scenes of a massacre in a rather normal looking low slung ranch house, and he imagined that he might be faced with that someday at Fort Barracuda. Mexico had been another life many years ago but there were men who hadn't forgotten the Barracudas.

Hardware, with a last triumphant jerk was freed; he yanked open the door as if it were cardboard and then lurched towards the house. It occurred to Chance that he could take off, could be away before anyone appeared at the window, before anyone realized. His fingers traced the grooves of the key and then abruptly he put it into his jacket pocket and opened the door and got out. For the benefit of any would-be miniature golfers, the outside speakers were blaring forth Doris Day as she sang the theme song from "Pillow Talk." So long ago, thought Chance. And no one ever imagined that Rock Hudson wasn't fascinated by the bubbly blonde, that he didn't love being kissed in the last scene.

Chance walked past the prancing flamingoes who were in a conversational group this time so Wesley had been out here last. As he prepared to ring the doorbell, the door opened. "Chance, my boy!" It was Wesley in a turquoise jumpsuit. There was nothing aqua about it. As if not to be outdone, Lesley stood behind him in a jumpsuit of orange, smiling widely. The brothers looked as if they'd been costumed by Howard Johnson. "Come on in! We've been waiting on you!"

He was led through the bare halls over the red linoleum to the map room, residence of DooDah, protagonista of all his nightmares. There in their same three chairs they luxuriated in the blast of air conditioning and considered Panama. "More troops down there today," said Lesley. "Up to six thousand now."

"Noriega's saying Panama's about to be a second Vietnam," added Wesley. He put down the bright green Sprite can and tilted his chair back farther.

"Afraid we're still in the same boat, moneywise." Chance paused. "It's there until the banks open but for the time being I've got money bypassing Panama. It's going through Mexico City, through Miami and directly from Las Paz and Medellin to L.A. Then I've got Roger getting it to New York. He has several extra couriers making the Thursday night flights to Geneva. Friday it's in. Two million roughly per suitcase."

Wesley nodded. "Sounds good to me. We haven't lost anything, have we? I mean," he laughed without mirth. "Since that fuckin' plane."

Chance shook his head. He resisted the urge to mop the dampness from his temples. His underarms were soaked. He told himself they weren't psychic, that they couldn't possibly know what he was planning. He desperately wanted to take off his jacket but didn't want them to see his damp shirt. "Every Friday money in suitcases is virtually pouring into those Geneva accounts." He used the plural on purpose and didn't mention the Italian/American film company. Ernie had fucked it up so thoroughly Chance didn't care if he never heard the name Zephyr again. And as for next year's taxes? Who cared. He wouldn't be around to figure it out. Zephyr as a tax write-off was down the tubes and Chance thought he might choke if he ever had to talk to that moron Melville again. Jesus. Chance didn't pause, just continued, "There are accounts ready and waiting for the funds from all twelve Panamanian shell companies. The Lichtenstein accounts are in order. And so far as the Caribbean goes," he shrugged."In good shape. Nothing to worry about. Cayman Islands. Bahamas. Costa Rica." Chance was ready for any questions they had. He realized he was giving an overview of every-thing which was unusual. He was tying up loose ends, giving a sum-mary. He hadn't meant to.

"Chance, how much are we taking in from the plantation?" Lesley was asking. "Still about thirty million a year?"

"Dollars? You mean dollars?"

"Yeah. Whaddya think I mean, francs?" Lesley snorted.

"Closer to thirty four, thirty five million." Is he testing me? wondered Chance. It's actually about forty-two, forty-three, but he won't know that.

"Not bad. Shame the market's so glutted and the price is so low. God, remember when we were selling wholesale for $65,000 a key and now it's down to $15,000 in Miami?"

"It's only ten thou a kilo in Miami the last few weeks," put in Chance. "Jason says there's nothing he can do except wait for a gang war."

The Barracudas were in a sentimental mood. Tab Hunter was singing "Red Sails in the Sunset." "Remember when it used to be just the Mafia? Just those Wops carryin' on?"

His brother nodded. "Shit, yes. Then the Cubans muscled in, then the Colombians and now all those Jamaicans. Those niggers scare me, boy."

"They lak to kill people. Gives 'em a kick. They are right out of a jungle." He reached for his root beer and belched.

Garcia appeared in the doorway and said, "Ready," with a strong Spanish accent. Through the open door, Chance smelled the latest stew, and tried not to screw up his face at the odor.

"You stayin' for dinner, Chance? Garcia's still going at that new recipe book. No tellin' what he's cooked up."

Rat casserole, thought Chance but he managed to smile. Rat sandwiches on rye, hold the mayo. "Sure. I don't have to be back in L.A. for awhile."

Slow was already at the table when they walked in. The midget had been pushed up too close as usual. The edge of the big white paper plate practically touched the second button of his red plaid shirt; his short legs hung down with the brown scuffed tie shoes dangling a good twelve inches off the floor. Chance greeted him with a smile and he nodded. Something was wrong with him, though. His face was pinched and he looked as if he wanted to speak, wanted to say something. Usually the midget nodded at Chance and looked down at his plate throughout the entire meal, as if willing himself far away. He never ate, never spoke.

Wesley and Lesley, a symphony of color, sat down with much puffing and groaning. Lesley was gaining weight and his girth threatened to tear the zipper right out of the middle of the absurd orange jumpsuit. The shiny red machete scar gleamed across Wesley's cheek. They both resembled very damaged kewpie dolls with pink plastic faces, perhaps dolls that a child had punctured again and again with a pencil lead.

Doris Day was singing 'Mister Banjo.' How perfect, thought Chance. The Barracudas classified women as whores or madonnas—the whores were in Vegas, Doris Day was the madonna next door.

Garcia ambled across the kitchen on his bowlegs. His pompadour had been thoroughly greased for the occasion and Chance wondered idly if it had dripped in the steaming pot as he labored over his newest five star poison. Each man helped himself with the ladle as Garcia stood beside his chair giving off an aroma in equal parts of perspiration and Vitalis. Chance thought, the last time and managed to look pleased with the portion he put on his plate.

"You oughtta get yourself out here more often for dinner," Wesley was saying. "We is plannin' a party on Friday night."

"A party?" They had no friends."What kind of party?" Chance had never known them to celebrate a holiday. They had given him another percentage of the take at Christmas last year, but he had already been helping himself so it didn't feel like a real present.

Lesley started to laugh. It was an unpleasant, gloating laugh. "Jose found out that Slow here's been holdin' out on us."

The midget turned dark blue eyes up at Chance. He looked precariously near tears.

Wesley boomed. "Yeah! Seems Slow's been keepin' a rabbit in his room! A big purty white rabbit!"

Slow swallowed loudly and looked down at his empty plate.

The Barracuda brothers were tickled with themselves. They chortled like fat little boys but the party idea was dropped. Chance turned the conversation to what Reagan would do about North and McFarlane and the Iran arms scandal. Wesley was adamant for a president is a president. "He kin pardon'em, sure as shootin.' It's his right. He's the president and he still says North is a hero to the 'Merican people."

"That Marine ain't no hero in my book," put in Lesley. "He broke the law by sending money to them rebels and now he acts proud of it. He got caught. So he oughtta shut up and go to jail. Save everybody's time. Instead he's gonna blow the whistle on Bush who's out there shaking hands and gathering up votes like pickin' daisies. Yeah, Colonel North has to go to jail." He grinned his yellow snaggle-toothed grin. "Do not pass 'go' and do not collect $200." He looked like a Jack-0-Lantern. "What dummies," he went on. "The whole crowd of 'em. For all those guys to screw up all at once is just mind-bungling."

"Who will you vote for if Bush and Dukakis run in November?" Chance was genuinely curious. The brothers devoured the television news and though uneducated, or perhaps because of little schooling, they cut through a lot of bullshit. They didn't fool easily.

"Ha! Ain't no question about it! If Bush is gonna go on like Reagan about drugs then he's got my vote."

Chance smiled. He had read and filed only three days ago a General Accounting Report printed in his Bible, THE UNDERGROUND EMPIRE by James Mills. It said more drugs were entering the United States now than entered five years ago. In November 1984, two years after Reagan announced his "bold , confident plan" to "be on the tail" of drug traffickers, cocaine imports had jumped 50 percent and heroin was more plentiful that at any other time since the late 1970's. An estimated sixty-three TONS of cocaine glutted the U.S. market in 1984. This had, unfortunately for the Barracudas, slashed the price by half.

"Sure! I lak all this 'jes say no' yacketty yak 'cause I don't think kids should use drugs. But if they want to it might as well be our drugs they use." Wesley leaned back in his chair and began to pick at a stained front tooth. The gold toothpick was shiny in the light of the bare bulb which was suspended from the ceiling. His eyes were dead looking. "Reagan's got his head in the clouds. The governments could stop drug trafficking in two days. It's a political hot potato. Look at Noriega. What a joke! They think he's gonna git on a plane and come to Miami with his hands out for the handcuffs? Nah. And why now? They've known about him for years. Everybody's known about him for years. And Mexico, same deal, right up to the President. The last one's in Madrid havin' a nice life with all his drug money in Swiss banks." He sighed at the ridiculousness of it all. "Reagan don't know his ass from a hole in the around." He put down the toothpick. "So his baby boy Bush'll be jes fine with me."

Garcia began to take the plates away. Even with the air conditioning the kitchen was like a sauna which suddenly smelled of rotting tuna fish; the white walls gone yellow with grease were damp with moisture. When the table was clear of everything save their water glasses and the paper plates had been thrown into the garbage can behind Slow, Wesley got up and went to the refrigerator. He returned, great belly preceding him, and opened a brightly colored cardboard box on the table. "Chance, you want grape or orange or Fudgsicle?"

They all of them, even Slow, sat is silence in the heat and licked their popsicles. The brothers' diamond rings twinkled as their hands moved up and down. Afterwards in a rare show of manners, the Barracudas carefully laid their little sticks on the sticky wrapping paper in the middle of the table. Slow and Chance followed suit.

"Time to go. Thanks for dinner. You call me if you need anything." Chance was standing. This could be the last time I ever see them. This could be it. Where is Hardware? Chance was perspiring heavily. The last time. The getaway he'd dreamed of. If- where was Hardware? He didn't want to ask. He was usually beside the chopper or like a shadow behind him in the hallway. Wesley and Lesley stood in the front door. Chance looked beyond them and realized the Mexican was not outside. Maybe this was what he'd been waiting for.

"Hardware's gittin' some other shoes," said Wesley. "You really oughtta come back on Friday night, Chance!"

"Yessirre bob! We gonna hav us a treat!"

"What is this party all about?" It was then that Chance felt more than saw the midget beside him. Doris Day was singing a love song. Slow's eyes were wet with tears but he didn't speak. It was almost dark and his brothers didn't even see him in the half light.

"Jose's goin to town on Friday to git us a microwave and we gonna put the rabbit in it!" Lesley was in high spirits. "Sort of a baptism. For the oven!"

Chance's stomach flipped horribly. He turned away from the dwarf beside him. What could he do? What was there to do? He had no power over Les and Wes. He had to leave this place. Now was the time. Chance walked quickly away from the house, away from the chortling Barracudas. They were round as tops in their bright jumpsuits like a cruel Tweedle Dee and Tweedle Dum. Sadists in polyester. Chance strode past the flamingoes and pulled himself into the helicopter. The key turned, the motor caught, the rotors whirled and then he saw Hardware, like a linebacker, running towards him. He allowed him to come aboard and waited for him to pant over his seat belt and only then did he begin the ascent. The last thing Take-A-Chance recognized as he floated upward in the coming darkness was a tiny figure that appeared to be looking up at him; someone no bigger than a child standing some distance from the house, alone in a barren landscape.

*　*　*　*　*　*　*　*　*　*　*

Chapter Eleven

It came in Saturday's mail. Teddy looked at the Chicago postmark and wondered who could be writing her from there. Typed. Signorina T. Starbuck. She walked slowly to the bar, greeting the Africans and stopping to bend down to pet the prancing Kiko. The Moroccan gave her a white rose when she asked how he was, was he happy it was spring. Teddy smiled and asked him to cut the stem for her; the rose was then tucked in with a tortoise shell comb at her right temple. "Grazie," she said and then "Ciao," to the little black chihuahua whose tail wagged like an electric fan.

Teddy paid for the cappuccino at the cashier's and Paolo teased her about a fidanzato. "Who gave you the flower? A lover?" Teddy grinned back. "A lover? Which lover is the question! I have so many lovers, Paolo. If they all gave me flowers at once I would have enough to fill the Colosseum." He laughed at her along with two old men in wool caps and corduroy jackets. She took the little cup to an outside table and opened the white envelope.

"Buon giorno," called Rolando's man from the other side of the doorway. Teddy looked up and said, "Ciao," wondering why she should feel surprised. He'd been at his post faithfully ever since she'd had dinner at Rolando's trattoria. "Come va?" How does it go? They nodded at one another and then Teddy pulled the single sheet from the envelope. In blue fountain pen the bottom line was handwritten. "I thought when I met you we'd be friends for a long time. Please forgive me. Love, Diane."

Teddy sighed and began to read the typed page. 'Dearest Teddy, I have left Rome as I am sure you have noticed and am staying here with my parents in Chicago. I have done a great deal of thinking since the dinner party at your house so long ago. At least it feels so long ago and not as if just a few weeks have passed. I don't know if you can ever forgive me. Or forgive what happened and I phrase it that way, because I honestly feel that I could not control the evening or what I felt or what began that night. I cry when I think of your inviting me to help you with Massimo and I cry when I think of wearing your dress and your make-up and how good you are. How trusting you were. Please believe me when I say I didn't do anything on purpose.

You know how I live—that I don't go to parties, that I don't meet men unless it's professionally in my editor's office, that I have not looked for anyone. I am not sure that I even yearned for anyone. I have pulled away from that part of life for seventeen years. In 1970 I was your age and in love with someone, engaged to be married. When he graduated from Northwestern he was drafted and we postponed the wedding until his return from Viet Nam. I won't, nor can I, tell you everything but we wrote and we were deeply in love and we had so many plans. He didn't cone back. Two weeks before his tour of duty was over he was killed by a land mine.

I gave my weddng dress to a cousin and returned all the presents and began an odyssey between New York and France, then those years in Spain and finally Rome. I have never been able to forget him or the way I felt about him. I have never wanted to replace him nor have I thought it possible. And then you invited me to dinner and you made me feel so pretty, almost beautiful....and you introduced me to your Massimo and I tried not to talk so much but I could not stop myself and I tried not to look at him, to laugh at his wit, but it felt good and I couldn't stop myself.'

Teddy's face streamed with tears. She remembered seeing Diane lean back, away from Massimo as he tried to kiss her and she remembered hearing the glass shatter on the stone floor. She skimmed the rest quickly for the letters were blurring. Diane begged her not to blame Massimo because 'he did not realize you were in love with him'. She said that he had called several times to say he was sorry but when he'd heard her voice, she'd always sounded upset and he'd been unable to speak. The phone calls, thought Teddy. Massimo. Yes. the familiar voice that one time had been Massimo.

She folded the letter as Rolando's man stood over her. "Tutto bene?" he asked and she wiped her face with the ridiculous little four inch square paper napkin and nodded. "Sto bene. Triste. Molto triste ma sto bene." She used his offered handkerchief and then tried to give it back but he said, "No. Piu tarde." He helped her up from the table and watched her walk quickly down the narrow street. I'm fine, she said to herself. It's okay. I'm fine. Diane and I can be friends again. She thought of losing someone you love and thought I've been lucky all my life until now. Olivier. Oh, Olivier.

Nino kept his eyes on her as she made her way through the knots of Saturday morning shoppers towards her building. Her head was down and she took quick swipes with his handkerchief every few steps. Her hair was loose and golden in the bright April sunlight.

＊　＊　＊　＊　＊　＊　＊　＊　＊　＊　＊

Hardware's nearly flat dark face was without expression. He stared straight ahead as if hypnotized; his massive body overflowed the dark blue tub chair in the center of the large hotel room. Chance wondered what he was thinking. Probably annoyed that I said I had a headache and he couldn't watch his Saturday morning cartoons. It's a big day for the Roadrunner.　　　Chance lay on the double bed with a pillow behind him and reached for the Heineken on the bedside table. "Sure you don't want something to drink? Anything to eat? I can call room service again." Hardware shook his bullet head. Jose had given him a haircut the week before and he sported white sidewalls over each ear. Looks more like a bullet than ever, thought Chance. Not one hair on the sides for wind resistance. He remembered how he'd come running for the plane the night before, like a bull charging. I could have left him, was the thought that nagged Chance. Why didn't I? Chance swigged the beer out of the green bottle and swallowed. Wasn't the time. Something was wrong. Time. He looked at his expensive watch. Nine oh five. Could be here all day if the flights from Mexico City are late. More mules with more suitcases of money. Chance decided he would finish his dealings with the Barracudas the right way…a way that would make them hesitate to come after him. He would do what no one else had. He would play fair in the last inning, leave them all the account numbers, all the banks neatly listed and the names of the men he dealt with. How they got in touch with them, how they kept the ball rolling was their problem. But they were nothing if not smart; after all, they'd had to teach him so much in the beginning.

Maybe they'd let me go if I did it that way, reflected Chance. He knew how they hated to be cheated, hated to be made fools of. That put blood in their eyes, that got them on the phone in the middle of the night and made them give orders to 'erase ' people. He wondered if they'd call Greaser Paul in Nuevo Laredo or if they'd go for someone they'd known back in Tijuana. Greaser Paul would be easy to find -he practically lived at the Cadillac Bar. But they'd be helpless about paying him unless it was via money order out of Vegas with Jose doing the driving and changing cars. Well, now Hardware will be with them, too. He took another swallow of the cold beer and looked at the beer gut on the Mexican which folded over the waistband of his blue jeans. Greaser Paul must be getting a little old for these jobs, considered Chance. He felt a wave of nausea and turned to check for the bottle of Maalox. It stood, ever ready, on the table by the phone. He swallowed a belch and thought, we all are.

Chance's mind kept returning to the midget. He didn't want to think of him, hated remembering the look in his eyes across the kitchen table, the look on his face in the doorway. Chance tipped the bottle and drank the last of the beer. It didn't taste good when he thought of Slow. He kept seeing the small figure in the desert looking up at him. Maybe he hadn't been, thought Chance. Maybe I imagined he was. Chance reached for the L.A. Times and read the headlines. 'Iran Charges Iraq with Chemical Attack,' 'Summit Planned May 29,' 'Truce Talks in Nicaragua.' He tossed the paper aside. So a dwarf has problems with his rabbit. I'm sorry, but it's not my business. Chance scowled as his stomach rumbled ominously and then said aloud, "It doesn't have anything to do with me."

* * * * * * * * * * *

"May I come over for wine later? Will you have dinner with me?" Vittorio never announced himself, never said 'pronto,' or 'buon giorno' on the telephone.

"Certo. Cuando?" Teddy was in a blue and white flowered bikini that tied on the sides and in back with nothing more substantial than what appeared to be blue shoelaces.

"Alle otto e mezzo? Va bene?"

"D'accordo." Teddy hung up then walked back to her bedroom and to her towel on the little balcony. Vittorio. He's not like anyone I've ever known before. He's not a Jeremy or a Massimo. He doesn't wear glasses and he isn't shy with women. Not with me, anyway. Teddy took off her top after leaning up on her elbows to make sure no one was across the street on the terrace above. She lay back again and wondered if she should tell him that the phone calls were no longer the least bit ominous. Maybe. Maybe not. She didn't want to talk about the dinner or Diane yet.

Vittorio. I couldn't pull the things I pulled on Massimo with him. He'd laugh at me. She felt embarrassed at the thought that Massimo had probably told Diane how she used to call him every day. I practically forced him to ask me to dinner. Teddy plopped the wide-brimmed hat over her face and cringed in total privacy. Vittorio is terribly handsome. What a smile when he does, and those pale blue eyes, and that dark skin and the white hair. Amazing combination. And he's so tall. She turned over on her side; her long legs werc golden brown. He's very elegant. Very attractive. Wonder why he isn't married. Wonder why he's never kissed me or even touched me. I wanted him to hold me, just as a person, the day I found out about Olivier, but he didn't. He was as comforting and good as he could be without letting me cry in his arms.

It's all right, decided Teddy. She resisted admitting that she would like him to care about her, other than the way he did. He does, though. He really does care. Of course. And that's enough, she insisted. He's a good friend and you can't have too many friends. She lay down on her back again and felt the comforting heat of the late afternoon sun. Besides, she told herself: Vittorio really isn't my type.

* * * * * * * * * * *

"Mmmmm," purred Teddy, appearing like nothing so much as a big cat, tawny and sleek, amber-eyed, bare-shouldered in the candlelight. "I like it. I've never been here before."

"It's called 'The Last Folly.' I thought it was appropriate for our plans." Vittorio's cheeks were pink with sun. His eyes were as blue as his shirt and he appeared excited. "Are you still in this? If you're not, say so. I won't be upset. I'll just do it alone. I want-"

"What do you think?" She took a sip of the champagne and it seemed to sparkle all the way down her throat. "I think I was in it when I let Mr. Consular Special Services assume there was nothing else." She pushed at the black and pearl comb above her left temple. Tonight, especially, Teddy Starbuck could have been described as 'clean-limbed,' for her slender arms were as lovely, like so much silk, as the suggestion of her breasts in the square necked black dress. She wore a narrow choker of pearls and clusters of pearls were at her ears. Her hair was gathered in combs and cascaded in waves halfway down her back. Her high cheekbones, dark eyes, the patrician nose combined to give her a rare beauty.

"I have decided we're all thieves one way or another. I am a thief now and so are you. Maybe Olivier was, too. Red is and whoever gives him the suitcases certainly is." She tilted her head to one side. "Oh, yes, I'm still in this."

"Teddy, I have to tell you something."

"I'm listening."

Their waiter appeared and proceeded to tell them the specialties. They ordered carciofini to start and he went away again. Vittorio changed his mind and when he didn't speak, Teddy did. "Do you think," she asked in a low voice, "we'll go to prison for this?"

"Don't be ridiculous!" Vittorio, the embodiment of confidence, was taken aback at the very idea. "I wouldn't imagine doing it if I thought I wouldn't succeed." He paused. "And success is not only getting the money, but getting away with it."

"Where will you live?" asked Teddy softly. Would he leave Rome?

"Oh, I'll live where I live now. But I won't work for Zephyr anymore." He stopped. "I can do as I please and not worry so much."

"What do you worry about?" Teddy stared at his face. Sadness had crossed it, his eyes stared down at the white tablecloth. He saw his napkin on the floor and reached for it. There was the clatter of his little pills though the bottle didn't fall from his pocket.

"What was that noise?"

"Nothing."

She reached over and put her hand in his shirt breast pocket. Teddy read the label in silence and then gave the bottle back. He dropped it in the pocket of his suit jacket. "What's that all about?" she asked.

"My heart beats too fast sometimes."

"When you're upset?"

He nodded and, with relief, thanked the waiter for the plates placed before them. "Teddy." He'd made a decision. "Will you come home with me after dinner?" She nodded as she picked up her fork. Not very romantic, surely he didn't…he wasn't…? He continued, "I want to show you something. Where I live. I want to tell you something."

Teddy nodded. The elegantissimo Principe was suddenly vulnerable, even tense. She'd never noticed it before. "Did you invite me here for a business meeting or for fun?"

"Lots of reasons I asked you here." He almost smiled back at her. "Why did you come?" '

"I was hungry."

He laughed when she gazed up at him wickedly.

"I hope you are thirsty, too." He sipped his champagne and then signalled the waiter. "Champagne all right with you instead of switching to wine?" She nodded. His eyes were so blue, so nearly transparent in the candlelight. It must be the candlelight, thought Teddy.

"It's good to see you smile," she said when the waiter had left their table. "Why don't you smile more often?"

He shrugged. "I told you. I worry. And maybe I can ask again why you only wear black and white or one or the other, not that you don't look…."

Teddy rolled her eyes in exasperation. She'd heard the rumors of widowhood at the studio. "It's really Olivier's fault," she began.

"Then you are in mourning?" he said.

She shook her head. "No, Olivier would prefer me in hot pink if he had his way." She liked to talk about him. It made him seem nearby. "It's because the night I left my husband Olivier was with me and he packed my bags." She hesitated. "I was a mess. I stood in the middle of the bedroom and gave long speeches. State of panic, I suppose. And good ole Olivier took over and tossed things into suitcases and somehow…" she swallowed thinking of all the times he'd been her rock. "Well, I used to have masses of clothes. And closets big enough to ride bicycles in." She spoke as one would say 'I used to have long hair but I cut it.' "Lots of clothes. And I had them arranged by color. And Olivier, while I was giving a soliloquy…." Another Diane word. "Simply tossed things in suitcases as he came to them…."

Vittorio was delighted. "I wondered if you had a black and white soul. I'm happy you do not."

"No. I don't. I think it might be green. Emerald green."

"Mine is the color of the ocean," he said seriously. "I think in colors all the time and you…when I look at you…" he didn't finish.

"I think in music some of the time. Do you ever walk around to sound tracks?" He shook his head not understanding. "Well, most of the time I walk around hearing the theme song of "Lawrence of Arabia" in my brain."

Vittorio thought, so that explains the long strides, the defiance in her posture. "For me, it's always colors. Before anything is big or small I want to know the color. That is my priority."

"How boring I must be for you!" erupted Teddy.

He shook his head as the second bottle of champagne arrived. "No, because sometimes the black and white of your clothes only makes more vivid how gold and tan and cinammon and bronze you are. You are hundreds of colors."

Teddy stared at his face and then, almost shyly, asked, "Do you paint? I saw orange paint on your thumb once."

Vittorio looked down at his wine glass. "What if I said it was iodine?"

"I wouldn't believe you. It was long after that."

He nodded. "I do. It's what I love most about my life." Suddenly he realized that wasn't true.

"Someday," said Teddy softly.

He read her mind and nodded. "Maybe someday."

They ate well and drank two bottles of champagne. Every table in the pink candlelit room was filled by the time Vittorio had asked for the check at midnight. Some Romans had just arrived for dinner and the pianist had seated himself and begun to play love songs.

Teddy excused herself and concentrated on not tilting as she maneuvered like a sailboat without a centerboard between the little tables. Once in the ladies room she pulled off her earrings and staring into the mirrored wall slapped her face. "Mio dio," she murmured. "I'm positively numb." She brushed her hair hard with the little brush in the gold evening bag. She'd read that it was relaxing and that husbands were supposed to brush their wives' hair when they were in labor. Gosh, thought Teddy. Last thing I'd want would be great hair at a time like that. Think I'd say, put down that hairbrush, please, and pass the Demerol.

Fifteen minutes later they were driving under the stone archway of the palazzo. Vittorio yanked on the hand brake and turned to her. "I...I haven't known how to tell you something for a long time now." He stopped. "And I haven't known how to ask you a question either."

"Ask." The fresh air had made a difference. The spring night smelled like peaches. In the middle of Rome, Teddy thought she was in a peach orchard.

"Why did you trust me enough to give me that account number? Why do you trust me now in this wild plan for Friday?"

Teddy shrugged. "I simply do. You won't betray me. I know you won't."

"Is it because you think I have enough money?"

"Maybe it's that." She paused and looked through the windshield at the purple flowers. He had not turned off the headlights yet. "But it's more. I don't think anyone thinks they ever have enough money. So whether you do or not, doesn't make a difference."

"What if I told you I had very little money?"

Teddy didn't answer at first. It was ridiculous. Why, look at his clothes, at the car, and he lives in a palazzo. Vittorio stared at her profile as she continued. "Maybe someone would say that I am poor. But I live well. I love my apartment and I have plenty of clothes. I'm outrageously healthy and wine is cheap and the sun is usually shining." She was reminded of Diane's outburst with Faith. Then she was reminded of something Eleanor had said. "Living well is the best revenge. Someone named Gerald Murphy said that. A friend of Fitzgerald's on the French Riviera before it was chic." Vittorio was listening to every word with great interest. She went on. "So maybe it's not how much but..." she turned to him in the dim light of the car. "But it's how much fun you have with what you have."

Vittorio didn't answer but got out and walked around to help Teddy from the car. She looked up at the sky spattered with stars. The building surrounded them in a square like a fortress or a child's arrangement of blocks. Their shoes crunched on the gravel of the courtyard as they walked towards the colonnade and then he unlocked the terreno door. Double doors were pushed open and Teddy followed Vittorio over the threshold. The ceiling was vaulted, that's all she could see, and very high above them. Marble stairs with a wrought iron railing curved upward and disappeared in the dark. Vittorio groped on a ledge until he found the white candle and then struck a match. The smell of paraffin dispelled the cool cellar scent.

"He can't ever hear me," explained Vittorio at the next door one landing up. "Cesare is very deaf. He's been with us for generations. His father and his grandfather and now his granddaughter will have her baby soon."

Teddy was confused. Why no lights? And who was Cesare anyway? He'd never mentioned him before. She found herself wanting to cling to his coat sleeve in the dark. There was so much space around them, full of darkness. It wasn't like being in a dark room, it was as if the world had gone black.

Vittorio used his key and instead of lights and warmth there was only more darkness when they walked into the large room. Large isn't the word, thought Teddy. It's the length of a football field. Another vaulted ceiling with light from enormous arched windows gave her an idea of frescoes. "My parents don't want to use electricity unless it's an emergency so they only use it for the television or for the music at night."

Teddy didn't say anything. She took his hand as he led her across the parquet floor. She liked the way it felt. Cool and strong. There were bigger than life statues on platforms here and there in the room . It was a ballroom of sorts, she decided. "Come with me. No, don't worry, there's nothing to fall over. I'm sure they're still up and would like to meet you."

Then several dark rooms later she heard it. It was a symphony. "Beethoven's Pastorale," said Vittorio as he opened the door. The room was the most beautiful Teddy had ever seen in her life. This was a palace and this was a dream. It was gold and blue and pink and angels hovered across a curved ceiling trailing scarves which barely hid their nakedness. The walls were panelled with bucolie scenes of rivers and hills, of lakes and serene landscapes. Clouds as fluffy as whipped cream were in corners up near the ceiling. And as her eyes went downward she saw the candelabra, maybe a dozen of them with six tall white candles in each. The nearly square room was quite bright with their light.

"Vittorio, caro!" called a woman in a blue dressing gown. She had purple flowers woven in her hair; they were the same as the flowers in the courtyard.

"Mama, I have brought Teddy to see you." He pulled her forward. Teddy took the soft hand in hers and smiled. The woman looked at her very carefully and then, as if satisfied, pointed to a little blue velvet chair and told her to sit down.

"Papa! This is Teddy Starbuck," Vittorio was saying. A man who looked exactly like an older version of Vittorio came forward and took her hand. He called her 'my dear' and dipped his face towards her knuckles only giving the appearance of having kissed her.

"Sit," ordered the Principessa. "We are playing bridge and I'm winning so he will do anything to interrupt the game." Her voice was teasing and loud enough for her husband to hear.

"Carissima," he pleaded. "Next you will be saying I engineered this lovely interlude!"

She laughed lightly. "Did you? Confession is good for the soul, Arturo!"

Teddy looked beyond the ornately carved table with the cards to the little black and white television set on a commode, gessoed, with scallop shell drawer pulls. Gloria Swanson was facing the camera, impassioned and pleading. The room behind her was a California 1930's version of a palace. Sunset Boulevard, thought Teddy. "Why aren't you listening to it?" she asked.

"Oh, we prefer the music, but I adore what these Hollywood stars look like. It brings back so many memories." The soothing strains of Beethoven continued.

"Teddy, I want to show you the rest of the palazzo." Vittorio had not sat down. An old man shouting "Prego!" entered the room bearing a tray with wine glasses.

"We can't stay, Mama," Vittorio was saying. Teddy followed him out of the warm candlellit chamber and into the corridor. When she closed the door behind her the man was still calling "Prego!" but the Principessa had already begun to deal the cards for a new hand.

"Teddy, may I take you home?"

She couldn't see his face but he sounded upset. Had she done something wrong? "Yes. I'll even invite you up for wine."

He didn't answer but took her hand again and they retraced their steps through the enormous high-ceilinged rooms which loomed over them filled with darkness. He didn't talk in the car and he didn't speak when he parked in front of her building. "You are coming up then?" she asked.

Vittorio nodded. They used the stairs and in minutes were in Teddy's cozy living room. Vittorio walked ahead of her, as if he lived there, turning on this lamp and that one. She took off her coat and went into the kitchen for white wine from the refrigerator. "I even have sparkling. Think we deserve it?" she called.

"Si. Si, certo. We do."

"Your mother is very lovely. I wish we'd had time to talk." Teddy sat down on the couch and handed him the bottle. She put the glasses on his side of the coffee table.

Vittorio expertly pushed the cork up as he turned the bottle and was rewarded with a little 'hiss' as the cork was expelled. The wine bubbled into the glasses and they each took one. Teddy waited for him to speak. He drank his first swallow as if he desperately needed it. "I'm not what you think I am. I tell lies."

"We all do. And how do you know what I think you are?"

"Teddy," he shook his head and put the glass down. He put his head in his hands, his elbows on the knees of his beautifully tailored suit. "You probably trusted me with that money, with the account number because you thought I had so much money I wouldn't steal from you." He still wouldn't look at her. His face was behind his hands. He has nice hands, she noticed not for the first time. Fine bones. "I have no money except what you see. You see suits and shoes and a car. That's it. The palazzo has been in our family since the 1400's. It was built by the Venturinis and if we have to starve in it we will." He sighed. "I'm sorry to disappoint you, but I must tell you. I can't let you become any more involved in the Friday thing until you know all the facts." She waited. "I went to all the best schools and when I was twenty my father said, we have no money. I was amazed. I thought he was joking. My father has never worked a day in his life. Has never had an office, has never made an appointment other than for lunch at his club. I am educated as he is.

I am not a businessman either." He stopped, wondering if this bold American would think he was hopeless.

Vittorio took a deep breath. He wanted her to know, to understand. "Suddenly there was no money? It was unbelievable. Because, believe me, there was always money. It was like air. We never gave it a moment's thought. My mother had fine clothes and a hairdresser who came to her twice a week and we had weekends at this villa or that castello and we never wondered how much anything cost." He took a sip of the wine. The bubbles rose to the top like tiny balloons in bunches. "So I...." His voice faded.

"Vittorio," she said softly. "It doesn't matter to me. I don't need to know this. It doesn't change things."

"You have to know." His voice was suddenly firm. "At least you have to know what happened beginning two years ago." He took another sip of the wine. There was pain in his face. "I went to a party. First, Romans, my friends know about me, they know about my money or lack of it. It doesn't stop the invitations or the women. Though most of the women would rather have a prince with money." He looked put upon. "But then, they, the women with money, think I am perfect." He sighed and obviously decided to drop the subject of women. "So I went to a party and someone introduced me to a man from California using my title and his ears pricked up." Vittorio's mouth was set in a frown. "It was Ernie Melville. Ah! A prince! he cried. And then he offered me a job." Vittorio's voice was nearly a whisper. "If I would consent to write the checks for the movie company then the money would be wired to cover the checks every Monday."

He took another sip of wine. "But I would have to pick up the money by signing a form at the bank which was illegal. Illegal for me, an Italian citizen, to receive dollars. I think this was to bind me, to trap me. This was the beginning and I thought it was just one time. So I went to the bank and I signed the form and I felt...I felt sick inside but Ernie Melville was offering me a thousand dollars for this." Vittorio didn't look up at her. He stared at his glass as though he could divine her reaction by the color of the wine. "I went to my father and asked him what I should do and we talked all through the night and early in the morning he said, this man from California is dirt and you are a Venturini. He told me to fool this man from California and to take his money."

Vittorio looked up at Teddy then. Her brown eyes were staring past him at the wall behind him. He continued. "My father told me that I would need the finest clothes and the best car to continue to convince this man that I had money. It all seemed to hinge upon that. The idea that I was so rich I didn't need the money." He smiled cynically. "Madness. What is it? Catch 22? So my father sent for his tailor whom we had not seen for years and he agreed and then the cousin of my father's old polo friend said, 'let me give you a new car every six months for as long as this lasts,' and the shoemaker offered hand-made shoes and my father's shirtmaker....you know the rest." He stopped. "Italians are like this. And all this was because they love my father and because being a prince means something to them more than money, more than living in a palazzo. Also," he did very nearly smile. "I think they liked the idea of putting something over on an American, especially an American who lived in Los Angeles."

Teddy smiled then. "So I'm telling you about a big game, a how do you say? A scam? I have no money. All the money I get from Zephyr goes to make me look the way I look and to pay taxes on the castle in Umbria, the palazzo you just saw, the castle in Tuscany, the little palace in Venice, the palazzo in Florence." He took another sip of wine. "All taxes. All to keep these huge buildings in our family."

"All these huge buildings as you call them, are they empty?"
Vittorio shook his head. "No one lives in them, if that's what you mean. But as for being empty, no, not exactly. They are full of Caravaggios and Titians and Tintorettos. Selling just one painting would be enough to take care of the family for ten years but..."

"Your mother and your father..."

"I know they are curious people. Eccentric, I suppose. They are happy. They never go out. They never see friends. They gossip about people as though they saw them yesterday or as if they died twenty years ago." Vittorio raked his fingers through his white silky hair. "I can't do anything but...but humor them. They want to play cards all night and sleep all day. The electricity would be minimal but my father feels he is helping me. He knows I hate Ernie Melville and Zephyr so he feels if he can save 30.000 lira a month then it is better for me." Teddy still had not spoken. Vittorio looked up at her across the table. It was late. "What do you think?" he asked.

"I'm proud to steal with you."

They lifted their glasses in a silent toast and then drank the last drops of the wine.

* * * * * * * * * * *

On Monday morning Vittorio signed the paper at the bank saying he had received the dollars. The day's exchange rate was checked and the numbers were punched into Alessandro Pertini's hand-held calculator. Another paper, with carbons, was filled out and signed, then the lire was counted. Millions and millions of lire. The obsequious manager who hovered over him had no idea it was the last time. The Principe did not smile as he shook his hand but then he never did. He went quickly to the glass capsule of a door and waited until one curved partition had closed behind him and the other had slid open releasing him to the crowded Roman sidewalk. He unlocked the car and slid into the driver's seat; in twenty minutes he had deposited all the lire to his personal account at the Banco di Roma seven blocks away. It would cover all the checks he had written the previous week.

Then Vittorio drove to Zephyr studios. He drove very fast, past the modern apartment blocks of EUR, past the sheep and the green expanses of countryside and within forty minutes was nodding at the guard and pulling through the gates as the red and white striped wooden bar was lifted.

The prince took the steps two at a time and was only at his desk long enough to draft his resignation which he instructed Anna to wire to Ernie Melville. She was astonished and held the paper in her hand, open-mouthed and disbelieving. She was still in the same pose when he closed the door behind him. His feet clattered down the steps and through the modern slate-floored lobby and in minutes the silver Lamborghini was heading back to Rome.

* * * * * * * * * * *

Teddy worked as usual trying not to think of anything other than how she could corral the director between the last scene before lunch and the shooting of the first scene after lunch. Maybe I could invite myself to lunch, she decided with trepidation. Tex Steinman was known for his terrible temper and kept his Italian secretary dabbing at her eye make-up all day long. She usually cried over the photocopy machine.

"Hey, Teddy," called Charlie sticking his head in Salvatore's office. She looked up from the pages of interview questions. "Guess what?"

"Dimmi." Tell me.

"The chief financial officer of Zephyr Studios has just checked out. Hit the road. Said 'ciao.'"

"My God! What about our salaries?" Teddy's eyebrows were raised, her brown eyes were panicked. It wasn't an act. The importance of Geneva on Friday had not really been absorbed.

It was still a game with Vittorio, even after his Saturday night 'confession.' It was a way to get them back for hurting Olivier. The money was not relevant yet. She was thinking in terms of being unfairly denied her salary. "Will they pay us? Can they?"

Charlie shrugged. "I can't stop work just in case filming starts next week for the brand new and highly improved 'Chainsaw Sisters Part III.' But if I were you, I would relax. Don't do anything yet."

Salvatore stood in the doorway. "You two have heard the news?" They nodded glumly. "Who wants to go to the canteen for a six hour coffee break?"

They both did but the coffee seemed wrong somehow and so they ended up with a bottle of white wine and paper cups sitting in the grass behind one of the soundstages. Teddy never did interview the tyrannical Tex.

*   *   *   *   *   *   *   *   *   *   *

"You got them, didn't you?" Chance spoke into the payphone in front of the dry cleaners. The sticker pleading for the chance to "Martinize" his raincoat was still affixed to the front window.

Roger stood in knee-high weeds on the edge of a Los Angeles shopping center. He leaned towards a large clear plastic half dome that reminded him of what his mother used to dry her hair under. The grass was so thick he could barely make out his topsiders. He stretched his left leg and rested one foot on the bumper of his blue BMW. His voice was happy. "Oh, boy, did I! Five? Five, this time? That's great."

"How about New York? Can they handle this all on Thursday night?"

"All set. My man has got two pals now and I'll have him dig up two more." He paused."Think they should all go on the same Swissair flight?"

"I don't see why not. Maybe you should tell him to switch the Guccis for some other bags. So they don't match. Or they could go on different flights. I don't care really." Chance was tired and he had a stomach ache. "But get everything to Pierre in time for the bank closing on Friday. That's an absolute."

"Okay. He's smart. I'll give him the options and see how he handles it." Roger was playing with his I.D. bracelet. He watched a young man with very blonde hair walk into the Shop Rite a dozen yards away. He wondered if he could follow him in and strike up a conversation. Something outrageously original like ‚'hot day, isn't it?'

"Okay, Roger. No problems?" Chance wondered why he felt like saying good bye, good luck, something in farewell. Hell, I don't even like Roger.

"Not a care in the world. Happy about the extra loot. Good times for the coke trade, right?" He laughed.

Chance hated that kind of talk. It was senseless. One never knew. That's why he hated using his car phone and forbid the others to ever conduct business on it. But the business was closing. "Yeah. Take care," he ended and hung up.

* * * * * * * * * * *

Roger hung up and dialed New York. The operator's recording came on and he was reminded that he had to put in money. He left the receiver dangling upside down and raced to the car to get the yellow plastic bowl of quarters. Such a pain, he thought as he fed the slot and heard the jangle of the money falling into the clutches of AT & T. "Hey, Red. It's me. You want to call me back or should we risk it?"

Red had been at McAllister's til three the morning before and was just now walking around. He was bleary-eyed until he recognized the voice. "Risk it. Hi! How are you?"

"Great. Believe me, I'm great. Now, look. No problem with Friday is there? Know what I mean?"

"No problem. All ready."

"Today I sent five. Should arrive late tonight or early tomorrow morning. Your doorman will get them if you're not home but I would strongly suggest you be home."

"Five?" Red breathed. He wore nothing but white undershorts and his pink freckled body seemed to flush pinker with excitment.

"Five." Roger was acting cool. Five. So what. Let him know I'm used to this stuff. No big fucking deal. "Do you have guys to take care of this? The same two from last week and two more?"

Red was licking his chapped lips. "Yeah. Five of us."

"Another thing. Maybe you should stagger the arrival. Use different flights. Another idea is to buy other luggage. Probably a good idea to do one or the other. Or both."

Shit. Aloud Red agreed. "Same deadline?"

"Right. An absolute. That's final. The most important thing. We don't want anything hanging around over a weekend. Except you and your friends, of course." Roger felt good. "Have fun."

Red thought of all that money and said, "You can count on it!"

*   *   *   *   *   *   *   *   *   *   *

Vittorio showed up at Teddy's as she returned home from work. "Oh, Vittorio!" she gasped when he came up behind her in the hallway. "I never did my interview with that real life monster Tex Steinman. He's been in a bad mood all week because he can't get his four poodles air-lifted from Beverly Hills to the Hotel Inghilterra in Rome." She shook her head. "Something about the Concorde...it won't take dogs. Not as passengers, anyway and the freight section isn't pressurized and his secretary, do you know Silvia? She is afraid as she said, 'The little dogs they will explode!'"

Vittorio helped her with her keys. "And do you know what else happened today?" She sank barefooted onto the couch. Her hair was back in gold combs with green enamel leaves on them. The white sundress was wrinkled beneath the black linen jacket; she'd put an emerald silk handkerchief in the pocket of it. "The chief, I mean the top gun, the biggest financial officer of all Zephyr just left! He resigned! Gone with the wind!"

"I know." Vittorio was tearing brown paper off enormous packages in the middle of the living room.

"You know? Were you there today?" What were those giant things? wondered Teddy. She sank back on the pillows.

"I was there long enough to resign." Vittorio winked at her.
Teddy had both hands over her mouth."You! Of course! I'm so dumb!"

Vittorio was still tearing at the paper, head down, bent over. "What is all that?" demanded Teddy.

He stepped away so she could see. "For Friday."

Brand new and very handsome, there they were. Three big Gucci suitcases.

* * * * * * * * * * *

"I hate them! I hate what they did to Olivier and I hate what they've been making you do! You can't talk me out of it!"

"I can do it alone and come back here and tell you every-"

"No, you can't! You need me!" Teddy was standing in the middle of the room now, hands on hips. The two of them had been fighting for over an hour and she showed no sign of backing down.

Vittorio stared at her. Determined, arrogant, angry. He surrendered. "Okay. I need you. Do you have any old newspapers?"

* * * * * * * * * * *

On Wednesday night Principe Vittorio della Santini Venturini had dinner with Rolando, King of the Thieves.

* * * * * * * * * * *

They've got plenty, decided Take-A-Chance. Plenty. He put in a handful of quarters and called Panama City, then Mexico City, then

Fort Lauderdale. To Lopez, to Carlos, and to Jason, the message was the same. "I'm getting out." Sweat poured down his face and under his arms in the light summer suit. "Don't send any more couriers north because I won't be in L.A. after tomorrow."

Each man wished him luck and in disbelief, hung up the phone. They all wondered the same thing: Christ! Does this mean all that money coming up from La Paz and Medellin is now mine?

Chance slid into the driver's seat of the chocolate brown Mercedes and stared at himself in the rearview mirror. Hardware's head was right behind his. I did it. It's official. Now, instead of the pipeline ending with me in California, it ends in three other cities; three other men will become richer than they'd ever dreamed possible. He started the car and swerved out onto the highway. The BeeGees crooned on the tape deck and Hardware stirred in the back seat. Not quite official, thought Chance. Not quite.

*   *   *   *   *   *   *   *   *   *   *

Edith was sitting in the middle of the bed on the brightly striped Mexican blanket regarding Slow with an intense stare. He was talking softly. "We have to go, Edith. It's the only thing to do. But it's all right. You'll see." He looked at the bookcases behind him mournfully. "I know you're just as sad to leave all the books behind as I am." Edith didn't move. Her ears were straight up, listening. He rocked in his red cowboy boots across the room, stopping to think at the refrigerator then standing beside the bureau, staring at the open bureau drawers. He dropped two plaid shirts into the small bag which lay on the floor and then his shaving equipment and his toothbrush. His watch said half past two. Nothing to do but wait until dark. He zipped the little suitcase and stood it behind the door then he took a book on astronomy down from the top shelf and settled himself in the blue rocking chair.

Edith leapt from the bed into his lap and the little chair tilted precariously. "Edith, we are going to be able to see lots and lots of stars tonight and the next night and the next. I don't want you to be frightened of anything, of a big person or a loud noise, because I will always be beside you, always take care of you." Edith's shining black eyes stared up at him and she pushed herself even closer. Slow smiled and then said once more, "It will be all right, you'll see." He turned to the index and looked up Milky Way and then found the page and began to read. The dwarf and the rabbit tipped back and forth together in that chair for the very last time.

*   *   *   *   *   *   *   *   *   *   *

Chance closed his bedroom door and then decided he never did that and it would look suspicious. He opened it and walked through the big white living room under the pretense of going to the kitchen for a Tab. Hardware was where he should have been which was on the couch staring at the television screen. Jesus.

California. Home of the twenty-four hour a day cartoon channel. Popeye was squeezing open a can of spinach and making slurp noises as it flew down his throat. Olive Oyl was shrieking for help. Chance went into the kitchen. He pulled open the cold pink can and took a sip. His stomach lurched and he wondered if he would do better with spinach. Radio to stomach, he said to himself. Radio to stomach. Come in for a landing.

Twenty minutes later he had sorted the files for the last time. All in order. Nothing to complain about. Fifteen years of moving money. And the culmination of that was in one briefcase on about a hundred pieces of paper, Chance sat down and critically examined his fingernails. Short, clean, okay. He wiped his damp forehead with his handkerchief. He still wore the trousers of the summer suit of all his phone calls, but now the jacket hung from the back of the leather and chrome desk chair. I could just grab the jacket, call a cab and go to the airport, couldn't I? I could walk out in the backyard, go through the back gate and keep walking. Why haven't I thought of these things before? Money.

Bugs Bunny screamed from the living room 'What's up, Doc?' Money. That must have been it. Maybe I never reached the point of thinking I had enough. Enough money. And I'm not calling a taxi and I'm not walking out the back gate. Chance took a deep breath and tossed the pink can into the wastebasket. No. I'm not. Maybe I wasn't waiting for enough money. Maybe I was waiting for enough courage.

*   *   *   *   *   *   *   *   *   *

"Boarding pass. Thank you, sir. First class, oh, you're right here, sir." The exceptionally pretty brunette flashed him a 500 watt smile and gestured towards his seat. Her uniform pulled tightly across her bust when she made the motion and he noticed appreciatively. Red settled himself and buckled his seatbelt. Nothing for the overhead rack. Nothing except a New York magazine on the seat beside him. And all that cash in the hold. Five suitcases. Yes, he was doing it all himself.

Swissair Flight 139 took off on time and Red dozed between champagne and dinner. Once you decide something, it's easy. One suitcase disappeared before. That fucking Oliver. I still can't get over that. I had him pegged all wrong. So now it's time for another suitcase to get lost. Not entirely my fault. After all I had to find extra people at the last minute. I did my best. He felt the corners of his dark blue U.S. passport in his shirt pocket. Anyone can open a Swiss bank account. And anyone with guts can walk in with a big suitcase full of hundred dollar bills.

Red watched as more champagne was poured then he reclined his seat as far as it would go, ignored the movie and thought about the future. Tomorrow at high noon Geneva time he would be a millionaire. A multi-millionaire.

*   *   *   *   *   *   *   *   *   *

It was dusk as the helicopter clattered over Fort Barracuda.

Everything was as always except no one was expecting him. Take-A-Chance spotted the miniature golf course and then the house and then the white star. There were no lights showing so either the blackout cloths were in place or they hadn't turned the lights on yet. Hardware grunted and looked down, not at the landscape, but at his seatbelt as though planning yet a new way to rip it open.

Why am I doing this, Chance asked himself. He was curiously calm as he hovered over the acres of sand in the clattering machine. He felt a surrealistic sense of inevitability as if he were about to be wheeled into surgery. There were a dozen other ways to take his leave, but here he was, for the last time. He set the copter down gently, almost tenderly and waited.

Hardware fumbled under his seat for the Fritos and when his big hand clutched them he was out the door and halfway to the house in seconds. The front door opened at the same instant that Chance saw a movement at the far wing of Fort Barracuda.

"Chance! Good to see ya!" It was Wesley in a powder blue leisure suit. He appeared to be wearing white loafers with the bullets tucked into the vamps. The rotors slowed and Chance could hear Doris Day singing, "Please Don't Eat the Daisies." Then he saw the movement again and realized it was Slow, the midget. And something else. He had another midget with him. It was becoming darker by the second and hard to see.

Chance got out of the helicopter thinking I didn't plan it this way, why am I doing this. He walked towards Wesley with the briefcase in his hand and said, "I'm leaving. Everything you need is in here." Hardware, Jose, Lesley were all behind Wesley, all wearing expressions of surprise. Chance turned. He knew all about the weapons, the Uzis, the target practice. Any second, he thought, I'll be ripped to pieces. Will I hear the gun first or just feel the lead tear through my back?

He saw the movement out of the corner of his right eye again and something in Chance responded. He yelled, "Come on! Hurry! Run!"

In seconds he was pulling himself into the helicopter, still expecting the bullets to begin. Five panicked seconds later he grasped Slow's hand and lifted him, cowboy boots and suitcase, off the ground and then to his amazement a giant rabbit leapt up in the air and into the plane and scuffled between the two seats.

Chance turned the ignition key and it caught—-drowning out Doris Day and the shouting. The rotors spun faster and faster and at last, seeming to take forever, Take-A-Chance and Slow and Edith all rose into the Nevada sky. There was pandemonium on the ground for the briefcase had come open and the helicopter had sucked the papers from it. Like a flock of white birds they circled zanily in the backwash of the blades as the Barracuda brothers scrambled to gather them.

They were far away. A fingernail moon was coming up over the desert when Chance and Slow and Edith at last heard the staccato echoing of the machine guns.

✳ ✳ ✳ ✳ ✳ ✳ ✳ ✳ ✳ ✳ ✳

Vittorio couldn't sleep. The white Egyptian cotton pajamas though freshly laundered were rumpled and baggy. Am I losing my mind? he asked himself. He grasped the bedpost. Teddy involved up to her pretty neck and me—I've never had a head for business! And I'm planning a multimillion dollar theft in the Geneva airport. Accidenti, he swore. Stealing in Switzerland! Of all places! Vittorio panicked. Life imprisonment maybe. Ten years of Swiss food would be enough. Mio dio! he paced back and forth at the foot of his bed. His slippers made a shhhh sshhhh noise across the marble floor.

✳ ✳ ✳ ✳ ✳ ✳ ✳ ✳ ✳ ✳

Teddy sat up in bed and turned on the light. She was bored with lying there like a dead fish. It was four in the morning of the day she was going to steal Gucci suitcases. Vittorio said he'd taken care of everything. He promised her they wouldn't be killed like Olivier. Well, that was comforting. Teddy turned off the light then got out of bed and walked to the window. She gazed across the street at Diane's dark apartment and thought of calling her in Chicago. Oh, what are you up to tomorrow? Playing tennis. Lunch with a friend. Getting my hair cut. Going to Geneva to steal some money. Flaming flamingoes, thought Teddy, as she looked out at the stars.

*   *   *   *   *   *   *   *   *   *   *

"Si. Molto bene. Benissimo." The doctor took the scissors and snipped away at the gauze. Then he took the little saw and split the cast in half. In minutes he had lifted it off and was flexing his own fingers and nodding at the patient. "Prova. Andiamo. Come questa."

The fingers moved slowly. They hadn't been broken, it was the bones on the top of his hand. The grunting began yet again behind the broken jaw. "MMMMMmmmm," he insisted. "Mmmmmmmm."

A pencil was brought and then the doctor lifted the prescription pad from the breast pocket of his white smock. The patient's fingers moved as if preparing to perform at the piano and then grasped the pencil tenuously. With great effort, great concentration he tried to mark the paper and then the pencil fell. The nurse placed it in his fingers again and once more it fell. "MMmmmmmm," he demanded and she placed it in his hand yet again. He began to print. "T E D DY STARBUCK PIAZZA BENEDETO.

He dropped the pencil as the doctor took the pad.

"Non e un nome Italiano." He tore off the page and spoke to the nurse. "Ever heard of Piazza Benedetto?" She shook her head. "No. Neither have I. I'll look it up when I get home tonight. This is the man with no identification, si?"

"Si, Professore. Niente. Arrivato tre settimane fa. Niente."

"Si. Maybe this is his family. A domani." With one last look at the young man he put the scrap of paper in his pocket and walked away. The patient made the "MMMmmmmm" noise helplessly one last time for Thursday.

*   *   *   *   *   *   *   *   *   *   *

"Pronta?"

"Si," answered Teddy. "Ready."

The two of them moved up to the Alitalia counter at Fiumicino and faced the woman in dark blue. She looked at their tickets and punched buttons on the computer for their seat assignments. "Any luggage?"

Vittorio lifted the three large suitcases onto the scales and winced. Signorina Alitalia shrugged, without even looking at the weight. "Non sono pesanti. No fa niente." She pulled the elastic of the green and white cardboard tags around the handles of one, two, three suitcases and then pushed a button. Teddy and Vittorio watched the bags lurch behind the counter, fall on their sides on the conveyor belt and disappear behind the same little flirtacious curtain of black rubber streamers.

"Our flying time to Geneva will be approximately one hour and five minutes. We will be flying at an altitude..." Teddy shut out the plastic voice on the intercom and turned to Vittorio. "So we take the train back to Rome. Then what will you do?"

Vittorio looked different today. He was wearing a white shirt and a dark blue knitted tie and a suit of such a dark navy it seemed nearly black. "I will take some of the money and go to Umbria and begin, with the workers, to repair the castle. My parents can go there for the summer. The baby can be born there."

"What baby?"

Vittorio smiled faintly. "Cesare's granddaughter is having a baby."

Teddy felt a little knot in her stomach. Umbria! I don't even know where that is but I bet it's far away from Rome. I won't see him anymore if he goes to live in Umbria. "Do you…will you live in Umbria all the time?"

Vittorio was staring out at the clouds, thinking he'd miss Teddy Starbuck. The only woman who hadn't asked him for something. She didn't care if he were a prince or not. The only woman who hadn't come after him with blood-red fingernails and bared fangs. "No. There are plenty of places to live. First, I want to get my family settled. I want them to have a life again, with friends, with more servants to take care of them. The money will make all that possible. My mother can have clothes, my father can pay all his back dues at the Caccia. His club," explained Vittorio. "And I can see that the little palace in Venice is ready for them in September and that the place in Florence has heat by next winter…" He had a faraway look on his handsome face. "It's a second beginning as if the events of twenty years ago never happened. My parents have never complained about all the money going for taxes. Suppose it seems strange to an American that they would never consider selling family property or a painting." He shook his head ruefully. "It's been difficult for my father who is quite proud but I think Mama has barely noticed. She has always loved candlelight."

Teddy felt like crying. The Vittorio she saw nearly every day, the Vittorio she schemed with, drank wine with, was already far away in another life.

They didn't speak again until the plane bumped down on the tarmac. Vittorio patted his pocket nervously and felt for the plastic tag. It was there. His heart pills rattled and he wondered if he should take one. "You're okay," said Teddy as if he had asked her. "You're all right." She impulsively took his hand in hers and squeezed it. The current of attraction surprised them both. They faced each other side by side in the airline seats and stared. Vittorio's eyes were like the sky and Teddy's lips were faintly parted, lush, sweet.

Vittorio turned away. "Andiamo," he said reaching down on the floor for the plastic bag. "So we go through customs together, but I'll be behind you. You go directly to the luggage carousel and wait for me. I'll come with a cart. Remember: you are no longer my friend. If you see the bags, grab them but otherwise just stand there in your mink looking imperious. I'll try to find out if the Swissair from Kennedy is on time or not."

Teddy nodded. She was pushing her hair up into the black wool beret. With her pearl earrings and the Jeremy white mink she looked like a very wealthy young woman. It was late in the year for mink but the Roman women still paraded around in them. When they weren't wearing sable. And anyway, she and Vittorio had decided it was okay because Geneva is farther north. She was wearing more make up than usual—beige eyeshadow and brown eyeliner, peach colored lipstick and two shades of blusher.

They seemed to stand forever in the aisle of the plane, forever in the line for immigration and at last, Vittorio left her for the men's room. Teddy's mouth felt dry as she approached the crowd watching for their suitcases. Were there carts? Would anyone see him in the bathroom? What if Red was hours late from New York? What if they'd decided to skip this Friday and he didn't arrive at all? Calma. Calma, she insisted. The first snag they'd considered had not happened. No strike at Fiumicino.

Teddy reached for the Gucci suitcase but another arm from behind her grabbed the handle instead. He spoke Italian to her. "Scusi, Signorina. Please allow me." Vittorio was wearing the hat pulled way down over his forehead. The hair that showed over his white collar was jet black. The plastic nametag pinned to his pocket identified him as Giorgio Massini; the photograph above the typed name was of a man in a chauffeur's black cap looking directly into the camera. Gucci number two came into view. Vittorio grabbed it and then the third. "No time to lose," he said very softly as he bent down. "New York flight is in early. Carousel number four. Follow me."

This was the part they hadn't been able to perfect. Teddy was to go to a nearby phone and thumb through her address book as Vittorio, in his chauffeur's uniform, was to put the luggage on the conveyor belt. Then he was to move aside and mix with the crowd for a few moments as though straining to identify the luggage of his mistress. He and Teddy had put a small adhesive tape 'x' on the top of each of their suitcases. It was near the handle and not easy to spot unless you expected to see it.

The bags from the New York flight were being unloaded. Vittorio watched blue ones, red ones, green ones, all come down the metal chute and fall on the conveyor belt where they went round and round. He swallowed thickly. Where was Red? Mio dio. He waited. Saw the Guccis from Rome go around once more. There was no crowd to mix with. Teddy still 'talked' animatedly on the phone. He wondered what on earth she was going on about. He wondered what language she was speaking. Where were the New York passengers? Maybe there was a problem at immigration but surely some should have come through. Then he heard the announcement in French. Problems with the doors of the plane. Mio dio. What luck! Vittorio picked up the first Gucci without an 'x' then the second and the third.

Teddy put down the phone and came towards him. Vittorio wondered if anyone would check luggage tags. Usually didn't. How would she explain arriving from Rome and her luggage taking a trip by itself from New York? But then if they open one Teddy will be shocked and say, "Where did that money come from? My God! I have the wrong suitcase!" and they will check her tags and voila! Maybe she will be questioned but we'll get through it.

Teddy was pointing at another Gucci. He shook his head 'no' but she insisted and then another and another. "You are my chauffeur," she hissed in Italian. "Even if only for the next ten minutes."

Vittorio was furious. Six Gucci suitcases for one person. For one woman, even a woman dressed in white mink like Teddy, it was unbelievable. Accidenti! he cursed under his breath. Merde. He swore in

French because he was in Switzerland. She'd gone crazy. Lost her mind. She was filling the cart with them. He'd be lucky if he could push the damn thing.

"L'ultima, Giorgio," she was pointing at one more. "No!" he raged. "Si," she insisted regally.

At the moment his hand grasped the handle and he swung it on top of the others, the hall was filled with arriving passengers. Obviously someone had freed them from the plane. Rumpled, excited, irritated, loud, they surged around Teddy and Vittorio and the leaning tower of Gucci. Tremulously, he started towards Customs behind the white mink.

We'll never get away with this now, he panicked. His heart was beating like a drum. Ha! and I used to dread going to the bank. The bank was a joy compared to this. I'll have to fight for extradition like Gelli. Mio dio. Swiss food for the rest of my natural life.

Teddy's black alligator pumps went click click click on the smooth shining floor. Piece of cake, she said to herself. Don't know what Vittorio's having a stroke about. Poor man. Not cut out for this. Teddy's inner bantering belied the iciness of her hands and the perspiration she felt under the beret. My hair is sweating, she decided.

Then it happened. One of the uniformed inspectors waved them aside. Teddy smiled and said 'good morning.' She held her American passport like a talisman before her. Perhaps he only wanted that. "Oui," he nodded and then pointed at the suitcases. All matching. All enormous. Teddy smiled aqain and began in English. "So much. Ridiculous, isn't it? My husband and children arrive tomorrow. They made me bring everything." Husband and children! Vittorio was screaming silently. We never decided she would have a husband and children. She's not wearing a wedding ring. Teddy sighed and smiled. The middle-aged Swiss was not smiling back at her. He walked towards Vittorio and tapped the top suitcase with one finger. He motioned for it to be put on the counter and opened. Vittorio couldn't hear anything except his heart. He saw Teddy's mouth moving.

The suitcase was lifted down. In slow motion. Vittorio, in his role of chauffeur knew he should assist but physically could not. His hands were numb. The zipper was unzipped and the top was lifted. All three of them gazed in surprise at the cut-up Italian newspapers. The Swiss inspector picked up what appeared to be part of an Il Messaggero headline.

Teddy was furious. "Oh, that little monster! How could he do this!" She picked up a handful of paper and tossed it back. "My six year old has a very peculiar sense of humor. I just…I am just….." She looked near tears. "Well, when he arrives tomorrow I'll be right here waiting for him!"

Then the unbelievable happened. The inspector's sharp eyes surveyed the Mont Blanc of other bags and he started to laugh. Vittorio began to laugh and then Teddy. The Swiss took a handful of newspaper and began to put it into a wastebasket on the floor. Teddy helped him. They were all laughing. Then the bag was closed and put on top of the cart again. Teddy smiled at the man and waved good bye, trying to look upset and amused all at once.

"Giorgio, we'll be needing a taxi," she demanded as the Prince trailed behind her through the airport.

They took a limousine instead and when everything was inside they gave him the name of the bank. "Our bank," gloated Teddy.

"Teddy!" shouted Vittorio. "Six suitcases! Husband and children! You don't look old enough to have a six year old! We never said you would have a hus-"

"Cool it, Vittorio," she said airily with a cat smile of triumph on her face. "It worked, didn't it?"

"Si," he admitted as he took off the chauffeur's cap.

Teddy began to gasp with laughter. "You look like a skunk! Put it on again!"

Vittorio swore. "I'd almost rather go to jail than be your driver!"

Teddy chortled happily. She was struggling out of the mink and turning it wrong side out. Then she pulled the beret off and shook out her blond hair. "Well, you told me I had to look different at the airport and at the bank. "

Vittorio was amazed at the transformation. There she was, all golden Teddy again. She plucked off the pearl earrings and replaced them with clip-ons of malachite. "Help me with this coat, Giorgio," she said casually.

Vittorio breathed, "Chauffeur or not, I'd like to spank you."

Teddy giggled and then put her arms into the coat which reversed to the palest possible, nearly ivory suede. She pulled the pockets through and jammed the black beret in one.

The bank manager had been expecting them. The limousine was unloaded quickly and all the suitcases taken to his office which was cool and furnished with dark wood and fragrant leather. Teddy stood like a wild flower in the center of the masculine room.

"A deposit, Monsieur Michel." Vittorio took off his hat and was stared at. Teddy began to laugh. Vittorio tried to explain but obviously couldn't so he began to laugh, too.

"It's a game," he smiled and started to laugh again. Teddy had never seen him laugh so much.

"I've always wanted a chauffeur," put in Teddy.

The Swiss shook his head but he was smiling. "Shall we open these and…I'll call in someone to count it."

Moment of truth, thought Teddy. She pulled open one and breathed, "Okay," as Vittorio did the same. In four minutes there were five 'okays.' Monsieur du Pont watched impassively for after all, he was quite used to this sort of thing. Money arrived in paper bags, in briefcases, in duffel bags. He was sophisticated when it came to such matters. The counter was making progress but it would take a while so two other counters were called in. They were young men in dark suits who worked methodically and quickly, drab cousins to casino croupiers.

Vittorio and Teddy sat on the dark blue leather couch with all the brass nail heads and did their best to look serious. Vittorio wore the cap again and Teddy kept smiling at him as though very near a fit of giggling. Monsieur Michel offered them coffee and they accepted. Then the three of them discussed the weather at great length and he returned to his desk to go over some documents. Shhhh shshsh shhhh went the ruffling of the bills.

Teddy asked if she could be shown to the ladies room and Monsieur Michel escorted her from the office. She thanked him and locked the door behind her. Minutes later she returned in a cloud of after shave, with fresh lipstick, her hair brushed loose around her face.

"Ten million seven hundred and fifty thousand dollars in one hundred dollar bills," said the counter with the slip of paper in his hand.

"Merci," they all nodded at one another and the trio in dark suits departed. "All for deposit, I assume?" Michel had his pen poised to fill in the number.

Teddy looked at Vittorio. "We don't have our train tickets yet and we haven't had lunch."

Minus suitcases and all the money save fifty thousand dollars each they were soon on the sidewalk outside the bank. Teddy had tucked her white envelope in the zipper pocket of her large black alligator pocketbook and Vittorio had put half in his trouser pocket and the other half in his suit jacket. "Vittorio," began Teddy. "Do you think we could eat on the train? I've never eaten on a train before."

Vittorio was horrified. The food. Or else there were rolls in the station. And the wine! It was better used to dress a salad. He saw her face and said, "I agree, let's get out of Geneva subito. Right away." Suddenly he had an idea. "And yes, Teddy, we shall eat on a train!" He put his hand up for a taxi and opened the door for her. Then he gave the address of last Friday's elegant restaurant. Teddy didn't say a word. She trusted him totally. He said we'd eat on the train and we will, was her philosophy.

And eat on the train they did. Vittorio purchased all the seats, all six of them, in a first class compartment. They settled themselves and then opened the hamper prepared by the chef of the Beau di Lac. There were glass flutes and white china and white linen napkins; there was champagne and caviar and quail eggs and cold roast beef. There were delicacies Teddy had never tasted. "Oh!" she moaned. "Tell me what everything is so I'll know what I love and can ask for it again!"

They had a quiet moment as the train crossed into Italy. Teddy spoke. "I feel that Olivier should know about this. Should be laughing with us. Celebrating." Her eyes were filled with tears. "Sometimes I feel guilty that I haven't gone into total hysterics about his dying. After all, it happened in Rome and he came to see me." Vittorio was shaking his head, no, don't do this to yourself. "But," she bit her lip and looked out at the Alps. "One reason I haven't grieved more is because," she blinked at the sudden bright sunlight reflected by the snow. "I just can't make myself think he's….dead. I don't feel it yet."

"You loved him so much that in a way, he isn't." Vittorio's eyes were moist.

The train swept past white peaks and dark ravines and midnight green spruce trees. The landscape for Teddy seemed like a miles and miles long Christmas card. Vittorio poured more champagne and they, both near tears, toasted the absent Olivier

*   *   *   *   *   *   *   *   *   *   *

"MMMMmmmm," insisted the patient as the doctor stood over him carefully examining the sore fingers. "Mmmmmmmmmmm."

"Can you write today? Take this. It's better than the pencil." He handed him a fountain pen and watched. "He's writing a book," smiled the nurse.

"Do you read English? No. Well, Professore Marinelli does. Take this to him and ask him to translate."

"Si, Professore." She disappeared immediately with the note.

"My name is Oliver Richardson. Someone took my wallet and my passport and when I tried to get it back we fell into the street. Please find Teddy Starbuck at Piazza Benedeto."

An hour later the doctor returned to the bed with Professore Marinelli. He spoke English very slowly, very concisely. "I have called the American Embassy and they appeared to have some record of you. A consular officer will be here this afternoon." He smiled when Oliver began the "mmmmmmm" noises again. "And as for your friend, we may be able to find him through the Embassy also. Is it, by any chance, Piazza Benedetto Cairoli?"

Oliver nodded and tears filled his eyes. The doctor patted his shoulder gently and said, "Va bene. E facile. There is no telephone listing but it's a little street next to where I live and I will have no trouble discovering an American named Teddy Starbuck."

I've been found, thought Oliver. And someone will find Teddy for me. It's possible. It will happen. Tears of relief streamed down his face and fell on the pillow. The nurse tenderly dabbed at his eyes. "Va bene, Signor Reechardson. Tutto bene."

* * * * * * * * * * *

"Why won't they come after us? You never told me that. I mean you'll be safe in Umbria but I'll be in my same apartment."

"I'm not going to be in Umbria all the time, Teddy. You know how much I love Rome." He sipped champagne. French. Wonderful stuff. He put the glass down on the window tray and pulled a piece of paper from the inside pocket of his suit. "Here." He handed it to her and she read quickly.

Then she looked up and said, "I don't know why you say you don't have a head for business. I think you're brilliant." Her eyes were amber in the sunlight and glowed with affection for him.

"Grazie." Vittorio looked away from her for a second and then cleared his throat as if embarrassed at the adulation. He would never confess that it had been partly Rolando's idea."It simply means that if anything ever happens to either of us, even if we just die in bed thirty years from…"

"Fifty. Give me another fifty years please." Teddy sipped from the flute.

"Va bene. Fifty years from now. Our wills will be read and the truth about Ernie Melville and all the names I can remember and the hotel and the bank, all will be made public. A copy of this is with my avvocato in Rome and in the bank with Michel and in a safety deposit box at the Banco di Roma. So, it's in their best interests for us to be very healthy for a very long time."

"I'm taking off my coat now," Teddy announced. The emerald green linen dress, sleeveless, simple, elegant, took Vittorio by surprise. "I'm not in mourning anymore. Not for my marriage or even for Oliver who would disapprove violently anyway." She sat down again and smiled across at Vittorio. Her masses of blond hair were streaked with sun colors. Her eyes were mischievous. "Starting today everything is going to be new. I'll get a new job on Monday."

Vittorio smiled. Yes, she probably would.

She poured more champagne in their glasses. The train is really terrific went through her mind. And this food. And this champagne. And so is Vittorio. "I miss you already," she said solemnly.

Vittorio looked at her lovely, sad face and was reminded of the first time he had ever seen her. Like Venus' wild younger sister standing in the scallop shell on the pale blue ocean waves. "Why?" he asked.

"Because…" she began and then shrugged her shoulders like an embarrassed child. "Just because," she finished.

Vittorio then said very quietly, "I love you, Teddy Starbuck."

She nodded, not speaking. "Yes," was all she said when he took her glass and put it beside his on the window tray.

* * * * * * * * * * *

They may have kissed for a thousand miles for Italy is a long country. The train raced through the Alps, past city after city, and through the countryside of Tuscany which was the same color as Teddy's dress. It was at sunset, four hours from Rome when Vittorio asked her to marry him and three hours fifty-nine minutes from Rome when Teddy said she would. By midnight when the locomotive pulled into Termini, Rome's big station, they had decided on five children. Vittorio's eyes kept filling up with tears. "We have all these palaces now," he explained. "And there'll be so much room for so many bambini."

They were a little bit drunk and terribly happy and took a taxi, with the hamper and all the empty bottles, to the Venturini palazzo to interrupt the card game.

* * * * * * * * * * *

It was still Friday afternoon in southern California. Chance was at the wheel, Carly Simon was on the radio, and Slow was in the front seat staring up at the sky with a big grin on his face. The top was down and the wind rushed past them and felt very clean. Edith sat right in the center of the back seat, ears back, eyes slitted, enjoying the ride.

"So, that was my plan," Chance was saylng. He wasn't so sure about England anymore. He didn't know one single person there. "What will you do?"

"I want a car like this one. This is a very special car."

Chance was surprised. "Well, I'II tell you, Sidney. It wasn't cheap."

"Oh, I have money."

Chance thought, oh, poor little guy. Probably has fifty dollars tucked in his left boot. He's led this isolated strange life with a pet he thinks is nearly human and he's lost touch. Has no idea of how things work, how much things cost. Chance looked in the rearview mirror at the giant white rabbit. How much better to see Edith there than Hardware. "Sidney, I have so much money. And it is because of your brothers. I can give you a lot of money."

"I have enough for a car. If I don't get one exactly like this I was considering a 1962 Rolls Royce Silver Cloud-"

Chance turned so quickly to look at him that he almost hurt his neck. "You have that kind of money?"

"I have..." he hesitated and then, though he trusted Take-A-Chance, modestly divided the number in half. "I have in the neighborhood of eight million dollars. Let's say plus."

Chance blinked several times behind the Foster Grant sunglasses. "That's great. Really really great." The Mercedes was on automatic pilot as he absorbed this news.

"The stock market. It's all money Wes and Les started sending to me and my mother years ago. I read a little bit and got interested and made some and lost some and then I started reading more and making more." Slow was unused to talking so much and was completely unused to having someone answer him and respond. It was a delight. "I sold off a lot in September and then went in again after the October crash." He looked up at another puffy cloud. "I did all right."

Chance was filled with admiration. "But you don't even have a phone! How did you..."

"Oh, I'd go into Vegas or one of the other little towns with Jose to get the mail once a month and I'd call New York, my broker, and tell him the way I thought the month would go and give him hiqhs and lows not to go above or below and we'd handle it that way."

"Wow!" Chance smiled and leaned over and patted the little knee on the seat beside him. "Wow!" he shouted.

It was mid-afternoon when they stopped at the Home of the Whopper and ordered hamburgers and milkshakes to eat in the car. Edith had a tossed salad with Roquefort dressing. "Always been a vegetarian," explained Sidney.

"So what will you do? You've got a lot of money and Edith and say, maybe you could become a stockbroker."

"Chance, do you think they'll come after us?" Sidney was wiping ketchup off his mouth. He was wearing a bright blue plaid sports shirt and the red cowboy boots for the first time in public.

"No. And I think they waited till we were out of range to start shooting. Just to give us a scare. They aren't going to bother tracking us down. First of all they wouldn't want you. You haven't done anything. And second of all, I gave them what was theirs. I don't think they'll bother us." Us. Us? thought Chance.

Sidney sighed. "Glad to hear you say that. I used to dream about DooDah…"

Chance smiled and then drank the last swallow of the chocolate shake. His stomach was not bothering him at all today. "So, getting back to what I was saying, what will you do?"

"Well, I like a few simple things. I miss my National Geographics but I guess, with money, I could replace them."

"Sure you can," nodded Chance. Sidney continued. "I think I'll replace all my books. Maybe I'll build a house with a library in it. Maybe with a fireplace in it. Maybe with a swimming pool outside." His eyes were bright. "And just being in this car has made me so happy. That's given me the idea I might want a car."

Chance liked the little guy. He gathered up all the napkins and papers and pushed them into one white paper bag. Edith was right in the middle of the backseat standing over the empty cardboard salad dish. A smudge of Roquefort was on her nose but as if she'd been told, as Chance watched, she delicately wiped it away with one fat white paw.

"Everybody ready?" asked Chance as he turned the ignition key. Sidney grinned. "I am! Are you, Edith? Are you all right back there?" Edith was sitting up very tall, staring ahead, quite ready.

Chance didn't say anything. So, Sidney was kind of eccentric. But he was such a nice guy. And he read so much. So intelligent. Take-A-Chance steered the convertible out onto the highway. It was a lovely spring afternoon, they had no place they had to be, and everywhere to go. The sun was shining, the top was down and the wind whistled in their ears, especially in Edith's.

Sidney's voice was heard above the purring of the chocolate brown Mercedes. "Chance, I was wondering....do you play chess?"

THE END

Clarissa McNair graduated from Briarcliff College in New York majoring in American history. In Toronto, she was a researcher for *Connections,* the six hour, award-winning CBC-TV documentary on organized crime. In Rome, she was a news writer, broadcaster and producer of political documentaries for Vatican Radio and was also the weekend news anchor for WROM-TV. While writing *DANCING WITH THIEVES,* she lived in Porto Ercole, a little fishing village off the coast of Tuscany. Having had adventures from Afghanistan to Zanzibar, she is now a private detective specializing in criminal cases.